THE
ULTIMATE,
ULTIMATE,
ULTIMATE
MALLWORLD

The Ultimate, Ultimate, Ultimate Mallworld

by S.P. SOMTOW

© 1981, 2000, 2013 by Somtow Sucharitkul
Illustratiosn © by Karl Kofoed

published as "Mallworld" by Donning Press in 1981
revised edition published by Bluejay Books in 1985
expanded edition as "Ultimate Mallworld" by Meisha
Merlin in 2000

this edition, published as "The Ultimate, Ultimate,
Ultimate Mallworld" is a reprint of the 2000 edition
with additional material released for the 35th
anniversary of the sale of the first Mallworld story to
Isaac Asimov's Science Fiction Magazine in 1978

Diplodocus Press
Los Angeles
Bangkok

Head Office: 48 Sukhumvit Soi 33
Bangkok 10110, Thailand

trade paperback
ISBN 978-1-940999-02-9
hardcover
ISBN 978-1-940999-03-6

0 9 8 7 6 5 4 3 2 1

S.P. SOMTOW

THE ULTIMATE, ULTIMATE, ULTIMATE

MALLWORLD

ILLUSTRATED BY KARL KOFOED

DIPLODOCUS PRESS

BANGKOK · LOS ANGELES

Ultimate, Ultimate, Ultimate?

What, you may ask, is so "ultimate, ultiimate, ultimate" about this particular incarnation of a 35-year-old concept? There is very little new material. It is, however, as complete a collection as I could manage, combining the first time not only the Kofoed illustrations which was such an important element of the original Asimov's appearances, but also the cover painted by the artist for one of the stories, which was later reused as the cover of the rare Donning edition.

For that Donning edition, Kofoed also produced a back cover which is in itself a satire. It's a sort of mirror image of the cover in which space vehicles are shown turning around and dumping their trash into the vastness of space.

The Donning edition has become a great rarity indeed. Only 1800 copies were ever printed in the first place. When they were distributed, it was discovered that a large number of the copies had one signature printed twice, and another signature missing. So, if anyone has an original 1982 copy of the book, they really must treasure it.

A brief online survey shows copies going for around $134, and amazon shows a new copy of the second edition for over $200. It also shows a used copy of the third edition, titled *The Ultimate Mallworld,* for a minimum of $63.

As the author of the novel, I'm certainly a little proud of the book is worth so much, but I'm also a little peeved that I'm not getting any of those big bucks. There must be a whole generation of young readers would like to read this book if they can only get their hands on a reasonably priced copy. Well, in the last decade, there has been a huge revolution in the way books are published. I've been able to regain control of a large number of my back listed books. No publisher today, in hot pursuit of such as J. K. Rowling, would be interested in an antique such as this. But oddly enough, I still am. And I hope you are too.

Thus, I want to welcome my readers, new and old, to a new edition of an ancient classic, an edition of which the author gets to keep a far higher percentage of the cover price than would have been feasible under the ancient system of publishing in which the book first appeared. If you bought this book, you've bought me a decent lunch. I thank you for that. You are what keeps those decent lunches coming, hopefully until the last lunch before I return to that great shopping mall in the sky.

Indeed, if you've splurged and purchased the hardcover, you've bought me a very nice dinner. And it's a long-term bargain, because you can hand it down to the next generation, who won't have to buy me lunch because I'll be dead.

These fiscal facts are in themselves enough to make the book ultimate, ultimate, ultimate, at least for its author.

Some 35 years ago, that author was a 25-year-old who had just arrived in the United States. My first career, as an avant-garde composer, was foundering, because I couldn't get anybody in Thailand to believe that what I was doing was actually music. That, despite some rave reviews from extremely respectable international journals, and being invited to perform in some of the more prestigious venues in classical music.

I had turned to writing simply in order to try to work myself out of a writer's block that I had developed as a composer. It did not occur to me that it would actually be a source of income. I sent some stories out to magazine almost on a whim. They came whizzing right back. That made me somehow more determined, because I'm not the kind of person who likes to give up that quickly. So soon, in between bouts of trying to write music, I'd be sending out short stories to all the big science fiction magazine.

At the time I had come to be living in a town called Alexandria, which is in Virginia, right next to the capital city of the USA, Washington DC. I was still eking out a living in music, because I had a very bizarre job ghostwriting music for a humming millionaire. Near Alexandria, in the suburban town of Springfield, that was a shopping mall.

You must understand that in the 1970 the shopping mall was the ultimate symbol of progress and futuristic advancement. I'd grown up in Europe, where we didn't have them. Subsequently, I had been living briefly in Thailand, where they did not yet exist either. I found this mall to be endlessly fascinating, and I spent much time with a small notebook — and by *notebook* I mean something with pieces of paper inside (one did not actually have such a thing as a laptop computer in those dark times) — and I would get ideas and I would jot them down. They were ideas about other worlds, about vast galactic civilization, about unimaginable technologies. You know, like cell phones. At times, too, I would imagine what the mall would be like if it went on forever.

It seemed to me that shopping malls were not unlike cathedrals in the Middle Ages. They were places where people from every segment of society met and mingled and interacted. They were edifices of great architectural creativity, towering walls of glass, gleaming corridors, lights and signs that screamed at you from every angle. In a society in which what passes for religion is a TV quack sucking dollar bills in through the screen of your television, malls had a numinous sense about them, a kind of awe, kind of mystic beauty.

The first story that I wrote which was set on an artificial planet called Mallworld was shipped out just like every other story, and I expected it to come flying back within a few weeks. Instead, I received a phone call from a man named George Scithers.

The man did not identify himself on the phone. He simply said, "Yes."

"Who is this?" I said.

The mysterious caller responded not in words, but by saying, "Woof woof."

In fact I would have hung up, but the caller eventually mentioned that he was the editor of *Isaac Asimov's Science Fiction Magazine*, and that they were going to buy the story. This was of course a rather exciting development in my life and the $375 which I was paid for the story was soon spent In wild celebration, indeed, it was spent for the check even came. Subsequently, I wrote several more stories set in that universe, and they seemed to strike a chord with readers of science fiction of the 70s and early 80s.

Perhaps it was only because I observed the mall with the eye of an outsider that I was able to catch its profoundly religious undertones. Perhaps, again, it was with the alien perspective that I was able to see all the levels of irony that the shopping mall lifestyle presented, and to predict how these commercial structures would eventually transform our world.

Many little things that were predicted in the stories came to pass very quickly. Widespread illiteracy for example. Also, roller coasters inside shopping malls. Although, one could not yet have sex on them. The stories seemed to influence people in other ways, too. There is a huge TV series called

Babylon-5, but the world in which it is set is first mentioned in my book — and described in the same terms. Coincidence? Unconscious, I am sure. There is, to my amazement, an app called *Mallworld* available on my iPhone — and I sure didn't license it. I hope they pay one day. Indeed, the word *Mallworld* itself, which I believe I invented, has come to be a viable word, uttered by people who have never heard of a thirty-click-long shopping mall floating in space.

Other predictions of course did not happen. People can still read, if only barely. There are no suicide parlors in Beverly Center, nor can you order a genetically engineered child from a catalog at the Mall of the Americas.

But, it'll happen.

In a very real sense, the Mallworld stories are of their time. The world moved on. When George was removed as editor of the magazine, I had a meeting with the new editor and the first being she said to me was, "No more Mallworld."

The glory days, in which I could publish a story in this series in two consecutive issues of the magazine, were over by 1984. But the collected stories had their own life, and the paperback was widely distributed.

For years afterwards, all I would ever hear from certain readers was "how about another Mallworld story?" And so I did produce a few more, and one appeared in collections such as *The Ultimate Alien.* Another, whose dark tone caused

George to reject it from *Asimov's*,   appeared in *Amazing stories.*

Another story, originally designed as a tie in to a role-playing game, was collected in the most recent incarnation of the *Mallworld* universe, the edition that appeared in the year 2000.

As far as I know, the book you're holding it's about as complete and it's going get. I do in fact as many other stories set in this universe somewhere in the cluttered recesses of my unconscious mind, but priorities are little low right now.

Nevertheless, I received so many questions over the years about where this book can be obtained, that I've put out my own edition. Now, if enough people show interest, if enough resurrected readers crawl out of the woodwork, or if enough new readers could be imbued with nostalgia and want to see more stories, it is not out of the question. I'm just like to sit back and wait and see what happens next.

— Bangkok, 2013

To my two honorary godsons,
Håkon and Jimmy
This is a future that was born before you were,
And no, I won't write a book report on it for you

Table of Contents

Prologue

Somewhere in the vicinity of Saturn

My August Many-n'huat*itudinous Fifty-tiered Father of the High Selespridar—greeting! I suppose you're here for the review session. You want to determine, as we Selespridar regularly must, once every n'huat of aeons, whether any of the worlds we have been…ah, babysitting…is ready to assume the full mantle of Galactic citizenship. Welcome to our little pocket universe, to the wondrous barbaric backworlds of the inscrutable humans! Are you ready to exercise your judgment, High One? Are you flushed with the lambent effulgence of ug'unnieth, and ready to interpret these short-lived creatures' understanding of the Meaning of Life, tempering your justice with compassion?*

Enough of this flattery, High One, you say? Proceed directly to the matter at hand? Oh, very well. I tell you, though, being among these humans, governing as I do from this magnificently gaudy floating palace at the orbit of Saturn, soaking myself in what passes here for their civilization, their art, their meager but earnest science, their monotonously hypnotic music…I've become almost as loquacious as one of them. Ah yes, they're certainly talkative. When I do pull the mindfiles that we're going to examine today, you'll see just how talkative they are. Their minds do a constant running commentary on everything that deluges in from all their senses. Typical of a backward race, I suppose, but it never ceases to amaze me. Did I tell you, my lord, of my last assignment? They gave me that funny star system of Shnang-Shnau-Shnu. Remember, where the inhabitants are enormous mountains of silicon, and converse with each other by means of puffs of smoke exhaled through their volcanic throats, dyeing the air a thousand brimstone colors? I had a terrible time babysitting them, and they still haven't reached anything like maturity, so beguiled are they by the meaningless patterns of their endless patter. I broke the seal on their universe barrier, once, to take a troupe of the chatterpuffers on a sort of zoo tour, but none found it edifying, and few found it conducive to greater ug'unnieth.

What? Shut up and carry on with my business? Why, it's strange, my lord, that you should display such impatience. Remember, won't you, that the next time we meet to analyze the human condition, every single mind we examine today will have been dead a thousand of their years. Peculiar, how close it brings one to the ultimate, to be so much in touch with one's mortality. My lord, my lord, such unbecoming impatience! Remember that you are a fifty-tiered Selespridon, incredibly close to the attainment of the final ug'unnieth, whereas I am a mere no one, a three-tiered, just another boring governor of a solar system. You are, my lord, Hyperion to a satyr. That's from one of their plays. Perhaps I digress. Perhaps not.

Would you care for one of these? No? It's Levitol, you know. One of their mind-expansion drug-things. They use them in an attempt to gain partial ug'unnieth, the poor dears! No? Allow me at least. See? One tablet and one's head hits the ceiling.

I'll deopaque the walls of this somewhat tasteless manse and show you what sort of a place this is. Then we can proceed to the main business of the day: that is, to determine, by looking into the minds of nine members of this alien species, whether or not they are ready for freedom, for union with the pan-Galactic civilization. And remember, my lord, to have patience with their perception of time…for though this examination will seem to us, and especially to one of such advanced z'ngenxip as yourself, to last but the twinkling of an eye, for them it will be half a lifetime or more…believe me, lord, you don't know the half of it. You live in such exalted splendor, I doubt whether you even utter a syllable in a thousand n'huat! You don't see how one's inner g'nurdef can be polluted by exposure to the constant jabbering of a trillion monkeylike creatures. Ah, yes.

*Look out of the manse. You see the border of their universe;
and within, Saturn, their outermost world, the last one we have
allowed to remain within their pocket universe. How long ago did
we shunt their system into this vacant cosmos? I don't know; at
least a couple of* n'huat *before I became governor here. They didn't
take it very well. Kept mumbling on about* the stars, the stars,
the stars. *What ludicrousness! Apparently, for centuries, the celestial
orbs have embodied all their dreams, their hopes, their futures. We
took this away, true; Earth's worlds have no more stars. But it's only
for a short time. We can't release them yet; they're a dangerous
species, dangerous, very dangerous—*

*What, Your Multi-*n'huati*tude? You'll be the judge of that?
Of course, of course.*

*Here we go. I have before me the mind-magician, an
instrument capable of pulling the mindfile of any creature under
my governance. We've selected a sample of several billion from all
over the system—*

*You've no time? You want me to just pick a nice representative
spot, one that most epitomizes their culture, and grab the first nine
minds the mind-magician can get a fix on? Surely that seems a
rather uncompassionate means of dealing with the life and death
of civilizations… but I bow to your superior* ug'unnieth, *my lord, I
suppose. Ah yes, a representative place. Well, how about Mallworld?*

What's Mallworld?

*I can't describe it, lord. It's a…commercial center, but…the
best thing for me to do, I think, would be for us just to zero in on it,
and take a look at it in all its barbarous splendor!*

Very well. On with it, on with it.

*Goodness! Did you hear that? Someone's coming through the
barrier right at this very moment! It's one of our ships, but the
mind-magician detects a human mindfile…it must be
malfunctioning, lord, I—*

*All right. It's too late now. The mind-magician has reached
into the subject's mind. It's spewing out its contents now, for our
edification and perhaps amusement, although I pray that my lord*

have a little compassion for what are, after all, creatures of exceptional inferiority, who are so far behind in the Way of Ug'unnieth *as to* deserve our pity, not our derision, and—

Shut up and start the projection? You want to see the worst of it, you want the nitty-gritty, the filth, lord? You're tired of my discursive meanderings, which add nothing to your contemplative z'neugma? *Oh, all right, all right.*

Let the show begin!

A Day in Mallworld

Now:

Why would a lonely, unsatisfied, bible-belt virgin teenage girl like me ever want to steal the family car, sneak off the colony, and teleport to Mallworld on the sabbath, anyway?

People have a lot of misconceptions about bible-belt people. In the first place, we aren't even all alike; there's four colonies, three of them relocated L-5 ones salvaged from earth orbit, the other one—the Catholics'—an azroid like most other colonies. Our colony, Godzone, is a good mixture of Amish, Buddhist, and Hare Krishnas...but I guess you "civilized" sophisticates wouldn't even know the difference. As for being in the boonies, bible-belt's only point oh one of an A.U. away from Interworld, just one million miles, and that's nothing anyway, with the new teletransportations...

The biggest misconception of all is that we're freaks.

Well, me, I'm not even religious. We live in a perfectly respectable ten-by-ten-by-ten six-person apartment, practice respectable birth control, only go to Temple once a week, have two cars (one long-distance one, of course) and a plot of land roofside. Apart from my plain saffron robe, you couldn't tell me from a Babylonian. I've got normal black hair, freckles, budding little breasts, regular periods, and a perfectly normal, unoutlandish name: Zoe McOmar.

And, just like everyone else in this whole godforsaken solar system, I want to get *out*...well, here's the difference: I *am getting out.*

The Sunday before my big escapade, we were in church. My little brother was crunching on his algae bar, his robe all askew, in the back seat, as our car hovered in its assigned churchlane. The cars stretched all around us, and above and below as far as I could see, all the way up to the ceiling-floor of Godzone…and past the dashboard, past a couple hundred vehicles, the mile-high words were glowing:

MECCA/JERUSALEM/BENARES
—TAKE YOUR PICK

The windshield dissolved into a bob-image of Ashoka Toscanini, patriarch of Godzone.

"The scourge of the Selespridar has been visited upon us, miserable sinners!" he intoned. He was about six inches high (our car is an old model), and his black robes were billowing in the godwind and his hair was aflame. "Atone, atone!" he cried. "Else the Selespridar will shove us even further into the abyss of Hell…"

I must inform the ignorant that it is the belief of the patriarchs of Godzone—and of a few other misguided believers, or "saved ones," that mankind's unfortunate present setback was due to his past sins, enumerated in the *Karmadharma-devaphasa,* an epic poem composed by Jesus Christ back on Earth, in his incarnation as the god Krishna in the Dark Ages of the twentieth and twenty-first centuries.

All the Godzonians *I* ever knew didn't believe a word of it; it was just a nice little myth…but the fact is, there is a great big barrier around the orbit of Saturn, a barrier that has thrown us into our own private little universe until such time as *"homo sapiens sapiens* attains a state of civilized enlightenment."

…just at that moment, there was a holo of a Selespridon on the windshield. He was *unearthly* beautiful. They all are: sleek, tall, .998 humanoid, except they're a vivid blue all over, with sparkling, fiery magenta hair that quivers and catches the light…I had been studying them, and I knew that this one, with his three-tiered tunic, was Klutharion, governor of the Solar System.

"And here's the very devil himself!" thundered the voice of Ashoka Toscanini. "It is these demons whom God has sent to punish us for our sins…repent, repent, you wicked children of sin…"

It was time for the litany. Dadmom whirred into action beside me, muttering in its mechanical voice: "Now, kids, say your prayers like good children. Now, Zoe, now, Amahl, be good little kids…" I winced. My parents hadn't readjusted the cranky old nanny for ten years. I glanced sidelong; my real parents were in the car to the right, hands clasped in a religious attitude. They were zealots, which explained at least seventy-five percent of my dissatisfaction with life.

I closed my eyes tight and I saw the Selespridon in my mind's eye. He was ten times more beautiful than a rock star (and they all use blue makeup, I swear), and I wanted him so fiercely it was everything I could do to hold back my tears. It wasn't just lust; it was the injustice of us humans being confined to our own universe while *out there,* the Selespridar lived in some inconceivable glory, technological gods. I just wanted to see them. Maybe to touch them. It's really a damper on the human spirit, knowing you're in a cage, even if the cage is a spheroid nineteen A.U.'s wide.

I opened my eyes (mumbling my prayers the whole time) and looked around and saw the ever-so-orderly ranks of cars and the flashing letters in the distance and the idiot preacher, and I knew that I had *had it.* I was going to *get out,* somehow, and when you say *get out* with the italics in your voice, that means *getting out* of the whole cage, and the only way to do that is to persuade a Selespridon to take you, and there are no Selespridon facilities in the bible-belt. I'd have to go to Mallworld…which is a shopping center thirty kilometers long, where they even have Selespridar sometimes, rich tourists, cultural anthropologists, administrators. Gawking at the natives. The trouble was, I was only fourteen, and I'd never been further than the Vatican.

The next Sunday I sneaked out of the apartment before Dawnbells and took out our long-distance car from the garage. I'd had my license for all of two days, and I knew exactly what to do.

I couldn't see a thing; the lights weren't on yet, and we don't have wasteful personal light switches like on Mars or Ganymede. I wasn't frightened at all. I'd worked myself up so that I simply didn't care about anything at all anymore, only *freedom.* It was all turning into sort of a David and Goliath allegory in my mind...

Quickly I punched the coordinates for *outside,* then my father's credit card number, which I'd secretly memorized years before. The dashboard was all buttons and pictures; like all non-bible-belt artifacts, it was designed for people who can't read like we can. An irrational worry hit me for a moment that the machine would somehow recognize me and give me a good hiding, but after a few moments, the car crashed into the ceiling and dematted to the surface.

Just like that! I didn't even breathe, but just set a course for the nearest interport (for an off-belt destination, you have to transmat, obviously) and—Then I really got scared. My colony was rapidly shrinking into a gray cylinder.

How could it all be so black? Weren't there any stars? There were always stars in the old holos, but...everything was totally black. It wasn't logical that there should be stars, but I always imagined space as, you know, before *they* came. It was brutal, the way the emptiness reminded me that man is *exiled.* I should have seen all the way out into infinity, and instead I was scrunched up into nineteen A.U.'s of black, oppressive *claustrophobia...*

But I went on staring out of the screen. I was petrified, but I was fascinated, too. It was all coming home to me. The prospects of meeting a Selespridon and persuading him to take me out of captivity seemed more and more remote. I was ready to turn home in despair. But the less likely it seemed, the more I wanted to make the dream real. And it was the dream of all mankind, even of the sophisticates.

I caught sight of the bible-belt in the corner of the screen. We were moving fast, though it felt like being absolutely still; the three cylinders, little silver slivers, were almost end-to-end at this distance, and the dumpy-looking asteroid which was the Vatican was a misshapen pearl...like links from a broken necklace. It was pretty, and maybe I wouldn't ever see any of it again, either.

Then I made out a single star...it was reddish. Only Mars. And the sun, a tiny, bright little ball, and Jupiter ahead, only just a disc and brilliant white.

And then the circle of buoys that ringed the interport. I punched for Mallworld so the car would have time to compute the jump angle and velocity. The technology of all this was Selespridar, of course; they were always trying to improve the lot of us poor humans, easing the centuries for us while we were being made ready for something we couldn't even understand.

The car sprinted forward. I felt some high g's for a second, and then it thunked into the interport field and transmatted. I was in Mallworld space now.

Mallworld! The biggest shopping center of all time, where you can buy anything you could possibly imagine!

It looked just like Godzone.

There was the familiar cylinder shape, glowing faintly in the blackness. But as the car coasted in nearer I could see the enormous banners of stiffened plasticloth shooting out from the docking gates, in gaudy yellows and turquoises and crimsons, declaring

> WELCOME TO MALLWORLD—
> WHERE *ALL* DREAMS COME TRUE
> OVER TWENTY THOUSAND SHOPS
> ONE MILLION CUSTOMERS DAILY
> FROM SOL SYSTEM AND THE STARS

(Who the hell can read those signs anyway, I thought.) And I was speeding into the parking lot, where the car anchored itself, deducted more money from Dad's account, and disgorged me. I had doffed my saffron robe—didn't want to look obviously

hick—and was in my monomolecular pajamas. I would, I hoped, look outlandish enough to pass as the latest fashion; and the iridescent peacock blue did highlight my eyes rather well, anyway.

I fairly dashed into the airchute, which tubed from the lot into Mallworld proper, which was quite an eerie feeling because the tubes were made of the latest Selespridar material: nothing. It was the same forceshield principle that was locking mankind into its human zoo.

As the tube wafted me down the two or three kilometers into the world, I thought bitterly, *Nice aliens, throwing us choice bits of superior technology, scraps from the table, trader beads*...(I know about trader beads because in bible-belt we do earth history, too; we're very old-fashioned and heritage-conscious.)

I was standing in the main hallway of Gate 507, and all I could do was gape.

I was leaning against a balcony, and looking up and down, I couldn't begin to guess the number of levels in this place.

It was bewildering. On all sides of me an endless stream of people scurried briskly into little booths—how did they all fit? Oh: they must be the fabled mini-demat-booths! No stairs, no elevators, no escalators! I was revolted by the energy waste, but then these were Babylonians, each of them bedecked like the Christmas tree in the foyer of the Hare Krishna seminary. Fat women bulged with parcels; svelte ones were followed by automatic shopping bags...but how did you know where to go? I was so frustrated I could have screamed.

"Well, where do I *find* anything?" I said aloud in exasperation.

A six-inch-high little man in a shocking pink uniform came flying through the air and hovered in front of my nose. I wanted to swat him, but he said: "I am computer simulacrum Mallguide 22214037. You called?"

I was embarrassed for a moment, and then thought, *Well, it's only a machine,* then said, "Well, I've never been here before!"

"Well, what do you want to buy?"

"Nothing. I'm looking for Selespridar."

"Well, we're not programmed for that, I'm afraid. Do you wish me to summon a more advanced model?"

"Er...no. Don't you have a guidebook or something?"

"Discontinued, miss. Who can read these days?"

"Well, where do the Selespridar hang out? Is there anywhere special, you know, native rain dances for the tourists or something?"

That remark went completely over the comsim's head, of course; I had to show superiority somehow, if only for my own benefit. Maybe I should buy something, I thought, slightly guiltily: spending money went against lifelong, inculcated habits...but I *did* have some of my own credit, actually, from last summer's job picking hops to make Godzbeer on roofside. I wondered how far it would go...

"Miss, I'm telling you, I'm only a Mallguide. For in-depth analyses you'll have to go to a paycomp and buy time on it. Shall I have one paged?"

"Er—no." (I multiplied the price of ten minutes' paycomp back home by three or four. I figured that that would be about right—and it was more money than I had ever seen. Of course, with the distance, there'd be maybe a minute's delay before my account rang red, but—)

"I see. Well, is there anything you would like to buy, in that case?"

"Well, I *am* hungry," I said. I hadn't had any breakfast. Then, I figured, a bar or caf...would be as good a place as any to start hunting for Selespridar...

"Restaurant level is H46. Just tell the booth." He went fluttering off. Like a little fairy.

I managed to barge into the nearest booth, shouted *H46* at it, and was instantly somewhere quite different.

Instantly, signs were flashing all over:

EAT AT JOE'S

GENUINE ARTIFICIAL RAW FISH

WE SPECIALIZE IN ALIEN GOURMET COOKING

and a lot of signs in languages I didn't know, too. *Who* reads *all this stuff anyway?* I thought to myself. Most of the signs were visual, though, with a few oral ones screaming in my ears...and people, running everywhere, jabbering away...I didn't know you could feel so lonely with so much going on...

Well, I really was hungry, so I thought I'd better play it safe. I'd no idea what any of the fancy foods were like. I once got sicker than a punctured p-suit, eating a genuine earthside egg. It was so disgusting, and when you think that it had actually come from *inside* a hen—No, it was home cooking for me. I walked right into it, a little side door in the corridor.

BUCKEROGEROO'S EAT-ALL-YOU-WANT STEAK HOUSE!

The *size* of the restaurant blew my mind, after those corridors. Three or four tiers of the place, and motor-booths whizzing through the air, and the six-inch simulacra of earth-type cowboys on horseback reciting the menu to customers, and eye-wrenching lights everywhere. All humans, though. Not a single alien.

I was feeling very small, so I took a seat facing the wall. I held out my thumb to the cowboy who hovered over my shoulder, and opted for the regular. Then I picked up a knife and started to saw off a piece of the table.

Delicious...it was just like home. I started to relax a little, idly watching the familiar sight of the steak reconstituting itself out of the fastclone nutrient bath.

Now, what?

"Good day." I almost didn't look up. That deep, unearthly voice!

It was a Selespridon. I gaped at him. He was two and a half meters tall, blue as the old earth sky, with that shock of purple hair flying free about his shoulders, and four tiers on his tunic. That meant he had to be even more powerful than Klutharion himself.

In which case, what was he doing here?

While these thoughts whirled around in my head, the Selespridon just gazed at me. It was really intense. I dropped my fork, and it accidentally turned on the motor mechanism and the booth began to levitate, and I didn't even notice. His eyes were so compelling, so hypnotic. I don't wonder that this was how they conquered us in the first place. I wanted him! It wasn't a sexual thing. No, there *was* something indefinably erotic about the way I wanted him, but there was more: what he stood for, freedom and adventure and the wide universe.

"I…I'm Zoe McOmar," I said, feeling stupid.

"From the bible-belt, I would imagine?"

"Wha…how do you know?"

"Only a bible-belter would eat in a place as…as *tacky* as this one. And I assume, also, that you are a runaway…?"

I was crestfallen. My type must be so common in Mallworld that anyone could tell straight off. Me and my big ideas! And now the booth was rotating slowly, jetting over the second tier of the restaurant…

"Do not be worried, little one," he said gently. "There are many runaways here, but few would have such an opportunity as you may have. For I have something you want, no? The power to get you off this godforsaken system, no?"

I looked up at him and I stared and stared and stared.

"Yes," the alien mused. "Humans do not take easily to confinement. I have not misjudged human nature. Even when that confinement is an entire solar system. Very dangerous species, very. Be that as it may, though—I think you could save my life. You would like to bargain?"

"But how? You're a fourth-tier Selespridon, and I am only a human, and—" He was playing with me, I thought. Tantalizing me, taunting me with my own dreams. Because he had me now. I would do *anything*…

"Well, frankly, I am about to be executed. Tomorrow I must give myself up to the authorities for a crime committed centuries ago. I am on quest, you see."

I nodded. It was a familiar concept. Selespridar who were of sufficient status could accept a deferred death and try to perform a quest.

"You see," he went on (and I could not really fathom his emotion at all, he was so alien), "my crime was one of uncompassion, and for this, the penalty is to be cast into the black hole A'anakoitha, some twelve parsecs from my homeworld. I shall die immediately, of course, but...because of time dilation, I shall seem to remain, a tortured corpse, in the perimeter of the black hole as an example for schoolchildren generations from now. This I could not allow, since my children would be subjected to much ostracism."

I didn't follow anything much of what he said, but he needed help, obviously. But more than feeling sorry for him, I was excited by what he was saying. He was tossing off black holes and parsecs as though they were nothing at all! And I knew that the official time period of a Selespridon quest was one *n'huat,* considerably longer than a human life-span.

So he was sort of a wandering Jew, or a Flying Dutchman, if you know your earth mythology.

"What exactly is your quest?" I asked in all ingenuousness. "Redemption by love, or something?" This was a concept from the earthmyth, and, besides, the patriarch of Godzone was always on about it in his sermons.

The alien laughed. It was a hollow, desperate kind of laugh. His emotions could not be read; his face was beautiful as ever. Inside, I cried for him.

"It's a quest only given when they are certain the criminal deserves death. I have to find the meaning of life."

I stamped hard on the booth floor, which brought it whizzing back to the ground. "But that's ridiculous!"

"It's the nearest translation," he said. "What I mean is...*ug'unnieth,* actually, which means...well, people *have* been successful in it before, they *have* brought back acceptable answers, and since your system is such a labyrinthine repository of ancient truths and primitive things which we in our enlightenment have forgotten, I thought—"

"Well. Hocus-pocus. You came here for magic, or something. Well, you certainly came to the right person! I *am* from bible-belt, you know, I know all about the meaning of life or whatever…"

"That is precisely why I came into this restaurant in the first place," the Selespridon said.

"First," he said—his name was Zhangif, I had found out—"you must not remain in those pajamas. *I* do not care, of course, but if one of the more fashion-conscious Mallworlders…"

We were strolling *(he* was; I was having a lot of trouble navigating) down a crazi-gravi corridor, cork-screwing from level to level and switching confusingly from gravi-up to gravi-down every five minutes. I was furious that he had noticed my pajamas.

"I haven't any money," I said bitterly.

"As runaways go, you aren't terribly knowledgeable," he said. "By the B67 entrance, there's a place where all the runaways pick up tricks. You can always make credit."

"Of course I've heard of that," I said sullenly. "It's against my religion." Then, seeing how time was flying and if I couldn't find an answer for his stupid question I would have to go back home and probably never have another chance to *get* out— "Look, don't you want to work on your quest?"

Again the despairing laugh. "It is a matter of supreme indifference," he said loftily. "I have been on this quest for *centuries.* It is the equivalent of the death sentence anyway."

"But your kids…and you—being made an example, perpetually dropping into a black hole…"

"Ha!"

(Of course! It came to me at once. Zhangif was in his *n'urdef* cycle by now, longing for union with his maternal cousins. As part of the almost incomprehensible Selespridon mating cycle, there were periods of intense manic-depression, I remembered from schoolwork.)

I'm never going to get out! I thought grimly.

"Let's get your clothes," Zhangif said listlessly.

We hopped into a booth, and I asked for an auto-couture. I knew I wouldn't be able to handle a full-service store. I got something very quickly and Zhangif absentmindedly thumbed the creditcomp for me...

I picked something conservative. None of these pornographic modern things where the breasts are all covered up to make them look lewd and *obscene.* I was so old-fashioned I was practically naked.

"Good taste," he commented. "The innocent little-girl look. Well, it befits your upbringing, I suppose."

Then he switched to a frantic, urgent tone. "Quick, we have got to find the meaning of life, I'm going to die unless I do, woman, help me!" The manic aspect of his cycle had blipped on.

"I guess we'd better start with religion," I said slowly. "That's a nice, primitive thing. I suppose there's a church somewhere in Mallworld?" I directed my question at the little pink man who had popped into being by my shoulder.

"One hundred cathedrals, six hundred forty-two chapels, and a Christian Science Reading Room," said the comsim smugly. "To which of these shall I direct the honored sir?"

Decidedly more obsequious, isn't he, talking to the Masters of the Galaxy, I noted.

"I guess I'll start with my own," I said. "Give me the level for neo-Amish-Buddheo-Krishna-ologism." (*We* just called it "the God Stuff" at home, but I knew there was an official name for it.)

"Recreationist, Reformist, or Reconstructionist?"

"I didn't know there were any sects. The Godzone kind, I guess."

"Reconstructionist. Innermost level. Take the cross-booth three down the hall to demat. It's nullgrav down there. Please thumb for magno-footware as you pass through."

Zhangif had already started, bursting with impatience. I watched as he walked, with an *animal* urgency I can't describe that made him *so* desirable, his violet mane flying behind him...he was a god. And he had the power to make me a goddess. I began to run after him. Not having to fake my way in pajamas freed my mind. I felt I could do anything!

We dematted into a huge, perfectly spherical room with mirrored walls. Only a few people, and all of them reflected a million times in the smooth walls, the reflections tiny as little dolls...I found the magnos in my hand and belted them on my feet. Wildly I grabbed for the Selespridon's hand—incredible presumption!—and we drifted to the floor-roof. Nothing new about the sensation, except being inside the vast, featureless bowl, feeling so tiny. I was awestruck, a little afraid even.

WELCOME, a voice sang, high-pitched and eerie, TO THE PERFECT CIRCLE OF RECONSTRUCTIONIST NEO-AMISH-BUDDHEO-KRISHNA-OLOGISTIC TRUTH.

"Wow," I whispered. "And I thought for once in my life I was missing church on the sabbath."

"Quiet. You are sure this nonsense will give some insight into the meaning of life?"

THE SERVICE WILL BEGIN SHORTLY. GRAVITY IS BEING REDUCED TO NIL...FEEL THE WEIGHTLESSNESS AS A SYMBOL OF THE SPIRIT OF MAN UNDER THE PROTECTION OF THE DIVINE *OM*.

And now I really needed the shoes. Otherwise I would have floated away. I felt a little bit drunk...

Just then the patriarch of Mallworld matted into the center of the sphere. I could only just see him, he was so far away, and he was upside-down. He looked just like Ashoka Toscanini, our own patriarch. The resemblance shook me, even though I knew that all patriarchs were cloned from the original founder of our faith.

He began to preach in an impressive voice. The instant he started I knew this would be no good. The sermon was, word for word, the same one I had heard last week, about the evils of the Selespridar! Every nuance, every turn of phrase, was identical.

"Cheated, cheated, cheated!" I stage-whispered to Zhangif. "And I was never told. The man's a robot or a hologram or something. I heard the same thing last week, and—"

"This is fascinating," said the Selespridon, never taking his eyes off the little figure. "Perhaps, perhaps indeed..."

I kept my mouth shut for the best part of an hour as the catalogue of diabolic Selespridarianisms droned on. If Zhangif could find what he wanted there, I wasn't going to disillusion him. We waited until the sermon was over; everyone had left long before the end.

Beaming, the patriarch came floating toward us. I'd never been within spitting distance of one in my life, and here he was, breathing down our necks.

"A fine sermon," Zhangif said ruefully. "But—"

"My child, my child, I am delighted! But whatever are you doing in that sinful fancy dress?"

"Father, he *is*—" I said hastily.

"Just so, daughter," said the patriarch. "You are forgiven."

"Well, sir," I said (I kept thinking, *If this is a robot, its circuits aren't being all that logical*), "perhaps you could help this gentleman? He needs to know the meaning of life..."

The patriarch wheezed a little.

"It's—it's rather urgent, sir," I added.

"Ha! No one has asked me a *meaningful* question since I began here!" cried the black-robed one, levitating away from us in broad circles and waving imperiously to the vanished crowd. "You don't know what it means to me...on this commercial, Mammon-thralled Mallworld, questions of philosophy are no longer debated. No, no, a great evil has indeed descended upon us, my children!"

He came drifting toward us. Suddenly his expression became rather menacing. "But you seek to entrap me with your diabolical questions, you with your innocent, childlike nakedness, indicative of the lies of Satan himself—and you, in the garb of a Selespridon? My boy...this isn't Halloween, you know."

Just as abruptly he became solicitous, fatherly. He put his arms on both of our shoulders, and said, "Here. Take this tape—only audio, I'm afraid, what with the Church's impoverishment, hard times, hard times—and listen well. A quarter-credit will automatically be deducted, the room has read your thumbprints. It is the *Karmadharmadevaphasa,* an epic poem composed by an avatar of Jesus Christ himself, after he won the epic battle against St. Joseph Smith the Apostate. *You* do not need the meaning of life! You need spiritual guidance. However, you are forgiven—forgiven—forgiven— forgiven—"

Father Ashoka (as I kept thinking of him) quickly shrank to the size of a demat-control-knob, then fluttered off, muttering "malfunction, malfunction," in a metallic voice, then dematted completely, leaving us alone in the huge chamber.

"Overload," I said.

The alien, talking mostly to himself, said, "No, no, this isn't it at all...when at first he was talking about the problem of evil, and the moral aspects of the Selespridon presence, then I almost got something. But the concept of *ug'unnieth*...ah, *ug'unnieth...* "

"Well, what exactly *is* this concept? I mean, if you explained it to me, perhaps I could help you better. I know about humans, but I can't figure out your unearthly concepts without some kind of help, you know."

"More broad-based," he said, "more universal, somehow, more reality-oriented. You know? *A'anuuk glemeshtoforsht, ang n 'passmolokhian sarod...* "

"Excuse me," I interrupted. "If you'll tell me in *English,* I think I could help, really!"

"Well, that's just the problem, little one. If it were translatable into your crude speech, I wouldn't need to be looking for it. That's one of its primary characteristics. But rest assured, I shall know it when I *do* see it."

We spent the next few hours exploring various religions. The Zens assured us that there *is* no meaning of life. I thought that was a pretty nifty answer, but the Selespridon didn't buy it. "Of course there is," he said. "Otherwise, why should I be searching for it?"

The Catholics—where we ended up—well, their cathedral was quite astounding. The Pope herself lived nearby; a recent Diet had decreed that the Church of "Rome" must become more commercialized, and what with the bombing of Italy on Old Earth, what better location than the greatest shopping center in the Solar System?

The whole thing was a holoZeiss projection, a landscape of heaven, so you saw clouds that seemed to stretch off into infinity, and *thousands* of simulated choirboys, each with electronic sitar or ancient synthesizer, warbling away like so many angeloids.

We caught a couple of self-lighting candles as they zeroed in on us, and he was looking around curiously, waiting for something to happen, but I was just enchanted by the sounds. I'd heard of the ancient singers, you know, Maria Callas and Donnyandmarie, the so-called "duo of truth," but I doubt that even the classics could be more beautiful...and the way the image of the Pope, naked as an innocent child, clutching the Christ Child to her bosom, wafted so gently through the sky, so huge and comforting...

On Godzone things are so unsophisticated. This almost made you *believe* in religion.

"This won't do!" Zhangif said, throwing his candle into the crazi-gravi corridor as we stepped out.

The gravity field made the candleflame dance and it flew upward, ahead of us, out of sight.

"It is almost what I need," he continued, "but alas, I recall that in the case of Nakulleh the murderess, who embarked on a quest before me, the Earth Catholic Religion was denied by the Council as an example of the meaning of life..."

"You mean people of your race come to Sol System often on quests?"

"Well, obviously, child! It's only the most barbaric place in the universe, with more ancient wisdoms and hokey half-truths than anywhere else...I am beginning to suspect that the only reason the Council keeps your system isolated is to provide quest material—"

That hurt. I was furious with them all. They were as bad as the patriarch said they were. Suddenly I felt a blind rage against every Selespridon in the Galaxy. They *used* us. Lower being or not, I had to *get out* now. I had to show them all that a human being wasn't just a piece of space offal.

"Well," I practically yelled, "what am I supposed to do now? You can't even explain to me what you want, and you think us humans are too dumb anyway, and we can't understand any of your highfalutin 'concepts'—"

"Of course you're too dumb," he said. "You're a race of perverts—murderers—cannibals—loonies!" He was trembling with rage, and he was so beautiful, and I was being torn apart by hate and desire.

We halted in front of a booth.

"Well?" I said.

"I understand that in your system mating rituals contain a lot of *ug'unnieth...*"

"Oh, that!" I was red to the gills, suddenly. "Well—" *Hell,* I thought, *I'm a progressive and won't do it with someone I don't like, even if the Church has culled it*—"I've never done it, you see. I have no experience with that sort of thing."

"Oh. I was thinking you might demonstrate."

"Sorry, Zhangif. What else is there I can help you with...? Give me some more ideas on this *ug'unnieth* of yours."

"Well, these religions of yours are all very well, but all unenlightened cultures have them. It's hard to describe *ug'unnieth* in your limited speech modes, but perhaps...something a little more...ethnic?"

"Oh. Drugs, maybe," I said listlessly. "Some of us think they can show us the meaning of life..."

And that's how I found myself dematting into a Place I Had Promised My Mother Never To Set Foot In. A veritable den of iniquity. A cesspool of vice.

It looked exactly like a hospital. There was a small room, oblong, crowded with about a hundred people levitating in various positions, like twisted manikins thrown into free-fall. I don't know how they managed to avoid each other; presumably they were still subliminally aware of their surroundings, even under the influence...

"Oh, this is the Levitol room," I said, trusting that I sounded worldly enough. (It wasn't hard; sometimes the school lavatory was just like this room here.) "We even have Levitol in Godzone. I imagine you'd need something a little stronger."

A couple locked in frozen embrace came barreling toward us, then cleverly deflected upward into a figure-eight around two suspended little boys who were too young to be there and whose faces had petrified into guilty grins.

Ignoring all these familiar sights, I said, "What you need is to try one of our mind-expanders...but...ethnic, too? The Acid Room, I guess."

He was oscillating now, faster than before, between fits of moroseness and hyperactivity. If he didn't mate soon, I didn't know if he'd even survive. I pulled him quickly past a long row of Self-Involvement Cubicles, through another Levitol Room, and he was muttering dejectedly to himself the whole time in his alien speech.

We came by way of a labyrinthine Reality-Simulating Corridor to a sign that said, in a seductive voice, FIND THE MEANING OF LIFE HERE!

"That's us," the Selespridon said, suddenly agitated.

LITTLE ROOM AT THE BACK, PLEASE...

The purple hair was standing on end, the alien was shaking violently all over, a wildly erotic odor was emanating from him. Trying to ignore all this, I said, "Now this is about as ethnic as you'll ever get, Zhangif. This is from Old Earth, you know, no less, and as such must be unimaginably ancient..."

(What a kid I was! "Unimaginably ancient?" Why, this specimen had probably been born before the first space flight!)

Sure enough the little comsims that emerged from the room and were now swarming around us had Afros, jeans, and dirty T-shirts. They simply *exuded* millennial wisdom, like little Apollos, Mohammeds, or Kennedys.

"Well, Zhangif, shall we go on?"

"Ah…" he sighed. We followed the swarm into the little room, which turned out to be an ancient receptionist's office. And there was a real human sitting there, lending the whole thing a very authentic atmosphere. She did look a *little* strange, though, since she had a vestigial head cosmetically implanted in her neck…

Obviously from Babylon-5, I thought. Richest colony, hollowed out of Deimos. I stared at the head, trying to compute how much it would cost to get one myself.

"What are you staring at?" she said. "Oh, that," she chuckled pleasantly. "It's my little brother. You see, Storkways Inc. messed up the delivery, and this was all they could salvage. You find it disturbing? I don't find it at all disturbing. Everyone around here—"

Her eyes went wide. "You're—a Selespridon!"

She crawled out from under her desk and began to worship him.

"It's plain to see what religion *she* is. A ufologist," I snorted. "Look, we don't have time, and my friend here needs to know the meaning of life."

"Oh, I am so blessed by your visit, sir…an attendant will be with you in a moment, pray sit down…"

Two chairfloats came down from the ceiling, and Zhangif and I began to relax. A couple of humans in Old Earth costumes—one in a business suit, another in a kimono—came in with hypodermic syringes.

"Not me," I said hastily. "Just the Selespridon here."

The two went over to his chairfloat. The secretary-receptionist began to give her standard lecture on the history of psychedelic drugs.

"The use of 'acid' is a very ancient earthie practice used by questors after meaning. Introduced to Earth by a sage whose name has come down to us in various forms as Tim O'Leary, Zeus, and Oscar Wilde, 'acid' was originally a highly dangerous organic compound. However, in today's journey into the halls of truth, you will be using a milder derivative of the compound. No other detail of the ancient ritual has been altered..."

Was this a hypnotic, ritualistic monotone—or was this simply a very bored, boring person? I could not tell. The room became dark; the two simulated Ancients hovered menacingly over Zhangif's chairfloat, their olden garments glowing softly in response to some ultraviolet light source (as though in an ancient "disco," I supposed). The receptionist droned on, giving the history of the drug, its empirical and structural formulae, its repression by the Earth Government during the Dark Ages, and many other facts known to all. The hypodermic syringe, I learned, was only an "authentic" fetish; the drug was administered orally...

It was all very soporific. I found myself drifting off, and the darkness grew deeper and warmer and more comfortable.

Zhangif was screaming.

I leaped off the chairfloat onto my feet and shouted, "Turn on the lights, someone!"

"I've been poisoned! I've been poisoned!" The lights burst on, blinding me for a second.

I hadn't even asked him if the compound would be toxic or not. "You really are as dumb as the aliens say," I told myself watching the Selespridon writhing in agony, watching the three attendants running this way and that in a hurry, and finally leaving us alone, abandoning us. Now I was really in it. If I'd been responsible for the death of a Selespridon...

"Quick..." he gasped. "A lavatory, I must regurgitate, or I will die, quickly..." I helped him down from his chairfloat and held his arm. We struggled out of the Escape Parlor, out into the corridor. He was heavy as anything, and I was practically lugging him. A sweet odor, so seductive, rose from my body where I had touched him...

Where was there a bathroom in this place?

EVERYTHING FOR THE WELL-GROOMED ANDROID, screamed a sign. I pulled him on. We staggered down the corridor together. I felt like crying, I was so frustrated. I yelled out, "Comsim, comsim, mallguide, somebody…"

YOUR HOLOGRAM IN TWENTY SECONDS
A COMPUTER-CHARACTER INDEX OF YOUR
BELOVED FROM A SCRAP OF TISSUE!

And then, abruptly, total darkness and silence. For ten or eleven seconds…I held my breath, feeling the weight of the Selespridon against my shoulders.

The lights went on. People flew by, jostling each other, falling over each other, screaming…

ANNOUNCEMENT. TEMPORARY POWER OUTAGE, thundered a deep voice over the tumult. EMERGENCY LIGHTS NOW ON. STAY IN YOUR PLACES, PLEASE. COMSIMS WILL RETURN TO DUTY IN ABOUT TWELVE MINUTES.

I was terrified. Now there wouldn't be any signs. None of the signs were talking anymore. People were walking past in a complete daze. The stores with visual signs were all right. People would recognize the pictures or holos and go in, but…the murmuring of humans without machines was different, eerie. I'd never heard it before. I felt the alien against me, gasping, his face turning from blue to a steel gray, and I thought, *If I don't get to a bathroom now, he'll regurgitate on the floor and I'll get caught and sentenced and sent home and—*

There was a little manual door to my right…

To my relief, it said LAVATORY right on it, in English, in *writing*. Thank God they hadn't obsolized the bathrooms! I pushed the door open and shoved the alien toward the nearest cathartic tank, clutching his hand while he—

Minutes later, he was his old, oscillating self again. We stood in the corridor. I looked at him wistfully. The sounds of Mallworld, power restored, hummed around us.

I had failed; I would have to stay in Mallworld forever, like every other runaway, become a child of the corridors...already I felt like I had lived in Mallworld my whole life. Home had faded completely.

"Well," I said, "I guess I tried."

The alien was in his dejected mood. "Yes. Now, in only an hour or so, I will return to my homeworld and turn myself in for the death sentence..."

"Well, good-bye."

"Wait...before you go...can I ask you a question?" said the Selespridon. "When all the signs went off, how did you manage to find the bathroom? I mean, do you humans have some instinct for self-relief? Is there some primitive homing mechanism?"

"Oh, no. I just read the sign," I said irritably. I wanted him out of my sight. I wanted to get used to being a Mallworld stalker.

"Read? The concept is unfamiliar. What precisely—"

"You mean you can't read?"

"What *is* this 'read,' then?"

"Listen!" I said, pointing to one or two signs that were in writing. "AUNT ABEDAH'S MONOPOLE-SKATING RINK...PSYCHIC PROBES: LICENSED...ARE YOU DEAD? RE-VIVIFICATION POSSIBLE!"

"...incredible!" said Zhangif.

And then I just laughed and laughed and laughed. "You mean—you aliens, with your fabulous technology, with your Galaxy-ruling powers, with all this—you can't even *read?*" Then I had it. "I've *got* your 'meaning of life,' Zhangif! If this doesn't convince your Council, nothing will!" And I tugged at his arm. He followed me, still depressed, and I waved to a pink comsim.

"A bookstore," I said. I knew how to order these things around now; I wasn't the scared little girl of a few hours back now! "I suppose you're going to tell me you have four thousand of them in Mallworld."

"Regrettably, there are none, miss," said the comsim, settling on my shoulder.

"What do you mean?" My heart was pounding. After having solved the alien's riddle...

"Perhaps you might find a book at one of the antique stores on level A1. That's the oldest level in Mallworld, you know..."

And we were off.

It was little more than a cubicle, with heaps of junk piled higgledy-piggledy all over, and one little man tending everything. "What do you want, kid? This is for museum collectors only...oh, beg pardon, sir," he said as the Selespridon followed me in.

"A dictionary," I said.

The old man looked at me, completely taken aback, then beamed. "My dear girl...!" he stammered. And then he pulled out an honest-to-goodness *book*. "It's a genuine, twenty-first-century *Shorter Oxford English Dictionary*, honored Persons," he said. "It will make a wonderful doorstop, or a *pièce de resistancé* on a tea table, or—"

"I'll take it," I said quickly, and Zhangif solemnly thumbed the paycomp. I picked up the thing...it was very heavy...and turned to the entry for *life*.

"See here," I said...Zhangif peered over my shoulder, mystified...LIFE: the condition or attribute of being alive. Opposed to death." I read out the entire definition, and added: "And this thing contains the meaning of every other word there is, too."

"It's astounding!" cried Zhangif. "How is it done? Telepathy? Mortification of the flesh?"

"No, no, silly...these little marks here represent *words*. A long time ago, everybody could read. But then they invented something called television, then something called holovision, and now only bible-belters learn it...it used to be the only way of disseminating knowledge, fancy that!"

Zhangif picked up the book and thumbed through it.

"It's upside-down," I said, laughing.

"Well," he said, "it is certainly new. Lost arts of the Ancients, my word...undeniably ethnic...ritual fetish...crystallization of universals into paper-ink symbology...little one, you have saved my life."

"They'll buy it?"

"My girl, this is purest *ug'unnieth!* Already my spirits soar. You have earned your trip to the stars..." and he flipped into his hyperactive state, and I had to run to keep up with him, up the corridor and into the demat-booth and into the airtubes and into the carport and...

"Close your eyes."

I felt motion. I was strapped into a car of alien design, everything in the wrong place. I shut my eyes tight. I was happy, not only because I was *getting out,* but also because I had known better than the aliens, I had won a small intellectual victory...

We accelerated. "Now open them," he said quietly.

I did. His odor was stronger now, so enticing. I hoped he could hold out until he arrived at his world.

I looked out of the screens, and saw—and saw—

How could there be so many of them?

The stars were everywhere, I could have died with crazy laughing, I couldn't believe it could be so beautiful...and it was all happening to *me,* Zoe McOmar, a little hick teenager from nowhere!

It was really *neat.*

Well, my lord, we certainly goofed a little there, didn't we? But what could I do? Zhangif out-tiers me somewhat, and one must make allowances for the wild actions of those who are condemned to death. Nonetheless, a human has escaped from our little barrier. Well, there's bound to be leakage, what with all the tourists, xeno-anthropologists, and so on who love to visit the lands of the backward and who get their jollies staring at vermin. Indeed. As long as they can't get back through the barrier, it'll be all right, I suppose; we can protect our little fledgling civilizations from cultural pollution…

Perhaps, lord, I should proceed apace, for I perceive that you have become somewhat agitated. Why? Do you honestly think that the young girl provided our Zhangif with some parcel of ug'unnieth? *Does this perhaps convince you, Your Multi-*n'hua*titude, that we should release the humans from their so-called cage? Why, lord, you are positively trembling!*

Let us continue, then. The mind-magician roves through the corridors of Mallworld now, plucking another mindfile from among its teeming shoppers… for there are, indeed, a million stories to be found there…I've a fix! Shall I continue? By way of contrast, it seems to be an older man, one of great wealth, an artist. He is sitting in some kind of projection room, making a recording that will later be seen by billions upon billions of these humans. I think you'll find it interesting.

(But first, a word from one of our sponsors.)

BUY B-O-I-N-N-G-G-G!!!
A NEW CONCEPT IN LEVITOL TABLETS!

Yessiree! Each tablet of Boinnggg! comes coated with three jucy layers of candy, chocolate, and levitative ingredients. Just like any other Levitol pill, you might think! But no.

Boinnggg! has something extra!

Through the miracle of Selespridon technology, we have implanted a miniaturized, localized, personality-imprintifiable GRAVITY-NULLIFICATION-DEVICE!

Yes! After the drug wears off, you won't bump your precious little derriere on the ground.

Indeed not!

The Selespridon device, which is fully biodegradable by the digestive fluids, and *completely non-fattening*, will sustain you in your floating pattern for as long as one hour after you have returned to consciousness from your Levitol "high". You'll never be caught with a nasty bruise on your behind when you buy Boinnggg!!! from quality drugstores everywhere.

B-O-I-N-N-G-G-G!!!
THE LEVITOL WITH BOUNCE!

Sing a Song of Mallworld

Well…I guess I'm ready to start.

It's hard.

I suppose you people out there—and I'm assuming, for my own sanity's sake, that there are people out there, people who have paid good money to hear the great Julian barJulian XIII pour out his heart—I suppose you think it's easy for an old pro like me. I'm here, alone in this room in Mallworld with my clavichrome, I've fixed all the settings on the machine, I've strapped myself in and I've stuck all the electrodes in the right places, and now I'm going to overwhelm the lot of you with sound and color…and you'll sit in front of your holovee with the tacto-olfacto inputs and fall into a world I created out of my pain, my love, my everything.

Well…I guess I'm ready to start.

I'm going to tell you how I became who I am. And yet—

Should I start with the wild party in the Gaza Plaza Hotel, when the gang got smashed on Levitol and floated down the corridors of Mallworld, pursued by gaggles of little six-inch-high security comsims, and Annetta overdosed and hit her head on the ceiling of a crazi-gravi hallway and got a concussion?

Or do I tell you about Mallworld itself, the thirty-kilometer-long shopping center that floats in the loneliness between the asteroids and Jupiter, that has *everything,* from robots to Rice Krispies?

Or do I start with the time I was five and we went down to Nick's Music Store on level Q91, and I banged my chubby fist on the mechanism and knocked out a whole level of Mallworld in a maelstrom of sound and light?

With multi-great-granddad, who won the choice of the title to half a million cubiklicks between the belt and Jupiter, or a lifetime supply of deodorant soap...and obstinately chose the former, out of sheer romantic holovision-addicted starstruckness?

Mustn't ramble...

When I was a kid, not many kids actually lived in Mallworld. They still don't. All the people who operate the twenty thousand shops, hotels, department stores, holo-palaces, brothels, psychiatric concessions, suicide parlors, and churches commute to Mallworld on the transmat, which is instantaneous, so they might live as far away as Deimos or Ganymede. But there were a number of us who did live there: for instance, the quads—Pico, Nano, Femto, and Atto LaGuardia—their mother was human arbitrator of Mallworld, a sinecure that coughs up a kilocred a day. Annetta's father is alien liaison, another sinecure since *homo sapiens* no longer runs its own affairs—and, as for me—

Mallworld just happens to be on a transmat nexus, which makes it a highly desirable location. And when they located it, a hundred and fifty years ago, where would that be but the very worthless semimegacubiklick of space that multigramps had laughingly taken instead of a ton of soap. When my granddad noticed—

My family is *rich.* Try figuring one percent of Mallworld's gross, over a hundred and fifty years, plus compound interest. My father stopped counting it; the amount can't be humanly imagined, it's just a theoretical geometric progression in the mind of a computer somewhere. We adopted a simpler way of collecting the rent: I just wander around freely in Mallworld and take anything I want.

Owning the world is as natural for Julian barJulian XIII.

Like everyone else who is *us,* I was spoiled, lazy, affected, bored, insolent, languid, decadent. Of the seven or eight in the gang, I was by far the richest, and consequently, by direct square law, the spoiledest, laziest, affectedest, and so on.

I only had two saving graces. One—well, when my dad decided to have me, he walked into Storkways Inc. on the maternity level and purchased the highest IQ that money could buy. And also, being an old-fashioned kind of person, he picked the standard soma, so I don't have wings or four arms or a green skin like many of my friends did—victims of the cult of individuality that the rich and bored profess to this day.

And then I played the clavichrome. Even before the events I'm about to tell you lucky people…I was pretty talented. Technically, I could outplay all my teachers by the time I was fourteen. I did the classic stuff, with each key linked to a specific chromawavelength and basically angular contours; I could also do a certain amount of the new virtuoso stuff with the variable color structures (random or controlled), and I was beginning to produce some highly derivative stuff on my own.

That's what I'm saying with hindsight, mind you. In those days I had a somewhat higher opinion of my own abilities. After all, there weren't any competent critics around, and who'd want to offend the offspring of Julian barJulian XII, and risk losing a substantial gratuity?

Well; that was *us,* the Mallworld gang, thirty or forty years ago. We were all in our late teens, finishing up from the same school—the St. Martin Luther King Traditional Style Strict and Snooty School, which took up a whole hollowed-out mini-planetoid in Jovian orbit.

As a counterpoint to this rich, bored and decadent theme, there was *them.*

You see them still, flitting in the shadows of Mallworld, in the corner of your eye in a corridor, slim things, just shadowshapes. They're the runaways who hustle by the B67 entrance. You can always tell them. They don't have a mothersurrogate robot in tow. They're not yelling for another algae bar or petting the Fomalhautan gaboochi in the live alien animal stand. There's no electric shopping bag laden with goodies levitating two paces behind their chubby heels.

No. You step out of a demat-booth onto a new level and you tell your shopping bag to make a left and suddenly you'll see one dart across your field of vision; and he'll look at you like he knows all of you down to the core, a haunted, hunted look...but innocent. The look'll last just a millisecond and he'll have vanished and you'll never see him again...or you'll see another face and you'll think it's him, but actually it's a *her,* and you'll never be sure...

And that's where I'll start my story. The day I found out where they came from, and where they so mysteriously disappeared to.

It was the day the seven of us came home for the Long Vacation. Our school, patronized by the "us" of various colonies, was very long on tradition and kept to the almost meaningless earthtime: and we had a "summer" vacation of three "months" every "year." It was a depressing last day; we'd been doing human history, and the teacher had taken it upon himself to take the class on a field trip to Saturn's orbit where we saw for ourselves the edge of the universe that we've been shunted into by the Selespridar until "such time as homo sapiens achieves maturity and is fit to join the rest of the Galaxy." We gazed out of the school bus into nothingness; and then the bus's holoZeiss segued into images of how the stars used to look, and it was like Saturn and all its icy rings had suddenly been stitched into a tapestry of burning lights...and then they turned it off again, and Saturn shone alone in the blackness. Then we bused past the Selespridon shield-stations which kept the forceshield constantly in place, knowing that just beyond them, but infinitely far away in a whole other universe, was everything that mankind had ever dreamed about.

It was enough to make you depressed for weeks on end; and in fact it was the school's policy (you know, one of the good old "traditions") to rub its students' noses in the human condition the whole time, so we'd never forget that we aren't free...*yet.*

And afterward we assembled in the gymnasium, and the principal gave a long speech about St. Martin Luther King, a former Pope on old Terra who was said to have led the holy war against the King Kong of Southeast Asia (hence his title)——

it was empty stuff, exhorting us by example. To show you just how "traditional" our school was: the Vatican had formally removed St. Martin Luther King from its canon some ten years before my dad signed my delivery contract! Be that as it may...

After that the teachers gathered in front of the principal, and he pressed the button that dissolved them all back into the computer, and then we sang a hymn, and then the gang gathered at the exit and raced to the parking lot.

I was the official owner of the *us* bus, a little thing I'd picked up from the Toyochev Carpalace on A46. We jammed into it, and I pressed the coordinates and promptly fell asleep.

It was my birthday; and a present from Dad, unopened, was in my autosatchel the whole time. Shows you how exhausted—and depressed—I was. I didn't come to until the car transmatted out of the ring of buoys and entered Mallworld space. The quads and Annetta were glumly puffing away on wads of chewing gum, stinking up the car...

We floated down the nothing tubes and burst into Mallworld. All of us were restless, rather hyper, and very, very depressed over the history lesson.

"Let's go and hit the monopole-skating rink!" said Annetta. Her gaiety was rather forced. Nobody paid any attention. "How about the human pinball game? How about a race around the comsim safari park?"

Mallworld was always impressive after two months in boarding school. I stood there, drinking in the sheer size of the thing. There was level upon level on either side of our corridor, down and up as far as you could see, and demat-booths every hundred meters or so, and signs and holo-ads yelling at you to buy the latest cars, whores, skating gloves, body changes, copulo-androids, breakfast cereals, pet gaboochis, pocket holoZeisses, mothersurrogates, monomolecular brassieres, babies...and the people! They rushed into demat-booths, they slidewalked along the mobiustripping crazi-gravi corridors, some in seemly nakedness, others in the most outré of Babylonian potato sacks, others with vestigial second heads and other becoming cosmetic surgery...and the constant jabbering, mumbling, bawling, and babbling was music to my ears after the silent, empty corridors of St. Martin Luther King's.

Well—

"Let's have a party, at least," Annetta was saying, fluttering her six-inch purple eyelashes languidly at the quads.

"But where?" I heard one of them say. I was staring at the mob, drinking in the sounds, so I didn't really take part in the conversation.

I found us racing into a demat-booth and materializing in *my* suite at the Gaza Plaza Hotel. I knew they were all mooching off me, the richest, but what did I care? I was too depressed to say anything. We entered the lobby, a couple of six-inch-high computer simulacra dressed in Turkish fezes bowed us up to my suite, I let them have the big party room, and I went into a bedroom to stew in private. It was a nice hotel; it was built in the shape of the great pyramid of Khufu on Earth, and each room was a pyramid, too; some of them were upside-down pyramids, interlocking with each other, with alternating gravi-ups and gravi-downs, all done by a clever Selespridon imported device. I banged the door on my friends—from my point of view they were standing upside down on the ceiling of the next room—and sat on the floatbed. I was in the prime of teenager-hood, and much given to fits of depression.

Something was wrong with my life.

And I wasn't smart enough, or objective enough, to have the faintest idea what it was. I knew that I had anything I wanted, and couldn't really complain. But life grated on me.

I thought of giving Dad a call, but I knew he'd get mad at me. He'd enrolled in the Xeno-Buddhist cult of nothingness and spent all his time staring at the navels of alien holo-scriptures. And all he would do would be to give me more money. It always worked...he thought.

I paced around, imagining myself in a turbulent maelstrom of creative achievement, once or twice almost reaching for the clavichrome console.

Then I thought of the present from Dad.

I subvoked an order to my school satchel; it came over to me and disgorged a little package. I broke the seal, and it was a little black box with electrodes sprouting out of it. I looked for instructions—St. Martin's taught reading among its more useless accomplishments, and so it was a rather silly, ingrained reflex—but found nothing; so I held it in my hand and waited. Presently, it spoke.

"Hello, Master Julian barJulian the Thirteenth. I am a present from your father, Julian barJulian the Twelfth, on the occasion of your seventeenth birthday, earthreckoning. I'm a new attachment for your clavichrome, only this year (earthreckoning) developed by the Clavichrome Monopoly Corp. in its Deimos labs. Happy birthday. We call it the *psionic amplifier* or psifi. Basically, it adds a whole new dimension to clavichrome performances by enhancing any 'psi' abilities that may be latent in you—which are rather limited in *homo sapiens,* according to the Selespridar—so that images from the unconscious, precognitive or telepathic, for example, that would never otherwise become conscious, may be imposed consciously upon the clavichrome's visual spectrum. At the first level, the psifi may be operated by inserting electrode A with the pink identifier into—"

Well done, Dad! I thought. *Your first* meaningful *present in years.* I listened to the rest of the instructions with half an ear. I was already impatient to try it out. The hookup was just like any of the other clavichrome add-ons; electrodes in the head (I'd had external DIN inputs connected up long before then, of course) and in the main body of the console. I cheered up considerably and told the bedroom door to accordion open.

The party was in full swing. The whole of *us* was there—and a few crashers too, acquaintances from other colonies or from school, whose parents had come to Mallworld for their shopping sprees. I spidered up the wall to the other room's gravi-down and plonked myself in a chairfloat. Everything buzzed pleasantly...

"Hey, play us a tune," said Pico suddenly. He had turned aside from some argument with Femto (easy to tell them apart: their names were embedded in fluorescent pink crystalchips on their foreheads). The others turned too, acknowledging my appearance (it *was* my place...) and then they stopped whatever they were doing and looked at me expectantly. I saw the identical idolatrous look in the quads' faces.

I've never been able to resist that.

So I hooked up.

I was still in the show-off stage then. I guess everyone goes through it, but in hindsight it gives me little shivers of embarrassment. You have this huge, four-layered twelve-octave keyboard, each tone adjustable to the sixty-six subdivisions of the octave, with selectable overtones. You have this gigantic chromatic apparatus that sends out spurts of color and spins exquisite patterns in the air, and you can key the colors any way you want. You can have each tone correspond to a point in the visible light spectrum—that's the standard setting—or any other settings; you can generate random correspondences or have correspondences in any pattern you want, simple, quadratic, whatever. The keys are so sensitive that the slightest pressure change in your fingers can alter the whole perspective. You can subvoke instructions to a hundred little black boxes for new patterns and images. And with the psifi, you'd add a whole 'nother layer of meaning and texture to the piece...

I couldn't resist trying out Dad's present, even though I'd never practiced with a psionically sensitive instrument in my life. But I was just a kid.

I hung on until the hush was complete. Annetta hung from the pointed ceiling, completely outside everything.

Then I launched into *Light on the Sound.*

That's one of the most famous pieces ever written, and I couldn't really play it. I started it too fast and decided to bluff the thing out. I sent out volleys of starclusters to counterpoint the dizzy four-note lefthand ostinato, then improvised some patches of glitter-whorls over a deep blue background that I sustained with the foot pedals. In the background I could hear them gasp—the gullible Philistines! Anyone can do fireworks on a clavichrome.

I got mad at them.

I bet they wouldn't notice even if I started making it up, I thought. Even though it's practically the most famous solo clavichrome piece in the world. I started fooling around. I threw myself into the thing—

I introduced a perky sort of boogie rhythm into the bass and matched it with fuzzy pink outlines that flitted nervously between the firetongues. Getting angrier, I lashed the light columns together with chains of crystal. I added a rain of high-pitched songpellets that threatened to drown the whole theme...

Then I remembered that the psifi was hooked on, and I wasn't quite in control of it. Horrible, dirty pictures of lewd women in potato sacks started prancing across the wall, silly adolescent fantasies—I heard them laughing, all my friends. They probably thought it was a neat party trick. And then, suddenly, out of the very bottom of my mind, a vision blurred into view and hung for a tiny moment—

It was a girl. Small and soft and vulnerable; green eyes that cut you in two, they were so piercing; and wild hair like the veldt in the comsim safari park; and she was about to speak and then she popped out of existence and I tore the plugs out of my head and turned the machine off in an angry impulse.

It sure wasn't Annetta. Purple eyelashes, pink pseudo-wings, and permanently zonked out on Levitol.

"Hey, Jules, why'd you stop?" said Femto. "That was some combustible chick you conjured up just then."

"Leave me alone!"

"Uh. The guy's demented with lust," giggled Atto prudishly. The LaGuardias were a somewhat prudish family; they limited their fooling around to their immediate family. Whether insecurity or narcissism I don't know—it was *their* problem.

"C'mon," said someone, "we have to cheer him up. Let's go and hit the corridors!"

"Coming?" said Femto and Pico in unison. Nano had spidered up to get Annetta off the ceiling. She was quietly coming to…

Nano turned to Pico and continued their argument…

"There are no stairs in Mallworld!" he said.

"There are so stairs in Mallworld," Pico retorted.

"Where the hell are they, then? It's always been demat-booths from the moment Mallworld was built, and everyone knows it's the historic first all-demat-booth colony world ever constructed!"

"What about while they were building the demat-booths? Are you going to tell me that the builders crawled along a thousand times thirty klicks of corridors just to install them? You're crazy!"

"Shut up, everyone!" I yelled. I couldn't hear myself think. What a useless argument, anyway. If there were stairs in Mallworld, no one knew where they were. No one used them…

"Hey," said Annetta in her shrill, affected voice. "Let's get a Levitol convoy going!" Everyone chorused agreement, and someone stuffed a Levitol tablet into my hand. I didn't want to seem like a spoilsport, so—

(That girl! The fleeting image jumped through my mind…who *is* she? Did the psifi bring out something I had subliminally plucked from the mind of one of the others? If so, she wasn't mine! I was angry at the thought. Or was it a flash of unconscious precog that the psifi had caused to surface? I—)

In a trice we'd all linked hands to toes and were buoyed up by the Levitol and were a chain hovering in the air. I was near the front holding on to Annetta, whose eyes were glazed over. A warm feeling came over me, and I couldn't think too clearly anymore.

"Let's hit the corridors!" Annetta shrieked. We snaked out the door, did a stomach-turning gravi-twist to adjust to a new down, and corkscrewed through the hotel lobby at about a twenty-klick clip.

Suddenly a swarm of six-inch-high little men in pink uniforms were flitting about my shoulder.

"Sir!" they buzzed. "We are computer simulacra of the security wing, serial numbers SEC3556 through 69! Levitol tripping is permissible only in designated or private areas! Kindly cease this prohibited activity this instant!"

"Buzz off, comsim scum!" Pico shouted happily, and we all started to cackle uncontrollably, warming to the end-of-school feeling. We swerved into a central corridor and did figure-eights around an elderly couple who were petting a lapdog. Then we collided with a stack of auto-shopping bags, and one of them tried to stuff Annetta into a half-open sack of surrogate cabbages. Femto, at the end of the line, swung forward and booted it hard and we were off again!

"Kindly return to your room!" the comsims chanted monotonously in the background.

The Levitol was wearing off...

I was diving; didn't quite know what I was doing...landed right in the fast lane of a delivery slidewalk and the chain broke. We broke up in hysterics as the slidewalk whipped past Gimbel and Gamble's Department Store and Feeliepalace and through a lightstreaked game arcade.

Suddenly the comsims materialized again. "You have ignored our repeated requests," they chorused. "A disciplinary robot will arrive shortly and will disperse you to the custody of your respective parents or parent-surrogates."

A burly clunker popped out of the nearest demat-booth and jumped onto the slidewalk and made straight for us. We did a wild obstacle race over bales of pickled Denebian whiteworms bound for the alien gourmet delis, and the thing rolled inexorably toward us, gaining at every step...

"Quick!" I said. "We have to get off this thing!"

"Into that pinball machine!" Atto yelled as we dived off the slidewalk and sent our friend racing toward the far horizon...

"Tickets! Tickets!" said the salesbot. "Oh, it's *you*," it grunted, recognizing me. "Ho! Seven—eight—nine freebies coming up!" We grabbed our free mallets and barged the line and crawled one by one into the little cocoons that were being fed into the giant air rifle.

I exploded from the boom tube, soared up, my mallet askew, into the middle of the pinball machine, then landed right on the center rotating circle! The 3,000 bell was just beyond my grasp, and I knew I could bang it with the mallet if I could just coordinate the swing with the swerve, right on the galactic pongo's luminous nose. I strained with the mallet and was just hitting it when the circle upended and tossed me into the friction-less dust; and I was on my back slithering down a slope and flailing at the emptiness, with the tingtingtinging of the pongo receding into the distance; and I was still spinning from the momentum of the circle—

I stared right up to the topmost spectator tier and could see my score in sixty-foot-long computer digits and the rows of gamblers, each with his little notepad, tier after tier of them...and the glass gangplanks crisscrossing the air about eight meters above my head, where repair robots scuttled along, monitoring the wild proceedings below...

A twister sprang up and shoved me upslope where I caromed off a *tingtingtingtitingtiting* bubblebeastie and veered to the left, just smashing the corner of the red button and it lit up and announced perkily TRIPLE SCORE WHEN LIT TRIPLE SCORE WHEN LIT! I saw two kids barrelrolling through the 200-point croquet hoops and narrowly missed them, slipped onto a randomspindisk and slung myself around a curve and caught a handle and braked to a giddy stop, still slithering in the frictionless dust. Pink and blue candystripe ripples rouletted in the sand...I was panting. I strained to see my score: 50,720. Not bad, and I was still a good 300 meters from the auto-flippers, Scylla and Charybdis. If I lost my hold on the handle before I had a chance to think up a strategy, I'd be off on random again...

My ears perked up. There was a commotion in the stands. People were yelling: "Stop her! Stop thief!" What was going on? I heard a patterclatter on the glass gangplanks eight meters over my head and saw legs of a girl in tatters, feet pounding the glass and a couple of metal clunkers clanking after her and a swarm of security comsims buzzing "Shoplifting prohibited! You are under arrest!" at her, and the girl looked down at me and—

Jumped and crashed right on top of me. In a split second I'd lost my handhold and we were off!

Her face was two centimeters from mine: I didn't have time to figure out who it—

It was *her!*

The green eyes piercing me, the yellow-green wild-grass hair, caught in the pinball airstream and eclipsing the candystripe lights—

We tumbled. I noticed some of the crowd standing up, yelling.

"Get your filthy hands off me!" she rasped. It wasn't at all the voice I expected.

"Who are you, you, you—" My eyes must have been wide as Jupiters; I could hardly speak, and I wanted to know so desperately...I clutched her as inertia swept us downslope toward Scylla and Charybdis, and she was pummeling me the whole time and telling me to let go and we rolled over in the sand and I kept stammering "Who are you?" and then I suddenly realized there was only one reason the buzzards would be trying to arrest her for shoplifting...

She was one of *them!*

I heard a thud behind us as the clunkers dropped down after her. One of them spun by, thrashing its steely cuff-tentacles vainly after us; the other gained steadily on us, gingerly stepping-stoning on the randomspindisks.

"Hold on, damn it, I'm trying to help you!" I said. The scent of her filled my nostrils, confusing me. I jammed a lever with my mallet *en passant* and flipped us upslope with a flop, and we shot past the clunker, and I childishly nyah-nyahed him as he slid helplessly into Scylla and Charybdis.

Pico, Nano, Atto, and Femto daisychained, whooshing into the open maw, and then I saw in dismay that the flippers weren't working—they'd jimmied them so's to catch us—and I clutched her, struggling, and we zoomed down the last hundred meters into the gigantic gaping blackness...

Into the arms of a dozen clunkers. We were in a cordoned-off area at the entrance to the corridor, and a crowd was already gathering to gawk, some of them shouting for their money back and complaining about foul bets.

"You are under arrest," announced the gaggle of comsims, materializing.

"Wait a minute!" I said. Was I going to lose the girl of my precog fantasy the instant I'd run into her? Was this all it was going to come to? "She's with me, damn it! Let her go!"

The crowd was silent suddenly. Hostile eyes glared at me. I put my arm around the girl and felt her yield just slightly, acknowledging me for the first time. I held out my thumb so the comsim could check my identity. It paused for a time, then protested, "Sir, the law..."

"Oh, you know what the law can go do to itself," I said furiously. "I'll give the store a kilocred if they don't prosecute. Two, three, I don't care." The crowd gasped at this unexpected turn of events.

"Now wait a minute," said the girl.

"I'll handle this!" I was starting to enjoy the scene. I was especially starting to enjoy the prospect of being alone with her afterward and basking in the warm glow of inevitable gratitude, and maybe a bit more...I mean, I'd just saved her from six months in a sanitization club, hadn't I?

There was a hardness to her that was different from how the psifi had shown her to me, but underneath it was incomprehension, hurt—only a wisp of tattered firefur clung to her body. Her hair swept over and obscured her forehead. And on her cheek, the left cheek—I hadn't seen it either, in my psifi reverie—was a white scar like a baroque pearl.

"Verdict: released into the custody of Julian barJulian the Thirteenth," came the voice of the Arbitration Computer, through the mouths of the comsims. The crowd began to disperse. She pulled away from me; I held on to her wrist and demanded, "What's your name?"

She broke free and bolted through the entrance into the corridor, knocking over a mothersurrogate and baby. I stopped thinking and just ran.

I could see her. She was fast! Already she was threading through swarms of gossiping matrons, barely skimming the floor, cutting across to the delivery slidewalks—

I was within a meter of her. I got nearer—

She fled into a demat-booth. There was just a centimeter between my hand and her elbow, and the booth didn't know the difference and the safety factor locked on and I was whisked off with her and we materialized on another level just outside The Way Out Suicide Parlor; and then she ran straight into the wall and pressed a stud on it and the wall started to slide…I wedged my toe in and caught hold of her and then I just gaped!

I blinked once or twice, straightened out my skimpy tunic, looked again…

"I guess it's no use," she said. "You're one of *them,* and now you know."

"Wait a minute," I said. *"You're* them. I'm *us."*

We both laughed rather nervously, and I blinked again and I still couldn't believe where this was…

We were in between two layers of Mallworld's skin. The metal gleam stretched up and away and down and away and to every side for as far as I could see, a mirror curved into forever…the far wall, perhaps fifty meters away, was connected to where we were standing (a sort of platform) by an intricate network of catwalks and strange twisted staircases that spiraled into infinity it seemed...it was vast. *Vast.*

Yes, Pico LaGuardia, I thought, suddenly remembering the quads' little argument at my party, *yes, there are stairs in Mallworld. What stairs they are!*

Winding like strands of giga-DNA.

And runged ladders hugging the sides. Snakes and silver ladders.

"Well," said the girl, "good-bye."

I suddenly noticed what it was that she had stolen, that she had risked six months in the clink for, tucked into her torn belt.

It was a doll.

She turned and started up a ramp, her arms catching at supports and metal protuberances with an easy familiarity. She swung herself up onto another platform.

I wasn't going to watch her recede into the metal vastness...Wait!" I shouted. The echo came, intense, frightening. "What's your name?"

A laughter resounded from all around, silvery as the walls themselves...

"Letisha!" (...*tishatishatishhhhhhhhh...*)

And she was gone.

It was a strange day to begin the Long Vacation with. I brooded after that; none of my friends seemed human, real. I saw her face whenever I played the clavichrome; and then I grew disgusted with my playing, for the first time. I saw her in dreams, hovering at the point of the ceiling in my bedroom...but it was a week before I screwed up the courage to go back and look for her.

And there I was, staring at the handle that led to another world...

On my left was the vestibule of The Way Out Corp. Its display sign whispered enticingly: "Tired of life? Why not...kill yourself? Over three hundred ways possible—most reversible! Money-back guarantee if not completely satisfied..."

I shuddered and touched the stud. The slam of the metal door re-echoed behind me and out into emptiness. I didn't want to make a sound, so I dissolved my shoes. Metal chilled my soles.

What was it about that girl? Was it her alienness, the fact that she belonged to a whole 'nother kind of life that I'd never seen before? I resolved myself and went up the ramp that was flung out over a drop to nothingness. Around me the hugeness was threatening; it was vaster than I'd remembered. A dim light shone from inlaid photopanels and was reflected back and forth across the silvergleam...the air smelled strange, ancient, and I expected dust on the ramp, but it was spotless.

I tried to remember which way she'd gone. Staircases twisted past me like elfin columns, vanishing to points in a gray loftiness. *She can't have gone that far...they must live here somewhere...*I swung myself up onto another level, the way I'd seen her do. I went up the stairs that angled out to the next catwalk; it didn't feel like *up,* more like sideways. I think there were leaks from the various gravi-control devices in the contiguous areas of Mallworld, so that my weight yoyoed and sometimes I had to do flips to stay on top. Spirals crossed overhead in not-quite-comprehensible patterns, and always the antiseptic virgin gleam of the metal shone, so that I passed through lightpools webbed by coiling shadows...

Then—

Voices. Echoshifted whispers in a slow circling around my head. I froze. I was enveloped in a steep curving of stairway, and I peered through a gap in the steel and saw them.

Across a two-meter gulf was a railinged platform. Some sort of weird ritual was going on.

Self-lighting candles, obviously pilfered from the Catholic cathedral on the religious level, glowed at the corners of the platform. About fifteen teenagers were crowded around in a circle. They were all nude and for a moment I thought the strange colors of their skins were just genetic mutapigment like some of my friends. But it was skinpaint—vivid greens, deep blues, fiery reds, with contrasting patterns in thick, angular strokes. They were wild-looking, like primitive earthies in prehistoric holo-movies...I couldn't make out what they were saying yet, so I leaned forward and stuck part of my face through the chink, hoping the light wouldn't fall on me.

They stopped suddenly and turned to their leader, the one with no bodypaint. He couldn't have been more than thirteen, and he had a classic, expensive-looking soma that suggested rich parents. He looked a lot like me...except that he had shoulder-length purple hair and—they shone clearly even at this distance—eyes of deep mauve. Something about those eyes...

There was an appalling emptiness in his eyes.

He waved his hand and they scrunched together, cross-legged, in a huddle. "Reports!" he said. He had a staccato, high voice with an aftertaste of wistfulness.

A girl spoke. *Letisha!*

"Two of us have been captured by *them* and sentenced to one year each in a sanitization club. We have acquired additional beddings for the two new members who have run away from bible-belt."

I held my breath. This was Letisha, all right, but how different! Blue paint covered her from head to foot, and from her navel radiated garish scarlet spokes of paint. There was something...*hypnotized* about her, about all of them.

I was scared stiff.

Mustn't breathe—

"We must say an act of contrition in remembrance of them," said the leader: again that curious voice. It had an attraction I couldn't define in it, the voice of that boy; it was at once totally authoritative and pleading, hurt. The whole group started to mumble incomprehensibly.

So this was where *they* came from, where *they* disappeared to. In this unknown world, they had thrown behind them all the overlays of civilization that they had brought with them when they ran away from their colony worlds, whether from poverty or from intolerable families or ideologies...they were savages! Superstitious, mud-eating savages like the bow-and-arrow-slinging, gas-guzzling Ancients!

I saw Letisha and realized that I wanted to be like her. Amid the whackiness, the weirdness, there was a solemnity that worried me but also made me a little envious. Because I hadn't had a serious thought in my whole life that I could remember. Oh, I'd been angry, frustrated, infatuated...but these people were obsessed.

That was new to me.

They began chanting a quiet litany whose words I could not make out. Then the leader spoke again in his curiously haunting voice: "We are all here in Mallworld for but a brief span, aren't we? And I have come to comfort you. There are hundreds of lost children lurking in hidden passageways, sleeping in the stairwells, emerging to gyp and hustle and shoplift. But we alone have the light."

The others started mumbling, their eyes fixed on the void that was their leader's face. He went on: "There's a world beyond the orbit of Saturn, beyond the Selespridon barrier. One day, when our little time in Mallworld is over, we will emerge from our cocoons and shatter the forceshield and enter the world of starlight!"

The mumbling increased, became a distant-tempest sound. I saw that Letisha was as drawn to the leader as the rest. And as for me—

They were beautiful words, and the voice was beautiful, and only the week before I'd had this dreadful experience learning about the rulers of the Galaxy and man's isolation, and the words seemed to offer some kind of mystical hope...I didn't believe it, of course. I knew it was metaphysical drivel. And yet—

That kid! Those vacant, mauve eyes! For a moment I even forgot about Letisha and was spellbound by the kid's charisma.

"Listen, all of *us,*" he said. "You love me, don't you?"

"We love you, Yitsakh," they chanted.

"You'd die for me, wouldn't you?"

"We'd die for you, Yitsakh…"

I was shivering. The echoes went on and on, diminishing infinitely into the curved metal. I wasn't equipped to deal with this.

Then the leader said, his voice rising. "The pact! The pact! Remember the pact!"

"The pact! The pact!" they repeated, and the echoes of the *-ct-ct* sounds clicked as they trickled past me…

They began to chant again. "Once a year a child is born, once a year a child must die! Once a year a child is born, once a year a child must die!" The chant grew and grew until the whole huge emptiness was resonating. And I knew that this strange religion the *them* were clinging to must contain something sinister behind the lovely images.

One of them pulled out a test tube filled with some kind of liquid. I pushed my face hard against the gap in the stairway and saw what it was—a Storkways test tube of the kind used for fertilizing ova. The leader took the tube and placed it in the center of the group and then twisted it with his wrist to start it spinning.

"Whomsoever this shall point to, let him join the Lord's anointed!" he cried in a singsong voice. The test tube slowed down…

And pointed to Letisha.

"Letisha!" said the leader. "You are the lucky one who will join the stars. What have you chosen to kill yourself with?"

I couldn't contain myself any longer. "No!" I screamed. They all rose up and looked around, the kid nearest me caught sight of my eye disappearing from the crack, in a second two of them had caught hold of the banister and vaulted themselves over and I was caught and pinioned. I was hot all over.

"Save yourself, Letisha!" I yelled. "Don't let 'em get you!"

I felt giddy as the two, still clutching me tight, vaulted expertly back onto the platform…I stared wildly around me. Fifteen kids in savage bodypaint threatened from all sides.

I had to brazen it out. "What kind of crazy suicide pact is this? What right do you guys have to go around ordering kids to commit suicide?"

"You're one of *them!*" said the leader, in a voice devoid of anger. I saw that he *pitied* me…"Who are you?"

"I'm Julian barJulian," I said, "the Thirteenth, and I own the space you live in."

"Who can own space?" the Leader said, mocking me gently. "Life is just a fleeting transience."

"You're crazy!"

Letisha spoke. Her voice was quiet, curiously convincing. "No, Julian. *You're* crazy."

"Shall we throw him over the edge?" said one of the kids, as nonchalantly as if he'd said *Shall I wash the dishes?* I opened my mouth and couldn't speak…

"What do you think, my people?" said Yitsakh. Again, no harsh emotions. "Letisha, you are the one that seems to know him. Why have you been mixing with these shallow, meaningless people, these people of the shadows?"

Letisha said, "Yitsakh, I don't know who he is. Last week he rescued me from the clinkerclunks. Don't ask me why. Maybe there's some good in him…"

"We can't let him go!" said a voice. "He'll tell on us!"

"Will you?" said Yitsakh. He didn't look at me.

"What do you think I am?" I said hotly.

"We *know* what you are," said another one, and I felt the incredible scorn in his voice and was stung.

"He won't tell," said Letisha softly. I looked at her in surprise. For a moment, our eyes met and I struggled against my captors. I thought I saw something there but she looked away quickly, as though ashamed of having shown me any part of herself. Then she said to Yitsakh, "He looks a little like you, Yitsakh. I think he came from the same batch. The only difference is that he has normal, dark brown hair, and—" She went on like this for a while, and I suddenly realized that Yitsakh was blind. "Yitsakh, you know I love you. We all do.

I know he won't hurt us, I'm telling you on my love for you. And now that I'm about to die, I think you should spare him…"

So much for all my delusions that the girl would fall into my arms in gratitude for my saving her hide! Touché! *That* debt was wiped out for sure.

"Very well," said Yitsakh. The empty purple eyes stared through me into…what? Did he see the reaches of space beyond our universe, where the Selespridar lived and the stars shone?

I was going to lose her! And now I knew for sure that I was in love with her. I had to save her for myself. I had to win her away from this mad prophet of the stairways…"I don't know the way back," I said. "I'm lost."

"I will escort him back," said Letisha—and my heart lifted—"and return for the rest of the ceremony." My heart sank again.

"You won't let this stranger tempt you from the pact?" said Yitsakh, suddenly a child.

I saw that this was what she loved in him. His vulnerability, his certitude. He had power, that boy…"Of course I won't let him tempt me," she said. And kissed him on the cheek, very lightly, and turned to me with expressionless eyes. "Let's go."

I was going to try my hardest to tempt her. And she knew it, too. I knew that she saw it as some kind of test. Inside I screamed, *You're in a trap! Come out and let me love you!*

Letisha beckoned once; they released me, and we left by a different catwalk from the ones I'd seen before. I saw that on a string around her waist hung the doll she had stolen.

"Ease onto this banister," she said. "Careful."

We slid down a straight stretch of stairway, slowly—it was a low-g section—and then were inside another spiral. She didn't say anything except to whisper directions in the same flat voice.

"You're coming with me!" I said as soon as I knew we were out of earshot. "You can't stay with them, they're monsters, and you deserve a better chance…"

"Shut up."

I stumbled on a jagged piece of metal. Without any fuss she picked me up and set me going again.

"Look, I'm rich. You can have anything you want. Just stay with me awhile, okay? Then you can go back to your weird savages…"

"I know all about you," she said. "More than you think. You have no idea how narrowly you missed being killed. If any of the others had actually *realized*—"

"What?" She was so close to me!

"Never mind."

All too soon we had reached the platform where the real world and the alien one converged. "Come on," I said, pressing the stud.

"No."

I couldn't stand it anymore. I grabbed her and wouldn't let go. She let fly with her free fist and got me in the nose. I felt the blood trickle but couldn't feel any pain. I was angry at them for brainwashing her into this ridiculous cult, I was angry at her for not coming with me like destiny had clearly intended—

I got hold of both her wrists. We were precariously near the edge. She kneed me in the stomach. I felt a dull ache, then more anger. I let go and grabbed her whole body tight, shaking her.

"Selfish bastard!" she screamed.

"I'm only trying to save you—"

She wrenched herself again and I held on tight and the string around her waist broke and the doll went sailing off into the void—

She stared after it, then broke away from me and bawled.

It was easy for me to hold on to her and lead her away. She didn't struggle at all. Now I was only angry at myself. Couldn't I do anything right? We stepped onto the first slidewalk, and I held on to her hand, and she sobbed without stopping, and I felt sick with self-recrimination and desire.

We made it to my suite at the Gaza Plaza, and she went straight to the cathartic booth to vacuum off the paint. She stepped out wearing one of my artfur tunics. Her eyes were quite dry now, and blazing.

"All right," she said very quietly, "Mr. Rich Man. You've kidnapped me, made me break the pact, and you're probably about to offer me a pile of money in exchange for my services as a companion or something. But you can't keep me here. You don't have the right."

God! She was more beautiful to me than any of my shallow friends. She *was* a dream come true, literally. I had to make her see reason, I had to show her she couldn't go on like that. "Please," I said, "just stay a little while longer, will you?"

She didn't answer me, but moved and sat down on a chairfloat. After a while she said, "I haven't got all the time in the universe, you know. Make your sales pitch so I can leave."

So I told her everything about myself. I told her about the way she had appeared to me in the middle of my clavichrome playing, how I had become driven by the vision of her…I went on and on. I think I started to tell about my school and about how Dad didn't love me but just sent me gobs and gobs of money and expected gratitude. I think I cried. I don't know.

At the end of it she was as cold as ever, and I was as hopelessly in love as ever.

Finally she said, "You talk very well, Julian. But you never once showed that you thought of me as a human being. You fell in love with a thing in your machine, without knowing who I was or anything. And I don't love you. I love Yitsakh. I believe in him…"

"You're lying!" I shouted. "You can't believe all that rubbish. You know you're not going to be reborn in the real universe among the stars when you die…you're just going to snuff out, like a self-lighting candle from the cathedral."

"Yeah, whatever," she said. She got up to leave—

"Wait!" I said.

We once did mythology in school. I remembered a tale retold by someone called Homer, a science fiction writer from the Dark Ages. It was called Orpheus and Eurydice, and it was about this singer who brought back his lover from the dead...in the days before optional-reversibility death, I mean...I remembered that he could sing so well that the very stones would weep.

Well, maybe if I played the clavichrome to her—

Damn it, I knew I was the best clavichrome player in the Solar System. All my teachers and all my friends had told me so.

"Just wait awhile longer," I said. "Let me play to you, let me show you how I really love you..."

"You're pathetic," she said. But she sat down again.

I took a long time hooking up, on purpose, just so I could look at the way she sat. In spite of her shouting at me just moments before, she was perfectly composed now. If I played to her I could swing it, maybe. Then I knew I could. After all, I was Julian barJulian XIII, and I *always* got everything I wanted.

So I started to improvise, watching her face the whole time.

I had to impress her, so I picked *Light on the Sound* again. That ill-fated piece...

I started at a steady tempo, not wanting to make a mistake. I didn't use the psifi; I was still too scared from the first time I'd tried it. But I was vain enough to turn on the recording box (when not in use, my clavichrome doubled as recorder, message-storer, minicomp) and to program the most dazzling, ambitious color-sequence into the keyboard that I knew.

I threw every interpretational trick I knew into the performance. I had extra arabesquing lightcolumns that rose and snapped, and filigrees of purple sparklers running in and out of them, and I whipped up the four-note ostinato until it segued into the big thundering section with the keening twitter of high notes fireworking under chordclusters that crashed in tandem with ocean-waves of blue light. I had inverted thunderbolts straining for the pointed ceiling. I had veils that fell one by one until it was a mist over the console, and when I got to the brilliant final section I couldn't see my own fingers...

The final echo died out and I turned to her, expecting applause.

She laughed at me.

"You have fantastic technique," she said at last. "But the way you play is just typical of your kind. You're showing off everything you've got. I didn't feel a thing when you played..."

"No!" I cried out, knowing underneath it all that every word of it was true—I brought my hands crashing onto the keyboard and a horrible jangle of sounds mixed with supernova dirty mud colors exploded across the room.

"Don't you see," she said, "why I prefer my world to yours?"

"Your world is fake!"

"I won't make the obvious rejoinder..."

"Damn it...this clavichrome is real, real, real!" I banged my fist on it and another volley of discords burst forth.

"Julian, your playing is very pretty, but it isn't real at all. You haven't lived near death the way all of *us* have. You've done everything, but you've experienced nothing! When you become a real artist, you won't play that way anymore. You'll show off when the piece requires it, and you'll build simple shapes as well as complicated ones...Julian, I really like you. I want you to know that."

She had a big heart, that girl. I realized how dumb all my pretentions had been, how I didn't even deserve to have her scolding me like this. But I still hoped—

"Will you stay awhile here?" I said. "I'll put a megacred in an account in your name so you won't have to steal. I'll do anything you say, I'll relearn the clavichrome the way you tell me to."

She smiled.

It was the kind of smile that would unfreeze the rings of Saturn. I called for a comsim and made the credit transfer. She didn't look the whole time I was doing it.

And then she yielded to me, but never giving any of her real self. I knew her mind was on other things. And the next morning she was gone, and the clavichrome had the light on that showed a message stuck in it...

I sat down and she materialized in the empty air.

"Julian—" she said. "Thanks for the money. By the time you scan this I will have signed a tight, irreversible-death contract with The Way Out Corp. No bribe you can give them will bring me back. I'll be in a million pieces. I do like you, Julian, but I'm loyal to my word...

"All of *us* who have known Yitsakh have sworn to uphold his vision. We don't know if it's true or not. We just know that we love him. We all came from broken homes, we all ran away to big, anonymous Mallworld because of intolerable situations; and Yitsakh gave us a new dream, something bigger than ourselves. If I didn't follow through with the pact, I think Yitsakh would be unbearably hurt...

"Good-bye, Julian."

I reached over to turn the thing off. I didn't burst out crying. I didn't rush into paroxysms of grief. I felt alienated, outside myself. Remembering the previous night and thinking of her...as particles of dust flung out in the loneliness of space.

But the tape wasn't quite over.

"I almost forgot, Julian—there's a story I have to tell you before I go. It might help explain a little better some of the cruel things I said.

"Once upon a time there was a very rich man. He had one son he didn't care for much; the son was four years old and precocious but very self-involved and didn't give anything to the father. So he decided to try again. He went to Storkways Inc. and ordered a baby—the most classically beautiful baby he could imagine. But there was an error in the manufacture, and the baby was born blind. The father rejected it at once and vowed to order no more babies.

"Human compassion being what it is, they did not pulp the child. He grew up in the hidden places of Mallworld, and instead of seeing the world around him made visions out of nothingness. He survived...

"His father's name was Julian barJulian the Twelfth, Julian. Yitsakh is your brother."

And then Letisha faded from my life.

I sat at the clavichrome console for a very long time. I thought I would cry but I didn't. This was too *big* to cry about. I'd cried often enough in my short life, mostly to get something I wanted. Or thought I wanted. I'd cried when my first clavichrome didn't have all the buttons I wanted. I got the extra buttons. I'd cried at the paltry size of my uncountable allowance. I got more.

I wouldn't get *this.*

I couldn't have had it even if Letisha were...were...

And all the new things I had learned about whirled in my head, undoing all the ingrained thought patterns, wrenching everything apart. I saw the huge empty void between the skins of Mallworld, with the echoes whispershifting over spirals of steel; I saw the holoZeiss projection on the school bus with the ghosts of the stars superimposed on the emptiness of our pocket universe; I saw Yitsakh's starry vision; I saw Letisha's face and how she loved someone enough to die just for the integrity of his vision; and I saw the empty purple eyes of Yitsakh, my rejected brother, who could have been just like me and was one of *them* instead, one of the outcasts...the eyes that could not see me saw right through me, right to the heart of what men desire.

I knew that I had to build something to replace the shattered patterns of the past...

And all the images began to crystallize into a complete thought. *Simplicity,* I thought. *A simple, pure statement.* Something so obvious that we've all completely overlooked it.

The thought came together all at once.

I set the clavichrome controls so that the waverange of the color blue was spread over the entire twelve octaves, in infinitesimal gradations. Quickly I hooked up and then turned on the recorder and printer so I could have a score...

I started with a single pure note, no overtones at all, and a single line of blue light. Just a simple idea. The note grew on either side into a slow cluster; and the blue light grew too, very slowly, until the whole air was singing with blues, ceruleans, aquamarines, ultramarines, turquoises, moving imperceptibly from one to the other and shifting in slow waves...time stood almost still. Gradually a heartbeat sound became audible, a faint throb that intensified the stillness.

I wasn't thinking about me anymore, not about Letisha, not about our brief relationship. I was thinking a little about Yitsakh's vision and about how mankind would be free one day. About how each of us has a little piece of the truth inside himself, how shallowness and stupidity could hide it...made the whole room around me into a deep blue sky; and I made the music deep blue and raging, but understated. And then I planted a star in the dark blue and counterpointed a new very simple theme in the treble, still using pure tones without overtones; and then I added another star and another, and more kinds of blue, and stars that did not move but just glittered quietly; and then I made all the keyboards burst out in song, building a fugue out of the simple treble theme and throwing star after star into the sky until the deep blue heaven blazed with men's dreams.

It's my most famous piece.

I don't even have to tell you its name, you've all recognized it from the description. Maybe some of you have kids who are struggling through it—it's not very hard technically.

I've told my story now. I guess I tricked you. I tricked myself too: when I started off I thought it'd be a brief, light, humorous intro and then I'd launch into one of my showy pieces—and I've written hundreds of those. I've written a lot of better pieces than that first breakthrough into art, too; but you know how whimsical the public's fancy is. Hell, you *are* the public.

I hope you're still with me, out there.

You know I often wonder what happens to those wild children when they grow up. I still see them sometimes, turning a corner, stepping out of a booth—sometimes I swear it's Yitsakh. But he probably is middle-aged now, if he hasn't succumbed to his own visions...

I'm going to play the song now, and I hope it helps you to see Yitsakh's dream. I hope you'll dream it with me, until the day the Selespridar open the universe to us again. Until we're free.

Quite an artist, my lord, don't you think? I was really quite entranced by the primal magnificence of his clavichrome composition, the first one he played. Perhaps, High One, you find this to be evidence in their favor, this art?

No? You don't understand what's going on? You want to know what a pinball machine is? You're ordering one to be fetched from Mallworld and delivered to your home, so that you can enjoy this primitive entertainment device for yourself? I told you, my lord, how infectious this native culture is...

But we're off again; this time into another tale of unmitigated tawdriness.

(But first, a word from another one of our sponsors.)

CULT-OF-THE-MONTH CLUB

Have you ever wondered what it's like to reach nirvana? To whirl yourself into ecstasy like the dervishes of old?

To suffer the joys of crucifixion, of expiating the sins of humanity, painlessly and without the need for devivification?

If you're lonely and depressed—

If the blandishments of suicide parlors and kinky vending machines have failed to snag you—

If your life needs meaning—

We may have just the thing for you!

YES! THE CULT-OF-THE-MONTH CLUB!

Religious rapture can be yours—a different one every month—you pay only for the cults you wish to adopt for the rest of the period, and all for the low low price of forty-seven point three credits!

How do we do it?

Well, it's bulk. Every year our board of directors sends experts to romantic, superstitious old earth to dig up new religions. They scour the ancient tombs of such mystical figures as Grant and Napoleon. They visit the temples of ancient leaders like Jesus, Nixon and Zoroaster. They leaf through ancient tomes and twodee videotapes. They hire priests— often aging human relics who haunt the streets and alleys of earth, preaching their arcane doctrines to beggars and anthropologists. A staff of analysts—who are all aware of the different needs of today's humans—sifts through the mass of data and then sends their findings to our religious tailors.

There the difficult part begins—for each of the cults finally selected must be condensed, abridged, *tailor-made* for the man and woman of today, who wants good value for money and isn't going to wait around for ten or fifty years to attain enlightenment.

And then we do a careful comsim study of each religion. Does it really have genuine meaning?

Does it contain an interesting, unique and colorful religious experience?

Does it involve effort or suffering on the participants' part? If so we offer mitigations or surrogate suffering, unless you opt for our deviants' special.

Is it truly a *fun* religion?

When all these stringent tests and controls are passed—

We bring them to you!

Yes, indeed! You, in the privacy of your own cubiclet, can experience—

The searing, erotic frenzy of St. Theresa!

All the carnival fun of the Samoan ritual pollution of fire hydrants!

The solemn, austere peacefulness of a Last Supper in a genuine reconstructed McDonalds!

If you were to join all these religions separately, you'd end up in a credit clink. Seriously. Many have vast initiation fees, and some demand that you give up all your worldly possessions—not something most people can readily afford more than once in their lives, let alone every month.

Are you convinced?

No?

Well, here's something that'll grab you for sure.

For a limited time only, YOU can get your choice of three religions for only one creed! We're giving you this incredible offer because you know you'll love the Cult-of-the-month-club. And we ask only that you take four more selections during the coming year.

Here's how it works—

Every month you'll get an attractive holovisual prospectus that pops right into your holovee. Our main selection, plus several alternates, will be described in tempting detail. You can experience *one full day* of any selection simply by voicing your desire to the convenient intelligence-level-Z comsim that is conveniently programmed into your package.

If you don't want religion that month, simply say so and your wishes will be honored. Absolutely no door-to-door preaching or surprise manifestations of deities, and especially no tithing permitted! Your pre-cult fee is absolutely *all* you ever have to pay.

To start, just pick three of the cults on this list and come down to our level, Alphomega Six Six Six, right here in Mallworld! (And if you saw this offer at participating psychiatrists, remember that you can pick a fourth religion, absolutely free! just give us your shrink's permit number when you apply.)

Choose from the following—

*** *Juggernaut Special.* Be crushed under the wheeled image of a gigantic primitive idol! Restorative surgery not included.

*** *Early Christianity.* Our best bargain of the year. Seventeen separate sects, counts as one choice.

*** *Pyramid Worshipping.* Be wrapped in linen bandages, drugged, and chanted over by priests in Egyptian robes! Watch their surprise as you come to life and terrorize a reproduction of the ancient city of London.

*** *Zennish navel-gazing.* Meditate for forty years! (time effect simulated with controlled Brevitol. Real time duration fifteen days.)

*** *Harried Krishna.* Sell plastic flowers in a reproduction of an ancient jetport—to bored and argumentative customers!

*** Thugee *Cult.* Kill androids in a veritable orgy of gore! Guaranteed harmless.

*** *Priest of the Sun/Cult of Moloch.* Double-header here! Spend two weeks climbing pyramids and sacrificing attractive young men and women to Tezcatlipoca, then another fortnight throwing babies into fires! Simulated victims only. Two religions count as a single selection.

*** *Priest of Heliogabolus.* Indulge in ritual castration! Completely reversible process allows this rite to be enjoyed as often as you wish, with friends or in the privacy of your own cubiclet.

WE GUARANTEE THAT YOUR LIFE
WILL HAVE MEANING
BY THE TIME YOU'RE THROUGH, OR YOUR
MONEY COMPLETELY REFUNDED!

CULT-OF-THE-MONTH!
THE MODERN WAY TO GET RELIGION!

The Vampire of Mallworld

Clement barJulian was a quadrillionaire with eyes in the back of his head. I was a reporter for the Holothrills-National Enquirer Syndicate, stiffly snapping at my live turtle soup in the middle of a gourmet restaurant in the middle of a thirty-klick-long shopping center floating in space, trying to get the man to talk about a vampire—and he wasn't talking.

"I hate to presume on our old friendship—" I was saying. Above, a holoZeiss projected a shimmering stardome. My turtle swam half-heartedly in its bowl of bluish nutriliquid, and I was only waiting for it to hold still a moment so I could jab it with my fork.

"You presume," said Clement barJulian, "too far. There *is* no vampire in Mallworld." The candlelight flared up for a moment, playing flicker-shadow with his face. It was, of course, a deliberately contrived effect; I knew that Clement liked to affect a menacing mien. "Go home, Milton. Aren't you supposed to be covering the atrocities of the seven-veiled sect or something?"

"Yes, I was. But they assigned someone else. Got some kind of notion that I'm slipping...hell, Clement, you've seen the ratings! I'm only the most popular holovee personality in the Solar System! Remember when I covered the time in Mallworld when the mini-demat-booths backfired and left six hundred shoppers minus their heads? Remember when the Selespridon governor of Sol System was molested by a hundred Girl Scouts from bible-belt? And here I am investigating filler material. Sticking me with a moderately gory carnival act when I could be covering the war in Luna or interviewing a Selespridon..." Carefully I maneuvered myself to get some good shots of barJulian. I was incognito, of course, covered with mounds of plastiflesh; indeed, the pot belly I'd snapped over my well-muscled torso was a pouch to carry my camera in, and it was operating surreptitiously through my navel.

"Always whining, Milton Huang, always whining," said Clement barJulian as he slurped the last of his Denebian whiteworms. "I know very well that whenever you get a Mallworld story you come to me first and whine and hope I'll bail you out—not to mention that I own a not bad share of the networks. But I've never heard of a vampire in Mallworld, and I don't even rightly know what one is—some kind of geek, no?—and if anyone would know, I would." He was right: his family *owned* Mallworld. He was worth enough to buy Phobos and Deimos and use them for juggling balls. And yet—he was edgier than I'd ever seen him. He'd always been very cordial with me, though you can't really ever know what the super-rich have clicking in their minds. But today he was downright hostile. Was there something going on?

"I'll investigate, of course," I said. My career was slipping and I could hardly do otherwise.

"That," said Clement portentously, "is life."

It was a relief to step out of the Galaxy Palace restaurant. Clement barJulian owned it, of course. It was the only place in existence where you could see the stars—the way they used to look, before the Selespridar came and shunted everything inside the orbit of Saturn into a pocket universe "for your own good"—projected via the last surviving holoZeiss recording. It's a beautiful restaurant; depressing, too. I'd gotten some good establishing shots there—only 2-D unfortunately, but they could be superimposed into a holo-collage, very in and arty that year, back at the studio.

Once in the corridor—

Mallworld was as it always was. Crazi-gravi corridors corkscrewing precariously and mobiustripping around straight corridors lined with demat-booths, and you could look up and see level after level after level on either side of you, vanishing into infinity, above and below; signs yelling at you, garish holo-ads with sensual young men and women selling perfume, airbeds, spacecars, relics of the Cross, pet salamanders, laxatives, compact sensuosurrogates for asteroid miners, rut pills, skating gloves—and the people, streaming by like space truckers' convoys, and the robots weighed down with shopping bags, and the jabbering, the jabbering...

Setting off at random—figured I should do some more establishing shots—I found a courtyard with upside-down fountains. An orchestra of Rigellian semisentients was playing squeaky music from their synthesizing rituals.

Perhaps I've been a little too Machiavellian, going straight to barJulian, straight to the top like this, I thought. Resolutely I turned to summon a comsim. Why not try the direct approach?

The comsim landed on my shoulder, a bearded six-inch man in pink.

"Hello. I am computer simulacrum Mallguide 227719," it buzzed. "Can I help you?"

"Yes. Uh, where's the vampire?"

"Hee!" it snickered, fluttering around my head. "You must be loaded! Show me your thumb."

Satisfied by my creditworthiness, it went on, "Honored sir"— it had suddenly become very obsequious, being programmed to react favorably to well-heeled thumbprints—"I cannot talk. But for one of such a bottomless expense account..."

"What do you mean, you can't talk?"

"You will be contacted!" And it was gone. I hadn't even been able to turn quickly enough to get a good angle through the camera eye in my navel.

All there was left to do was find a hotel and wait, so I got into a booth and asked for the Gaza Plaza, and in a split second I was walking into the hotel that was a scale model of the Great Pyramid of Khufu. Or perhaps it *was* the Great Pyramid—the ads were deliberately ambiguous there.

I felt a bit strange in the pyramid-shaped room, which was kept at a half-g for comfort. There was a crazy, queasy feeling in my stomach...but wait! It wasn't the gravity!

All right, you can come out now, I subvocalized. My belly ripped open at the command from my throat gizmo, and my camera flopped all over the bed, wires and tentacles and micromikes wriggling like Medusa's head.

"Well," I said. "What do you make of it all?"

"Pretty weird," it said. "I still think it's a hoax, but what do I know?"

"Hell," I said, "it's just some guy drinking blood. Why should Clement barJulian get all defensive about it? And what about all this cloak and dagger stuff with the comsims? I don't like it—"

Suddenly all the lights went out. "What the—" I stuttered, thinking, *Uh oh, not a repeat of last season's blackout!*

An eerie green light flickered on, cold and faint as in a dream. Then a comsim matted in: almost a foot tall, hovering in the air, with a dark black cloak that trailed behind him and rippled ever so gently. Its eyes were closed, and its lips were thin, red, sensuous.

"Quick, Clunko, get this on tape!" I murmured.

"Whaddya think I'm doing, dummy?"

I just stared and stared at the comsim. I almost recognized it; it was like a forgotten childhood image, an old story, a racial memory even.

The eyes flashed open. They were bloodshot. I was transfixed. Terror lanced my stomach for a wild moment before I could regain control.

Then—

A horrible cackle reverberated around the room, the mouth opened, the hideous fangs glistened, death-white, the eerie light shifting, darkening. gigantic shadows twisting...

"Good evening," it said. A sinuous, cold voice. "I am a comsim reproduction of Bela Bartok, the most famous vampire of the ancient earthmyths. If you will kindly follow me, we will demat into the Cellars of Doom...participation is twelve credits only, observation twelve thousand credits to ensure only the most discriminating clientele...and now, the secret

Vault of Horror of The Way Out Corporation. Your credit identification, please...this way! this way! this way!"

So this was it! I resisted an impulse to clutch Clunko's tentacles, abandoned myself to a deliciously creepy shudder, and followed the comsim through a wall that had begun to shimmer and turn to mist.

TIRED OF LIFE? said the sign in a mellow, father-image sort of voice. WHY NOT...KILL YOURSELF? 300 WAYS POSSIBLE AT *THE WAY OUT CORP.!* MOST REVERSIBLE! MONEY BACK GUARANTEE IF STILL ALIVE AFTER PROCESSING!

I noted with some perplexity that The Way Out Corp. was a subsidiary of the Clement barJulian Group. "The plot thickens." I subvoked to Clunko the camera. I'd discarded my pot belly and donned a cloth-of-iridium loinshield; Clunko clattered behind. I still did not dare reveal my true face, of course, since I had some pretty overpowering fans.

Our personal comsim led us inside. Abruptly, a soundscreen cut off the crowd and we were each immersed in our own little silence.

"Your seat, sir," said the comsim resonantly. A dim green light shone on an antique coffin, done up to make a padded couch.

"Yes, but what about the vam—" He had dematted. I found a piece of paper with writing on it on the couch, program notes or something: since I can't read, of course, I scrunched it up and threw it behind me. *Okay.* I subvoked. *Spread yourself out and start shooting.* Clunko subdivided into little cells—ah, the miracle of subatomic circuitry!— and began to drift around the place. For holovee you need at least four or five shooting angles or you can't get a good "in-the-round" feeling.

In the dimness I could make out some breathing. When my eyes adjusted I saw others in the audience. The bored and rich, all of them. Not since Pope Joan the Fifteenth's funeral had I seen such an array of garish clothing and outlandish, extravagant soma-models: purple skins, vestigial heads and other paraphernalia, grafted-on limbs and appendages, lewd-looking women wearing gilded potato sacks, and all of them heaving with a sort of vulturelike ecstasy. I even saw a Selespridon, occupying a couch by himself—tall, blue-skinned and magenta-haired and looking decidedly uncomfortable. A subtle, sickly sweet odor pervaded everything. It was so dark there wasn't any scale to it. I mean, there could have been thousands of people there...I subvoked an amplicommand to the olfacto track: there's nothing better than a wicked, nasty smell on holovee to really drive a point home...

A voice broke the silence. It came from everywhere at once, as the darkness deepened still more.

"Humans, aliens and semisentients," it began, "we are proud to present a genuine reconstruction of the day-to-day life of an ancient mythic vampire. The vampire of Earth—whose name has come down to us in various forms as Bella Abzug, Bela Bartok and Clarabelle—was a monstrous alien who devoured...human blood.

"Today we have the Vampire of Mallworld. A psychopath of unknown origin, this vampire came to The Way Out Corp. wishing for a release from life. Today, instead, he has earned a permanent place to live out his dread fantasies...all his victims are our customers. All the death scenes are genuine, and no victim will be revivified; each has signed an irreversible contract with The Way Out. We warn you—many who have come to watch as members of the audience have eventually found their way onto the stage of death!...And we sincerely hope that the desperadoes, the depressed, the schizoid, and the merely bored among you will think of us when the time comes for *you* to seek—*The Way Out!*"

Spotlight on a single coffin on a dais, old and dirty. The audience was quite still. Slowly, agonizingly slowly, the lid creaked open. The sound system was hyperamped to give you the shivers. It creaked...creaked...and then crashed onto the floor.

Very slowly he stood up. He was tall, over two meters. A black cloak flapped from his shoulders. His face was painted white, unearthly white with a glowing tinge of green. It was a long, bleak face, the black hair merging with the black cape, the lips Mars red and seductive, the eyes empty, dead. He hardly seemed to notice the audience.

"The first victim," said the announcer. "Miss Emily Smith."

A little old granny tottered onto the stage. She was shaking all over as she crossed the stage's lines of shadow. The vampire took her into his arms, towering above her. She seemed to see nothing but his compelling eyes.

Teeth glistened. She whimpered once before he ripped her apart, and then she fell to the ground with a crash. A robot dragged off the body.

That's all? I was thinking. I looked around: couples in the audience were intertwined, some shamelessly indulging in erotic little games. *Talk about the rich and bored!* Clunko buzzed in my ear. *Shut up,* I subvoked. *Keep filming.*

A few more victims, mostly women. And then—number ten or eleven, I forget the name, but she was shatteringly beautiful, only a girl…she wore a white gown, and her long black hair streamed behind her in the stagewind they had set up for her…she just stood there, half in the shadow, deep brown eyes moist and meltingly lovely, and I was on the edge of my seat. So was the audience. A throaty murmur escaped them, was stifled.

"Come, my dear, my little one…" The voice was heard for the first time, and the sound system distorted it into a terrifying, nightmare voice. She advanced as though hypnotized. The vampire caressed her face with a large, slender hand that half-glowed with some luminous grease paint; they embraced chastely, then more passionately, and then she was flinging aside her gown and he was biting her all over, and pools of red were spreading all over the white, and her sighs turned into shrieks of terror—

The whole audience cried out all at once. She flopped lifeless to the floor.

A burst of thunderous applause, cheering, the vampire bowed and dematted and the lights came blindingly on—

"We hope that you have had a pleasant fright," the announcer said warmly. "and thank you so much for choosing The Way Out Corp. for your entertainment today...Good evening."

I glanced cursorily at the audience. Many were still under the spell. Then I got up to look for the stage door.

This was stupendous! This man had turned a simple geek act into a work of art. I could imagine him wowing them all on the lunchtime news now—the ratings'd put our rivals Astroco in the sanitization club for bankruptcy. Mind you, he *was* a psychotic...but one might daydream. He had an air about him. There was no vulgarity here. This had power. This had panache. This had class.

It wasn't just a filler. This had to be a special. Pocket History of Earth's Ancient Vampires. Panel of psychologists— human and robot. The works. There was a fortune here, if only I could get the right angle on it.

...found a little autodoor that whispered STAGE DOOR, AUTHORIZED PERSONNEL ONLY, so I muttered "Holovee, holovee" in that urgent, well-rehearsed tone of voice that I always used to get into forbidden places. It accordioned open. Then it banged shut behind me and Clunko, and I took a look.

I found the vampire alone, being helped off with his clothes by a rusty-looking robot. Everything stank of poverty and degradation in the dressing room. Cloaks and props cluttered up every centimeter of the floor. And then I looked at the vampire's face.

He was standing in front of a mirror. I saw him first in the mirror, a dazed, sad face, a trace of blood on his lips. With a shock, I realized he was only a meter-fifty tall or so. He'd been wearing leviboots.

He had an earnest young face, mousy hair, freckles, a mild, undernourished look.

"You the vampire?" I couldn't believe it.

"I'm the vampire," he said sadly. The robot had whisked the cloak away and he stood naked in front of me. His soma was emaciated, pitiful. I was still in shock as he went on. "I don't know how you got in—"

"I'm Milton Huang!"

"Who?" The man didn't even watch holovee.

"I'm a holovee personality. I want to do a special on you. You look like you could use the money," I added in a confidential sort of tone. "Listen, what do I call you? Mr. Vampire? Vampey?"

"My name is Federico barJulian," he said emotionlessly, "and my friends usually call me Fred. But then again I have no friends."

I was shaking inside, the way you always do when a terrible humdinger of a story is about to break. "You're a *barJulian?* How could the scion of one of the richest families in the universe—"

"I told you. My father owns the place. Now leave me alone."

"You're *Clement's* kid?"

"Leave me alone!" I saw his face freeze and a look of deep tragedy come over it. It would be perfect for holovee: this man was a born actor. Lucky he didn't know everything was being committed to tape. "Can't you people leave me in peace?" he said. "You've already turned me into a ridiculous parody, a stage show, forcing me to abase myself because of my terrible hunger…"

"Look, I just want to do some filming. Name your price, for god's sake! Holothrills-National Enquirer is willing to pay any amount within reason…" I walked around him slowly, thinking, *Why does he need to do this? With his kind of credit he could buy up an azroid full of pretty people and bite them all to death.*

As if in answer to my thoughts, he said, "I've been disowned. Father wishes to hush me up, completely. I make a living the only way I know how." The pathos was just stunning. Loonies are always good material; they're so unpredictable, so *genuine*. And a quadrillionaire loonie geek was the acme of ratingsworthiness.

He stared me full in the face and said, "I just want to be normal."

"Huh?" I was taken aback. "You can't mean that. Hell, look at what you've got; they all love you out there. Your show has everything an audience could possibly want: a little bit of sex, a little bit of sadism, and a whole lot of archetypal, mythic mystery…come on," I said frustratedly, "you can't be *that* psychotic. Money's money."

"But you don't *understand,*" he said, practically in tears. Nothing could have been further from the imposing, terrifying figure he had portrayed only a moment before. "I loathe this life. I don't want to be a freak! I want to be normal! Help me! Help me!" And he had gripped my arm so tight that it was hurting. Gently I twisted loose. I took a long, stern look at everything I'd seen. Should I cut my losses…and lose the most potentially staggering holovee special I'd ever had the chance to make? There was pathos in the way this little man, childlike and torn by uncontrollable desires, was weeping his heart out in the dressing room. There was tragedy, even depth.

Then I got my brainstorm.

"Look here," I said, "we'll *get* you cured! We'll buy you the best psychocomputer in Mallworld. We'll have experts come and root out every trauma, every complex. We'll even slip you back into society afterward; we've got the megacreds to do it, and—"

"There's a price," he said truculently. "There's always a price."

"Let us tape everything."

"Well…" I saw a little gleam in his eye now and smiled smugly. How well I knew in those days that *everything* has its price.

Taking advantage of his confusion, I went on quickly, "Why, don't you see? As a sensation show it's pretty cool. We could maybe get a thirty-five to forty on the ratings. But as *human interest*—the private anguish of your tormented soul as it finally finds peace—it's incredible! I can see the whole thing," I went on, losing all caution in my enthusiasm, "a three-hour feelietape special. We can get the sponsors. Hell, The Way Out Corp. will do it for the publicity, maybe even the Vatican! The eyes of billions, in their living rooms, in their spacecars, in their azroid hideouts, eyes, ears, tacto-olfacto electrodes all glued to the holo-screen, from Titan to Mercury…'The Vampire of Mallworld finds truth and meaning, and a new life.' It's warm— it's wonderful—"

"Help me! Oh, help me!" cried the Vampire of Mallworld.

Time passed and the best psychocomps in Mallworld were unable to extract any but the most extraneous information from Fred. We drugged him with every drug we could think of. We had him trussed up in a booth on the fifteenth level of Auntie Annetta's Do-It-Yourself Shrink Shack, alternately pumping him with sensory dep and sensory overload. A biochemcomp stood by, flashing every molecule of his endocrine system onto a strobomanic vidscreen. Even tried some medieval therapy from an old recipe book where you electrocute the victim— patient—half to death…I toyed with the idea of getting help from the Selespridar, even…

The best shrink shack in Mallworld was by definition the best shrink shack in the Solar System, and this was all it yielded:

Federico barJulian had shown a propensity for bloodletting and other violence from the earliest. He was virgin at twenty-two, twice the normal age. His obsession had crystalized when he watched some ancient two dimensional tapes of mythological vampire epics from Earth: his favorite was a character called Dracula after whom he was later to model his act most consciously. Every six hours, the hunger would come upon him and he would rush down to the suicide parlor for

another session. They were certainly milking him for all he was worth, paying him peanuts, and screwing the creditful thumbs of some fairly heavyweight clients...the Selespridon, a xeno-anthropologist, for instance, being one of the regulars. The six-hour interval between each feeding session was totally reliable. You could tell time by him. In fact, I gave up checking my eyelid calendar completely.

For a person with such a peculiar social problem, he was astonishingly sane: witty, full of tragicomic one-liners, and a great holovee personality. He seemed undaunted at first by the constant failure of the therapy machines. I had a great time with his steadfastness, his courage, his obvious longing to be normal. But it was all wearing thin, and you don't make a good holovee show with failure. The audience has to have a satisfying climax and denouement, or you're stuck with three hours of pathos and gore and sex and human frailty and witty characterization and not a peg to hang the story on...

My boss called me while I was taking a respite in the hotel's automassage-sauna. It was a transmat call; must have cost a fortune, all for the convenience of not having to wait ten minutes in between remarks. The boss materialized right in the middle of my tub of water. It was only a holo-image, but nonetheless unnerving.

"Got anything yet?"

"We're working on it—"

"Now see here, Huang!" The boss began to gyrate wildly around his tripod. "I don't want to catch sight of you in a sauna again, you hear? You've run way over budget and I'm giving you a hundred hours—" Abruptly his twenty seconds were up.

It's hard working for a machine; they have no sense of human dignity.

That was the day some kind of breakthrough happened—

I was too depressed after the boss called, thinking of my career going to seed and my ratings tumbling. After being poked at, prodded by machines, Fred was not feeling too hot either, so we decided to walk through Mallworld. We floated through the corridors in a holo-bubble, because I'd donned my all-too-familiar true somatype and I didn't want to be mobbed by the fans.

"It's not Bela Bartok anyway," he was saying, "it's Bela someone-else. They don't give a damn about accuracy at The Way Out, all they care for is their lousy show."

We turned a corner and sailed past the Galaxy Palace restaurant. We both shuddered, knowing who owned the place. I was becoming quite fond of Fred, even outside my professional capacity. We streaked past a bevy of shopping bags, their wares fairly bursting their seams, sauntering down a slidewalk as if they owned the place. A huge animated tomato demonstrated dance steps on a whirling dais flanked by twittering comsims. Up a crazi-gravi corridor that gravi-flipflopped so we saw the whole world upside down—

"Tired of this?" I said.

"Yeah. How about some nature?" We turned into the Earthscape Safari Park.

Striding boldly out of the holographic sea, one of Mallworld's most famous landmarks, the Statue of Limitations, patroness of merchants and thieves...

As we winged down a klomet-wide pathway lined on either side with Grecian columns, with lions (actually leonoids) and tigroids and zebroids and okapoids and crocodiloids acting out the primal drama of nature, and shadows from distant dueling triceratopses blotching the wild wheat brown savannah, we did not speak much. I saw that Fred was moved by what he saw. I sensed that he felt as they did, was part of this savage world. And then, without warning—

"Mommy!" he shrieked. He crushed me in his arms and tried to bite me, then began to wail like a baby and press hard against my chest, sobbing, "Mommy, Mommy..."

"What's wrong?" I looked ahead and saw nothing but a herd of chimpanzoids, playfully cavorting inside a plastiflesh carcass of an elephant.

"Mommy—"

I was shaken. I mean, I knew he was crazy, but he'd never *acted* crazy before, except for this little quirk of sucking people's blood. I tried to calm him down, but he would not rest until we had gone way past the chimpanzee exhibit, into the aquarium hall where they showed dozens of fish being happily devoured by larger and larger fish…

This new turn of events would keep the studio happy for a day or two. But now we needed results, and fast.

I beckoned to Clunko, who was trotting along behind, and asked for its advice. Meanwhile, Fred was staring at the chains of fish eating fish, smiling happily to himself.

"Maybe he was raised by apes in the jungle—" my camera began.

"Oh, be quiet."

"And acquired carnivorous habits, and when he was adopted back into civilization—"

"Watch enough ancient twodee tapes, you'll soon be as crazy as he is," I snapped. "Besides, he only bites humans. Besides, we found out that he was born right here in Mallworld, at Storkways Inc., in fact, who have never been known to deliver a defective baby—"

"Or so they claim."

"He's never so much as stepped off this thirty-klick hunk of metal! And what place could be safer than Mallworld? Where in hell could he possibly have picked up a chimpanzee-specific mothersurrogate response? I think…that it's time for a human psychiatrist, Clunko."

"A witch doctor?"

"Don't be silly. They have had human psychiatrists for centuries—"

"What are you, some kind of back-to-nature ecologizer?"

"You machines are such impossible chauvinists," I said, thinking of my boss.

We spent the day trying to relax: watched lion eat lion, vulture eat vulture, shark eat shark, and, in a rousing climax to the park's entertainments, a passably convincing tyrannosaur eat tyrannosaur…and then Fred shambled off to assuage his six-hourly hunger, and I went off to look up Dr. Emmanuel Varhite. He and I had gone to St. Martin Luther King's Traditional Strict and Snooty School when we were kids, so presumably he—like Clement barJulian himself—was on the Old Boy Network.

I found him running a psychiatric concession at Gimbel and Gamble's Department Store and Feeliepalace on level T67. He'd come down in the world, and had also grown inordinately portly. He accepted the case at once, insisting only on one condition: that Holothrills buy him at least one meal a day at the Galaxy Palace restaurant. That was how low he had sunk, my old schoolmate. It was his own fault for picking such a pointless career, though. As useful to have chosen alchemy or window-washing, or to have learned how to read.

A few hours later. Emmanuel Varhite was wolfing down Denebian whiteworms with great relish beneath the dome of artificial stars in Clement barJulian's restaurant. We had a table right beneath the starfield, and special wraparound seats that really felt snug. Invisible, too—they were Selespridon forcemechanisms—they made us look as though we were spacing out on Levitol. Clunko was casually disguised among the cutlery. Above, the "stars" shone—fake, but still beautiful. It was a masterstroke, I thought, to film in the Galaxy Palace: the stars were dazzling, and every human being yearns for those outside our space and time…

Here the tables were turned, and we, the underdogs, got served by real people dressed in exotic alien costumes. Probably inaccurate.

I'd settled for the echinoderms stuffed with soft-shell malaprops; Fred, in full Bella Abzug attire, was eating a steak. Rare.

Varhite, whose face resembled a trampled rosebush, was expostulating at the camera. "We know," he said, "that the subject likes to drink blood—preferably killing the victim in the process."

"Come on, Varhite!" I stage-whispered. "Try to sound a little more witch-doctorly...our audience can be a little dumb, you know?"

*"Relaxen Sie...*I mean, relax, my boy," he said, warming to the image I'd created for him. "There are other clues. For instance, he reacts violently to chimpanzees, calling them 'Mommy, Mommy' in a petulant child's voice...clearly an anguished plea from the Unconscious.

"He is a product of Storkways Incorporated, the most blue-chip, influential baby factory in the Solar System, whose main showroom is, of course, in Mallworld..." As he spoke he never stopped sucking in the whiteworms as they wriggled in their death throes, thus releasing the intoxicating hormone that was the whole secret to their appeal...for sheer taste, give me spaghetti. "He first, as it were, concretized his urges when accidentally exposed to an old twodee movie. Now he watches it every day, in between meals, in his little one-room apartment tucked inside the labyrinthine corridors of The Way Out Corp. And every six hours—"

"They've heard that."

"Now, from these facts, what strange, tortuous, twisted trauma can we glean? Ah—"

"Not much to go on, is there, Doctor?" I said glumly. "Frankly, Doctor—my boss is thinking of dumping this whole project."

"And not cure me?" Fred suddenly looked up from his steak with those hopeless, despairing eyes.

"Come on, kid," I said, patting his hand. "Doctor Varhite and I, we *believe* in you." At that moment, I confess to being moved. He seemed so helpless...a baby, really. Trying to look professional, I skewered another echinoderm, watching as it deflated in a messy splat of rheum. "We *will* cure you!" I was almost choking. I'd lived with this thing for days now.

"And yet," said Doctor Varhite, "it seems to be most difficult to isolate the primal trauma. It must be very deep, very deep."

I knew the doctor was up to something, so I subvoked to my camera. Several forks and spoons levitated to surround the doctor from all sides. He pulled out something from his armpit pouch and threw it on the table. It was an inflatable hologram. He touched the stud—

A chimpanzee was sitting on the table.

"We've already done this a hundred times, you don't have to be cruel—" I began.

And the vampire screamed! He tried to clutch me, the empty hologram's throat, tried to bite it, began to sob. I was so involved, subvoking instructions to all my hardware, that it was practically happening to me. And then he sank down on the table, wracked by convulsions, as other diners on their motorized tables swung by to see what all the fuss was about.

"Ah-*ha!*" Doctor Varhite cried. "Positively Pavlovian!" Abruptly the screaming stopped. Fred pulled himself together, whispered "Mommy" very softly, and gathered his cloak up around himself. He stood erect and tall in his levi-boots, menacing in his deathpale makeup.

His face seemed to shine with a pallid, luminous coldness.

"Blood," he whispered harshly. "Blood, blood, blood!" Then he swept out of his seat and strode to a demat-booth in the middle of the restaurant and disappeared, leaving behind him a giggling audience of diners.

"Well," I sighed, "that's another thing we know."

"*Ja,*" said the doctor, "regular as clockwork. In the middle of a word, in the middle of an action, when the six hours come, the urge comes. It's uncanny." With a fingertip he deflated his hologram.

"Well, let's go back to the hotel and talk more strategy, eh?" I said. But I wasn't feeling very hopeful.

"What about dessert?" I sighed; the contract was binding, of course, so we ordered. While we were waiting, a six-inch-high hologram of my boss appeared on the table.

"Oh no," I gasped, "not another holo! And this time *I'm* going to get the convulsions."

"Huang!" spluttered the hologram. "Something terrible has happened! Holothrills-National Enquirer has been completely bought up by the Clement barJulian Group!"

I could feel my stomach turn. "Does this mean—"

"Yes it does! Now look, you have twenty-four hours to come back to Soaprock, or your expense account is up. Orders from on high say you're fired...whatever the cost! Someone in the new administration's after your ass, Huang. Now this is a regular real-time call. I'm not waiting ten minutes just to see you answer, lounging about in a sauna or...dining at the Galaxy! I bet that's where you are, isn't it? Now see here—"

He vanished and was replaced by two chocolate sundaes.

I shuddered. There was my whole career, flashing before my eyes. I tried not to think at all, and applied myself greedily to the sundae, an exotic dish made entirely from the blubber of specially cloned whales.

"You see the situation I'm in," I said. "I've raised the kid's hopes sky-high and now I'm to dash them all." Maybe I should have been thinking more about my own career than about Fred the vampire. But I'd seen his show, I'd been touched by it. The kid had fallen all the way from riches to rags because of his obsession, yet...in the moment that he killed, he was a king. I'd seen it, I'd captured it on film, and I was starting to see him as a martyr symbol of the human race...or maybe just falling victim to my own skillfully worded holo-scripts. I don't know.

"We still," Doctor Varhite said kindly, "have twenty-four hours."

"What can we do? We've tried everything!"

"Except...confrontation therapy."

"Oh?"

"I have already figured it out. This will be so dramatic that you can run to the competition with it if you have to—"

"BarJulian owns the competition."

"You want to help Fred, don't you? Regardless."

"Regardless." I knew this was the wrong time for altruism, but I was in too deep to quit.

"Confrontation therapy was a popular Dark Ages treatment," Varhite explained as Clunko whirled around the table, "invented by one Marcus Welby, whose tapes have survived the ages in truncated form. It involves confronting the patient with the locale, the flavor, the *presence* of his infancy, in order to drive the hidden trauma or *engram* to the surface. Tomorrow, then, we will film at Storkways, Inc., and the patient will come to find himself, there, at the very moment of his birth."

"It sounds very farfetched to me."

"My boy," he said, "what do you know about Storkways Inc.? Did *you* have the good fortune to be a Storkways child?"

"Of course not! I was born in the regular way, with an android host mothersurrogate, delivered by Caesarian straight into my mother's arms."

"That's the problem, then. You don't understand the peculiar loneliness, the *angst,* of a baby factory. I'm sure we can find an answer there...won't you give it a try?"

"What's in it for you, Emmanuel?"

He shrugged. "It's complicated. I guess I want to vindicate us 'witch doctors' and destroy the ascendancy of the psychocomps. I've been on a downhill trend lately and I need something. And besides, another day of the Galaxy Palace's food—"

Just then a waiter slunk up to our table. "Excuse me, sir," he said, floundering about in his half-donned fuzzy suit. "Mr. barJulian has asked me to inform you that you and the doctor are no longer welcome in this restaurant. A comsim will escort you—"

With a grand gesture Doctor Varhite slung the remainder of his sundae in the waiter's face. He stood dazed for a moment, then toppled into a heap of arms, legs, fur and chocolate sauce.

Clunko had filmed the whole thing. "Bravo!" I said. "Let's get out of here."

"You have no idea," said Doctor Varhite, "how much it cost me to do that."

It was a sorry troupe that matted on the level Y99 an hour or so later; we had just caught the last of Fred's act at The Way Out, and he had just done away with a pair of beautiful tangerine-eyed twins. Varhite led the way through a conch-twisty passageway; I followed, not even caring that, even in my normal soma, I was not attracting the attention of any rabid fans. Clunko trotted behind, and the Vampire of Mallworld lagged in the rear. I knew I wouldn't get a chance to see the act again—not at twelve kilocred a throw and no expense account—and so the killings had been tinged with an exquisite sadness. You might wonder why…these people have elected, of their own free will, to die, and the exhibitions of suicide parlors are a natural consequence of man's innate commercialism…but I found myself thrust into a state of profound longing which no competent newsman should have felt. I began to wonder about myself. Did I really belong in the holothrill trade?

Too soon we reached the lobby of Storkways Inc., a gigantic stylized uterus, painted pink, with transparent walk-levels jutting from the sides, which you approached from below by means of a diagonal slidewalk through a tubular passageway. The symbolism lent a grave dignity to the proceedings. Storkways was the oldest of the baby production firms, and was known to be incorruptible. No one had ever purchased a faulty baby from Storkways…or so they claimed. The primeval womb would make an excellent final scene, I decided, my spirits lifting a little. I could almost hear the script: *Here, in the very womb of humanity…*

I had to stop and remind myself that I was just doing the day's filming as an empty gesture, an attempt to wring every last microcred from the coffers of the company.

Soon we were greeted by a buxom human attendant in an oversize diaper and nothing else. She was wearing Storkways' Radiant Motherhood Smile.

"Ah," she said, not at all perturbed by the strange sight of a vampire in full regalia, a fat little psychoanalyst, a talking camera, and me. "A charming ménage you have here, I see! What kind of baby were you interested in, and at what price range?"

I looked a bit indecisive, I suppose, so she quickly went on, "Aquatics are in this season, as are little fuzzies and of course our ever-popular normal model, and—"

She looked at us expectantly. The smile hadn't changed at bit: I knew that it had been soldered on surgically.

"Why don't you nice fellows just browse through our catalogue?" she said. Instantly the air was full of holographic toddlers, solemnly filing past our faces. "Just point to the one you want...oh!...you're...*Milton Huang!*" she shrieked suddenly.

It was the only thing that happened all day. "I'm sure you'll be wanting a custom-made, then," she said thoughtfully. "Are these your husbands?"

"Miss—"

"Could I have your thumbprint, please? Just a formality, credit check, you know, and—well, actually I wanted it for my collection, I watch your show almost every fourday—"

"We'd like to do some filming here. If you'll just thumb this release—" I fiddled around with spools of minitape from my loinshield.

"O-o-o-o-oh!" She just stared at me, hardly taking in a word, while I explained the situation. "I'll get the manager. Oh, we'd be proud. Very proud indeed," She hopped into a demat-booth.

"What do you think?" I whispered to Emmanuel.

"Let's be patient," he said. Then, "Oh, look at all the darling babies!"

A seductive voice was saying, in warm, motherly tones. "Number 17 of our 'exotic' line is green-skinned, adapted for Deimos gravity, with a power-steering option for those difficult visits to high-gravity worlds. Choice of three hair colors and two basic personality indexes—'passionate and profound' or 'excitable and extrovert.' Actual personality will depend, of course, on environmental factors and your own parental proclivities."

The baby spun around and toddled off in midair.

"Number 18. The two heads are perfectly adapted for—"

"Can't we turn this thing off?" I shouted impatiently. Doctor Varhite nudged me gently, and I saw that our friend Fred was gazing, spellbound, at the tot parade.

"Normal...normal..." he was murmuring, as a charming little number with vestigial wings, four arms, and belly-gills drifted by. Poor Fred. I made sure I got a shot of his wistful face. I was in my element now, capturing the very essence of the man for the audience that was never to be. More and more the situation was getting urgent—anyone who'd envy an 'exotic' baby for being normal...they're usually intended for Babylon-5, and if you call anything to do with *that* colony normal, you really have flipped your chips.

Miss Perfect Mother came flouncing in with another matriarchal figure, this time in a golden diaper that radiated higher authority. This was Mabel Murray-Pentecost, regional manager of Storkways Inc. She too sported the infamous patent smile.

"Welcome!" she boomed. "I am most honored to be able to conduct you through our venerable halls myself, though I am *sure* that whatever is troubling that poor, poor young man will not be found here. And let me say for the benefit of the audience"—she certainly was making the best of her airtime, not knowing that she'd never make it on to the holovee screen—"that Storkways is *dedicated* to the infinite recomplexification of our human gene pool. Why be the same when you can be different? I know it's conservative and old-fashioned of us, but let me say that I *believe* in those values. Here at Storkways Inc. we always say: 'A clone no more!'"

Having said her piece, she beckoned us into a booth.

"Fred has been tranquilized," Varhite was explaining, "so that only the most primal memories will precipitate his convulsions." Nevertheless, I noticed that Miss Murray-Pentecost was keeping her distance and even seemed a little leery of Clunko as he clambered after us.

"...and this is the viewing room," she was saying, "where the little dears all rest and where they can be examined by prospective parents through a sophisticated audio-video-tacto-olfacto projection device in the privacy of their own holoview cubicles."

We were standing in a tremendously long hall lined with floatcribs, five in a row, with narrow lanes between each row, and little comfort-robots whizzing back and forth between the rows. The din was really heady; with some reluctance I resisted the cheap trick of switching up the audio track. I was damn well going to be artistic even if no one was going to experience this show.

"My god!" I exclaimed for the camera. "How many babies do you have here at any one time?"

"Three, four thousand," she said. "We change them every sleep shift."

"But...don't they ever get misplaced?" said Doctor Varhite slyly.

"What, sir? Incompetence here at Storkways Inc.? You ask the impossible. Are we not *dedicated* to the preservation of human life? Are we not a byword for ethical behavior throughout the Solar System?"

"All right, already!" I said. "Varhite—any luck on the patient?"

Fred was stalking up and down the aisles. He seemed a little restless, with his cloak flying behind him and his hands trembling a bit, but benign enough for now. Every now and then he stopped to croon over one of the babies.

"He won't...you know, *eat* one?" asked Mabel Murray-Pentecost anxiously.

"Oh, no. His 'attacks' come every six hours exactly, and he's just been fed," said Doctor Varhite.

"Curious," said the matriarch. "We've just had our feeding too—we run the feeding system every six hours, and it's all computer controlled, obviously—"

Doctor Varhite and I exchanged a quick look. "It's probably fortuitous," I said. "It seems a pretty unlikely connection to me..."

I subvoked Clunko and told him to heel. We had a lot more
to squeeze into my last day and I was getting impatient. We weren't
going to find a solution anyway. Clunko had been having a grand
time snapping all the babies—his 'human interest' programming
was very deeply ingrained. I had to squeeze to negotiate the aisles,
and the manageress's fixed smile had become extremely wearying
to look at. The hall was *not* designed for people, but for robots;
and the nearest demat-booth was a good five hundred meters of
squashing and squeezing away.

The next hall was a very murky one. It was two meters
across but seemed to stretch forever. The walls were high—
about twenty-five meters—and lined with shelves. On each
shelf squatted a row of bored-looking chimpanzees, each with
a baby in its arms.

"Ah-*ha!*" said Emmanuel. I saw his point. Now I was sure
there was a connection, but what was it? I glanced at Fred,
who was shaken but still in one piece—thanks to the massive
dose of tranquilizers.

"This," said the guide, "is our feeding room, where our
little ones are breast-fed by genetically altered chimpanzees,
as you can see. It's ever so hygienic, and you know it's much
better psychologically for the child to be able to relate to a
living creature."

Now I knew that all the pieces belonged to the same puzzle.
But I still couldn't see the answer. Nothing fell into place.
What could possibly be traumatic about being breast-fed by a
chimpanzee? The idea certainly didn't worry me, and I had
been a regular baby.

But they gave me a creepy feeling, those rows and rows of
apes, each clutching a baby in its arms, each with a dead, glazed
look which betrayed...what? Genetic tampering? "What
now?" I asked Doctor Varhite.

"Is there anything else?" He turned to Miss Murray-
Pentecost.

"I don't think so—this represents all the stages that a baby
would go through..."

"And yet the patient has exhibited no unusual anxieties— yet." Fred had retreated into his cloak but was still calm. "You've never discovered"—the doctor began to hem and haw, choosing his words with great care—"any instances of traumatization from these breast feedings?"

"Heavens no, Doctor," she said with some revulsion. "Our research department—not to mention our discriminating clientele—would never have let us get away with such a thing!"

"And the babies are placed with chimpanzee mother-surrogates immediately after parturition?" said Doctor Varhite.

"Well, yes, of course."

"And if no chimpanzees are available?" I said.

"Well, it sometimes happens, and then we take some of the older babies off the chimpanzees temporarily to make room...we have excellent temporary facilities, of course, for the temporarily displaced little ones..."

"Show me," Varhite said grimly.

"You don't ask for much, do you?" she said through her implacable smile. "Come with me." Her golden diaper gleamed in the half-light.

"I do apologize for our lack of demat-booths here," she said, "but we usually only have robots here." A little passageway opened up at our feet, and she motioned us to descend. "We don't usually want any unnecessary infection, you know, and one can't very well put a prospective parent into an autoclave..." She chuckled heartily at her own joke.

The steep passageway was cramped: we had to go single file. Fred and the doctor lagged; I think Fred was reluctant and had to be coaxed. A strange unease hung in the air. The manageress and I were the first ones to enter the little room. There were perhaps ten circular tables, stacked with hardware.

"On peak seasons," she was saying, "we do sometimes use these."

She indicated one of the round machines on a table, from which half a dozen padded cribs jutted, in some of which babies lay, some gurgling, some asleep. A plastiflesh pacifier extended over the mouth of each infant, and was connected to a vat of milk under the table. Most of the berthlets were empty.

"Seems efficient enough," I said.

She beamed maternally. "It's usually only for a day or so, until a new shipment of fastclone chimps can be transmatted from the farms on Earth."

"What's this here?" I pointed to one of the unoccupied cribs, where a pacifier looked a little odd.

"Why," she said, "I've no idea."

The plastiflesh had broken off, rotted away somehow, revealing the pointed steel of the milk-injector underneath, sharp and ugly. A baby could...

"Are you telling me—" I began.

"Oh, no, our equipment is inspected *daily*. That must be why the crib is unoccupied, you see." I thought I could detect a slight wilting of the permanent smile, even though I knew it was anatomically impossible.

"But isn't it just possible that, if you had a defective pacifier, that a baby could accidentally get assigned to it *before* the daily inspection, and—"

Just then the others came down and crowded around the table. I was just pointing out the faulty pacifier when—

Fred gave a hysterical cry and began to pummel the machine with his fists. Doctor Varhite and I stepped back in shock. He was banging, now his fists were sore and bloody, he was yelling over and over, "Mommy, Mommy, Mommy, you betrayed me you hurt me you made me drink blood you gave me blood Mommy Mommy Mommy—"

My blood was racing with excitement. I sent the camera flying every which way. Fred was beautiful. The way he clawed at the metal, the way he moaned and shrieked—

"Inspected daily?" I turned to the matriarch grimly.

"I assure you, sir," she said without losing her smile for a moment, "your accusations are impossible! We'll sue! We'll sue!"

"Mommy Mommy Mommy—"

How big a story could you get? Incompetence—in *Storkways Incorporated*—within the very bastions of everything we held good in society! I'd shot the show that would undermine the very foundations of our beliefs! No matter that no one would see it—

"I'll sue, you can't go exposing us like this, I can explain!" screamed the matriarch, smiling beatifically and grotesquely the whole time.

Above the tumult I turned to Emmanuel Varhite. "And now let's talk to the expert himself," I said in my suavest holovee voice. "Now that the pieces have come together, what are your conclusions?"

"Dark are the ways of the Unconscious," he began dramatically. (The screaming in the background never stopped. It set the babies off, and *they* were all hollering their lungs out.) "The essence of Confrontation Therapy is truth, sheer truth. Here we have seen an unfortunate trauma: the patient was made to substitute pain and blood for a mother's love and milk. No wonder he felt hostility toward the chimpanzee-mothersurrogate who came too late to aid him from his terrible torment! No wonder he could not forgive! Yes! It was in this very womb that the seeds of schizophrenia were sown..."

"Mommy Mommy Mommy—"

"I'll sue—"

"Waaaaaaagh—"

Seizing the moment, I gathered up my most melodramatic phrases and stood in a heroic pose, full face in front of Clunko. *Go, Clunko,* go, I subvoked, and then began rhetorically: "What have we seen here, friends? We have traced this unfortunate, tragic man's career back to its very roots. We have shown him the source of his terrible inner conflict; and now we have freed him to emerge, a fully *human* being, from the living hell that was his domain. Yes! What we have witnessed today—is Death and Rebirth! Total Catharsis! In monumental, heartwarming victory for the human spirit!"

I spread out my arms in the famous "crucified" pose that has since made me a household word, held for ten seconds, and turned around to see if I could stop all the screaming.

"...so you see," Clement barJulian was saying to me, "I had to see the finished product. Federico was—is—my son." He downed another glass of angels' tears. "I should have believed that a cure was possible, and yet—and yet—"

"I know." He had wept four times when they showed him the rough edit of the special. He'd rehired me. He'd re-adopted his son. I didn't want to go into all that again—I was trying to ferret out some scandal about his sister-in-law. After a whole year in which I'd become rich, in which Storkways had paid damages through the nose—and hush-up money, too, when a dozen other cases of criminal negligence came to light, and vampire imitators popped up all over Sol System, and glamorous Fred being chased everywhere by an army of amorous groupies begging for a gentle nip on the neck in memory of the old days—

Yes. Things certainly turned out right for him. And yet—

"Clement," I said, "I don't like what I do anymore."

He hardly looked up from his main course, a succulent crablike purple thing with splotchy tentacles swimming in a bowl of strawberry Jell-O. I looked away, watching the stars wheel. "Eh?"

"I'm a phony, you know," I said. After a whole year I had to blurt out my heart to someone. "All holovee personalities are. We're really drab. And yet, when I think of when I first watched Fred's show, and saw love and death and beauty and mystery all mingled together, and I knew that this was *Art*...nothing *I* do will ever be as beautiful, or as terrifying, or as *real*, as Fred the vampire's lunacy. Will it?"

"He was crazy!" Clement said. "You cured him, and earned a few creds yourself from the whole thing. You should be happy."

"But I'm scared. I'm scared. I feel like I've destroyed something very personal, something like a soul, I suppose. I almost regret it..."

"Come on!" Clement roared. "Here, take your mind off it, let me tell you some juicy gossip—"

I could not bring myself to confess to Clement barJulian that, for a few moments, when his son the vampire squeezed the life out of a particularly beautiful woman in a passion beyond ecstasy and terror, I would have given anything to feel what he felt...for a few seconds that will haunt me forever, I had envied the Vampire of Mallworld.

It can safely be said, my lord, that the tale we have just witnessed weighs negatively rather than positively in the balance, don't you think?...Oh, on the contrary, Mr. Huang's final contrition and self-awareness you find quite charming, and not as devoid of ug'unnieth as you were previously led to believe all humans must be? Oh, how far you have progressed on the road to final compassion, lord! I envy you.

Oh, what's that? You want tickets to the vampire show? Alas, their time moves so much quicker than ours. It is long since over, and we, despite all our Galaxy-dominating technical feats, have solemnly signed the pan-Galactic time treaty, which binds us to not going backward in time; you know how awkward those paradoxes can be!

So what, you say! It's not even our universe anyway! The treaty doesn't cover vacant universes! Perhaps so, my lord, but I don't know, I don't...all right, sire, all right, just this once...

Well, what did you think of that! He saw you in the audience, lord! It's in the mindfile, remember, seeing the high Selespridar the first time he taped the geek show?

You are visibly moved, my lord. Perhaps a little break, before we go on to the next creature under consideration.

In any case, I must take a moment to welcome my superior Gdazhkeh, who rules twenty times as many star systems as I do, and might want to join us in our deliberations...oh, I guess not. He's heading straight for Mallworld.

The mind-magician has climbed aboard his vessel...it is following him...soon it will zero in on yet another inhabitant of this peculiar place...we have her now. A female, I think.

(Now a word for all our adult readers.)

(Kids please do not read.)

COPULAND!

Now you can do it all—in one convenient setting, right here in Mallworld.

Conceived by the twisted genius of Tiberius barJulian Sinistre, half-scion of the most celebrated family in the known universe—

Copuland!

The solar system's first amusement park-theme brothel!

Get the urge suddenly, in the middle of your boring shopping duties? Enter the mini-demat booth and whisper the magic level number XIII and you'll instantly be transported into a world of wildest fantasy and delight!

Here are some of the thrilling rides you'll experience—

The ultimate! The most sensational, mind binding old fashioned-style roller coaster ever realized by the human imagination! The Copucoaster! Fifty full kilometers of loops, twirls, spins and heart stopping falls—comsim controlled functions so you never know which way the coaster's going to roll! Ride with your partner (or partner of any sex provided for a small extra charge) in a completely sealed-off, polarized car with bed float for two! Carom through holospectacles of orgies through the ages! You'll never be the same once you've done it in the Copucoaster!

For a change of pace, there's the Tunnel of Sensual Delights. Ride in a genuine reproduction of an ancient earth gondola through the canals of a reconstructed Venice! See the breathtakingly beautiful "Sensuality through the Ages" panorama—in complete audiovideotactolfactory immersion!

Fly on the backs of winged pterosaurs through the Cave of Time! Each pterosaur comes complete with four-poster auto massage vibrabedfloat and operational android harem slaves! You won't be bored for a second as you watch lifelike recreations of the reproductive cycles of titanic dinosaurs—of our ape-man ancestors—of birds, bees, and balucitheria!

And introducing the symbol of Copuland—the universe's first giant, scrumptiously screwable cotton candy sculpture!

For a respite, watch our live Carnal Ballet perform—in the water—in the air—in the gigantic Ovoid Theater at the center of Copuland!

And patronize our kinky vending machines. Greatest selection known to man...this week only, quadruple bonus stamina points!

But don't think we've forgotten what this is all about. No, Tiberius barJulian Sinistre's *Living Kama Sutra* caters to every possible act! (Of course, acts involving pain, degradation and humiliation are available only with android surrogates—this is a family park!—but you'll never know the difference.)

So don't wait...copulate!

Come to Copuland today!!!!

Ten percent off entry fee with proof of purchase from The Way Out Corp., Storkways, or The Shrink Shack Psychiatric Handyman Franchises throughout the Outer System.

Rabid in Mallworld

Here's the universe—

Flickersparklepinpoints dervish-dancing through darkness. Whorls, whirls, and swirls of fiery stippledust. Giddy worlds wheeling on unseen slings. Starspills out of cosmic salt-and-pepper shakers. Frozen fireworks—

They're not my words anyway. All I am is Joni Gryphon, dishwasher extraordinary at the Galaxy Palace in Mallworld, and I certainly can't wax poetic about anything off the cuff. But if there were a subject that would make me, the most down-to-earth person I can think of, go all dreamy-eyed…that'd be it.

The stars.

That aren't ours.

Yeah, I guess every human burns inside about the stars. I know. Because they were taken from us. Because a couple of hundred years ago the all-wise all-powerful, all-sexy Selespridar took over the Solar System, stuck a forceshield around the orbit of Saturn and shunted us into a very exclusive, very private, very claustrophobic universe all of our own. Until we get *civilized.* Which sure doesn't mean in *my* lifetime.

And no stars.

Let's talk about something else…this is beginning to hurt.

The Galaxy Palace in Mallworld. Home of alien gourmet cooking. The most glamorous dinery in four worlds and sixteen moons and a thousand azroids.

If you're wondering about why people would pay a kilocred for one meal—when that same amount will feed a starving family of fourteen for a year, earthside—you've never heard *anything.*

Why come to Mallworld in the first place?

I must tell you first that I come from Eggroll, an azroid halfway from nowhere, whose only claim to fame is as a caterer's planet and home of the St. Betty Crocker School of Culinary Achievement. We lived in a one-room plastic hovel on Rigatoni Level and dreamed of a better life. Well, of course, when I was of jobbable age—eighteen—my family looked up the dazzlingest family connection they had—which was Great-Uncle Agrippa, maître d'hôte of the Galaxy Palace in Mallworld, a familial patriarch spoken of only in the most reverent of tones...and bang! I got the job.

Mallworld took some getting used to. Teleporting in on the transmat, floating down the nothing tubes into a world of wonders. Tier upon tier, level upon level, serpentine crowdstreams pouring into demat-booths, holosigns blaring and flashing, little pink men buzzing around yelling slogans in your ears, corridors crazy-graving and twisting into doughnuts and crullers, slidewalks snailing and snaking alongside you, autopushers handing out free Levitol pills, robots dispensing candy, kinky sex, encyclopedias and fluffy toys...I hope you're getting the idea.

Well! I thought. Me, a slovenly, unpretty girl from the back azroids, and I end up amid tinselglint and glamor! How's it done?

There I was, in a thirty-klick-long shopping center floating in space, between the belt and Jupiter, where any dream was there for the asking if you could pay for it—and, well, I wasn't just another shopper. I *worked* there. I was one of the gang. Thrills, thrills, thrills.

I soon learned that the glamor was strictly surface. Unless you had a really well-heeled thumbprint.

I hitched up with a guy called Dunny Lorenzo—for warmth and to save money—and moved to a closet of a room in Cramp Concentration, a little azroid towed out to the Mallworld area for people who worked there, to save on transmat bills. Commuting might have been instantaneous for the customers...for me it was an hour or more in the car, bumper to bumper across the blackness of space as the Mallworld work shifts chugged to work in their thousands of identical toyochevs.

So, far from accumulating spacecars and holovee sets and other possessions, I worked my tail off, washing dishes at the most glamorous restaurant in the whole Solar System. They had no robots to do that sort of thing at all—the labor was all human. That was part of the glamor. Actually being waited on by human beings. Yeah, I netted high for this work. But hours were long, and I never had time to spend it.

Mother always said to me, *You'll meet interesting people, Joni dear, you'll be mixing with the crème de la crème, we all struggled up from nothing to do this for you...*

Sure. Shelling malaprops in a kitchen.

Here's why people come to the Galaxy:

First there's the alien gourmet cooking. Courtesy of our Selespridon masters' trade routes, there's soft-shell malaprops marinated in angels' tears, roast Vegan dingwort, klitterbungas fried in oyster sauce, sweet-and-sour ice turtles with chocolate chips, as well as ancient earth dishes, whose recipes are extracted—by the restaurant's research department—from ancient, decaying earth documents (so the propaganda goes): bird's nest soup, roast boar, London broil, corned beef hash.

It's about the only place where you'll see aliens, too: where you'll run into one of our masters, two meters of blue-skinned .998 humanoid with their flaming magenta hair and their sensual, erotic odor...or some of their confreres. The plasma beings from the heart of Arcturus, glowing from their shielded magnetic-fielded bottles. Rigellian plants, humming as they sip their scented sugar-water.

Second—envy. The customers want to turn the tables on our masters; so they have people dressed up as aliens, serving their food and bowing obsequiously as though the humans were masters of the Galaxy.

But the most important reason people pay to come and eat there was and is—

The stars.

I guess we always come back to that subject sooner or later.

It was the only surviving holoZeiss recording of how the sky *really* looked, in the old days…and when I was first working at the Galaxy Palace they played it twice every standard day, lunchtime and dinnertime, against the huge dome of the main ballroom.

Soft starlight would shine down on the diners.

It certainly brought in the credits. It made me angry at first, the way we humans exploit the anguish of our own condition, the human tragedy…for a buck.

The very first day on the job, I was on waitress duty and jaunting out of the kitchen with a tray and they'd just turned it on.

The ballroom, wonderstunned, hushed as a cathedral. My eyes getting used to the dimness, and then—

Starlight stared down from a past when men had a future. Oh, god, the pain in my guts, the anger, the longing…*Why do we even go on?* I thought. *Why have children, why live?* I dropped the tray. Glass splintered. I heard it as if it was worlds away.

My kid's going to see them the way they really are, I vowed as I bent down to mop up the mess. Uncle Agrippa began scolding me from somewhere behind; it sounded like a fly buzzing through the intense quiet: "I'll dock you a week's wages for this, you imbecile!"

My kid will see them as they really are, I swore hopelessly, fiercely, wincing as a piece of wineglass nicked my wrist.

Day 23 of my job began routinely enough.

0695 standard metric time: woke up. Dunny woke up. Lights blazing; bed deflating rapidly, me clawing around and bumping into the wall and then rolling into a heap with Dunny; the dispenser disgorging two cups of caffoid.

I watched Dunny pull himself together. "Sheeeeesh," he said, testing the caffoid with his finger.

"Hot," we said together. It was a little game. I knew what he was going to say next, too…and he did.

"Let's make a baby," he said.

We were saving up for one. We'd been hitched for two weeks now...and it looked like it might last a year or more. He was gentle. He had soft eyes, dark gray with just a hint of tangerine...and flame-orange hair with streaks of gray programmed into it, and the colors shifted when he shook his head. It was hard to believe that he was a cop. Or rather, a security comsim overseer—"cops" are for the backworld azroids like Eggroll.

Then he said something different. He said, "Why don't we do it the new way, I mean, just make our own baby—mingle our genetic material and all?"

I was shocked at him. I don't believe in the newfangled, reckless babymaking that allows nature to take its course and accepts any old thing, any old one-arm bandit combination of genes. I'm old-fashioned, I guess, coming from somewhere like Eggroll with its values and traditions. "When I get a baby," I said softly, "I'm going to *buy* one—preferably from Storkways Inc. Nothing but the best. My baby's got to have all the things I never had—"

I was being more emotional than I realized. In fact I was starting to cry and couldn't even control myself.

"What's wrong, honey?" He put his arms around me. I felt the room close in on us like the walls of the Solar System itself.

"My cousin Walt was a natural," I said. "I used to watch him gangling around the kitchen. I used to get angry for him, angry at his stupid parents who trusted to the cosmic dice..."

I'm a good Catholic. Why, I was remote-confirmed by the Pope herself at my Bar Mitzvah. How my parents loved me! They'd saved up for years, got me from a subsidiary of Storkways on Deimos...nothing but the best.

Later the commuter convoy snaked through the blackness to Mallworld, a silver sliver glinting in huge nothingness. I remember looking up and seeing one star, a reddish Mars— not a real star at that—and thinking: *Why even bother to have children, if they're going to grow up and be slaves to a power that they can't even see?* And I thrust the un-Catholic thought from me like a piece of dirt, but it nagged there still, like a robot salesman.

Dunny said, "Remember our date, darling. After your shift today we're going to go monopole-skating, and then we'll eat our lunch together in the simulated earthscape park..." He kissed me and got out of the car; we'd gotten to the parking lot in a state of sheer somnambulism.

"I love you," I said, trying to sound tough. I didn't want him to think he'd won our daily argument. But his wanting to have a "natural" baby disturbed me more than I could say. It went against...you know, there was something almost *dirty* about the idea. Even though I try to have an understanding attitude toward newfangled ideas.

Shrugging it off, I sprayed on a work smock and headed for the nearest demat-booth.

"Late, late, late!" Great-Uncle Agrippa shouted as soon as I'd winked into the kitchen. "And today of all days!"

"But Uncle Grippie—" I saw him pacing up and down, pausing now and then to bang the counter with a rolling pin.

"Enough, enough. I'll have you know that today, today, *today,* girl, a five-tier Selespridon is coming to lunch. Lunch, lunch! Now. You and Vanessa get to shelling those malaprops at once." He paused to subvocalize a command to his rolling pin, set it to kneading dough, and raised his arms for an attendant to spray on his work clothes. Then he waved at the pile of malaprops that lay quivering in a basket. Fresh from the Selespridon home planet...

I shuddered. A five-tier Selespridon! Why, even Klutharion, governor of the Solar System, was only a three-tier. I turned to Vanessa, a round, blue-skinned woman— cosmetics, I knew a woman of *her* means couldn't afford a genuine blue skin—and said, "We'd better get going. I think he means business today."

"I certainly do!" Uncle Agrippa said. He turned his back to direct some more attendants, and the arm he'd had grafted in his back waved a finger sternly at us. He was very proud of that arm, Great-Uncle Grippie was. He could stir a cocktail and light a flambé and pour wine all at once, and the arm was removable, too.

"Sweet and sour, sweet and sour, damn you!" he screamed at a chef who was struggling into a fuzzy suit so he could pan-fry a dingwort authentically in front of his customer. "Sweet and sour, that means chocolate sauce and oranges, stupid! Don't you know the most basic of traditional recipes?" He stormed toward the demat-booth and dematted with a flurry of distraught attendants.

I looked at Vanessa in the sudden silence. We cracked up at once, then stifled ourselves.

"Well," I sighed, "let's start shelling."

Malaprops are curious creatures. They're from the Selespridar's own planet and are a favorite delicacy of theirs; and they are the ugliest things imaginable. They're a cross between a lobster, a rabbit and a zucchini, with a sort of tortoise-shell in the middle. It's the shell you have to pry off—with a knife—ever so delicately—and since they come frozen, you can just feel your fingers numbing and you can just imagine them dropping off from frostbite, and you can't get a new set of fingers with the insurance, either; it's specifically excluded for workers in alien gourmet restaurants...

We got to work.

"You look fazed," Vanessa said, throwing a reddish-blotchy shell into the basket. "Had a fight with Dunny?"

I nodded.

"About babies?"

"Uh-huh."

"Oh, Joni," she said. "It shouldn't bug you so much. After all, you won't be hitched forever, will you...?"

She could be very annoying at times, as best friends always are. "I have no idea—" I began.

"You're in love with him, then?"

I nodded dubiously.

Just then—

A malaprop leaped up from her lap. She screamed. It pinched her hard on the cheek. She shook the thing off, and it started to shamble toward the demat-booth.

"Oh my god, oh my god, it's alive, it's alive," she shrieked. I grabbed a bottle and tried to hold the thing at arm's length.

"Someone, come quickly, come!"

The malaprop shuffled around and around me. I jumped up on a chair, still brandishing the bottle. Its claws made a rasping squeak on the metal floor. I heard a crash as Vanessa fainted and crumpled to the floor. "For god's sake," I said, "someone do something!" It looked like it was about to hurl all two feet of claws, pincers, tentacles, and furry paws right at my face.

A commotion. I turned around and saw some attendants come in, aimed the bottle at the malaprop's head and resumed my screaming. The malaprop sprinted to the booth with astonishing swiftness and vanished. *My god,* I thought, *how did it ever learn to operate the thing?*

Great-Uncle Agrippa was shaking me. "Damnation!" he was saying. "We're one worker down and the things not shelled yet, and this five-tier Selespridon, heir to twenty-two stellar systems or something, is going to come here—I'm through, through, through!"

"Get this woman to a medicomp," I said calmly—I hoped— as my great-uncle stormed around. "And look, those things are meant to be *dead,* Great-Uncle Grippie! How could that ever have happened?"

"You mean a *malaprop—*"

"Yes, and it's disappeared down the demat system. It could be absolutely anywhere in Mallworld," I said as I watched them cart Vanessa away on a gravi-stretcher.

"Well, I don't have time to deal with that now. It's only a piece of food anyway…look, I'm assigning you on waitress duty to the Selespridon's private table. For god's sake don't make a mess of things. It's only that we're so understaffed."

"Thank you, Great-Uncle!" I said, and kissed him.

Despite his talk of understaffing, I knew he'd done it for me...just imagine, I'd be talking to one of the Masters of the Galaxy! I couldn't wait to tell Dunny later when we went on our date.

Uncle Grippie detailed a couple of extras to help me shell; I was too squeamish to go on even though I figured the chances of *another* live one were probably very remote indeed. I stood and watched them shelling and shucking, and as lunchtime and the first rush of the day came nearer, I decided to tiptoe out of the kitchen and take a look at the customers.

As I peeked out of the little opening in the wall, I saw the dome and saw they'd already turned on the stars. Even after twenty-three days it was enough to make me catch my breath.

I caught a whiff of him as I bent to serve him a goblet of genuine Earth mineral water (eighty-nine creds per half liter). They were walled off, the Selespridon and his guests, inside a cunning arrangement of sliding, curving opaque walls. The booth was candlelit, the flames playing shadow puppets against their faces—above, the stars wheeled. He smelled of musk, or something even more erotic...the hair rippled slowly, deep purple in the flicker. His eyes met mine for a moment: deep, dark, unfathomably alien, set into a sky blue face. We'll never understand the Selespridar.

His name was Gdazhkeh, and he really was heir to twenty-two star systems.

His guests clustered on couches. The cream of earthling society, nodding obsequiously and sagely in unison like marionettes. There was a pleasure girl from Deimos, decked in an outrageously concealing muu-muu; a poet who declaimed between fits of snoring; and an old man with eyes in the back of his head—the quadrillionaire Clement barJulian XII, who owned the restaurant and god knows what else besides.

"*Sacre bleu!*" said the Selespridon—he'd picked up a very strange accent in his peregrinations, for he'd spent twenty years in Greater Calcutta, capital city of Old Earth, among all the dirty earthies—"You human beings are endlessly fascinating. *Scheisse!* I've brought my young son here today—he's newly adopted—on his first grand tour of the Galaxy. I *had* to have him confront himself with the very pangs of a civilization in the throes of being born…"

I'd finished pouring, but I hung on every word. Maybe he'd even drop the Big Secret: when were the Selespridar going to release us from our bondage?

The poet was saying, "And where is your son now, Gdazhkeh? This scion of your noble race, this flower of the Galactic Masters—he must surely be a wonder for us poor mortals to observe—"

"Oh, he's back at the hotel," said the Selespridon, dunking his fingers in the fingerbowl. "I had to punish him for tweaking an earthling's nose. So hard to inculcate the proper respect and compassion, for, you know, those less fortunate than us, *n'est-ce pas?*"

(I bit my lip and turned up to watch the sad stars, haunting me in the flickering semidark…)

The smell of charbroiled malaprops.

"I've ordered something special for you, Gdazhkeh," said barJulian. "Your planetary delicacy."

"Ah," said the Selespridon, sniffing appreciatively, "How flattering! Thus do the simple folk of the simple worlds show their touching respect for us…*Mamma mia!*"

The waiter waltzed in. "This tray," he droned, "is genuine Styrofoam, salvaged from the Temple of Colonel Sanders on Old Earth." He started to slice the malaprops and to tong them onto the plates. (As a good Catholic I objected to this mumbo-jumbo. A little self-righteously, I fingered my St. Betty Crocker medallion, a first communion gift from my grandfather.)

Lips began to smack. Skewers elevated from the tabletop and adjusted themselves to each guest's feeding speed.

Just then—

A chorus of screams ran around the hall. Someone knocked the holoZeiss over and the stars swayed chaotically. The guests rose and babbled, the booth dividers were yanked up into the air, all the lights blazed on, and I saw—

Vanessa, running around the room, scuttling from table to table. An army of security clunkers clanked after her, overturning tables, Vanessa cackling wildly. Then she'd jumped onto a tabletop and was throwing pieces of fruit at all the guests.

"For god's sake, somebody stop her!" It was Great-Uncle Agrippa charging in, wielding his rolling pin. Guests clattered into corners like bowling pins.

Vanessa jumped on my Great-Uncle and bit him in the cheek. I screamed. Great-Uncle froze and fell face-forward into a tureen of soup. "See to him, you fools!" I shrieked to a couple of waiters, who dashed up to him and began to carry him out. Vanessa was still jumping up and down and pelting people with food. Finally two burly clunkers clapped metal arms around her and carried her off, still cackling like an uncooked goose.

I rushed to Agrippa's side. Embarrassingly, the whole congregation of the human race's elite gathered around me and I found myself in charge.

"She knocked the orderly on the head, pulled the medicomp's plug and escaped," a waiter said. "What's going on?"

"Damn that damned malaprop! It's all your fault, you…you Master of the Galaxy, my foot," I yelled at the Selespridon. "If you're so clever, how come you can't even make sure a food shipment is properly dead, huh? Civilized, my foot. Get out of the Solar System, get out, get out, get out…" Then I started to cry.

"What's this? A malaprop bit the woman? That's impossible!" someone muttered, and then—

The Selespridon let out a cry of what seemed like sheer anguish. He reared himself up to his full two meters, and—

visibly straining to be calm, said: *"Mince alors!"* You have to
find that malaprop. Alive. You must. I don't dare think what
would happen if you don't. The fate of twenty-two stellar
systems is at stake. If it's not found, I'll personally see to it
that you're all destroyed—" He paused. More coldly he said,
"I apologize for this outburst. I extend my compassion to all
of you. Get me security now! Summon the cops! Do
something!"

What was wrong? Why was this suddenly so important to
him?

Then the Mallworld police force trooped in. Uniformed
cops in sparkling bodystockings, in strict formation, a gaggle
of six-inch-high computer simulacra hovering like a swarm of
bees, an armada of clunkers beeping and buzzing and waving
their metal arms.

At the head of this impressive force—

My own hitchmate, Dunny Lorenzo!

I was confused. I like order and I didn't like seeing him
without warning like this, especially after our fight.

He ignored me. "I'm on duty," he said to Gdazhkeh.
"What's the trouble?"

Everyone started talking all at once. "Hold it, hold it,"
said Dunny. "You mean a live malaprop is on the loose and
biting people who are in turn going rabid and biting other
people?"

The Selespridon said, "The effects are only temporary,
officer. Twenty or thirty hours at the most. But you must find
the malaprop! In the meantime...ah, if only I had not punished
my poor little child! I must find him...before it's too
late...*merde!*" He strode to the nearest booth and dematted
before anyone could ask him any more questions.

Dunny was barking orders, and cops were filing out in all
directions. I'd never seen the cops at work and I was impressed
despite myself. Clunkers rolled after the men and women;
many sounded as if they needed a lube job. Mallworld Security
sure didn't look after its robots very well.

Then we were alone together, Dunny and I. Except for Uncle Grippie who lay in a pile of debris, algae soup dribbling down his face. I clutched Dunny's hand. "We had a *date!*" I said unreasonably. I knew what a mess things were in, but still—

He didn't listen. I knew he was still subvoking instructions to his aides as they spread through Mallworld. "We had a date, damn it!" I said. I had had important things I wanted to discuss. Like settling the problem of babies once and for all— fixing a price limit, choosing the options, stuff like that. I wanted to get it on credit, if only it'd tie the man down for a year or two...

"Well, damn you all," I grated. "I don't give a Pope's boobs about anything anymore!" I knew it was unreasonable to expect to be noticed, but I couldn't help it. It was such a wretched day.

Dunny went right on subvoking. Overhead, the lights blinked on and off and sometimes there was half a starfield, splintering the dome in two. So pathetic-looking. *We're worthless fakes, all of us!* I thought, despairing.

I picked up a skewer of malaprop and pitched it at Dunny as hard as I could. It missed, scudded across a table, and plopped to the floor. I huffed off to the nearest demat-booth in a grand funk.

...Found myself slidewalking down the C12 level, getting angrier and angrier. The slidewalk slung around a corner, and I passed a suicide parlor with fluorescent skeletons doing a song-and-dance number in the window. In a grocery, cucumbers waltzed. The walk slithered past a head shop with a dozen heads grinning grislily... *Too many people here, damn it!* I thought. A bevy of gawkers pattered past with an entourage of auto-shopping baskets.

Trying to make sense out of the events. Why was the Selespridon so worried about a missing bit of food? What did his son and the future of his twenty-two star systems have to do with anything? And what strange chemical in the malaprop's bite was making everyone crazy and setting off this biting spree? Who had Vanessa managed to bite before being restrained...and how in the Galaxy were they going to locate a missing malaprop among twenty thousand shops and feeliepalaces and amusement parks and cathedrals and restaurants?

Just then—

A crowd, gibbering, jabbering, a kid snarling and biting, scattered screams, clunkers rushing out and dousing everyone with sleepitoff gas—

That does it! I found a booth, leaped off the slidewalk and just yelled a random letter/number at it. I breezed out of it into a chromeglitter corridor curving upward, bumped right into a vending robot giving away free deodorant pills—

A voice, in carefully synthesized, comforting tones:

Alert! Alert! Do not panic, please...Stand by for announcement. There has been an outbreak of biting madness—mordomania—which is highly contagious. The bitten victims are affected within fifteen minutes to half an hour and become violent biters. The effect is due to a chemical secreted into the victim's bloodstream which catalyses the production of more of the same until it reaches the victim's saliva. This is only temporary, repeat only temporary. Do not panic. If you have been bitten in the last few minutes, report at once to a security officer. All attackers are now being restrained. For your protection, a shelter has been prepared at the neo-Amish Temple of Level Q91. All demat-booths have now been rerouted. We apologize for any delays and all bitten will be compensated on application to Mallworld Surety Co.— the insurance company that makes you feel loved! Special rates for the discorporate! Please proceed to the nearest demat-booth in an orderly fashion for processing. Alert! Do not panic—

A shrilling, impossible scream, and—

Stormclouds of people stumbling tumbling rumbling toward me, scrambling for the demat-booth I was in. Racing in the slidewalks, helter-skelter down the aisles. They pushed me off balance. I hurtled backward, fingers slithering across the chrome wall...*let me through!*

Here and there a six-inch-high comsim in a pink uniform helplessly trying to keep order. Shopping bags clattered aimlessly, trying to sniff out their masters. People bottlenecking into the demat-booth, converging from every corner—

An exaltation of zonkies, spaced out on Levitol, whizzed by, daisychaining around the crowd while an attendant from the drug palace tried to steer them toward the booth—

Do not panic do not panic do not panic

This the worst day of my life, I thought bitterly. I elbowed a shopping bag, stepped over a bawling brat, and dived into the booth.

The crowd exploded into the neo-Amish Temple in midair. The Temple was one of the seven wonders of Mallworld, a gravity-controlled 400-meter-across perfect sphere of dazzle-polished mirrormetal. I didn't have much time to appreciate it. I was feeling queasy—and not only because I was a good Catholic zooming into a den of heathen vice. They were turning down the gravity to nullgrav so's to pack in the mob, and they were dropping the gravity too fast. My stomach churned as I swooshed into a fat gentleman who was twirling like a top.

I guess it's a good idea to use this place, I thought bitterly as the momentum whirled me into the ocean of sardine-packed people—maybe 100,000 of them—floundering, grasping at each other, vomiting in the nullgrav, writhing as they tried to navigate past each other...several had fainted and were just floating aimlessly. The zonkie chain, still spaced out on Levitol, were figure-eighting and obstacle-racing through a school of terrified nuns.

The din was staggering.

Kindly stay calm please kindly stay calm please—thundered a voice, sparking off renewed screaming.

I was just about to abandon myself to chaos when I thought I saw Dunny. A little head poking out from—yes, it was! I hurled myself against a passing nun, trying to gauge my angular momentum right, caromed off a little boy with a security blanket, careened past a woman who was chasing after her disconnected hand—

Suddenly my nose was impaling his armpit.

"Joni, Joni—" he screamed above the roar while I desperately tried to lipread. His hair was all matted, and I'd never seen him so haggard. He kept trying to direct the traffic with a whistle. "This is the biggest to-do Mallworld has ever had! Do you realize there's a megacred reward out for capturing this blasted malaprop alive?"

"What's going on?" I yelled. A boy in full skating gear pried us apart and sent us flying in opposite directions. I managed to bounce off a fat man with gray sideburns, and then I threw my arms around Dunny, clinging hard to him. With all the sweat the gray in his hair was melding into the orange—"Goddamn it, Dunny Lorenzo, we had a date! Isn't there any way we can leave this bedlam?"

A momentary glitch in the gravity control sent the whole crowd barreling toward the walls, then released us again. I hung on to Dunny for dear life. He was saying, "I'm sorry about our fight," or something, and I was fending off a drunk with four arms who was trying to use *all* of them on me...

"I've had enough!" Dunny yelled. "Hold on tight! I'm supposed to be running this show, but I don't seem to be able to do anything at all! Just hold on, will you? I've got a demat-scrambler—" He turned on his boot jets and we were lurching wildly through the crowd, whistling past floating people left, right, and center. We fairly smashed into a demat-booth in the mirror-wall and—

Silence like a slap in the face.

Not the water-torture drip-thrumming of Cramp Concentration but a deeper silence. Like the whole Mallworld sucking in its breath, waiting, leviathan in repose...

I reached for Dunny's hand. After a while I heard surfwhispers from the signs in shop windows, and I realized that they were calibrated to roar over the crowdswell and now they'd turned down their volume to save energy. The corridor glistened, rainbows darting across plastichrome. I held his hand tighter. We picked a slow slidewalk and stood still, our hands our only contact, while the slidewalk corkscrewed and merrygorounded past walls that spun and kaleidoscoped and holo-ads that strobed and jaunted back and forth, over and over…

We walked then.

Faster.

Ran!

Bolted like children playing tag while the giant slumbered…

"This is a fantastic date," I whispered when we'd slowed down.

"Yeah…"

> ACME AUTOMATED SOAPBALL!
> DEODORIZES AS IT MASSAGES
> —STOCHASTIX UNLIMITED:
> CREDIT ALLOWED ON
> PROPHESIED FORTUNES—

the signs whispered to us, each sign a miracle of encapsulated sensuality.

"I wish we could catch that malaprop, though," said Dunny. "Then I wouldn't be in trouble with you over the baby…"

"But I keep thinking, why are we bothering to consider it, Dunny, when there's no future for any kid, now…" I was still enraged at some of the things the Selespridon had said. He had no right to be so callous about a whole solar system—no matter how inferior.

> TRY CLONESEX!
> ANTICIPATES YOUR EVERY WHIM
> IMITATE YOUR FAVORITE HINDU GOD!
> LIMB GRAFTS—100 CHIROMATS—NO WAITING
> ARE YOU UGLY? COME TO SOMA NOVA INC.
> TRADE-IN CREDIT ALLOWED
> ON YOUR HEALTHY, WELL-TUNED BODY

"Where shall we go now?" Dunny asked, still holding me. We hadn't let go after half an hour.

"Anywhere, anywhere…"

I thought of the whole of Mallworld crammed into that Temple on Q91. It was hilarious, I suppose. But I also wanted space, space, lots of space. This whole pocket universe they've caged us in—all nineteen A.U.'s across of it—isn't big enough for one human being with a vision.

"I want to go somewhere with lots of room," I said, "or at least the illusion of it."

We ran for the next booth like children. We found a monopole-skating rink and donned our skating gloves—no one to collect the rental fee—and hung-skated across the field for a while, feeling the pseudowind in our faces and the perfectly blended scent of fresh air and salt and ozone…

Soon we were tired out, so we halted and dematted and thumbed a robovendor in the corridor for two milkshakes. We stood awhile for the little capsules to take effect. Soon the cool chocolate sensation was running through our veins, and then—

"Let's go to the earthscape park," said Dunny urgently.

I knew we'd end up enjoying a little more than just the view of a simulated Old Earth. We grabbed a slidewalk and raced upstream on it, giggling as it tried to reverse direction for us.

Then, through the booth again and…

A forest of dendroids under a full moon. Soft howling of wolves, continuous-looped chirping of strange extinct earth insects: A dark shadow, a flurry of feathers in our faces—

"Don't worry," Dunny said. "It's just one of the ornithoids, probably an owl."

We walked on, through the Sphinx-dominated Sahara, to where the shadow of the Statue of Liberty crossed the breasts of the Venus de Milo as it swung gently under a weeping willow. A brook babbled the latest lovesongs. I began to feel very romantic.

"It feels like it was made for us, doesn't it?" I whispered. I thought of the hundred thousand people crammed into the

Temple, and the whole wide Mallworld all around us and only the two of us, together, alone...

Dunny said suddenly, "If we save up for four standard years, we can just about buy any kind of baby you want, Joni, if we pool our two incomes..."

I gave the Venus de Milo a little push—it was light as a helium floater—and watched it pendulum slowly back and forth. "But we'll have to stay hitched for four years," I said wonderingly. "How are we going to know we want to be together that long?"

"Come on!" he said, grabbing me fiercely so that I couldn't breathe for a moment. "Can you stop being so bloody down-to-earth for one moment? Can you dream for a while, Joni? Just because we're in a cage doesn't mean we have to stop living, stop being human!"

I threw myself at him. "I wish it could always be like this," I said. We stepped across the brook, past a thin little tundra patch, into a perfumed garden full of rosebushes and gilded swings. A pair of white ornithoids fluttered by, cooing. Above, the simusky glowed cool and blue, and pretty clouds in the shape of lambs skipped merrily—a pleasant conceit on the part of the designers.

I was just about to say "Let's make love" when I distinctly heard a child sobbing. "Shh," I said. "Listen—do you hear it?"

"Wait, what?"

The wailing cut across the singing brook, across the chirping and cooing of the background synthnoise...

Dunny was beginning to get hot! "Look, over here, next to the simulated rosebushes..." He started to drag me over, when the wailing came again.

"For god's sake, Dunny," I said, "there's a lost kid or something around here, and we'd better help it—"

"Oh, all right. Just as the mood was perfect...what a day! It's just one thing right after another!"

"Look!"

There ahead of us, in the shadow of a low wall, vine-brambled and moss-mottled, was a child. Huddled under a bush, with only an arm and the top of the head showing, and already I knew what it was—

We dashed across to it to cut off its escape. It was about a meter tall, in a flowing four-tiered tunic, and purple hair that rippled in the shadowlight, and the scent, sensual, unmistakable—

"You're a Selespridon!" I blurted out. The child just went on whining as if the world had come to an end. I didn't know that the Masters of the Galaxy ever cried or showed grief…quickly I went to the child's side and held him. He was shivering with terror.

"Well," Dunny said, "there's only one Selespridon child *in* our Solar System right now…Gdazhkeh, Junior! And his father, in between yelling on about capturing the lost malaprop, has done nothing but sit in his hotel and mutter about his son, his son, about how it may be too late…"

"We've got to take the kid to his dad," I said.

Suddenly Gdazhkeh Junior squirmed out of my arms and started shrieking in terror. "Leave me alone! Leave me alone or I'll show you!"

"Must have learned our language on his grand tour," I said to Dunny, turning, when the child began to shimmer and blur at the edges—

And suddenly he was a malaprop! "God Almighty!" Dunny groaned. "You were the one who bit Vanessa and injected that mordomaniac compound into her and…you mean, all the *other* malaprops…are baby Selespridar?" I said.

I mean, the adult Selespridar looked so human, it never occurred to me that they might have a metamorphosis cycle…I just gaped at him.

And then another grotesque thought surfaced for a moment, but it was so absurd that I choked it back down at once. "Come on, honey," I said to the kid. "Change back, be a dear."

He did so. "Neat trick, isn't it?" he said. "My cellular structure won't be completely stable in the adult shape for another ten or eleven of your years."

"So let's have an explanation," said Dunny.

"Well…" He started to cry again, and I had to hold on to him. "I didn't like staying at the hotel and I was just sneaking around following my father. So I saw him on the restaurant level and I wandered around till I hit the kitchens, and the malaprops looked like a good place to hide, but—they were shelling them! My father was going to eat them!"

"Well, I think I'd better take you to your dad now," said Dunny, who turned around to subvoke an order to the security department.

"No!" the child screamed. "I'll get eaten, I'll get eaten—"

The thought I'd just pushed aside now hit me like a sledgehammer. "God!" I shouted. "They're monsters! They eat their own children! Oh, god—"

"And I'm only two weeks old!" the kid managed to sob. "I only just came to on the river bank on our home planet and I didn't know—"

I couldn't stop to think that this was an alien creature, that there might be different motives, different feelings involved. I just knew it must be desperately frightened and it all got mixed up with how badly I wanted to have a kid and how poor we were and how we couldn't afford it and how much I wanted to give myself—

I clasped the soft blue thing hard to me, rocking it like a human mother would, not afraid that it might turn into a malaprop and bite me…finally, when I had gotten the Selespridon child calmed down, I started to sob hysterically myself, and I'd cried myself silly by the time security arrived.

I tried to be brave as we matted into the Presence.

A hotel room in Mallworld, I didn't know which hotel. I suppose it was much like any other room, except that I'd stayed in hotels only vicariously, through watching holovee shows.

Fluted columns, delicate fragrances from a scent-varigator, a bedfloat three meters long to accommodate the extra height of a Selespridon…and pile carpeting woven on Old Earth itself, so I felt almost as though I were standing on a cloud. At the other end of the room, in front of a French window that afforded a simulated view of a Martian sunset, the Selespridon sat in his own pool of darkness; his chairfloat was of beaten iridium. The air was permeated with the smell of him. A simubreeze played with his soft magenta hair. He was so beautiful, so powerful, so…monstrous! What sort of creature was it whose child feared to be eaten by him?

With a graceful wave Gdazhkeh dismissed the guards, clunkers, and computer simulacra who had brought us from the earthpark. That just left me, Dunny, and the cowering kid.

"Thank you for returning my son to me," he said. *"Gott im Himmel!* Your reward of one megacre has been deposited in both your names; any creditcomp will confirm it on your way out."

The kid clutched me harder.

"Now look here," I said. "We don't want your dirty money!" When Dunny started to say something I shut him up with a dig in the ribs. "This kid is scared to death, and besides, we saw him change form into a malaprop. Something very terrible is going on, and I'm not going to give you the kid! Okay, I suppose you've a lot of power, and you can probably give me a permanent somatectomy. So be it! Over my dead body, damn you!"

Gdazhkeh started to laugh.

"Well, come on, this isn't funny!" I screamed, and made a mad rush across the room. He held me at arm's length. I hadn't realized how strong he was. And the smell of him, so erogenic and overpowering, stopped me dead.

"All right, you humans. You have shown compassion, even though it is as a result of a rather ludicrous comedy of errors. I admire that." He let me go, and I walked back to the other two rather sullenly. "I suppose I ought to tell you some little-known facts about the life cycle of the Selespridon species…"

I listened open-mouthed as he began.

"After a gestation period, we Selespridar give birth to several million tiny eggs not dissimilar to your frogs' or fish eggs. Our pregnant ones (they can be either male or female) either wade out into the nearest stream or make use of special drains in our houses—the eggs then recapitulate, more or less, the evolutionary history of our species.

"The fact that malaprops are eaten as a delicacy on our home planet is an evolutionary necessity, genetically programmed. You see, the malaprop is the last stage before a Selespridon attains consciousness and becomes self-aware; it is therefore the last stage at which a weeding out process can compassionately occur. The malaprops undergo a final metamorphosis, crawl up onto the dry land, and stagger into the nearest Selespridon habitation; there they are shipped to an adoption center and prepared for their entry into the civilized community. You see, just because, in our developed stage, we happen to have parallel-evolved a surprisingly similar somatic form to humans, doesn't mean that our genetic makeup is anything like the human one."

"But still!" I said. "You would have eaten your own son, wouldn't you?"

"Of course not!" said Gdazhkeh. *"Mamma mia,* no! For the first few years of life the infant Selespridon retains a certain cellular fluidity, and in times of stress will revert to his old form. But you think I wouldn't have recognized my own son?"

"But," Dunny said, "he was afraid of being eaten!"

"Alas, yes. You see, the trauma of achieving consciousness in the river-mud and realizing who and what one really is...is one of the central problems of being a Selespridon. You have your human condition, we have ours. One way that many of our infants react is to cling to the earlier, more primal form. The pressures of being a sentient being, all at once...can be very overpowering. Besides, there may be an unconscious memory of the malaprop trapping devices that proliferate in every pond and lake on our home planet. That's one of the reasons I brought my boy to your system, by the way; I wanted to get him out of the usual growing-up environment! Take his mind off the awareness-acquisition-trauma..."

"I guess you're right," I said dubiously. "But I still think it's disgusting to eat your potential children!"

"No more so than to swallow human semen, for example, though. And how would you feel if nature had ordained for every single ovum and every single sperm produced by your race to reach babyhood?"

There was nothing I could say to that.

Suddenly the kid said, "Can I stay with these humans, Daddy, please? I like them!"

I looked at Dunny and said, "Well, if he's here to learn about our barbaric ways, I don't see why we shouldn't have him around for a while..."

The Selespridon said: *"Baka yaro!* You've succeeded where I've failed...you've made my son sympathize with an alien species! To think I punished him for tweaking an earthling's nose..."

"All it takes is a little understanding."

"Well," said Gdazhkeh. "How much more money would you like for this...ah...babysitting work?"

"You really don't understand, do you?" Dunny said. "We'd *like* to do it!" I remember thinking then how *good* Dunny is. And yes, I really *did* love him.

Gdazhkeh smiled. "We have a saying—"inscrutable as a human,'" he said. "We'll never understand you people..."

"Of course," I said slyly, "there is something we'd like...if you really wanted to repay us." There was a trace of bitterness in my voice.

"Money?" said the Selespridon. "Well, I daresay I can let you have enough to afford anything you want, *nicht wahr?"*

"Our freedom!" I gasped. There was a long silence.

The Selespridon came toward us, quite close. With one hand he toyed with his child's hair. "You humans, you humans," he said softly. There was irony in his voice, but compassion too. "You're a promising, dangerous species. You know how many 'human' jokes are going around the Galaxy these days? Well, listen to me. We Selespridar have been babysitting various species for millennia...longer even. And when we see one of our babies shooting up, wayward but undeniably brilliant...can we help it if we are a little oversolicitous, a little overprotective? How does a father feel on the day he truly realizes his son will ultimately replace him...?"

His tone was light. But somehow I was really moved.

"Because you have taught me some very important truths," the Selespridon said, "I will give you a very important gift. I want you to take the child for a few weeks, let him learn something about the inscrutable humans—but I also want both of you to come down to the Galaxy Palace tomorrow, early, before opening time. An hour or so early. I have some arrangements to make—first I must contact the Universe Outside, you understand, and get their permission, and arrange for the appropriate machines to be set up—but your gift should be ready by that time. *Capisce?"* His eyes twinkled.

Like starlight.

So they've turned on the holoZeiss, I thought.

The Galaxy Palace: hushed, empty, starlit.

Above us, the stardome slowly wheeling. The Milky Way splashed over darkness. Just me and Dunny, waiting...

A voice. Gdazhkeh's.

"I'm not here This is a precord. I wanted the two of you to be alone here to appreciate my gift. And before you decry it, and say that it is something insubstantial and a mere symbol and totally useless...I would have you know that it was necessary to use up the entire mass-energy of a star as a power source to bring this gift to you. And it is a gift that only a civilized being would appreciate; judge then, how fair I am to you, members of an uncertified race.

"If you don't mind, I can't resist a little lecture. As you know, there is an infinity of universes; the one from which we originally took you, and the one into which we have thrust you—for your own protection—are two such. With enormous power expenditure it is possible to force open a transdimensional window, and this is what has been done with the dome of your Galaxy Palace restaurant...if you see what I mean. The dome is now a window into your former home. But don't try to break through into the other universe—the forceshield that protects it is as impenetrable as the one that surrounds your entire little universe at the orbit of Saturn.

"I cannot give you the stars yet, *mes enfants,* but I can at least give you *hope.*

"Listen carefully...you think the holoZeiss is on, don't you? But why isn't it humming?"

I was chilly and I moved closer to Dunny for warmth. There was no sound at all. I strained. No humming. This could only mean that—

The stars! They were the real thing!

I couldn't stop crying.

Well, the Galaxy Palace restaurant is the only place in our little pocket universe where you can see out into the real universe. So you can imagine how long the line to eat there has gotten and how much they're charging. Clement barJulian was so happy he made me a partner. Money comes easy now.

Every day the shoppers in Mallworld walk by and hear the same hypey holo-ad screeching in their ears—

Here's the universe! Flickersparklepinpoints dervishdancing through darkness! Whorls, whirls, and swirls of fiery stippledust! Giddy worlds wheeling on unseen slings! Starspills out of cosmic salt and pepper shakers! Frozen fireworks!

Yeah.

We bought a baby last week. We didn't even feel our budget pinch. We don't live in Cramp Concentration anymore either; we commute in from Deimos on the transmat like decent folk. I got the baby from Storkways, and it really was the best baby money could buy...

I brought him to work one day and held him under the stardome so he could watch. He stopped crying suddenly and began to gurgle and laugh.

You know, I always used to wonder why the Selespridon's gift was so important. I mean, it doesn't make any difference whether the stars in the restaurant's decor are real or fake, does it? You can't touch them. You can't tell the difference. They're unreachable as ever.

I think I understand now, though.

I think it means this—

It isn't the past up there anymore.

It's the future.

Did Lord Gdazhkeh really have to do that? I wonder...

Oh, not to worry? The spacetimebending device will deteriorate after a few years and leave nothing behind? It is only a transient transformation after all, then?

Perhaps, lord, a little break for luncheon; I've ordered the most delicious malaprops from back home and...oh. Understandably, you feel a little sickened. You're thinking of your young ones, back there in the real universe, floundering at the river's edge.

Let us then, my lord, hasten on to our next victim...er, subject. If Your Magnificence doesn't mind. Here we go...yes, yes, our mind-magician has snared yet another specimen. But the image wavers! I do declare, Your Multi-n'huatitude, that the creature's lifeline seems to have split in two! You tell me that the filthy reproductive habits of these inferior beings are not our concern? But, Your Lordship, I assure you that these apemen do not reproduce by mitosis. I'll have a technician work on it right away. Oh. We've solved the problem. There was a flickering between parallel universes, my lord; for a moment our barrier did not quite hold, allowing a similar-yet-dissimilar cosmos to coexist with this one...yes, yes, it's been fixed! I don't think there's been any leakage. At least, nothing of consequence. Perhaps we should proceed?

(Kids, we haven't forgotten you. This one is just for you!)

KIDS! BUILD YOUR OWN MALLWORLD!

All you wonderful children out there! Isn't Mallworld just your favorite place? Isn't it great to be able to come to Mallworld and buy everything in sight? To explore the infinite wonders of consumer utopia?

Well, now you can build a scale model of your favorite place...right in your own room!

It's MINIMALL!

It comes in a sturdy, inflatable box.

It's got more than three thousand pieces for many fun-filled hours of hand-construction...and if you'd rather not go through the inconvenience of building the model yourself, MINIMALL comes with a comsim-operated auto-productive mode! Builds itself in three seconds flat! You can also use the Autoprod Mode to take it down again if you have a small room and you want it out of the way for a while.

Here's what you get—

Mallworld shell with cutaway.

Spare parts for dozens of stores.

Miniature people, comsims, gaboochis, even a Selespridon!

And two dozen toyochevs of all models to seed your parking lot with!

Yes, kids, you'll be able to play make-believe games with your realistic MINIMALL kit—perennial games like Buyers and Sellers, Clunkers and Shoplifters, and Raid the Warehouse! And even if you can't think of games to play, the minicomp inside the MINIMALL will think of something to do from its store of thousands of shopping games. Tells you stories, too! Tales like The Prince and the Consumer, Little Red Shopping Bag, and Sleeping Booty entertain you in miniature, right there in the MINIMALL's model of Mallworld's feeliepalace complex.

What's more, the MINIMALL is fully expandable!

Here's what you can get (each sold separately)—

Sound-system/muzak originator! Have your MINIMALL come to life with singing commercials, *muzak concrete*, and more!

Store-packages! Get a miniature Storkways! A suicide parlor with model Vampire! A scale model Statue of Limitations with working arms and legs!

Package of fifteen assorted clunkers—that listen to your every command and answer with programmable responses!

A working micro-demat booth! (Your parents must assemble this one—and don't get your fingers stuck in it or they'll have to pay to get them replaced!)

Yes, kids, you'll love MINIMALL—the toy that grows as you grow. New expansion sets will become available every season! MINIMALL will never go out of date! Daddies and Mommies love to play, too!

To get this wonderful model kit, get on your instybuy right away and call the toy department of Gimbel and Gamble's Department Store in Mallworld! Or come by and see for yourself! It's the ultimate adventure in true-to-life fantasy role-playing!

Note to parents: MINIMALL is completely non-toxic.

Mallworld Graffiti

She used to squeeze the filet mignon from the middle of the tube. She wore potato sacks to respectable parties instead of wisping around in seemly nudity. Her mothering instinct drove me crazy—forcing me to meet the mortgage on our kids (the little angels with their squalid, uneugenic faces, that bootleg genemonger look, and their acrid, intractable personalities)—pestering me to buy new clunkers for our kitchenette, new caffoid-carts, new sleaz-o-matics for our bed...

Oh, and the children! Running amok, tripping the clunkers over the dinner as it squirted from the computer, leaving their toys around for me to trip over, spraying their underwear all over the door so it couldn't iris open...

I couldn't stand the pack of them, but what could I do? I was under contract, a contract stupidly thumbed under the Great Seal of the Holy Judeo-Buddhist Matrimonial Agency itself, renegement punishable by three years in a sanitization clinic or a fine of twelve kilocreds. In those days I managed an instant pet store in Mallworld, and I certainly couldn't afford an annulment *and* pay the baby company *and* my share of the condo-azroid with time-sharing transmat and simcom facilities too! In short, I was a member of a silent minority which the philosophers of our time have deemed extinct since the Dark Ages...the harried husband.

Small discomforts, you may say. And yet...

In their own little way, it was these minor aches and pains of life that gave birth to a masterpiece.

Not to mention the Selespridar...

You know, after a while it becomes very easy to get into the habit of thinking of the Selespridar as "the Gods." After all, they are *so* powerful—didn't they thrust that unbreachable barrier all around the orbit of Saturn, walling in our Solar System, and shunt our whole shebang into a vacant little parallel universe—for "our own good"? Without so much as ruffling one strand of their wild magenta hair. As my personal comsim-cum-bedtime storyteller used to tell me when I was a kid, "Yes, Robbie, you can curse them all you like, and dream about the universe that we've lost—but you must admit they haven't done badly. There are no more wars—or only little ones, anyway, and everything seems pretty prosperous."

Oh, yes, the average person thinks of a Selespridon and he thinks *omnipotent* and *infallible* and all those things we humans aren't. Certainly more so than those hokey religions whose evangidroids blare forth recondite doctrines on every level of Mallworld, hypeing and entrapping the unwary shopper.

Personally, I never thought much about them. They were there and they were presumably all-wise and all that, but I didn't lust after the stars, even though this was very fashionable in the circles of prestigiopretentiousness of the milieu in which my parents (and therefore I as a child) moved back in Babylon-5. I mean it was a huge scientific wonder that they managed to keep that mighty forceshield in place around the Solar System, but beyond that—

Until the Selespridar changed my life.

Quite without knowing it. You could hardly blame them for one little glitch in the forceshield, could you now?

One little glitch in two centuries?

Oh, no, you're saying now. Not *another* story about That Famous Glitch.

Okay. You saw it on your holovee. But chances are you weren't one of the thousands who were working *in* Mallworld, or who happened to be whisking their autocarts through their weekend shopping spree, or were just plain hanging out, when it happened. And I was.

And for most people it was a nine-day wonder, to be marveled at, stored, forgotten. But it changed my life.

But to see why, you have to go back about twenty years, Earth reckoning.

Life in Babylon-5 was the closest thing *homo sapiens* had to an ftl drive. Fashions changed every twenty-four hours and were regulated by android proctors who would spray the new clothes on you on the spot and fine you a cred. Every one was either an artist or an aesthete, and both my parents were aesthetes. Dad ran a holovee lecture series on "Myth and Archetype in the Architectural Ambience of Ancient Fast-Food Restaurants." Mother was a disciple of the Xeno-Zen cult, finding meditative fulfillment in the contemplation of the tripartite navel of Kmengdreft, a Selespridon who'd escaped from their equivalent of a loony bin and found us dumb earthies a little more congenial.

With parents such as those, I, Robo Ishi-Leone, was bound to be a great artist—or so my parents said. By the time I was seven they'd bribed me into the best art school on Deimos, and I'd begun to make my mark as a snowman.

It seemed like a good choice. I was antisocial, and snowmen are lonely artists. I enjoyed scooting through space in my beat-up old toyochev, squirting water into little ice platelets, each with its little stasis-motor, and then sitting at the controls and waldoing each teeny flake into place so that they caught the light just right and became an image...classic pointillism was in by the time I reached puberty, and also the new trick of having concealed light sources buried in the mass of iceflakes; I was doing some pretty workmanlike stuff. I did a little ice-garden for Mom to meditate in just a couple of transmat stops from home but far enough away to be by itself in the starless blackness that is the human race's prison. She used it a couple of times, and once she even got Kmengdreft to perform his little tea ceremony there. Afterward I had to clean the tea leaves off some of the ice-chunks, practically by hand. I also made Dad a charming little ice McDonalds set in a delicately shimmering lawnlike tapestry of icicled french fries. A simple, dumb idea, but it was Art.

I had no intention of making a profession of it. I wanted—
like every kid—to be a big league laseball star.

Time passed; my parents ignored me as was then the fashion.

One fine day in early adolescence, I'd hopped into the toyochev,
crashed through the ceiling of my bedroom and matted into deep
space, towing a reservoir of water behind me. I'd just popped out of
a ring of buoys somewhere between the belt and Jupiter, bumming
by my lonesome as was usual for my teenaged self; and right then and
there, I decided to create an extraordinary ice-sculpture. The sort of
thing that academic bores like Dad would lecture about five hundred
years from now.

I made my car whirl madly in the darkness, sending water-
spurts sparking about me like a laser buzz saw. After I'd gathered
quite a cloud of the things, and I'd used the autostick to plaster
an invisible stasis-thing on each, I began playing around.

First I moved the iceflakes abstractly. I spun sort of an icy
spiderweb, using one of the presets in my field controller, and
then I put myself at the center and prowled about. Gradually
I introduced shifts into the web, making the lines of ice
undulate, collapse into irregular hundred-meter-long
polyhedrons, and now I was an insect buzzing in and out of a
mobile of ice, rotating slowly in the blackness. There wasn't
much light except what I generated from the car itself, and so
the construct changed constantly as paths of colored light
crisscrossed it...

I was in a kind of daze, I guess. You get into quite a power
trip, alone in space pushing great gobs of glitter around. In no
time I found that I'd been working for a couple of days.

Of course I wouldn't be missed—my dad was on a field
trip to Earth, excavating a Gino's in Old New Delhi, and my
mother had signed up for a year's hibertrance as part of her
cultish activities. But I'd had enough. I decided to circle my
latest abstract thing one more time and beat it.

I planted a light source at its heart. Then I spun out and
drifted around my creation. It was utterly chaotic, but so was
my life at the time, I guess...

Thousands of waterflakes gathered into sparklets that ringed a fluffy-soft center where the strands of the discarded web had fallen into folds of a gossamer mist-veil. Sometimes you could get so lost in the sheer *prettiness* of what you were doing that you forgot what you were trying to do completely.

Well, I'd worked *that* out of my system, and I was all ready to go back and do a little *real* work. When—

Out of the corner of my eye, I saw a car. A toyochev, but like nothing *you've* ever seen.

Talk about gaudy! It was solid gold and shaped like an ancient galleon, with winged gargoyles spouting colored jetstreams from the stern and flapping their gilt-feathered wings. I rubbed my eyes. Yes, this…monstrosity that reeked of megacredits was banked right beside me, and when I started to maneuver toward the ring of buoys that marked the transmat gate to the next nexus, *it followed me.*

I dodged, plumbing the ice madness I'd built. Sending flake-shards flying. The galleon kept pace easily. I carved great holes in the polyhedral center of the ice-thing, and the galleon sailed right through them.

Now they weren't doing anything wrong—I mean, space is free and all—but they were getting the hell on my nerves. To an artist, especially to a young, undeveloped, hypersensitive and antisocial one like me, being observed in mid-doodle is worse than being watched *in medias* doo-doo.

I subvoked some mean commands to my car's pilot. My stomach did aerial back-handsprings as my car vaulted around the shambles of my two days' sketching. Until I finally heard a voice over the intervoke—

"Want to come aboard, cute little snowman?" I froze. That voice! It was like…

Aha, I thought. *She's been spying on me, she's the type that goes for lonesome artists, and I'll make a quick conquest right here in the middle of nowhere.* What an adventure! The voice—

Like lolling on warm fur by candlelight. Like—

"Sure," I answered in what I hoped was a sensual, adult voice. "Right away, at your service."

The demat-instructions came through in that same sensual voice, and in a moment I was standing in a little whitewalled chamber in her toyochev, looking at the most beautiful woman in the world.

I wanted to rush right over and pull a number on her, but she motioned me away. The room was divided in two by a little brook, and her side of it was taken up by a gigantic fluffbed. The bright red artfur of it was rippling and rustling like flames.

"Art," she said at last. "So transient. You wrecked your toy picture running away from me, my cute little snowman..."

I stared at her, dropping all politeness by the wayside. She had incredibly long grass green hair that twined around her nude body, wreathing the soft curve of her breasts and veiling those parts that young men love to see. To be nude is of course to wear the completely innocent, unconcealing yet untouchable little-girl look, and yet the copious hair made it all so voluptuous, so desirable...I just gaped at her.

"Shall we?" she said. I could only nod.

And then afterward she said, "I'm just a cradle-snatcher after all, my little snowman."

"You're not old!" I protested—how innocent I was!—and I took a handful of her hair and I twisted it, boa-constrictor-fashion, round and round our shoulders, our bodies...

"I am a hundred years old, my child."

"A hundred ye—" I backed off, lost my foothold on the fur, stumbled into the brook. I got up sopping, feeling like a fool. "Sorry, I mean I didn't mean to criticize your age, I mean I—"

And then I looked into her eyes.

She *was* that old. Those eyes, a clear gray-green, had an oldness like mountains, like the sea...to summon up all the imagery of ancient dead poets. Her face—that could have been built yesterday. It was perfectly formed. Not a flaw, not a scratch, not a wrinkle.

"Science can do wonders if you have the money. Especially Selespridon science...I've been old for so long, little snowman, I've become morbid, my dear...you turned up at just the right moment."

So she'd just been using me to relieve some pent-up tension! I'd just happened along at the right time! But when I gazed on her she looked so perfect...what did I care that every particle of her flesh had been lovingly crafted by the magic-cum-science of our alien overlords? This antisocial, hyperaesthetic social misfit was in love!

"When...will I see you again?" I stammered. I didn't even know who she was.

She sighed, a murmury music at once languid and jaded and strangely entrancing. "You're all alike, you young ones. Always into permanence."

"I'm different—" I cried desperately.

"Yes, yes." Again, that throaty sigh. And then she handed me a crystal card. "Don't read it till you've left. And by the way, I'm having a little soirée next week. I'll see you there."

And, abruptly, she had walked over the bed to a demat-booth and vanished.

I didn't have a plan of her car—more palace than car—I wouldn't have known how to pursue her. All I could do was step into the booth on my side of the brook and order it to send me back to the car.

Afterward, I took out the card and waited.

My broken ice-sculpture, shattered into a thousand momentums by our chase scene, was flung out all over the next few cubiklicks by now. I just saw a couple of chunks floating forlornly by. In the blackness shone the white point that was Jupiter; but of course there were no stars. The stars were outside our universe, beyond the Selespridon barrier.

And then the card spoke to me in her voice. Just two word. Her name.

There's class and there's *class*. I'd always thought my family were pretty exalted—coming from Babylon-5's artistic enclave and all. But the name that the card breathed to me, in its languorously seductive voice, was more than class.

The card said, *Theresa barJulian.*

I had heard of her. She was a member of humanity's most powerful clan. She was Mistress of Mallworld.

I had just made love to the richest woman in the known universe.

Dad was standing six inches high on the kitchen table when I got back. You didn't get much background on the transmat call system, but I could vaguely make out the outline of a crumbling fast-food restaurant against a kaleidoscope of tumultuous earthie traffic.

"Dad," I said, "Dad, I've been invited to a party by Theresa barJulian!"

"I'm coming right back!" he growled. "This has gone too far—" The connection snapped.

In the morning Mom matted into my room. "Your father called me," she said.

"For that you climbed out of your religious hibertrance, Mom? You shouldn't have—"

"I forbid it!" she screamed. She looked haggard. On her way home she must've been stopped by the fashion proctors, because I could see tatters of last week's flamboyant firejeans peeking from underneath today's silk-striped sackcloth muu-muu.

"Forbid what?"

"Theresa barJulian's too frightening for words. She owns half the universe!"

"Pope's boobs!" I swore. "You're just scared of losing control of me, that's what! You're just jealous because you're not the only woman in my life; you're stuck in your reverse-Oedipal shtick or something. And because she's a million times more rich and powerful than *you'll* ever be—"

"We tried so hard to raise you to be artistic, not to be part of that tacky, decadent life—"

"When are you going to understand, Mother? Staring at navels and speculating on the eating habits of primitive earthies isn't what I want out of life! I don't even want to carve ice-blocks anymore! I'm in love, and I know what I'm doing!"

In about half an hour I found myself with nothing but a beat-up toyochev and fifty creds to my name, hauling it through the blackness of space on my way to Mallworld.

Mallworld!

Oh, I'd been there before...I was never a hick. I knew Mallworld was a thirty-klick-long shopping center coursing through space, somewhere between the belt and Jupiter, and that it is the place where all dreams come true, to quote the old romantic song. Mother had sometimes whisked me through there when we were out of some rare alien incense for one of her weird rituals, or to get Dad a souvenir from the only store that wasn't earthside that sold relics of the ancient temples of Colonel Sanders and the other hokey antique religions. But we'd avoided it on the whole, and usually I never had time to drink it all in, what with being constantly on the leash, as it were, and with my parents incomprehensible (though fashionable at the time) anachronistic disdain for commercialism. Oh yes, they were back-to-nature freaks. Our home air conditioner used gasoline extract to simulate the peaceful, unspoiled air of primal Earth...

But this was different. I was alone in Mallworld, I had run away to be with the goddess of commercialism herself!

Well, the first few days, while I was waiting for the party—

I walked the tall halls, level upon level of corkscrew corridors and gravi-looped walkways, tier upon tier of brash shops festooned with color-screeching holo-ads, sensuous androids selling sex, rambunctious robots peddling insurance, flying auto-shopping-carts that disbursed free samples of deodorant, expectorants, and autosuggestible sycophants, demat-booths that popped you in and out of churches, restaurants, shrink shacks, suicide parlors, skating rinks, feeliepalaces, zonkie hangouts, grandstands, bandstands, and copulands, and—

It was heady. Very heady.

And when I found out that Theresa barJulian's little card was a passport that thumbed the way open to an infinitude of freebies...

I ate at the Galaxy Palace under the simulated stardome. I hit the autocoutures and decked myself out in a different outfit every few hours. I stayed at the Gaza Plaza, the hotel hollowed out of the Great Pyramid of Khufu (so they said) and hauled to Mallworld at excruciating expense. When I was bored with splendor I raced the slidewalks—there were always a few other kids, but I didn't speak with them, I was proud of my solitude— skipping from hi-speed to mid-speed to lo-speed and trying to trip up the clunkers as they clanked by on their errands. If I wanted anything, a computer simulacrum, buzzing boisterously as it flitted past, would tell me where to go and to hell with the cost. I laughed when I thought of Mom and Dad kicking me out and *knowing* I wasn't well-thumbed enough to throw my credit around.

But I saw Theresa's face everywhere I looked. And I still had eight days left before the week was up.

On the third day I discovered Levitol.

I tripped in the drug palace at first. Then I started floating around the corridors, telling myself how fantastic I felt. After that I gave up completely on caution, and I began to drift in and out of demat-booths in a state of stupefied bliss, my eyes glazed over, dreaming of Theresa's hair, flying figure-eights and other nifty aerobatics around the heads of the throngs of shoppers...

They say that Levitol leads to Brevitol...

That was a much more dangerous drug. It didn't make you hover around harmlessly for a couple of hours. It made an hour seem like a minute or a minute seem like an hour, you couldn't tell in advance, and it knocked me out.

Two seconds later, it seemed, it was time for Theresa barJulian's party, and I was a confirmed addict.

A zonkie.

I came to, collared a passing comsim for directions. The miniature pink man buzzed around my face, confirming my identity and running some kind of security check, and then he whispered the level number in my ear.

"There's no point in trying to memorize it," he jabbered in his tinny voice, "the number changes automatically at indeterminate intervals." Then he vanished.

Eagerly I elbowed aside a troupe of Boy Scouts who were walking a dozen gaboochis on leashes, trod on the toe of a passing anchorite, kicked aside a sulking shopping bag, nearly got beaned by a zonked-out spiderman in a toga, and hopped into a booth.

I couldn't believe my eyes.

The cream of human society—not to mention the odd Selespridon—was drifting by my eyes. We were in an intimate sort of...bedroom; it definitely contained a monster of a diamond-shaped fluffbed, curtained by some smoky material and supported on kaleidolithic columns. Trays of hors d'oeuvres putted and pranced from guest to guest. They were as outré a bunch as I'd ever seen. Weird, custom-built somatypes with more arms and heads than a Hindu god; members of the new "minimalist" school who had had all their limbs amputated at hideous expense, and now winged it about in prostheses or, worse still, had been reduced to heads on hovering silver platters; and the few Selespridar, who must have been as scandalized as I, two meters tall with rippling magenta hair and that strange, feral, erotic odor that wafted behind them wherever they went, surveying the scene in a befuddled befogment.

I didn't know any of them, my Brevitol high had begun to wear off, and I was embarrassed to be there. I recognized some of the people from the holovee—I mean, I could have wagered the Pope's bra that that four-tier-tunicked Selespridon munching a drumstick in the corner was none other than Klutharion, governor of the Solar System, I mean we were talking *that* class of people—and I wanted to go home.

I was scared.

And then I saw *her!*

The curtains dissolved. She was lying on the fluffbed in all her glory, cloaked in her shimmering hair, and she was as beautiful as I remembered her; and beside her, smug and smirking and horribly handsome, was a naked young man who wasn't me.

Well! You see how ridiculously naïve I used to be! But I was in love, and what else was there to do? I charged.

She looked at me. Her eyelids fluttered for a moment, and I knew that she was searching her memory.

"Why, it's Robbie," she said. Her lips curved, ever so slightly, into a graceful smile. She tossed her head; her hair shuddered and parted a little, giving me a tantalizing glimpse of thigh. "How sweet of you to come. I was getting all depressed, and thinking of death and being very morbid, my little snowman, and that's why I threw this party. *Everyone's* here. Why don't you join me on my bed?"

Everyone was listening now, even the ones who were pretending not to. It was like being in one of those Byzantine imperial courts in the bad old gas-guzzling era.

"Come on," she said, "Don't mind *him.*" Reluctantly I climbed aboard. "I do so love your dark hair and your snow-pale skin and your little button of a nose and your blue-marble eyes. You look just like a little snowman, no?" I glared balefully at my rival, who only sniggered.

"I can't hope to compete with *him,*" I said archly, "on the physical appearance level. But—" I stopped. The whole imperial court was in convulsions. I suddenly realized they were laughing at *me.* "What the—"

"Terry here," said the young man whom I was attempting to treat with amused disdain, "gets about three unrequited lovers a day, and one in twenty gets a contract with The Way Out suicide parlor within the week. What today's youth is coming to!"

"How dare you call her Terry!" I cried hotly. "She's a— goddess!"

"And I'm a god," he said. "I'm Julian barJulian the Fourteenth, Terry's brother, and I'm old enough to be your grandfather, little snowman."

My humiliation was complete.

Or so I thought...

I'll never live this down. Never, never, never. "I—"

"Don't worry, dear, dear little snowman...you are *so* charming, don't you see? It was naughty of you to charge up to me like that, even Klutharion wouldn't dare do it, but your naïveté is so *touching,* so *authentic.* I've half a mind to keep you in stock for a while."

"So that's it, huh?" I said. "Keep me in stock like a breed-animal. Well, I'm more than a toy! I'm a—I'm a—" But what was I? "I'm an *artist,"* I finished lamely. Mocking guffaws echoed across the room. I flushed. "But I *am* one!"

She shushed the crowd with a finger on her lips. I wanted to spring upon her and devour her, but..."So you are, little snowman, so you are."

"I'll prove it!" I said, knowing I'd gone too far now.

"Very well." There was dead silence.

"Lately," she went on (she spoke so softly I had to strain to hear her), "I've been thinking about dying a lot. I want a mausoleum for myself. Even with all this alien magic-medicine, I doubt I'll last another year—" (A chorus of sycophantic cluck-clucks ran around the room. Her eyes flashed, silencing them at once.) "You see, little snowman? Build me...an ice-sculpture worthy of me. Light it with the light of Saturn, the farthest planet of our human universe. A huge ice-statue of me, a thousand times life-size, standing at the gateway between our universe and the *real* universe outside the Selespridon barrier...I shall have my coffin placed in its navel."

Thunderous applause now. "I'll do it."

She laughed, but not really *at* me. "Do you love me that much, little snowman?"

"Yes! Yes!" I said, my cheeks burning.

"Enough to devote your life to a foolish old woman's whim?"

"Yes, already!"

She was silent. Julian barJulian spoke. "You'll have a pension, of course. Let's say—a megacred an earthyear, as long as you keep working, plus all expenses. You'll draw your pay from any creditcomp in Mallworld, so long as you can show you're working on it. Terry is always kind to her young men. She always provides for them."

I closed my eyes and tried to imagine it. A millionfaceted sparkling Theresa of ice, lighting the gateway to the other universe, an effulgent beacon for all our dreams...it was staggering. Even then I knew that I couldn't do it. I was no real artist, I was just your typical product of Babylon-5, all jargon and no vision. And yet—

For *her,* I would do it.

Besides, think of all the Levitol and Brevitol that money could buy...

But what about the Great Glitch, you ask? And surely Theresa barJulian is not the rather drab woman described at the beginning of the story.

Patience...

Work on the mausoleum began at once. I hired a crew of ice-cutters—the dirty work could not all be done by one person, with a project this large—and transmatted off to Saturn's orbit. I had to pick a spot far enough so that the ringed planet wouldn't overpower the composition, close enough to make use of it as a natural light source. It was a pain to tow so much water out, so I picked methane ice as the base material...it'd worked well with the Rings, hadn't it?

In my no-longer-beat-up toyochev I now had a mini-transmat-intervoke for making real-time calls anywhere in the Solar System; I had full eating, drinking, entertainment, and sleeping facilities; and I had five hundred inflatable holograms of Theresa barJulian.

I had as yet no idea of how difficult it would be.

I studied the holograms. I studied Saturn. I studied the starless blackness until I felt, at last, the loneliness that is the human condition…I studied the dots that were Saturn's moons, racing across the dark. But Saturn itself—

Saturn was a monster. Saturn was stunning. Saturn dominated the endless night, haunting me, taunting me with my talentlessness. I—

The planet was huge and silent and watched me, never reproaching, as I blew up the best of the holograms to a forty-klick-long image and laid down the space-buoys that were the preliminary sketches for my Theresa's face…and in the back of my mind was a voice, a conscience, perhaps, telling me I was massacring a mightier work of art, I was sticking a mustache onto the Mona Lisa of ten billion years. I would swallow a pill and forget.

After about an earthyear, a ghost of Theresa began to emerge in the blackness. Wisps of sheer silk hair. From the approach angle, I wanted it to look like she was holding Saturn itself in her arms, embracing it, a madonna and child if you like.

Now I had to begin fleshing in the ghost, and this had to be mostly my own work, not the assistants'. I would order the iceflakes for the day, they would go shave them off wherever the nearest moon happened to be at the time, and they would affix the invisible stasis motors (a Selespridon device, this, making even our arts subject to *their* technology) and then I would go to work.

In six more months, all I had was a smile.

A smile—and a terrible, terrible hunger for oblivion. I remembered my first days in Mallworld, I remembered my first fix of Levitol and my flirtation with Brevitol, but now things were worse. I was into the stuff you had to send to Old Earth for, and my salary was starting to split at the seams. I remembered watching the addicts drift hopelessly along the slidewalks, lost in themselves. And now I was getting to be one. A zonkie.

It had been great sometimes—a dose of Brevitol and then I'd drive my car slowly along the massive lips of ice, and it would seem to take days, I would linger lovingly on every chunk of ice, every jagged crystal, every faceted polyhedron, and every sculpted snowflake, and I would dream of touching her lips, of kissing them and breathing warmth into their city-stoneness. It was beautiful. Until it wore off, and then would come pain.

I was doing less and less work.

And some days I would see Saturn scowling, I would be mocked by a beauty I could never hope to equal, and I would throw in the towel and do nothing and reach for another pill and—

More and more I wandered through Mallworld, but the rush of shoppers reminded me of a dance of death. Theresa would not see me.

Eventually I found the Graffiti Globe.

This was one of Mallworld's most famous landmarks—it was rumored that if you sat down in the park around it, the whole human race would eventually pass by…and I passed by it often. There was this metal globe, see, about three hundred meters in diameter, and gravi-down all around it so you walk on it in any direction. The whole thing was a massive recording device. You could kneel down anywhere and vent your wit or your frustrations and the globe would retain them for a while…sometimes, some clown who knew how to write would even scrawl some gibberish on its shiny surface, but of course only a scholar could interpret such things. But if you wanted some fun you could lie on the Graffiti Globe and put your ear to the cold metal and hear—

A thousand layers of murmurings. Anguished laments for lost lovers. Obscenities, some humorous, some vituperative, lacing through a texture of faint filthy songs and sad songs and songs that lampooned the Selespridar…*Meet me at three point fourteen o'clock. Selespridon science sucks malaprop manure. I love you. Help me, help me, I—. Kinky for slinkies, will fornicate for expenses.*

A million whispers. A million souls bared naked for any stranger to hear. A million cries for help.

It was beautiful to lie there all zonked out and listen to this sussurant mourning. You could be lulled to sleep by it. You could forget your own troubles. *I* did, for a while.

And when I awoke it would be back to Saturn, back to shunting small shards of methane-ice around, switching them back and forth and knowing that they never looked right and that Father Saturn was always watching...

In the end I did it.

I matted into the level of Mallworld where the Graffiti Globe was. I hadn't been able to afford my daily ration of chemicals. I jumped up onto the Globe and found a foothold and then I yelled into it, "Help! I'm a zonkie! Get me out of this!" And I gave them my address. The cold metal kissed my lips; for a moment I imagined they were ice-lips of my Theresa, smiling in the soft light of the huge cold beautiful planet—

A woman came to my suite at the Gaza Plaza Hotel. Her somatype spelled poverty, hard work, all the things I'd been brought up to disdain.

"Robo Ishi-Leone?" I did not like her voice. It was whiny, thin, too little-girlish for me.

"What do you want?"

"I've been sent to you. We heard your cry for help. I'm a pet store owner from level W77, but I also work as a volunteer for Zonkies Anonymous."

"How the—"

"I work as a graffiti monitor, Mr. Ishi-Leone."

I started to cry. In between bursts of incoherence the whole story came spewing out like an undigested gourmet dinner. And then I noticed that I was in her arms, and that we seemed to be...making love.

"What was that all about?" I said finally, settling back on the floatbed. Her technique had been deplorable, but there was something so sincere about it, unlike all the women I had known. Something I hadn't known was in me was responding to her. Perhaps it was that I was becoming a man now, and not a pampered hedonist of a kid.

"I don't know," she said, And she started crying too. It occurred to me that she wouldn't be working for Zonkies Anonymous if she hadn't been one herself, once.

"It's all right," I ventured, hugging her. She clung to me. I'd never had anyone *cling* to me before: I felt needed. It was alarming. "Got to go," I murmured quickly, and dematted before she could even tell me her name.

I was angry with myself by the time I was bursting through the buoys and into Saturn's space.

There was the planet. There were the rings, a perfect ice-sculpture, the cosmic snowman's masterpiece.

And there were the lips.

I'd betrayed them! I was unfit to finish Theresa barJulian's mausoleum. The lips smiled their enigmatic smile; the face was outlined only, with kilometer-long streakstrands of ice, liquid methane squirted by a stunt-flier and crystalizing instantly in the cold vacuum. The body was vaguer still; the navel, where a temple to Theresa was to be erected, was a mere pebble-azroid of ice.

I lay down in the car's auto-life-support pod, where I usually slept, and decided it was time to take an overdose.

I reached up to the shelf where I kept my pills. Two Levitol, assorted strong stuff, not really enough even to get a good high on, and a whole cache of Brevitols. That was all. I scooped up the sachet of Brevitols and swallowed the lot.

As I sank into the trance I realized I wasn't going to die. The life-pod would see to that. I couldn't even commit suicide properly! I panicked, tried to clamber out, but pretty soon I was too dazed and glazed to worry about anything.

When I awoke, a few minutes later, my earthtime timer informed me that a whole year had passed.

Groggily, I turned the toyochev on and circumnavigated Theresa. None of the workmen's cars were there. There were no tanks of methane, no masses of quarried iceflakes.

I was alone, alone with Saturn and with my aborted creation.

I set the car for Mallworld. Soon I was zeroing in on it. Mallworld beckoned to me, a sliver of mirror-bright silver gleaming in the darkness. I parked and floated down the nothing tubes into Mallworld proper. I had nothing in mind except the vague notion of getting the crew back together and starting work again. But, faster than I could think, I was already matting into a drug palace.

As I slipped off the slidewalk a comsim buzzed up to me. "Do something for you?"

"Just let me in there!" I snarled.

"Credit check."

"Don't you know me by now?" I shouted, trying to elbow past the little flying man into the palace. He kept darting in circles around my head, and I couldn't get past. "All right, all right." I held up my thumb,

"Sorry, but your file is closed," the comsim said. He perched offensively on my shoulder,

"Whaa—"

"Oh, there's a closeout message with it. I'm instructed to give it to you. It's from Theresa barJulian." He uttered the name with great reverence. He'd probably been programmed that way.

"Go ahead," I said testily.

Incongruously, the comsim began to speak to me in *her* voice—*Oh, my funny little snowman, I see you didn't make the grade after all. Well, there's a price for everything and you wouldn't be human if you didn't know that...and you haven't delivered, I guess. But I'm no cruel tyrant, my dear little snowman. Anytime you want to go on with my little project, I'll reinstate the salary and I'll even admit that you're a stronger breed of human than I thought you were. But for now...bye! Or, as the Selespridar put it—g'meng* taft psh'thoni, *"may your flowers push through the recalcitrant soil of life," if that means anything to you. Theresa, Goddess of Mallworld...*

"Some dame, eh?" said the comsim in his own voice.

"Get stuffed!" I screamed. I ran for a demat-booth, knocking down two clunkers with one blow.

I'd go to the Gaza Plaza, pick up my things...

The woman from Zonkies Anonymous was standing in the foyer.

"They've thrown out your things," she said. "I heard you were back."

"Leave me alone." I started out of the hotel.

"But don't you understand?" We slid past some nuns of the Acrobatic Order of St. Nureyev, arabesquing and doing cartwheels as they vended Bibles to passersby. "I love you! I've been waiting for you for a whole year!"

I jumped to a faster slidewalk. "You were so vulnerable, your story was so moving...I can help you, cure you of your zonkiness, we can work together slowly..." Two animated lampshades exhorted us to light up our lives with Loyola Lipton's Luscious Lemonade.

I jumped into a booth—not quite fast enough.

COME TO FIDO'S FEELIEPALACE!
FEATURED PRESENTATION
"GAS-GUZZLING GODZILLAS OF GANYMEDE!"

"We can get a nice place with plenty of breathing space for our kids, and bring them up nicely, and you can be a partner in the pet store, and—"

What? How had we gotten to that point? Well, I was tired, dead tired. In a second we were holding hands, vrooming down a mobiustripping slidewalk past Eve's and Adam's Love Nook, past a Society for Creative Anachronism rally where knights in antique helmets and business suits jousted from reconstructed motorcycles with deadly ancient pool cues, past simulated earthscapes and moonscapes and marscapes and starscapes, and we were kissing, I was sinking, sinking, sinking, and she was the only straw...

"What's your name?" I said at last, managing to surface through her nonstop gabbing.

"Lynnie LaBarber."

I saw her face: an unbeautiful, dumplingish face on which two raisin eyes were planted. *Oh, no!* I thought, sinking further. Desperately I tried to conjure up Theresa's face, her dazzling eyes, her taut-arched eyebrows, her lips that I had lived with for a year and more, and I could remember nothing. Nothing. That was finished.

I knew I was never going back. The smile on the unformed face would stay there forever, probably; those stasis motors ran on light. But I would never look on it again.

Two hours later I had thumbed a perpetuity hitchcontract with the woman with whose unflattering description I began this tale. I had hocked away my life's earnings for a couple of babies, sight unseen, and I had signed up for a course at Zonkies Anonymous. Before the year was out I had volunteered to be a Graffiti Globe monitor...

Needless to say, I could not possibly have known that I had just thumbed myself into ten years of sheer hell.

Nine months passed ("I want this to seem *natural,*" Lynnie told me—she was always *telling* me by the end of the week's marriage) and we took delivery of our first child, not the most trendy of models, and not from Storkways Inc. either, but nonetheless a human being of sorts. Another child followed, and another...

We called them Lynx and Lionel and Lem and Lamb and Lunkette, and still she kept ordering them. One custom-made from Storkways would have out-thumbed the credit we used up any day, but I wasn't rich anymore.

I tried to see Theresa once or twice, but the comsims wouldn't give me the code. I knew she was still alive— despite her assertion that she only had a year to live— because every now and then the holovee would carry an announcement of some great philanthropic project she was contributing to. One project she seemed especially fond of was the Institute for Eternal Youth Research on Phobos.

The babies piled into our condo-azroid. Lynnie got them from mail-order, she picked them up from the Mallworld Pound for the Unwanted, she scavenged through the catalogs of orphanages and fly-by-night freeze-a-zygote outfits. And I couldn't do anything, because I'd thumbed on the dotted line. Damn it, the contract had been in *writing,* and who the hell can read?

We had a baby a year, packed four and five to a closet, for about ten years. I worked hard at ousting my zonkhood. I worked indefatigably at the pet store, trying to forget what I could have become. I still had some high-up friends, some of them even promised to put in a good word for me with the Goddess...but I was through.

I labored in the store, cleaning up after the chimpanzees, birds, gaboochis, rocks, and comsimsurrogates. I turned to my childhood dream of being a laseball star—not much I could do about that, so instead I took to coaching Little League. I needed activity, activity, activity, if I was ever to forget.

I threw myself into helping zonkies. Whenever I closed up the store I would go spend hours scouring the Graffiti Globe for messages for help. I counseled a hundred sorry characters and more, reliving my own agony as I watched their withdrawal symptoms, trying to find niches for them in the society from which they'd fled...

And Mallworld, which had enthralled me and enchanted me and overloaded my senses, with whose Goddess I had once conversed almost as an equal...Mallworld began to lose its charm for me. I hated the daily traffic jams at the gateway to our time-share transmat, hated the way our toyochev (beat-up again, of course) had to grind and groan through to the non-shoppers' parking lot. I hated buying food by the megapellet. I hated—

The worst of it was having to vaculax the alien animals, the ones with exotic excretory habits...

It wasn't me!

Well, it has been said that when one is tired of Mallworld one is tired of life.

I was tired of life.

I didn't even think of Theresa anymore. I didn't think of the lips that waited in the eternal cold and dark. I was too tired to do anything but dive into the bed, too tired even to kiss my wife, let alone...no wonder she wanted a sleaz-o-matic. I thumbed for one. I thumbed for a hundred things, knowing I'd probably end up in a debtor's prison or worse, because it was better than wasting my time arguing.

And then, at the lowest moment of my life, on a tedious day like a thousand other tedious days, the Great Glitch came.

It was going to be a tough day. I had to work at the store, do a round of Graffiti monitoring, and then appear promptly for a laseball game at the stadium in the earthscape park. It was the Pet Store Parakeets—which included a sizable quorum of my kids—versus the Suicide Parlor Vampires, mostly kids of the staff of The Way Out Corp., grisliest and slickest of Mallworld's self-serve meet-your-Maker outfits. I wasn't looking forward to any of it.

I'd seized a sniff of caffoid snuff and driven to the transmat like a fury, cutting in front of the other commuters and provoking a chorus of snarls on the intervoke. I'd popped through the circle, raring for the mad dash to Mallworld.

Chaos! Cars were colliding in mid-space, the transmat was spitting them out and they were careening crazily around, all the lanes were scraggled into zigzags of spyrogyring toyochevs...

"What the—" I stabbed my intervoke into general reception, hoping someone would tell me what was happening. But all I could make out was a cacophony of imaginative cussing. Traffic's always reasonably smooth in space—how can it not be? How in Buddha's name—

And then I peered over to where Mallworld should have been hanging, a silvery stub of light suspended in the darkness, and what I saw made me jump clear out of my monomolecular underwear.

There were—

There were *two Mallworlds!*

Two cylinders of mirror-gleaming metal! *Two* sets of klicklong pennants that streamed out stiffly with welcoming messages for people who could read!

And, ahead of me, hornets' nests of cars, exploding out of duplicate transmats, like a wilderness of colliding galaxies...

I finally fought my way through. Now, which Mallworld was I supposed to go to?

It finally dawned on me. They weren't *quite* the same. Here a crinkle in a pennant, here a parking satellite set at a slightly different angle...it only took a moment to ascertain which Mallworld was *my* Mallworld, and soon I was parked and drifting down the forcetubes.

Some publicity stunt, I was thinking as I popped out of a demat-booth and matted into the store. I snapped at a couple of mini-clunkers; they scuffled obediently away and began sweeping the floor. I looked up and was rewarded by a bowel movement in the eye. I waved frantically at the miscreant parakeet, a pedigreed two-headed model and spoiled rotten, trying to aim it at the waiting forcecage which Lynnie was valiantly brandishing.

"Quick!" I shouted. "This way—whoops!—" and I was banana-peeling across the floor. I crashed against a monkey cage and stubbed my toe on a pet pumice.

"How do you like the new Mallworld?" Lynnie said as she expertly scooped the bird and assorted droppings into the forcecage and plonked the whole operation beside a giant beehive.

"Confusing," I said. "Whose idea of a commercial is that? I guess it must be the barJulians'; they're the only people who could afford such a thing."

"Oh, no," said Lynnie, absently helping one of our kids, Lynx, I think, into his laseball uniform and sending him out with a smack on the bottom. "It's nothing to do with *them.* It's the Selespridar. They—er—goofed."

"The *Selespridar?*"

"Uh-huh...I heard it on the store holovee. It's a real live emergency, and they pre-empted all the soap operas and everything! Klutharion was explaining it himself! He said that...the Selespridon force-mechanism, I mean the one that holds us in our pocket universe, is a very delicate device. He said there's jillions and cumquatmafrillions of universes, parallel universes, you know—"

"Science fiction," I muttered.

"Klutharion didn't seem to think so. Anyway, there's been a...slippage of some kind...two parallel universes are intersecting. Anyhow, Klutharion said that some-times...those *other* universes...aren't exactly *empty,* you know? Sometimes they're populated. And anyway, this one was, and *our* Selespridar are negotiating with *their* Selespridar right now to fix the breach. It's only about a megacubiklick of overlap, really it's nothing to worry about, and we're not supposed to go to the other Mallworld or worry about it or even think of it as being there, and it's only for a day or so anyway, until they sew up the fabric of the universe again."

"Oh," I said, disappointed. A big-time commercial would have been worth watching. But this was something that was none of our business, that was strictly between the Selespridar. So today would be business as usual. I couldn't possibly hope for the laseball game being canceled or something.

"Oh, and another impression I got—" Lynnie said, sidling up for an obligatory kiss. I obliged perfunctorily.

"What?" A customer had come in, and I wanted to wriggle out of Lynnie's overwhelming embrace, even if only to vend a white mouse or a lump of granite.

"I kind of got the impression that *our* Selespridar don't think very much of *their* Selespridar."

"Oh." I struggled free and went to the customer's aid.

Ten hours later I'd completely forgotten about the Great Glitch. I'd spent two hours listening to a theological argument between two high priestesses about whether or not buying a pet snake would violate their vows of chastity; I'd explained the feeding habits of sharks at some length to a faded flapper who wanted a novelty for her jacuzzi; I'd chased a Fomalhautan snotwort halfway down a slidewalk; and I'd sold a pet shale, a mouse, and a bag of birdseed. Lynnie had left long ago to prepare the kids for the big game; I closed up and set off for the Graffiti Globe with some relief.

Action was hot there today. I guess the dual Mallworld thing had really stirred up the deep-seated urges of people to compose hideous doggerel. I sprang up onto the globe, held out my amp-ferret, and listened. In the inane pun department, "I mall doubled up" seemed to be in the lead, followed closely by "a Mall two far." I tried to ignore these feeble witticisms as I hunted for messages from zonkies.

They were crawling all over the globe, like slugs, like caterpillars. The bedlam from my amp was incredible. It was like getting high all over again. I stumbled about, not paying much attention, and then I tripped over an old man in a nightgown and mitre.

"Of all the—" he began.

"Sorry, already!" My nose hurt. I started to get to my feet when I heard—

"Robo Ishi-Leone. Robo Ishi-Leone. If you hear this, for god's sake meet me outside the pet store at ten point oh, as close as you can make it...I beg you! I—"

It broke off. I think it was sobbing.

That voice! Suddenly, irrelevantly, an image of Theresa flashed through my mind. I knew this man's voice and I knew it had something to do with *her*. But how?

I got up. Only five minutes to ten point oh. I had to hurry.

I ran to the demat-booth and yelled the level number.

I leaped onto the fastest slidewalk.

By the time I rounded the corner, I knew who would be standing there. And it was.

I saw his face, swimmingly, through a haze of frantic human faces. He smiled a wan smile. I elbowed my way through the mass of jabbering shoppers.

It was true. There he was. He must have broken the Selespridon injunction, made it over to *my* Mallworld.

I smiled at Robo Ishi-Leone. I smiled at *me.*

"Come on in," I said, trying not to look flustered. But he had already thumbed the lock with nary a peep from the burglar-bugle. I followed him into his—our—store.

"Much the same, is it?" I said. He nodded.

His face was just like mine, and yet...there was a defeatedness about him which I didn't think I had. He hung his head and shuffled around, uneasy. *My god,* I thought, *is this how* I *look to other people?* "Sit," I said, motioning to a chairfloat. But he'd already found it and was already sitting. Of course. It stood to reason that we'd think much alike.

"So how's the store?" I said. He had sprung out of the chairfloat and was wandering from cage to cage, stopping now and then to mop and wipe. He seemed a lot more diligent than me. "Nervous, huh?" I said.

What the hell do you *say* to yourself? "Coming to the game?" I trotted over to our laseball shelf—being a pet store, we were able to breed our own versions of the photosynthesizing quasi-sentient alien beings, originally imported by the Selespridar as a gourmet delicacy—and selected a half dozen or so, making sure they were completely covered with sleek green fur and testing each of them with a little lase-goad to make sure they flew true.

"What game?" the other Robbie said, ducking as one of the laseballs went askew. It missed him and careened into a bundle of little pet granites.

So the two universes weren't exactly alike, then. "The kids. You know. Laseball. Pow, pow, ping, ping? Parakeets versus Vampires today." He nodded confusedly. "You don't have kids?"

"They're…away." Something about the way he said it, I couldn't quite put my finger on it—

"Planning to stay for a while?"

"Don't know."

"You're very laconic, you know that?"

"Yah."

"Why are you scrubbing everything? It's not even your store."

"Habit, I guess."

"Doesn't your wife help out? Lynnie, I mean."

"You have Lynnie? She isn't…away?"

Again the funny way he said it, fearful and with a half-sob thrown in. "No," I said. "I have her all right. Although you know as well as I do that we'd be better off without her…"

At last, someone who would understand. I wondered if he still saw Theresa, but I felt too embarrassed to ask yet.

We stood awkwardly for a few moments, listening to the chittering of the monkeys and the eerie, passionate outgribing from the gaboochi cage. Then I said, "Hey, Robo—"

He reached out to touch me, then. "Are you real?" he whispered. He looked like he was on the verge of crying.

"For god's sake," I cried, "What's the problem, huh? You can talk to *me*. I understand, don't I? I mean, are you still on the stuff or something, is Theresa bugging you still? Let me tell you, Robbie, snap out of it, cope, feed the kids, look on the bright side—" I didn't feel that great myself, but I had to say something, I mean, this was *me* out there, and maybe wading through a worse existence even than mine…

"Come on. First you visit here awhile, then I'll go over and visit you awhile. Okay?"

"You don't want to visit me."

Something was wrong. But I knew me well. I knew I was too proud and bullheaded to come right out, so I decided to watch him and see. "Here, catch," I said, and tossed him a baseball. He caught it neatly with an elegant wrist-twist.

I locked up again, we meandered up a coilspring corridor up to H56 (for the exercise) and then dematted to the earthscape park. There was a Little League-size laseball field there, nestled nicely between the Sphinx and the Taj Mahal. I saw that the circular field had already been set in motion, that a few parents and relatives were already installed on hoverbleachers that stretched all the way up to the Eiffel Tower (which also served as an umpire's control box).

The Vampires were out in force. Crisp black cloaks covered their mirror-coated leotards, and exaggerated fangs of flash-polished metal protruded from their mouths.

I raced over to our stand, with Robo Two frisking behind. Already he seemed happier. I reached the enclosure and shouted, "The fangs! Who passed them? They're an extra light-deflector! They're out to cheat us again!" They shrugged. I added, "By the way, this is Robo Two, from the other Mallworld." They shrugged some more.

Robo Two looked at the kids and stared and stared and stared, and then he looked at Lynnie and got all lump-in-the-throaty. I thought he was going to cry again.

Clearly the Vampire team were going to win. With Federico barJulian as their sponsor, how could the Vampires lose? There wasn't even any point in playing. I saw three of my kids scrambling into their reflective tights, balancing their mirror-disks from hand to hand, and trying out their fingerlasers (all with appropriate sound effects—theirs emitted great electronic wolf-howls, ours squawked in twelve-part harmony). The Vampires were strutting about outside, testing the spin of the field by cartwheeling and somersaulting this way and that. Great strands of colored gas where the lasers had burned through lingered in the specially treated air.

Above, the bases were being lowered into position; for the kids they had to be low enough to spring onto from a rotating playing field, yet high enough for them to show off their acrobatics for a few extra decimals.

I helped Lynx, who pitched, strap the fingerlasers onto his index fingers, and whispered some half-hearted words of encouragement ("Don't even *try* to outsmart the speed of light. Set up a phalanx in the outfield. You all aim for the ball at once, use your cyberinputs, don't rely on your eyes.") to my team, adjusted the decorative parakeet wings on a couple of the younger kids, gave Lynnie another obligatory peck on the nose, and then sank back into a chairfloat, subvoked for vibromassage, and prepared to fall asleep.

And meanwhile Robo Two was gazing with such longing at the kids and at my wife...

The Parakeets were up. A chorus of hisses went up from the hired claque on the hoverbleachers.

And they were off! A ball flew, a burst of ruby red laser light spurted from Lem, twisting his lithe little body and setting off the ball's laser-sensitive photosynthesizing device, so that it shot off an explosive jet stream of oxygen and by-products and soared off toward the short stop! A Vampire sent out a bright blue lightbeam, but it bounced off the stadium's mirrorwalls with a zingpingwhoosh of sound effects! The ball was whirling now, a dozen Vampires charged, trying to outguess the lightshaft, trying to change the ball's vectors, but their momentum shifted the field and made it spin madly, and Lem made a dash for the base doing a neat cartwheel onto where it was, but no! The bases whirled away, and a back-handspring later he found himself backing right into third! Just as the lightbeam came reflecting back and missing him by a couple of centimeters. The field spun to a halt, and I saw Lem crowing nastily at the nearest Vampire, who kicked him in the shin and sent him sprawling to the base's railing. The bleach-boys were booing now. We'd lucked into a good first move. Third base was a good fractional of a homerun, and he hadn't been hit by ball or laser, so there were no penalty decimals, and he must've gotten at least a three for elegance. Sure enough, the announcer said, "Four point oh seven two runs." Somehow I didn't think it would last.

Suddenly I became aware of a raucous cheering, in a voice horribly similar to my own—

Robo Two was out there at the field's edge dancing and waving and making an idiot of himself! I shrank a little further into my chairfloat, and turned up the massage to maximum, hoping I'd get pounded into oblivion and not have to get embarrassed to death.

They were off again! And there was Robo, yelling encouragement and harping on every homer. At the end of the first dozen innings (half an hour later) the air was thick with the tangle of angular burnlines and you could hardly see. Three balls had died and Robo Two insisted on a ceremony. "But *nobody* does that anymore!" I protested weakly, but the team shouted me down. It occurred to me that my double was a little better at appearing to be in tune with the spirit of the game than I was...

Now it was time for Lynx to pitch, and he always liked to do it standing on his head. You could double your team's score that way if you were good, but Lynx was all arms and legs and looked sort of like a postcoital, preprandial male spider. He always miscalculated the angular momentum of his headstands and made the playing field spin the wrong way, too. I retreated a little further. What I wouldn't give for a Levitol now—

But there was Robo Two, screaming advice, and what do you know?

And in the end we only lost by 2.78 runs! And afterward, the kids crowded around Robo Two and hugged him and made much of him, and they even started hauling him around on their shoulders and dragging him through the park, crashing into the Venus de Milo and slashing a gash in the hundred-meter scale model of the Mona Lisa and then the park police were there, clanking after them...

Afterward (I had to post bond on the kids—another kilocred down the drain) my alter ego and I strolled back to the store by ourselves. I was grumbling bitterly, and my other self was happier than I'd ever seen him.

"You're so lucky, Robbie!" he said. There was so much wistfulness in his voice.

"As far as I'm concerned," I said, "you can have it all."

"You mean it?"

"What?"

"That I could...change places with you? No, you don't mean it, you couldn't possibly mean it if you really knew what you were saying..."

"Take the damn lot of them!" I shouted, really angry now. Or was I jealous because they'd clustered around him and not me? "I don't want any of them! I want to turn the clock back. I want to be a snowman again and finish my ice-sculpture and—"

So I'd said it. After all those years.

Damn it, it was true! I'd never dared admit it aloud to myself.

And suddenly I saw those lips in my mind, those lips of ice...could it really have been so many years?

"You haven't finished it?" he asked me wonderingly.

"You have?" He didn't have to answer. He must have done it! Which meant that in his universe, he must be in with Theresa barJulian, he must be up to his neck in megacredits—

"I'll take it!" I said. "There's nothing for me here except debts and an unattractive wife and a dozen uneugenic brats. I'll change places with you! No one need ever know..."

And then a terrible sadness came over him. We had just passed a funeral home ("We'll give you everything you missed in life") and a minimalist store that supplied automated utensils and life supports for those chic floating heads on silver platters—that wasn't an exclusive somatype for the well-heeled anymore, anyone could get a cut-rate somatectomy for a song—a couple of them were hovering outside, window shopping, handle in handle. Perhaps that was why he was depressed, I was thinking, so I hurried on. But he still wouldn't come out of his mood.

Finally I said, "What is it? Aren't you happy?"

"You're *me!*" he screamed. "How could I even have thought of...taking all this away from you? You've got everything! And you're tempting me so much...you don't know what you're getting into! Just leave me alone, Robbie, just leave me alone!"

"Please," I said, "Let me be the judge of that..."

Theresa barJulian, straddling the universe in all her glory! Madonna's knickers, I wanted to see it. I had to see it. I had to see what I would have done if...

"Leave me alone!" he shouted again.

"Okay, already," I said. And to think that I could have escaped from that punitive marriage contract..."But look, a deal's a deal, huh? I showed you mine, now you show me yours."

"Okay," he said sullenly.

We were in his toyochev, and we were off, thrusting toward the second Mallworld. His car was just like mine; here a different dust-speck, maybe, there a different rip in the padding...but there was one enormous difference.

In the front of the driver's console, where you'd normally order your food and drink, stood a row of miniature holograms.

Lynnie and Lynx and Lem and Lionel and Lamb and Lucifer and Laurina and Lunkette and a couple others I wasn't sure I could identify. In solemn, muggish postures, not smiling, completely blank-looking. As though their souls had been stolen.

I didn't want to be rude, so I said, "Nice pix, Robbie."

He laughed hollowly. "Come on," he said, "don't rub it in, Robbie...they gave them to me, those filthy stinking bastards, just before my family went...*away*...don't you understand?"

"Who, Rob?" I was bewildered now. "What stinking bastards?"

"Oh, you re just mocking me!" I could see that he was on the verge of breaking down again, so I didn't pursue it.

"Hey, that ice-sculpture of ours—yours, I mean—must be quite something, huh?"

"Sure," he said. He didn't sound too convincing.

We had reached the space of the other Mallworld now. A few transmat-signs circled the Mall, and I realized suddenly that we could mat right out of there and be in his universe completely and when they stitched up the breach nobody would be the wiser.

On impulse I said, "Look, I know what Mallworld looks like. You don't have to show me. We have the condo, right? You have it all to yourself here, don't you? That's fine. I'll take it, I'll take it—"

He couldn't meet my eyes. "All right," he said.

"But now I want to see the ice sculpture! I want to see Theresa barJulian with my own eyes!"

We zeroed in on the rings of buoys; Robo Two subvoked a few instructions to his car, thumbed a creditcomp, and then said, "Who's Theresa barJulian?"

I gulped. "But—"

And then I realized that he had never once mentioned her name. That I had assumed our lives had been pretty much the same, that the same emotions had motivated us. I had blithely discussed "our" ice-sculpture while assuming the whole time that it was the same one.

Well, this might be even more interesting...to see who his Immortal Mistress of the Gateway might be...to see if our taste in women coincided...and then maybe it *was* her, and she just had a different name in this universe or something.

We burst out into another region of space. We had left my universe behind now. And then I saw—

I choked. "You've got the—the—"

All around me, uncountable, Christmas-tree-glittering in the darkness.

"The *stars,*" he said. The bitterness in his voice was unmistakable.

But now I was lost in the wonder of it. The stardome of the Galaxy Palace in Mallworld was nothing to this. This was—

I felt like I'd been fettered all my life and now I'd been freed. I was drunk on the glory of it. My vision, stopped by cage walls nineteen A.U.'s across, was touching infinity now. If I'd seen this before, when I was a kid, I think I could have finished the ice-sculpture. It was like waking from a dream.

For the first time I understood how men had gone crazy with having lost the stars, how there'd been suicidal riots during the first days of the Selespridar, and how even after they showed how completely benign they were, we still had to struggle to live with our grief, our loss...

I must have been silent for a long time. I closed and reopened my eyes and they were still there. Like a cosmic crystal shattered into shards and blown out over the darkness. I don't think even the worst metahallucinizers I took ever matched the grandeur of this...

"Robbie, Robbie, come out of it!" my alter ego was whispering.

The car turned. Ahead was Saturn, a different Saturn from mine, for his Saturn floated in a glorious star-stitched darkness. The stars softened things, made the rings and the moons smile. And then I saw the ice-sculpture. It was not Theresa barJulian.

"What?" I couldn't believe my eyes.

'Klutharion.' So the two human races had the same governor. "He forced me to build this...monument to his arrogance! He bribed me with a promise that my family would never be taken—*away,* but he didn't lift a finger to help me when the draft came!"

"Wait a minute!" I said. "What do you mean, *away?*" He pointed wildly outward. At the stars. "You mean...humans travel freely to the stars? I'd give anything to be here! Let's trade places now, before you change your mind!"

Robo Two laughed again. It was the laughter of someone who's signed an irreversible-death contract with The Way Out Corp. He didn't answer me, but gave the car new instructions. We were in for a grand tour of Saturn.

I saw a whole moon, carved into the face of a Selespridon. I saw huge marble asteroids chiseled into Selespridar figures, blue-faced, magenta-haired like *our* Selespridar and yet somehow—menacing-looking.

Skimming the surface of a scarred azroid, I saw an environmental bubble under which humans were toiling, chiseling, drilling, and I could see a Selespridon face already beginning to emerge.

"He loves monuments to himself," said my double. "He thinks we'll worship him if he builds enough of them."

We rounded the planet and I saw something that took my breath away.

Someone had been sculpting the cloud layer, working in dyes of different colors, and there was a ghostly image, in tints of red and brown and yellow, etched upon the other face of Saturn.

The image showed a Selespridon. He was laughing savagely, it seemed—although their emotions often seem inscrutable to humans—but there was no question about what he was doing.

He was wielding a whip, and a human was cowering beneath him. The Rings, the beautiful Rings, separated them.

It was an image of utter brutality, an image of a fear hidden so deep down in the psyche of civilized people, and yet so unmistakably clear...

"Slaves," I whispered.

My double showed me first his right thumb, his credit-thumb that he'd used to unlock my store. Then he showed me his other thumb. Inscribed in the center whorl—I had to strain to see it—was a squiggly symbol. "It's a draft-mark," he said.

I closed my eyes tight, trying to squeeze the stars out of the sky.

He told me more. In *our* universe, the Selespridar are, by and large, a kindly race; they are Masters of the Galaxy and so on, but mostly they are enlightened and they spend a lot of time babysitting immature cultures like ours—"until such time

as mankind achieves enough maturity to become acceptable
to the Galactic community," as they put it.

In *his* universe, the Selespridar had achieved Galactic
mastery through the slave trade.

Yes, they'd brought prosperity to humans. At a price. The
price was the slave-draft, an annual culling of the human race
for the labor markets of a jaded, cruel Galaxy. And the humans,
given no choice, had acceded. Even thrived, after a fashion,
endeavoring with all their hearts to forget their friends and
relatives who had gone...*away.*

To the stars about which all men dream.

They had the dream all right. They were human beings
after all. But their dream was a nightmare.

I felt outrage burning inside me. I wanted to break the
neck of one of them. "You're staying with me," I said. Then,
"I could have been you!" I voiced my deepest terror at last. "I
can't let you stay here—"

"Perhaps," he said then, "I should show you one final thing."
He made the car drift back to the ice-sculpture.

"I don't want to look at it again!" I cried. To no avail.

Ahead, glowing softly in Saturn's light, stood the Enemy.
Twenty klicks tall—almost as big as the whole Mallworld—its
thin lips twisted and evil, its eyes glittering with blue fire. Its
arms were outstretched, yes, clasping Saturn, just the way I
had planned to make the statue of Theresa. But here it looked
obscene.

"Take me away," I said. "I've had enough."

"No." We were diving straight into the statue. Soon we
were deep inside it, the car dodging the larger iceflakes and
heading straight into the statue's chest. I had to admire Robo's
technique. It must have taken him ten years to build this thing.

Jagged ice-chunks turned and churned here, center of a
slow whirlpool that scattered the available light and fractured
it and made the Selespridon's tunic glisten with rainbow colors.
We were flying through the hurricane's eye, a tunnel in the
statue's guts...

And then we stopped. There was a heart-shaped piece of ice, a hundred meters maybe, big enough to stand on and walk around a little.

"They haven't found out about this yet," Robo Two said. "When they do—" He made a throat-slitting gesture.

I hesitated. "I've got a p-suit in the back," he said. "Only one. You'll have to go out by yourself."

For a wild moment I thought it was some kind of trick— to abandon me here in mid-sculpture and rush home and abscond with the wife and kids—

I controlled myself. I was getting paranoid, what with having found out the truth about their world. I slipped into the suit and airlocked onto the mini-azroid of ice.

What did he want me to do? I saw his face from the car. He signed me to go ahead. And then I saw—

Etched on the Selespridon's heart, about fifty meters in diameter, was a laseball field. And the Pet Store Parakeets were playing. Each one was a perfectly carved piece of ice with his own little stasis motor. Little hairstrands of ice showed the laserbursts, and a miniature snowball hovered in stasis above the field...

The other team was a bunch of Selespridar. Big, mean, fiery-eyed and Goliathlike.

And my children were creaming the baloney out of them.

They seemed to be using deadly lasers, not the toy ones in the game. Selespridar were tumbling off the hoverbleachers. The big, mean players in the game were running scared, ten or more of them huddled inside a single base. And, in the enclosure, there was Robo Ishi-Leone, in the arms of his loving wife, laughing his brains out...

And then I understood—

How men were always going to fight back, in little ways when there are no big ways left, just for the joy of being human. My universe had it a million times better than his. And still, oppressed beyond belief, driven into slavery, given the stars and yet denied their freedom, the people of his universe were still my people. Still humans.

Forced into building a hubristic monument to his hated masters, Robo Two had risked death to leave a message, to thumb his nose at the masters, to show his love for his family.

I was proud of him. I was proud that he was *me*.

I watched the laseball game with the figures cold and crystalline, frozen in time, and there were tears in my eyes. I couldn't help myself. I stood there, frozen in time myself, a sculpture of ice myself, until my tears had blinded me altogether.

Later, in the car, I said, "Run away. Come back, be with us. The kids love you, Lynnie will go ape over having two identical husbands..."

We set the car's controls and sped straight to the transmat. My heart was pounding as we reached it, popped into Mallworld, saw with relief that *my* world was still there—

And then, halfway home, we turned and we saw *his* Mallworld pop out of existence. Snuffed out.

We were alone together, surrounded by impenetrable starless blackness, weeping for joy.

The official refugee count was twenty-six. Maybe there were more. I doubt that any of us defected to their side though. Unless they'd driven out, seen the stars, gone wild, hadn't been told in time...

Apparently such anomalies occur fairly often—every dozen years or so—but so far they'd always been very tiny, they'd always happened in some area of empty space, and we'd always had the good fortune to intersect with an unpopulated universe.

After Robo Two was settled in—it was good to have an extra hand in the store, and the kids doted on him, and we all had a lot of fun in bed, even without the sleaz-o-matic that the credit sharks found necessary to remove—I found myself wondering how we'd ever survived without him. To my surprise, I found that I was growing to love Lynnie and the kids a great deal. It had taken a chilling dystopia to show me this love. And yet—

I still had some unfinished business.

One day I strode out of the store, summoned a comsim and instructed it to send a message to Theresa barJulian. I would resume work on the mausoleum immediately, and requested that my salary be restored.

Inflation had taken its toll, but a megacred a year was still a small fortune. As soon as word came, I and the other I set out to my old hunting ground.

And there it was. The lips still hovered, half-parted in an almost-smile. They tell me that, among lonely miners at the universe's edge, legends had sprung up about those lips.

But they were not Theresa's lips anymore. I remembered nothing of her. They were just the lips of a woman.

We set to work. In a few days the place was crawling with workmen again. It was almost like the old days, except that there were two of me giving the orders. And then, one day, when the torso was taking shape and the eyes had already been kindled and some of the hair strands had been set in motion, so that they swirled gracefully about her nude body, Theresa came for a visit.

No golden galleon this time. This time it was a silver zeppelin, with a palatial reception hall and a monster of a hovering swimming pool graced by a school of live dolphins.

Theresa barJulian drifted toward me. I was shocked. She had become a minimalist. Her head—the hair still flowed everywhere, like an empress's train—rested on a golden life-support platter inlaid with bas-reliefs highlighted with iridium.

I and I were standing by the pool's edge when she came. The platter flitted back and forth between us, and she laughed, a silvery, musical laugh. She was as beautiful as ever.

But this wasn't *our* Theresa.

Our Theresa will not be any woman. She will be the soul of the human race, poised at the gateway to the future.

"My little snowman, darling," she murmured. "You've split in two!"

"Yes," I said.

"And you *are* finishing my little project for me, after all. What a charming diversion. Oh," she added, "I suppose I wasn't in this soma when we last met...they tell me you live ever so much longer with all the prostheses, and it's so much more *severe* and *classical,* isn't it, to be a severed head? Think of all those ancient busts..."

And then I realized that, for all her wealth, she was a pitiable creature, bored to distraction with her existence and yet too much in love with life to give it up. I said, "You'll like it, Theresa; it'll remind you of what you used to look like..."

"Ah, human vanity!" she said. "Far better to relinquish our hold on the karmic universe, no?" She spouted a few more of the platitudinous wisdoms of some fashionable sect. I listened politely, wanting to get away.

And then she said, "You still believe in true love, little snowman? Are you still doing this just for me?" Her mind seemed to wander a little, as though she were reliving the scene at the party, so long ago, when I had made such an ass of myself.

"No," I said. "It's not for you anymore."

I was thinking of the little tableau I was constructing within the statue, engraved upon its heart.

Yes, sculpted in miniature on the cold heart of our Madonna of the Gateway, a little picture of little Lynx beaning Klutharion with a laseball. And other assorted asnides.

And when we're all dead, I thought, *I and Lynnie and all the kids will still be laughing and lording it over the space lords, slugging the snot out of the Selespridar.*

"Oh? Who is it for, then, snowman?"

"The human race."

"Posterity!" She hooted with laughter. "Vanity, vanity, my little children!"

"You wouldn't understand."

No.

She was senile now, drained of everything, pathetic. But I could not hate her. For I was full of life and I had people to love and statements to make...

I winked at my partner—snowman to snowman—and then we turned our backs on her and made for the demat-booth, not looking back.

Oh, how horrible! I shall have the offending individuals captured and sent back right away. Yech! How my z'neugmeshk quivers at the disharmony between the two universes! I apologize for the leakage, Your Magnitude; it shall not continue. What? You don't care? You think I should simply allow the escapees from that universe of unspeakable evil to remain here? Your compassion does you credit, my lord, but what of the balance of the cosmos, the inner harmony between the parallel universes? I see you shrug, my lord, but these are serious questions. Don't just sit there guzzling Levitol! Powers above, you're going to bump your head on the ceiling! Sometimes I wonder about you multi-tiered types. Oh, I know I'm just a dumb old governor of a star system, and shouldn't poke my nose into the business of running the Galaxy, but surely your levity, your lack of a high seriousness, is demeaning to our status as babysitters of a less mature race? Why are you laughing at me?

Come, Your Magnificence! I see you can barely talk coherently through your giggling. What's the joke?

Ha! You say that I must learn to see the humor of the situation? To become even as one of these children, full of a sense of wonder at the universe? You jest, surely, at a poor system governor's expense. That I should for a moment lower myself to their level—you call that the meaning of life? You think that a meaningful search for ug'unnieth can truly be carried out amidst such degradation?

I'll never understand you High Ones.

Onward. If you thought compassionately about the humans before, forget it now. Let me show them to you at their most unloving, their most unlovable.

(The perfect gift for the person who has eveything!)

THE FOOD PROCESSOR AND SCULPTOR THAT DOES EVERYTHING!

Aren't you sick and tired of having a dozen different machines in the kitchen just to plunk a simple, wholesome food tablet on the table?

Listen. I know all about it. I, Doctor Theophilus Phinkham, Chief Chef at the Galaxy Palace in Mallworld, have been through it all, believe me.

Kelp de-dessicators! Chemistry sets for flavor and preserving! Messy tubes of icing or filet mignon! Self-raising roughage capsules! Can vaporizers! Transmutators! Dicer-slicers! Random food-pattern-generators! Radiation-content analyzers!

Lord help us! Even in the Galaxy Palace, the acme of haute cuisine, we have our problems...

But *you* don't need any of this.

No indeed! Not with—

FOOD SCULPTOR!

Here's what you get—in one cubic meter of miraculous micro circuitry and magic.

Pellet production: for your day-to-day needs. Throw in anything! Genuine food, even! If it contains any nutritive content whatsoever, it will extract the good bits, add fully programmable flavorings, and reduce it to a convenient, nourishing pellet that will sustain you for as much as three hours. A liquid-productive attachment (available separately) will create beverages in any flavor, from pepsoid to caffoid! You'll never have to look at those disgusting food substances again. After all, we're not cavemen, are we? We don't go around guzzling gas or raw meat. The pellet making function is the clean, modern, convenient way to go.

How much would you pay for a thing like this?

Just how much, for a device that removes *all* the unpleasantness from cooking?

Before you open your mouth, there's more!

Yes, my friend, more!

For special occasions, when you might want to impress your friends with arcane ancient cooking...

Food sculptor comes into action. A wholly dramatic technology that actually creates lifelike reproductions of every gourmet dish! You'll think you're dining on Denebian white worms sautéed in oyster sauce. On chocolate-chip-chitterlings. On rainbow-sparkle-Jell-O with delicious turkey gravy. And all when you prime the *Food Sculptor* with one kilogram of our patent *plastifood nutrient simulator product!*

And every one of these culinary masterpieces is heavily seeded with pulverized food pellets—so that they contain the *actual estimated nutritive content* of the food they are simulating!

Your friends will never know you didn't call the prohibitively expensive Galaxy Palace Subsidiary Takeout Service.

Yes, my friends, yes!

Just how much would you pay for such a marvel?

Five thousand credits?

Ten?

But wait till you hear this! Food Sculptor comes complete with three weeks' supply of plastifood product, with genuine styrofoam dinner service for four, and a souvenir medallion of St. Betty Crocker!

And, if you order *now*, you are eligible to compete in a prize drawing—the first prize of which is a *real dinner* at the *Galaxy Palace* in *Mallworld*—all expenses paid, as the personal guest of Clement barJulian!

Fifteen kilocreds? Twenty?

No way.

Just one little kilocred, payable in ten installments at only ninety percent annual interest!

Be the first on your azroid to own this radical new invention!

FOOD SCULPTOR!
THE INTELLIGENT FOOD PROCESSOR
THAT BRINGS CUISINE ART
TO A NEW PLATEAU OF BRILLIANCE!

The Dark side of Mallworld

Mallworld, thirty-klick-long shoppers' citadel in space where every tacky dream comes true, was receding in the starless darkness as my car reached the first ring of transmat buoys. I didn't pay any attention, although the sight was remarkable enough. I was busy spraying my face with the memory-plastiflesh that transformed my appearance into the rheum-dripping, bug-eyed horror that symbolizes my profession.

I'm Dollie Salvador, and I work for Storkways Inc.'s main office in Mallworld. Oh, no, not as one of those diaper-clad, ever-smiling matrons who take your order for a classy, eugenically genegeneered bundle of joy. I'm the one who comes after you when you renege on your payments. A child repossession agent. A bogeyman.

The plastiflesh began to settle, hugging the nooks and crannies of my face. I blinked on the mirror-walls of the car and took a look at myself, shuddering, as the car popped through the ring and emerged somewhere on the other side of the belt. The blackness was utterly featureless. There have been no stars, of course, since the blue-skinned, magenta-haired Selespridar with their supertech magic came down to the Solar System to babysit the human race and ended up locking us into our own little pocket universe "for our own good." It makes space feel lonely.

I was very lonely in those days. Being a bogeyperson was— well, I joined the profession out of altruism. I grew up in a used kid lot myself, you know. Heard stories from the older kids. About parents. I knew that a parent who would do *anything* rather than not pay the mortgage on his kids was a perpetrator of the worst possible form of child abuse...but it was painful to be the tough one. Wearing this hideous uniform,

I used even to forget I was a woman. It makes you sexless, this blotchy, warty, gangrenous travesty of a human face. It's supposed to scare your skin off. Usually it does. Everyone at Storkways shunned me. It seems that another evil of parents is that they tell you lying, libelous stories about bogeypersons, and frequently threaten to call them in to take you away. Their horror stories still cling to people when they grow up, and they often just can't cope with being confronted with, even working in the same company as, a bogeyperson. How lucky I was to be an orphan, I was thinking as my car darted into another transmat nexus.

Today's was a perplexing mission. I had to make a collection on twelve-year-old Hyacinth barJulian-Davies. It didn't seem possible. The barJulians are the richest family in the human race, and anyone who could claim a name like barJulian-Davies had to be at least wealthy enough to buy up Storkways. Hell, one of them owned Storkways. Hell, one of them owned *Mallworld*. And the kid was almost old enough to be an adult! It was fishy, very fishy. But they don't pay me to think.

I emerged in the region of space where the barJulian-Davies residence was supposed to be.

Vast stone faces, half-shadowed, peering out of the blackness, eyes that sent out lightbeams, crisscrossing the blackness—

The mansion of the barJulian-Davieses was an exact reproduction of an ancient castle in Bavaria, Earth—I recognized it from an old holovee docudrama—except that it rose dramatically from the center of the chin-cleft of a huge stone visage. It was Mount Rushmore—whether carved a second time out of some luckless azroid or dredged all the way up from Old Earth, I couldn't tell. The four anonymous heads were a charming setting, both eye-catching and quaintly reeking of antiquity; laserlight swaths flooded from their eyes, the only illumination in the lonely darkness. I put the car on search—to find the parking lot—and subvocalized the secret code that gets a Collection Officer through any forceshield...

And these were the people who couldn't pay an insignificant little payment on their child! I was suspicious, very suspicious. Surely people this affluent couldn't be so barbaric as to...I drifted toward the mountains, readjusting my bug-eyes one more time for luck, observing as I got nearer that the mountains appeared to be plastimolded over a chrome frame—bits of it peeped, like broken bone through a wound, out of the spraytextured rock. Just beneath the castle, a door in the neck irised open to receive me, and I caught, as I slid in, an artist's signature (I can't read, but I know writing when I see it) and a number. This whole architectural phantasmagoria wasn't even an original, then. It was a cookie-cutter-style, signed-numbered reproduction, one of dozens or even hundreds. What kitsch! I didn't like the barJulian-Davieses already.

The hall into which I dematted was vast, covered in imitation antique deep-pile shag carpeting, and brimming with peculiar art objects. I had materialized right in front of one, a swirling mass of chunky particles that encircled a pile of pirouetting lumpy brown rocks. Overhead, a chandelier-mobile put together from a phosphor-coated brontosaurus skeleton rotated slowly as it tinkled out an arrangement of one of the new *muzak concrete* hits. The place stank of megacredits, and yet was almost militantly tacky.

"Ah, hello." I turned to see a middle-aged woman in a potato sack, which her ample body filled to bursting. It was clearly a classic, expensive somatype—though I didn't recognize the Storkways ambience—which had gone to seed from overindulgence. "Well, well, well," she said, "you must be the new Giacometti reproduction we ordered from Earth! Come along, dear, and I'll show you your little niche..."

This wasn't going right. I started to interrupt. Why wasn't I frightening her? She went blithely on: "Let's look at you...yes, so lifelike! An ancient sculpture, brought to life, as it were, in full color, moving and breathing, another miracle from Pygmalion Enterprises, the fine-art-repro-store that breathes life into the master-works of antiquity! Ah, ah..." She sighed, and I tried to say something, but she went straight on. "Yes, it will be nice having you here, you know, none of the other art talks, of course, and our cousin Julian barJulian, you know, of the Mallworld barJulians, he's just bought an animated, talking reproduction of Picasso's *Demoiselles d'Avignon* for his suite at the Gaza Plaza, so of course we had to get something from Pygmalion Enterprises too, and—"

"Mrs. barJulian—"

"But my goodness, how lifelike! Let me show you the rest of the collection. This swirling brown thing, why, that's *Faex Vivenda,* one of the earliest twenty-fourth-century coprokinetic sculptures—so *stunning,* isn't it? And so relevant to the human condition, too, this juxtaposition of the septic with the sublime...hanging from the ceiling—" I looked dutifully at the brontosaurus, desperately waiting for a hole in her chatter that I could dive into—"is *La Brontosaure Danglante,* by Michelle Ford—"

"Stunning," I said, "but I'm not—"

"I'm sure I'll hear all about you in good time, my dear. I'm so glad you're here, because the barJulians look down on us so much, and you'll add a bit of *class* to our little gallery, and then maybe the barJulians will stop making fun of us—"

I couldn't help smiling a little. These people had *clearly* had riches thrust upon them somehow. Surely they weren't to the manor born, as the dirty earthies say, if they couldn't tell good art from junk. Even *I,* who am an utter Philistine, knew why the barJulians must think them preposterous. "Mrs. barJulian-Davies, I've got to tell you that—"

But she was off again. We traipsed past an iridium-plated model of *La Bedlam sans Merci* ("The Ungrateful Asylum") by Praxiteles, which depicted a wild bunch of madmen seeking political refuge at the Feminist Embassy during the Ninth World War—the original, almost two millennia old, is very beautiful, but the iridium plating made this version look gaudy and pompous; we donned antigrav skateboards and circumnavigated a scale model of the Baths of Caracalla in

the middle of which sprouted an organoplast rendition of the
True Cross on which St. Vlad the Impaler was crucified; we
skirted a wall of religious icons—a plaster of paris *Buddha
and Child,* a laser-holo-crochet-by-number *Iphigenia in
Schenectady,* and so on…I was being worn out. The strain of
being treated like a sculpture—I guess I knew now how the
boss felt, why machines always seem so irritable and defensive.
We neared the end of the grand tour—I nearly tripped over
the tabletop miniaturization of the Sistine Chapel ceiling—
and Mrs. barJulianDavies was going full steam: "So you see,
my dear, whatever those dreadful cousins of ours say, we do
have taste, don't we? And don't agree with me just because
you've been programmed to humor me, now! Be honest!" She
didn't wait for an answer but began calling, "Herbert! Herbert!
The Giacometti's here!"

"Oh, bother!" I turned around and had to restrain myself
from laughing. Hyacinth's father had matted into the room.
He was a maximalist.

You all remember the minimalist craze about ten years ago,
when everybody was getting somatectomies and wandering
around as severed heads on life-support platters? There was a
reaction against that when the plebs got hold of the fashion,
and did the pendulum ever swing! Mr. barJulian-Davies must
have had dozens of pairs of limbs. He had had an extra eazi-
stretch abdomen put in, and it had made him into a chimerical
half-human, half-caterpillar.

"My dear," he said to his wife, "that's not a sculpture, it's a
person!"

"Oh, nonsense, darling. You've got no artistic sense
whatsoever! No wonder the barJulians laugh at us…it's *exactly*
what we ordered."

"Don't be silly. That's a plastiflesh mask she's wearing. I
do believe, dearest, that she—or perhaps he—is an interloper,
perhaps *disguised* as a Giacometti sculpture, who may well be
planning to abscond with our valuable works of art—"

That was it. I started to giggle.

"Rubbish! Even the sculpture's laughing now. If it was an interloper, how could it have gotten into the house? We've an unlisted code—"

"Well, why don't we ask it, you stupid woman?"

And they both turned expectantly to me.

I cleared my throat and activated my voice-rasper to maximize my frighteningness. "I'm Salvador of Storkways Incorporated, Child Repossession Division—"

"Oh, my god!" she said. "A bogeyman!"

"Why, relax, my dear. It's obviously a mistake...where is little Hyacinth? Perhaps we should summon her...why dear Officer Salvador, you can see by our—ah—surroundings that we are hardly the type who would commit a—a—financial impropriety! Allow me to shake your hand—" He extended three or four limbs in my direction, but they became all tangled up. "Pardon me, these new *fashionable* somatic metamorphoses that my wife *will* insist I undergo"—he shot her a blitzful glare—"take some getting used to...I'm all arms and legs...ha, ha, ha...now, what seems to be the trouble? Julian barJulian is our cousin, you know—"

I went on grimly with the official announcement. You can't perform a legal repossession without a formal announcement. It was a formula I had had to memorize, which I must have recited a thousand times during my work as bogeyman for various tiny baby farms, finally through a merger for the greatest baby farm in the Solar System. "I must by corporate and overcorporate law inform you that, in repossessing your child, in whose mortgage agreement you stand grievously in default despite three official warnings, Storkways Incorporated does not act in violation of any of your child's human, cetacean, or sentient extraterrestrial rights. Only the right of parenthood, which has been legally defined as a purchasable commodity, is at issue here. Custody has now reverted to Storkways Inc., who may attempt to recoup their loss by offering the child's parentship for lease or sale at any period until the child's majority." I paused, expecting the usual terror-filled faces; I should have known better. There was nothing normal about this family whatsoever.

"That's absurd," said the father. He slithered around the Michelangelo coffee table and rested six of his legs on a chairfloat that dangled from a papier-mâché reproduction of Alexei Shamborg's *Man Fleeing from a Tower*. I noticed that, toward his rear, a pair of purposeful arms was methodically knitting a sweater. "Absurd! Why, do you realize how much money we have? I mean, we're no Julian barJulian, but—"

"Stop mentioning that name!" His wife was shouting suddenly. "It's always Julian, Julian, Julian! Don't you realize we're going to lose our daughter? You bastard! You've been deliberately not thumbing the house creditcomp and the payments haven't been getting through—"

"Don't be silly, dear. If there's been any sabotage, it's been *your* doing. You only wanted a child because the barJulians ordered one from Storkways and you had to keep up with them—"

"You—you vaculax! *I* wanted to keep up with the bloody barJulians, I suppose. They're your damn relations, you greasy, social-climbing—why, you practically invited yourself to Theresa's navel-embedding last year! And *I'm* the one you let them snicker at, your own wife—"

"Pope's pantyhose, I haven't the time to listen to a family row!" I yelled, hurling myself between them and prying a dozen hands off me. I felt a sudden rip, and...my rubbery plastiflesh skin was beginning to peel off my backside! "Now hand over the kid, huh?"

Mrs. barJulian-Davies backed off a little, knocking over a suit of imitation armor astride an ancient pennyfarthing. "Look what you've made me do," she said. "Besides, you know damn well, Herbert, that you haven't been able to twiddle your thumbs over the paycomp since your metamorphosis, and you've been telling *Hyacinth* to manage all the household payments—"

"Are you accusing your own daughter of sabotage, you pretentious baggage?"

"What's going on, mother?" A sweet young voice from far away, in the middle of the room.

I whirled around. I couldn't see anything at first; the junk was thick as jungle. "Oh," the voice came, nearer. A childish, breathy voice: I recognized the Storkways *class* about it. "It's the bogeyman. Welcome, I've been expecting you."

The two parents stopped dead, aghast. I'd seen the artistic horrors of their art gallery and I expected the worst of their child. Some outlandish, garish custom-made somatype with three vestigial heads or little purple wings or...

She stepped out from behind a corner of the Baths of Caracalla. She came right up to me.

"Can we go now?"

She was a classic model—one of Storkways's best. Even working where I did, I had seldom seen a child so beautiful, so poised. I understood now why a family as wealthy as this one would have to get a mortgage for this girl. An artist had designed the soma. She had black, shoulder-length hair and a pale complexion specked with light, well-placed freckles; and she wore a gossamer sari, innocently revealing, that rustled in an artificial wind. Her eyes were all tans and beiges and yellows and grays and umbers melded together like little Saturns, and the iris-designs were perfect mirror-images of one another. And with this kind of beauty, the kid couldn't fail to have all the other standard features—the super-IQ, the whole bit.

I was furious now. I was remembering every horror story I'd ever heard about a parent. I hated the barJulian-Davieses. I had to snatch that kid away from them, fast, irrevocably. "You're pretentious, petty, little-minded people," I said. "This kid is the only real piece of art in this whole mansion, and you've been careless enough to lose her—"

"We'll get the credit to Storkways—as soon as my thumb is working properly," said Hyacinth's father.

"I don't take bribes," I said. "Work it through channels—
and fast, because someone's going to want this kid. And maybe
whoever it is will have more affection than you frigid phonies
have." I turned to leave, but the girl was already leading the
way, her sari fluttering prettily behind her.

"Well! You sure showed them," she said, settling back into
the seatfloat. She hadn't struggled at all. Mount Rushmore
was retreating into the distance and the transmat ring was
centered dead ahead. She looked at me as if I were some kind
of hero, not a bogeyman on a routine assignment. When she
stared at me all wide-eyed I could see that her irises *were* mirror-
Saturns, I could even make out the rings, they were capillaries,
rerouted and tinted with glitter-pigments, truly a virtuoso bit
of genegeneering. "So where to now? Are you going to pulp
me or something?"

"Of course not." But I could tell she was scared. There
are outfits who pulp 'em actually; fly-by-nights operating out
of filthy earthie territory, where they still have governments
and other corruptions. I shuddered to think of it.

"Well, where to?" she said. I could tell already that she
was a very persistent person.

"The used kid lot," I said. *"You'll* get special treatment
though, no doubt about it. You should see our used kid
lot...you'll love it!" But suddenly I didn't really believe it. How
could anything be like a palace after the affluence *she'd* known?
I became insecure, defensive about how I'd grown up. I threw
myself into toeing the party line, describing the carefree joys
of living in a used kid lot, how they were really means of
avoiding the overcorporate tax structure, how kids lived out
their minority in considerable luxury there...

"Well, no place could be like the family house. When I
grow up I'm going to buy it back and turn it into a Museum of
Tack and Kitsch." I laughed. "You're not a bad sort," she said.
"I'll remember you when I've sorted out the guardianship
papers."

"What do you mean?"

"Idiot, don't you get it? I couldn't stand this hellhole any longer, so I sabotaged myself out! My stupid father hasn't got control of any of his new arms and legs yet, so he trusted *me* with the house paycomp!"

"Figures. I got a Croesus-rich juvenile delinquent in my car." She certainly had pluck. I tried to hide my admiration behind a mask of grumpiness.

"Can you blame me? Do you know I've never left that monster of a mansion in my life? That they only trotted me out at parties to annoy the barJulians, 'cause *I'm* the last creation of Master Genegeneer Lauren Klink, he did the DNA graphs just before he died and nixed them as soon as the zygote took? That I'm the *one* thing in that whole house that gives them any status whatsoever in the eyes of their exalted cousins? It was prison, prison, prison all the way! I went to school via a brainbox. I shopped in holocatalogs. I watched the feelies in my private viewroom..."

"I'm sorry," I said. I couldn't really imagine her kind of life at all. I lived in a swingles condo-azroid. But even with the hothouse sex going on frenetically around me, I had failed to find anything satisfactory. Well, when you're a bogeyperson you choose a lonely road. Nobody loves a defender of the law. They told me that a thousand times in training.

But at least I'd had a *chance* at a social life, even if I'd muffed it. She never had. I *hated* the barJulian-Davieses! "I hope your next parents are better. Even *I'd* make a better parent than...but why talk about the impossible?" I said quickly, avoiding the thought that had just flicked into my mind.

"Why's it impossible? I could easily give you the money and—"

I evaded the subject. For some reason, it made me much more nervous than it should have. "Besides, it's only for a year. I doubt anyone can afford to pick up your mortgage anyway, except maybe the barJulians, and—"

We crashed through the ring of buoys and sped through more blackness. "*I* can afford it," she said. "I've been saving up…don't you see, dummy? I'm going to buy my own mortgage and get custody of myself—"

"Hold it," I said. "That is most certainly against corporation law. You can't adopt yourself unless you're over thirteen— and then there's no point anyway, because you *automatically* adopt yourself."

"Well, you're not going to hold me to a stupid law like that, are you?"

"Yes."

She started crying.

I lost my cool. I got all unprofessional, I don't know why; whether it was all that hideous artwork or the unendearing personalities of the barJulian-Davieses, or whether I had somehow reached some karmic turning point in my life, I said, "There now, it's not so bad, Hyacinth—"

"Cindy," she sobbed. "I *hate* being called Hyacinth…"

"Cindy, I'm not arresting you or something, you know. Your human rights are intact. Damn it, it's my job to protect them! You wanted to leave your parents, didn't you?"

"I've been saving up since I was five. I want to get to Mallworld, sure, but this isn't how they said it would be—"

"They? Who's *they?*"

"Oh…I shouldn't say anything—"

"What are you talking about, Cindy?"

"My voices." The car swam through a cluster of rebuilt L-5-cylinders, strung together and trailing from a big azroid like *just married* tin cans in an ancient ritual. Cindy tugged at her sari and pulled out a neckchain with a pendant, a little Saturn that she held up gingerly by the rings—the tiny planet whirled around, without strings, without a thing holding it up. I knew it must be a Selespridon device. "It's an intervoke. A *Selespridon* intervoke." She handed it to me, and I saw that it matched her eyes exactly. "Oh, you can't hear anything; it's mated to my brain-patterns alone. I subvoke into it and I hear voices in my head."

This tiny thing must be worth a fortune. It slipped into my palm, hovered above it, spinning, not quite touching it. "Klutharion—you know, the governor of the Solar System— gave it to me at a reception at the house. He never came back, of course, even though they invited him many other times. Once was enough. Although naturally he was *captivated* with me."

"So am I," I said. Why had I said that? I could have swallowed my tongue. I was out of line.

"*Everyone* is. Lauren Klink made me that way. Everyone except my parents. They're oblivious. So now that you're under my spell, how about dropping me off somewhere, out of sight, in Mallworld, and not bringing me in at all?"

"I can't do that."

"I'll pay you."

"The company would sue my ass. *And* they'd catch you in a second. There's sensors that record everyone who steps through a demat-booth in Mallworld."

"That's not what the voices told me."

"What voices? You're not one of those loonies, are you?"

"No, I told you I hear voices! In the intervoke, you know! Klutharion wanted me to be able to talk to the outside world, he had compassion for me...I hear voices from Mallworld! They call themselves the Mallkyries, and they're calling for me to join them...that's why I had this crazy idea of tricking the paycomp and manipulating this repossession...oh, don't you see, you've *got* to let me go! Otherwise it's just from one prison to another..."

"I told you. I can't. Besides, you don't really mean Mallkyries. *Valkyries* now—learned about 'em in school. They fought on the Norse side during the American Sybil War, a couple thousand years ago. You know, over Helen O'Loy. It's just a myth, anyway, and—"

"You don't understand!" she cried, and burst out sobbing again. "I've made a deal with them, they've got to help me now, all you have to do is get me to them..."

"I'll do no such thing!"

"*Wild and free,*" she sang softly. It sounded like some kind of slogan. "*We sweep through the ghosts of mallworlds past, we ride through the corridors of emptiness, shrill war cries thrilling through the dusty air—*"

What was she on about? I saw how lost she was. We were alike, more alike than I wanted to know about.

"You don't like me." More crying.

"There now. There now." The head office could deal with it. Clearly I was way out of my depth. She was bright all right—her stratagem for running away from home proved it amply—but being alone with those neurotic parents for so long must have unhinged her mind. Her veneer of easy, smartass banter hid the hurt well. My heart went out to her, even though I knew I was in way over my depth. She couldn't really be in contact with mythical creatures in a shopping mall. She needed...she needed...

"You want to have sex?" she said suddenly, in a childish parody of a seductive voice.

"One," I said, "I don't like girls: two, we don't take bribes; three—stop crying, damn you, child!" Then I took her in my arms and held her for a while, as the car raced on through the featureless blackness. Night would be so beautiful if only we had stars.

"Why don't you adopt me, anyway? I bet you could use a kid. I've heard about you bogeypersons. You're a sad, lonely lot. I could cheer you up pretty good..."

Crafty, I thought. *That's the first time I've ever heard that ploy, in all these years of ferreting out kids...*and then, for a moment, I thought of having her as a daughter. I tried on the idea for size, but only for a moment! I shrank away from the thought at once. No! *Be professional!* I froze, concentrated on subvoking needless commands to the car's pilotcomp. "No."

"Pretty please—"

"No!"

"I'll never get away!" she kept saying over and over. And sometimes she would hold her intervoke in her hand and seem to be listening to something, and she would nod her head and seem to be subvoking a response.

And I was feeling...involvement! Oh, of course I'd felt sorry for them before, I mean, you wouldn't be human if you didn't, but this was different. It wasn't a clinical, *professional* kind of sorry.

For a split second I was tempted to let her go. To drop her off and run away and bury myself in my floatbed in my condo-azroid and never come out again...But I couldn't do it. My years of training were in the way. I could only hold the kid and feel sorry for her.

So, to pass the time between transmat leaps, we talked.

I told her about growing up in a used kid lot.

"Did you like it?"

"I loved it," I said sullenly. It occurred to me that I might be lying to myself. I waxed loquacious, revealing things about myself that even *I* hadn't known before. I fantasized about Cindy being my daughter again; for a few moments, that fragile absurdity seemed almost real.

And the girl listened. That flattered me.

And then we were silent for a long time. Afterward we breached the last ring of buoys and were in Mallworld space. Mallworld gleamed mirror-silver out of the darkness. Thousands of cars poured in and out in lightshafts that were traffic lanes, each car a dust-mote quantum in the beam...we merged into a lane and Mallworld grew until it filled the sky, its beacons flashing, its holo-ads dancing over the surface, its pennants waving, its bouncy muzak dunning over every channel of the car's intervoke. I called the office and shouted over the roar—

"Boss, I have the barJulian-Davies kid here..."

"Good!" came the hated mechanical voice. "We'll only be holding her for a while; her parents have already paycomped the penalty and back payments in over the real-time transmat. They're on their way to get her."

"No!" screamed Hyacinth. "You can't make me, I'm not going, I won't let you, you've got to help me escape—"

No time for regrets now. I was a bogeyman and Hyacinth
was my case for the day, and now it was time to come down to
earth. "There's nothing I can do," I said with as much coldness
as I could muster. "Will you come peacefully, or what?"

"No!" She raked her fingers across my face, scarring the
plastiflesh and ripping it so hard that it yanked away hair. I
yelped in pain, grabbed her arms and subvoked the child-
restrainer. Spider-arms came twisting out of the seat and held
her fast. "Now for Pope's sake," I said, "don't make it any
more difficult for me. This is hard for me too, damn it...forget
I said that, okay? Now do I have to zonk you out on sleepitoff
gas?" I think she could see how unwilling I was. Hell, why
couldn't I hide my feelings? She nodded. As the car docked,
I quickly stripped off the rest of the uniform—leaving my
skin raw in places—and sprayed on a regular worksmock. "Why
do you have to wear that thing anyway?" she said, all charm.
"You're really *pretty* underneath it."

For some reason I was touched. I've said it before, in this job I'm always forgetting I'm a woman, even an attractive one. Take it back. Actually I don't forget, but everyone else does, and it's easier on me if I pretend to forget too...I smiled.

"You're smiling," she said. "My parents never smiled. You care a lot more than my parents ever did," she said in a very small voice. I didn't answer. We didn't speak until we had floated down the nothing tubes and stood at the B63 entrance of Mallworld. I had her under restraint—snakelike metal tendrils held her to my wrist—and she wouldn't budge. She was staring at Mallworld.

Up and down as far as you could see the levels went, with rainbow-walkways soaring and crazi-gravi corridors twisting and plastic airtubes rocketing people back and forth like flies in a drinking straw and slidewalks racing each other and wedges of shoppers converging into demat-booths and popping out of them...

"Must be some overload," I shouted over the din. Some young kids were playing at hang-gliding from overhanging slidewalks, letting go at the last minute; shopping bags marched purposefully about; and in a few seconds I had rejected offers of insurance, sex, and stretch-o-credit from loudmouthed vendingbots. Half-zonked-out on Levitol, a six-armed man hovered in the air just ahead of us and juggled shrunken heads, croaking, "Two for a credit! Little heads from NeoBrazil reside in your mouth and don't eat much and do all your talking for you—guaranteed knowledgeable on seventeen selectable subjects—"

"Damn it, you can at least unlatch me," said Cindy. "I'm not a criminal, you know." I thought about it for a while, and then decided that I could trust her. I subvoked a command; the restraints dissolved; we hopped onto a slidewalk. I made sure she didn't wander more than a couple meters away from me. I didn't tell her I had a stunner, either.

We whipped past Ali Baba's Flying Carpet Mart, where old men with hookahs were hovering around on prefaded, prefrayed shags and linoleum rugs. Above our heads, a pro laseball team streaked by on an upper level slidewalk in glittering wings and sequined uniforms, followed by a xylophone and port-a-piano pick-up band and a dozen leg-kicking pom-pom girls wearing wooden barrels and ostrich feathers.

"Impressed?" I said. "This is going to be your home, you know."

"Uh-huh," she said. She was fingering her Saturn-intervoke again, and she seemed far away.

Fantasizing again. Dreaming about her "Mallkyries"... whoever they were.

"Slow down—" I hopped onto a new slidewalk, following her. I knew there was no way she could escape, but I was edgy. I was too involved, I might make a slip.

She bolted.

"Don't be stupid!" I shouted. She sprang two slidewalks in one leap. I hurdled a shopping bag and missed her slidewalk, jumped again, kicking a salesbot and sending it sprawling in a shower of plastic fruit. She was outdistancing me. I knew I should call for help, but I was burning with embarrassment. Why had I ever trusted her?

I clutched at a fold in her sari, and she went diving into a demat-booth with me in tow.

"I'm coming, Mallkyries!" she was screaming at the top of her voice. *"Wild and free—"*

A fakir started from his Bed-o-Nails—"the holographic fluffbed that makes you look like an ascetic"—punctured his hologram and fell groaning into the bedframe. I trampled the painless nails and sprinted onto the slidewalk, caught up again, went through another booth—

An emptier corridor now, just the imitation amethyst brick walls of Gimbel and Gamble's Department Store with its chorus line of trunk-wiggling Christmas trees touting bargains to the one side and the metal-curve walls of Aunt Abedah's Monopole Skating Rink on the other. I had just come within a centimeter of her again when—

Vroooom!

A rush of wind blew me over, kicking helpless against the slidewalk. I pulled out my stunner, but a big black *thing* knocked it out of my hand. I looked up—

Soaring motorcycles were pouring out from the nearest demat-booth! Clouds of noxious gas billowed! "Cindy!" I bellowed above the roar—

Holy vaculax! I thought. *She's tricked me!* Anger blinded me. I wanted to punch her in the face. To think that I'd told her the story of my life! To think that I'd considered— daydreamed about—adopting her, the scheming, sneaky little bitch! I—

Gloved hands reached down to grasp her. I saw her astride a motorcycle now, they weren't real reconstructed vehicles, they had bulging bug-eyes where their head-lamps should have been, and they flew in figure-eights around my head, and the women who rode them wore horned helmets and screeched forth primal sounding ululations, and then I oozed my arm out to where the stunner was and lost my cool completely and let loose, firing randomly into the black pungent fumes—

I hit one of the motorcycles. It began to yelp. *Pope's boobs, it's alive!* I remember thinking, as a black shuddering mass of flesh plummeted toward me and knocked me out.

When I came to in my office, with the voice of the boss ringing frantically in my ears and a moaning motorcycle tossing and turning on the hover-stretcher beside me, I found out about the dark side of Mallworld.

And about many other things. For instance, that there was a tiny clause in my job contract (which I had not, of course, read) that rendered me totally and utterly liable for the missing kid, to the tune of life in a "credit rehabilitation clinic"—all right, debtor's prison.

"Shut up, you damn machine," I said wearily. "How could I have possibly known that those Mallkyries existed? Who are they, anyway?"

"Listen, Salvador," it said, its voice reverberating from every curve of my uterus-shaped office. I waited. "You've really thrown the cat into the fishtank. Heavens, woman, you've even put *my* job on the line! I want her back!"

"How?"

"How? How should I know?"

"Who *are* these Mallkyries, anyway? What do they do?"

"They're from Darkside, probably."

"Darkside?"

"My god, woman, didn't they teach you anything in basic training?"

"I didn't go through the Storkways training. I came with a merger."

"All right, all right...look here. Mallworld has 57,000 cubiklicks of space. Half of it's fallow. Understand? Level upon level of empty gray metal, waiting to be leased out. Levels of ghost malls, abandoned levels...the skins between the levels, too, that no one visits now...they say all these places are inhabited. Julian barJulian XIII found one tribe of wild children, roaming the hidden stairways and stealing to survive. But there's more than one. There's dozens. *Hundreds,* maybe, somewhere. You say the barJulian-Davies girl was communicating with one of these gangs?"

"I thought she was imagining things!"

"Idiot! Never make such presumptions about a class-A+ IQ Storkways product! Her mind would never have malfunctioned before the guarantee ran out."

"So why can't we run a demat-booth trace on her? Surely she's left enough cells scraped on a booth for us to run a DNA check through the standard surveillance comps. This can't be that big a deal," I said nervously. It didn't answer me for a while...I watched the motorbike as it stirred in its sleep. It seemed to be having a nightmare.

"You don't understand!" Its voice was buzzing in frustration. "If she's gone over to Darkside, we *can't* trace her. We can tell what booths on our side she went into, but we can't tell what booths on Darkside she came out of. The detectors have stopped working in Darkside, or maybe they never worked...we don't even have accurate maps, we don't even know the right letter-number codes, you'll have to try them at random, probably. Wait a minute—I don't think we *will* be able to check out DNA traces anyway. Wasn't she a secret model? We don't even have a copy of the gene-patterns in our files!"

"But sometime in her life, someone *must* have taken a tissue sample or something—"

"So that's why they never let her out of the house!" said the boss grimly.

"They didn't want her tissue scraped, they didn't want even the chance of a clone..." What selfish, self-serving bastards those barJulian-Daviesses had been!

"Well, you'll simply have to find some other way."

"I'll have to—"

"Well, damn it, you're responsible!"

"It'll take the rest of my life."

"Would you rather spend it in a credit clinic?"

I gulped. "Then get on with it," it said.

"But I don't even know how to start!" I said. A comsim image of the boss was flying around the wombroom, haughtily sniffing the motorcycle, which was puffing fume-cloudlets and whimpering.

It said, "They say that only three people know anything about Darkside. They're old women who were around two centuries ago, when Mallworld first started. The Selespridar keep them alive, sort of as living fossils, and keep replenishing their RNA so they'll remember *everything* and amuse them with stories about the old days. Sort of repositories of ancient lore. The Selespridar are very into humans as a bunch of, you know, naïve primitives, but somehow closer to the 'meaning of life' or something than they are...well, you know they're always looking for this untranslatable *ug'unnieth,* this transcendental epiphany of the alien condition...these ancient women might know something about these 'Mallkyries.'"

Why am I even bothering? I thought. *There's no hope, and besides, she's exactly where she wants to be. But is she, though?* I remembered that—sophisticated as she was—she'd never had any direct experience with the outside world. Maybe she had been lured by these people. Maybe they were going to hold her for ransom or even torture her or something.

And then I brushed aside these unprofessional, oversympathetic thoughts.

No one gets the better of Dollie Salvador, I thought. *No one! I'm going to get her back just so I can punch her in the face.* Getting angry was just the right thing to do, because if I was worked up enough I wouldn't worry about losing my job or about how nearly I'd come to being thoroughly seduced by the girl's charm index into committing a crime against the bogey persons' ethical code. I didn't want to think about any of that. My rage burned, and it felt *good*.

"So what do I do? How do I find these three old hags I'm supposed to consult?"

"They work for Stochastix Unlimited as fortunetellers. Just ask for the Weird Sisters."

I was nervous as hell as I dematted—wearing my full uniform—into the roulette-cum-Ferris wheel structure that was Stochastix Unlimited. I don't believe in fortunetelling myself, but the paraphernalia is disturbing. The ancient Earthies with their jet planes and oxcarts used all sorts of methods to divine the future: examining entrails, looking at the stars—we can't even do that anymore, we can't even see the stars to make up lies about them—consulting their witch-doctors and their weathermen. But the old things haven't lost their scariness, or their primal power.

I was in a little room. In front of a bank of sensors, three wizened heads rested on a life-support desk. There was an old-style, unyielding chair which would not adjust to my body. I looked at the three heads in turn.

"Uh, are you the Weird Sisters?"

One of them—they were all eyeless, hairless and toothless—suddenly snapped to. "A visitor!" she croaked. "You want a stock market report? Or do you want the general reading with optional love-life analysis for an extra three credits?" Then she blinked out. The next head came to life. "I see by your bearing, sir, that you are a nobleman...let me see, your cards indicate—"

"I'm a woman," I said. I was used to people not knowing my sex, but one day my poor camel's back was going to crack.

The third head broke in, "—that you have reached a karmic nexus in your chain of being. Beware of the dog. You are crossed by the Ace of Spuds, reversed. Potatoes will give you dropsy. In the immediate past, you have Ineptness and The Meaning of Life reversed—"

"I didn't come here for a tarot card reading," I said angrily. I noticed that they only spoke one at a time, in turns, and when it wasn't one of their turns they would seem oblivious to me; they would either freeze as if dead, or gibber quietly to themselves. Sure enough, I saw that the sensor bank was only connecting with one head at a time, and there was a comsim waldo triggering a simple switching device. "Where are the Mallkyries?" I said. "I'm with Storkways repossession, official business, you'll be rewarded..."

They all screeched raucously. "Five credits for your fortune," cackled the one who was 'on,' "double or nothing option if we're more than fifty percent wrong as determined by an impartial compalyzer. Ten credits for extra service."

"But maps of Mallworld—hee hee hee—priceless!" The third head glared at me and stuck out its tongue.

"Damn you!" I marched over to the other side of the table and yanked the cord off the sensor waldo. The three heads began screaming.

"We can't see!" they shouted all at once. "Turn us back on—"

"Only if you answer my questions."

I got the level number.

Loonies, I thought, every last one of them. And these were the women to whom the Selespridar had given the gift of immense longevity...who entertained the gods themselves with their anecdotes! How preposterous. I hopped out of the building and turned on my wrist tracer so that the heavies could come after me if anything developed out of this. Somehow I didn't think it would. A child with a pet gaboochi in tow ran screaming when he saw me. For the first time in my life, I wasn't really enjoying my role as bogeyperson...

No. I'd never enjoyed the role, damn it! But I was admitting it to myself for once.

I was a washout as a bogeyman anyway. I'd succumbed to carelessness. I should've known better than to fraternize with a repossessee. Now I was on what could be my last mission. I could vindicate myself with the bogeypersons' guild, or I could get credit clink and blackballed for life.

Frankly I didn't give a Pope's feminine napkin either way. I entered a demat-booth...

I was going to step out into uncharted Mallworld now. Maybe the booth wouldn't even work, and I'd get accidentally decapitated or worse. I closed my eyes and called out the strange number: QQQ222.

When I opened my eyes I was in a ghost mall.

Gone were the strident holo-hypesongs; instead, there was distant echoey whispering of ads that were running down...mournful deep voices that sang of forgotten brands of deodorant soap...a lone light flickering in a restaurant where man-size steaks still waltzed in agonizing slow time in the window...still slidewalks. Musty, dusty air. So this was Darkside.

What to do now? I had no leads other than the word *Mallkyrie;* my only weapon was the standard issue stunner; and I looked ridiculous in the bogeyman's garb, with nobody around to shriek in terror. I stepped onto the nearest slidewalk. With a thunk it came to life. How many decades had it waited to be awakened by the pressure of a human foot? The slidewalk bore me forward jerkily. What was I to do? "Cindy, Cindy—" I called out, feeling like an imbecile. A deactivated salesbot rocked back and forth on a chair. A mechanical plant-band, left to photosynthesize in the half-dark, twittered and twanged and disgorged an occasional cacophony of music and white noise into the stillness. Sudden local breakdowns of the pseudogravs made me queasy and the dust dance. "Cindy! Cindy!" I was so angry I think I would have stunned her on sight.

"Cindy, come out of there, you crazy girl!"

A lightfleck in a demat-booth. A wisp of sheer sari...I sprang off the slidewalk. "Cin—"

They were crashing out of the booth. I couldn't see in the darkness; the air was thick with fumes. A motorcycle raked against my face and sheared off plastiflesh. I was bleeding. I grabbed my stungun, but a fist came pounding down on my face. Pain shot through me. I saw stars, and then, through the stars—

I saw *her* standing by a decaying sushi bar. Light from a phosphorescent plastic tuna in the window played over her soft, innocent features...I was so relieved I almost forgot what a nuisance she'd been. "Get me out of this!" I yelled.

She looked away. "Damn you! Rescue me or something, it's me, your friendly bogeyman, remember me?" She turned her back. Had I seen a flash of guilt in her eyes? Then she leaped onto a slidewalk and vanished into distant darkness. I was pinioned, strapped to the bottom of one of the motorbike things, choking and spluttering, the whole corridor was purring now, the convoy levitated and thrust into the darkness...

My eyelids were getting heavy. The fumes were addling my senses. We were going down a long dark tunnel, like a terror tunnel in a funpark, now and then a sign touted wares across the thunder of motorcycles...

PRIME AZROID REAL ESTATE,
GUARANTEED NO NEIGHBORS WITHIN SEVEN
THOUSAND KILOMETERS...CLONESTEAK...
DOUBLES WHILE YOU GOBBLE...
BE A HAPPY MISANTHROPE WITH
HOLO-PROJECTION! FOOL YOUR FRIENDS

After I don't know how long, I passed out.

I'm alone. The stars are shining, so I know it's a dream. The stars appear in all people's dreams, though no living human has seen them.

Cindy's running toward me. We're hugging each other. I'm warm all over, just like in the Storkways holohypesongs. This is ridiculous, *I'm thinking to myself,* me, the self-sufficient one, throwing away my career, my hard-won stake in real estate, the condo-azroid...

*She's laughing, her Saturn-eyes are laughing too...*I want it to last forever, *I'm thinking. And then—*

Her smile becomes a feral shriek, a cry of bloodlust, like a wild Earthie in a feelie. She hops onto her motorbike and zooms away. I'm lost now, I'm a little girl again, and now I turn around and see the bogey-man waiting, gibbering, arms outstretched, his claws are dripping rheum and eyes are ember-red and I'm screaming, screaming, the way I never did when I was a kid, he's saying You thought you weren't afraid, didn't you, you thought I wasn't real, but I *am* real, I'm inside you, I'm eating my way out and soon the outside and the inside will all be one, one bogeyman, *and I scream and I scream and I scream—*

I groped around. My feet were shackled. After a while I got used to the darkness. I was in a dank room. A sharp smell of Levitol lanced the air. This must have been a storeroom in a drug emporium once. I was starting to feel fluttery on my feet just from the scent; then I noticed the casks of it, leaning by one wall. A fractured ceiling-grille let in scatters of colored light. I strained to see more.

On the floor were stacks of plastiglass motorcycle-shapes...molds it seemed. Some of them were part-full of some furry, fleshy substance, dark and sometimes bulging with darting bug-eyes. Beside them I noticed racks of gaboochi eggs. So that's what they were, I realized. You can break the Fomalhautan gaboochi egg into almost any kind of mold and it'll grow into the shape you want. That's why they're such popular pets—you can custom-mold them into dogs and cats and all sorts of almost-extinct creatures. One of the helmeted Mallkyries could probably control the gaboochi through its ears—modified into handlebars—and I guessed that they must fly by being pumped to brimming with Levitol. It was cruelty to animals of the first order. I got angrier, pulling at my restraints and cursing colorfully into the emptiness.

I thought of the bogeyman inside me, eating his way out—

That girl! What she's gotten me into! I wanted to turn her lovely hide black and blue even though one square centimeter of it was probably worth as much as my whole condo-azroid. *If I ever get out of this alive—*

And then she matted into the room. She came to me. She had a laseknife stuck in her sari. My stomach jumped. "What's going on now?" I said. "You're not going to kill me, are you?"

"Well...actually...yes," she said, sounding apologetic. "It's not my fault! It's the initiation rite. Every Initiate has to *collect* someone before they can become a full-fledged Mallkyrie." She started to pull out the knife.

"Be careful with that thing—"

"Oh, bother," she said, fooling with the adjustments. I had to talk quickly or I'd find myself placed among the stars.

"Look," I said, "you don't want to do this, do you? I mean, did they tell you all along when you were listening on the intervoke that you were going to have to kill people?"

"Well, not exactly...they sang of freedom, of whooping down deserted mallways, of singing wild songs, of merry comradeship, of the wisdom of Odin—"

"Who's that?"

"The Leader, of course. He holds court in Mallhalla." This was becoming incredible. I couldn't believe that I was going to die for this...hideous distortion of a myth. My dream had lied to me. *They* were destroying me—it wasn't my doing!

"Hold it!" I said. "Listen, I'm your friend, remember? I talked back to your parents, I told them off for you—"

"You wouldn't let me go," she pointed out. "You wouldn't even adopt me after I offered to pay for it!"

"How could I? I had a job to do—"

"So do I."

"Yes, but…We were getting along so nicely! I trusted you, I didn't tie you up, you remember? How the hell can you just waste me like that? I bet I'm the first friend you ever had in your whole life—" I was gabbling now, confused and terrified. "Look, you really like it here? You really enjoy doing this?"

"I hate it! I hate it!" she cried, all at once emotional. "I never expected it to be like this—" She threw the knife down. "It seemed so *exciting* and it turns out they're just a gang of cutthroats! What's more, there's some kind of stupid tribal war on, against the Amazons or something, and it's deadly serious and they're offing people left, right and center—"

"Unshackle me, Cindy. I'll get us out of this somehow. I don't know how, but—" *(The wrist tracer!* I was thinking rapidly. *If I can only hold out long enough for them to miss me and do a scan and send reinforcements…)*

"How can you get us out?" She was weeping now. "I'm tired of this game, I'm trapped, they're going to kill you and then I'll be stuck in Darkside forever and they'll train me to shoplift and ride mutant gaboochis and—"

"Fun," I said. "Until—" She picked up the laseknife and cut me free. "Now what? Can you get us a couple of those"— I indicated the motorbike molds—*"things?"*

"I doubt it. Those aren't due for another six months and they're mind-mated as soon as they're released, *that* one's"— she pointed to a motorcycle mold that was full almost to bursting with the brown fleshy stuff—"going to be mine."

"We'll have to use our wits, then," I said dubiously, rubbing my sore wrists. "Where's my stungun?"

"Don't know. Look, why don't you just let me kill you, and if they come for me I'll say they *forced* me to—"

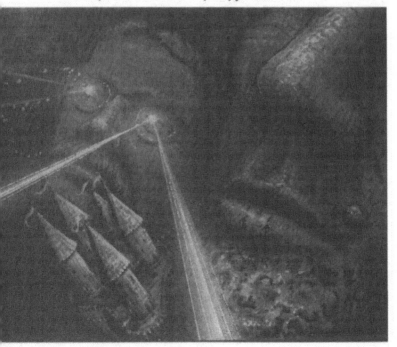

"Forget it."

"Yeah, I guess."

"Ever taken Levitol?"

"Some, at parties, only socially though."

"Where's the nearest working pan-Mallworld demat-booth?"

"Two hundred meters, maybe a quarterklick from here. There're guards, though."

"It's dark, right? If we use those faulty slidewalks they'll go chug-chug and waken the troops, right? So we'd better OD on Levitol and sail right over their heads."

"Sounds dangerous."

"You want out or don't you?" Maybe I was being too hard on the poor kid. I was thinking—irrational, since she'd just tried to snip me—how confused my feelings were getting!

We tiptoed to the nearest Levitol cask and I broke the seal. Pure Levitol—not the kind in tablets at the drugstore—came fuming out. The gaboochis in their glass prisons twitched, straining to break loose. I put my mouth to the hole and took a gulp. The next minute I'd practically conked myself out on the ceiling. In a moment Hyacinth had joined me. "Okay," I said, "let's hit out."

"I love you," she said.

"Don't give me any of that," I said. "I know you. You'll say anything to get by. Just because your IQ cost twice as much as mine did—don't cry, for god's sake!"

"There's two of them at the local demat-booth," she whispered.

"I'll take the one on the left." We both maneuvered into the booth, popped out, fists raised, swooped down, clobbered, left two neatly knocked-out Mallkyries in a little heap. Their motorcycle-gaboochis were tethered to a pole by the slidewalk. We held hands, giddy, skimming the vaulted ceiling of the corridor. The one working demat-booth that would get us out of there was blinking in the distance.

CREDIT BAD?
BETTER DEAD THAN IN THE RED!
LOW-COST SUICIDE PLANS!
LAYAWAY AVAILABLE

...headless skeletons in the window were juggling skulls that hummed barbershop harmonies. I shuddered, floated onward—

A shrill caterwauling rent the air! I tried to brake myself but couldn't because of the momentum of the Levitol. "The motorbikes! They're mindlinked with their owners! They must've sensed trouble!" Cindy said. Sure enough, a pack of Mallkyries had matted in from nowhere and were zeroing in on us, yelling their war cries, expelling thunderclouds of gas fumes. "We're doomed!" she screamed. She clutched me hard. We clung to each other, still flushed with Levitol and still whooshing inertially toward the demat-booth.

"I can't stop—" Adrenalin and Levitol don't mix well, and we were figure-eighting and doing involuntary aerobatics as the Mallkyries closed in.

Then—

Ahead of us, another dustcloud. Perched on flying unicorns, women in flowing robes with one breast bare, brandishing laserlances, were bursting through the paneless windows of a half-eaten gingerbread cathedral!

"Holy vaculax!" screamed Hyacinth. "It's an Amazon attack!"

"We'll be caught in a crossfire!" I said, holding her tight as we veered toward a wall and ricocheted like a flatulent balloon. The Amazons were whooping now, their unicorns—more altered gaboochis—were bucking and rearing as they hurtled toward us. The lances flashed! The motorcycles baroomed as we managed to duck, and they crashed headlong into the wall of unicorns—

"We're done for!" said Cindy, as the Levitol wore off more sharply and we began to plummet toward the chasm between two slidewalks.

"Hold on to the slidewalk!" I shouted. I put my arms out and caught the edges of two slidewalks and I dangled stupidly for a moment, and then I realized with horror that the pressure of my arms was making the slidewalks lurch to life and they were different speeds and if I didn't let go I'd be torn apart and—

"Hyacinth! Hyacinth!" All-too-familiar voices were squealing over the war cries. I managed to push myself up onto the slower slidewalk and to haul Cindy up. Above us, the carnage continued madly. Running toward us on the opposite slidewalk were the barJulian-Davieses!

"You come back with our daughter, you...you monster, you!" the mother was screeching. She leaped with astonishing agility onto where I was standing and began pummeling me with her fists. The Mallkyries and Amazons had left their steeds in midair and were now jumping down onto the slidewalks for hand-to-hand combat. From the corner of my eye I could see a clanking army of servoclunkers with sleepitoff wands charging into the mob and dealing indiscriminate instant sleep, and I could see bogeymen here and there directing them. At last! We were being rescued! They'd finally traced my tracer!

I grabbed Cindy's hand, gave Mrs. barJulian-Davies a sharp kick in the shin in an explosive seizure of hatred, and started toward the nearest bogeyman.

Without warning there was blinding light everywhere. Thunderclouds materialized in the passageway, and bolts of lightning shot out of holes in department store walls. I couldn't see a thing. There were shouts of "Zeus!" and "Odin!" and the gangs seemed to be scattering.

And then there was this cavernous, menaceful, mocking laughter coming from everywhere. Resounding through the corridors. I felt light-headed suddenly, as though I'd taken another dose of Levitol. I felt as though I were dissolving almost, becoming ethereal...and I was. The laughter echoed round and round my head. "I'm going bananas at last!" I said to myself. "Finally this job has gotten to me!"

And now we were in a vast hall. The floor seemed to be of cloud. Fog drifted around our ankles. There was just me and Cindy and Mr. and Mrs. barJulian-Davies, who had withdrawn to a distant corner under a pillar and were consoling each other. Hyacinth's father had draped his caterpilloid abdomen around the pillar and was *still* knitting a sweater with his eighteenth or so pair of appendages, and was still utterly awkward with all the other arms and legs. This must be one of the old fantasizing palaces that were so fashionable some decades before, somehow still in working order. I'd sometimes gone to one when I was a kid and pretended to be an olden princess, ordering her slaves around and guzzling gas from jeweled goblets. The hall was walled in naugatimber, elegant and old-fashioned. Drinking horns hung from the fakewood columns; it was they who exuded the perfumed cloud-stuff that swirled all around us...

The laughter went on and on. And finally we saw its source, materializing on a dais at one end of the room. It was some kind of godlike figure: tall, hairy, in a tunic sort of costume with a horned helmet like the Mallkyries'.

"Who the hell are you?" I said.

He went on laughing. Finally he spluttered, "Who do you think? I'm God, of course! Odin! Zeus! Whatever..."

"Let us go," Mrs. barJulian-Davies demanded. "I'm sure we can come to some financial arrangement, and besides, my cousin Julian barJulian, you know, of the Mallworld barJulians, won't like it at all when he finds out you're holding us prisoner here...when all we wanted was to come and pay for our daughter in person; the house paycomp was acting up, you know, and it kept telling us we didn't have any money—"

God went on laughing.

"Will you tell us what's going on?" I said, marching right up to him. "You're obviously mad, you should be put away. You've been recruiting people, gulling them, filling their heads with romantic dreams and then making them fight your costume-party wars. What kind of a messed-up ego do you have, to be able to—"

"You're right." His voice boomed, filling the whole hall easily. "I *am* mad, of course—ha, ha, ha!" He tore at his face. The plastiflesh fell to the ground. A musky, sensual odor emanated from him. His face was blue. Magenta hair fell from the crown of his head in waves and rippled softly behind him.

"You're—a Selespridon!" said Cindy.

"And a mad one, no less," said the alien, stepping down from the dais and proffering his hand to us. Cindy's parents had by now retreated into a quiet, gibbering hysteria. "My name is Kmengdreft the Crazy. I've been exiled from my home world, you know, doomed to wander forever among you primitive species…"

"What excuse does it give you to hide in a shopping mall and play god?"

"Academic curiosity…I'm fascinated by your legends, your myths. I'm quite a xeno-anthropologist these days, you know. Hee hee! Of course, most of the evidence of your Dawntimes has been destroyed, but one does one's best…did you like my motorcycles? Some experts think the Valkyries weren't in the same period as motorcycles, but…one must be creative, mustn't one, when it comes to times so remote? And sending out random intervoke-temptations to people, luring them into this closed, controlled world so they could live out their primeval past with utter abandon, with a god to turn to when they feared responsibility…what an *exciting* experiment. Exciting. Maybe my peers will even summon me home, away from this *merde*-eating hole, and acknowledge my brilliant achievements, eh?" He paused.

"You bastard!" I said. Everyone knows that the Selespridar are a great and wise race, and that they love us humans like fathers and are full of compassion…of the three or four last straws of the day, this one was as shattering as it was unexpected. I couldn't believe it. "You're a Selespridon!" I said, bitter because I would soon have to give up Cindy and go back to letting the bogeyman eat me away, bitter because the Selespridar had stolen the dreams of all humans. "You have everything! Why can't you teach us great things, instead of going native and messing with our lives? You live a million years or something, and we only last a century, but you want to snuff even *that!* There's so much you could help us with, and yet—"

"Oh, I tried it, I tried it. Became a Zen master for a while. No fun. I'm just a lousy Selespridon after all. Nobody loves me." He began to laugh again. "I don't *have* to let you go, you know," he said.

That should have scared me; the Selespridar have unthinkable powers, and they're *aliens,* you can't really understand them even when they're acting almost human. But instead of terror I felt numbed. All I wanted was to hand Cindy over and go home and hide. But Cindy saved us.

She spoke up. "It's nice to know," she said ever so sweetly, "that even though you Selespridar are Masters of the Galaxy and all that, you can still go bonkers too…makes us feel, you know, *closer.* More like a kindred race. We go crazy all the time, you know. I'm crazy. My parents are incredibly crazy. And bogeyman Salvador…she's crazy as hell. She bluffed me into not bumping her off, and she's been saving my life all day, even though she knows I've been manipulating the baloney out of her all day." I started laughing, helplessly. There wasn't anything left to do. So did she. And he. We were all cackling and guffawing until we cried. Except the parents, who seemed totally out of it.

"You know," said the Selespridon, "that's the nicest thing a human ever said to me. Maybe I will attain *ug'unnieth* after all." He became grave then, and said, "I guess I'll let you go and give up this whole thing…one of the reasons I'm insane is that I only have an attention span of about ten of your years…and I'll just turn myself in to the Selespridon authorities. Just as I was having fun, too!"

"But…what'll happen to you?" said Cindy. The poor kid, she was concerned about him! She'd followed her dream to its source and found it a mockery of those dreams, and she still cared! She moved me, that child.

"You, a human, show compassion toward me?" he said sadly. "I am truly shamed...I am so old, so senile, so insane now..."

"But what will happen to you?" I said.

"Oh, *furengillat*. The Grand Ending. I have committed the ultimate crime, have I not? The crime of uncompassion."

"They'll execute you?" said Cindy.

"It's nothing. Tomorrow's my 7,266th birthday anyway. You get bored. You think I *like* being mad?"

"At least you know it. Most mad humans don't."

"Oh, get out of here," said the Selespridon, not unkindly. "The demat-booth's just behind that pillar"—he pointed—"and you ask for level W444 to get out of Darkside. Your fellow bogeymen will be waiting there." And then—after a perfunctory display of thunder and lightning—he was gone.

The parents snapped to right away. "You're coming straight home, young lady!" said the father.

"But—" She looked at me imploringly. I looked at her. We'd been through a lot together. I wasn't the same person as when I had gotten up—was it only that morning? No, longer, surely, longer ago than that—and rolled into the office for the day's instructions. She was a beautiful kid.

And she needed me.

Something *had* been missing from my life.

As the girl looked at me, the Saturns whirling in her eyes and the delicate sari fluttering in the scented mist, I suddenly understood...

Damn it, Dollie Salvador, I thought. *Maybe it's true that nobody loves you. You've moped about it for years, blamed it all on belonging to a loveless, unlovable profession—but maybe it isn't all because you're a bogeyman. Maybe you have to give more too, maybe you should start off by loving somebody—*

"I've been scared of committing myself. All my life I've been scared," I said to myself. And then, aloud, I said something incredibly foolish. I said, "Actually, she's not going back with you. You see, she'd just deeded me just enough credit to buy up the remainder of her mortgage, and seeing how neglected she's been in the past, it seemed like the right thing to—"

"Rubbish," said the father. "We thumbed the payment through the minute you left. There is absolutely no way that you could prove that our claim was not the prior one."

"I'll sue!" I said angrily. I was committed now. In at the deep end. And I didn't care anymore. I wasn't afraid. I knew who the bogeyman really was. The bogeyman was my unwillingness to love or be loved, and he had been gnawing out my guts, piece by piece, all of my life. Now that I'd made the admission to myself, it was like throwing off thirty years' worth of shackles. "I don't care if you sue me right into a credit clinic! I don't care if I have to kidnap this kid and bash my head against the Selespridon barrier until it cracks open!"

"You won't have to," said Cindy suddenly. I saw the triumphant grin on her face, the one that meant she was on top of things.

"What do you mean?" said her mother.

"Well, since Papa trusted me with the house paycomp, I took the liberty of messing around a little with our holdings."

"What? How dare—" began Mr. barJulian-Davies.

"I paid eighteen supermegacredits for all the mercury mining concessions on Mercury!" she said gleefully. "And in case you're wondering about the trouble with the paycomp and why you had to take the trouble to come personally to haul me off…the answer's simple! You're bankrupt!"

"Utter nonsense, you foolish child. We'll simply sell the art."

At this I couldn't contain myself. I started giggling and Cindy took it up too, and we were in stitches.

Calming down, Cindy said, "Since you *are* my exparents, I suppose Dollie and I will let you live in that monstrous house with us. Everything that's left belongs to me now, you know! You can't do anything about it because I had power of attorney under overcorporate law…actually I only kept the house and the art."

"You have some taste left, I see," her mother said bitterly, eyeing me furiously. "We scrimped and fought for that art."

"Indeed," said Cindy. "But as for selling the art...I've got other plans. I'm going to swing from the brontosaurus chandelier until the bones break off, one by one—"

"Heavens! What will the barJulians think of us?" wailed her mother.

"Then I'll kick your coprokinetic sculpture into little pieces and—"

"No." I said, as my immense fortune finally dawned on me, "*I* get to kick the shit sculpture into little pieces! I'm the parent around here and I'll give the orders! *You* can spill coffee all over the Michelangelo coffee table—"

"And you can unstitch the laser-crocheting of *Iphigenia in Schenectady*—"

"We'll paint mustaches on Mount Rushmore—"

So this was what being a mother was all about.

Tawdry enough for you, Your Multi-n'huatitude? No?

Even considering the fact that one of our very own, Kmengdreft the Crazy, should be involved?

By the way, I understand he's turned himself in, and he's on his way back to the homeworld for the usual Ceremonial Discorporation. We all extend, I am sure, our fullest compassion to him.

Now, if the mind of our previous miscreant wasn't enough to put you off your malaprops, assuredly this seventh one will be!

On with it, you say? I should shut up and let Your Lordship do the deciding around here? Very well. All I can say is, my lord, that you asked for it.

OWN YOUR OWN VACULAX

Things were different in ancient times. Simpler. That most deeply personal of human activities—elimination of waste—was a very private, even a religious act, a veritable communion with nature.

For it was the law of the jungle then. Some of these men—and you must remember that they were as human as you or I—eliminated in forests, by roadsides and airfields, in lakes and rivers, expressing their creativity in the places they selected for becoming one with all humanity, all nature, all life. Ah, what joyous days they were!

But today things have changed. We live in nice, safe neighborhoods of a few million people instead of the jungles of wild trees or concrete that the earthies inhabited.

But inside us, isn't there a little thingamajig that longs for the past? The wide, open spaces of fabled New York City, where houses were but a hundred levels high? The atmosphere that went on for miles and miles, sensuously scented with gasoline and flowers?

Ah yes.

And now, from the Vaculax Corporation...

Yes! You too can communicate with nature, your *own* way, in your *own* time and place, in your *own* glorious solitude!

For the private vaculax is no longer the purview of the well-heeled thumbprint alone. With our new long-range credit plans, you can have a vaculax of your very own in your cubicle today! This very second, should you be plugged into the instybuy network!

Our top-of-the-line model, the maxilax, is for the home. Powered by a quantum black hole, an approved Selespridon import, the maxilax has a family attachment so as many as five can be "on the john" simultaneously! Great party fun as the vaculax becomes a stirring centerpiece for communal elimination and conversation!

And for today's single-person units, the mediolax: convenient to use, can be installed in any chairfloat at no extra charge.

And, for people on the run, try our economical new minilax. Fits right in that secret place, and only you know it's there! Absorbs, vaporizes, deodorizes in seconds! Works anytime— in business conferences...in the theater, so you don't have to miss a second of the show...at dinner or luncheon dates, when that exotic food gets you down and you don't want to inconvenience or embarrass your hosts.

So think about it. A caveman wouldn't have shared his toothbrush with anyone. Can you, a child of a time far far more sophisticated, do any less?

Join the millions of happy people who have opted for something personal, something that will add meaning to their lives.

Buy a vaculax today!

Our Mallworld showroom is on the F54 level. A wide range of demonstration models is at your service, should you feel the urge coming on at any time during your visit.

Vaculax Corporation—*we* do give a shit!

The Jaws of Mallworld

Time was when I hated the very idea of Mallworld. For three years I'd been a member of the copout sect. I'd made my pile in the azroid futures rat race, and all I wanted to do was withdraw into the contemplative existence. The copouts, in common with many of the crankier cults, frowned on commercialism, so there I was, enjoying my private azroid in the Cluster of Austerity, reveling in solitude, and steeping myself in the doctrines of the gurus of copoutism, and I was in my thirties and had never even *been* to Mallworld. In the rat race days I'd done all my shopping by remote.

It's inevitable, I suppose, that it would be a member of the barJulian family who first enticed me there. Although Tiberius barJulian-Sinistre was by no means your typical barJulian either...he was definitely a twig off the crooked branch of that gaggle of googillionaires, and the only reason I paid any attention to him at all when he trespassed within my personal azroid space was that we'd been to school together, he and I, back when St. Martin Luther King's Strict and Snooty still had a little class and hadn't yet been inundated by the Babylonian nouveau riche.

I was hopping mad, too, because he'd caught me cheating on my regime meditation.

I was surfing.

See, I had the random-wave-generator, the only evidence of human habitation on the surface of my azroid, turned on full. There was nothing at all in the blackness of space but the rock I called home, glinting in the distance; the elaborate interlocking patterns of space-bending gravitons my generator was spewing into the vacuum for a hundred klicks or so; the surfboard, really a colony of graviton-sensitive, space-dwelling bugs from beyond the Selespridon barrier, wriggling around in their protective corallike communal exoskeleton; and me, Kestrel O'Keefe, nude in one of those newfangled colorless odorless untactile p-suits, riding the waves in the midst of a holographic simurama of the primeval ocean that extended around me for a radius of one kilometer and followed me wherever I went.

I stretched out, gave into the crest of a huge one, and the sea-muzak was roaring in my ears, when the surfboard's emergency autobrake went *dong!* and the ocean vanished. My stomach was on the verge of turning itself inside out, the gravi-waves stopped, leaving me in free-fall for a moment before the homing device began to tow me in. And to top it all, the gaudiest toyochev I had ever seen in my life was bearing down on me.

The car was shocking pink with metallic turquoise stripes. It had monstrous flapping wings. It had a functional chariot, drawn by mechanical griffins, proudly poking from the hood. It had statues of ancient goddesses in lewd postures holding up a canopy of plastisilk. It had a double-barreled fake exhaust pipe that released limitation noxious fumes into space, just like a historical Old Earth vehicle. It had antique windshield wipers that swabbed away at the emptiness of space. It had baton-twirling, tutu-wearing clockwork elephants going before and after, and hideous, over orchestrated circus-band music blared into the inputs of my p-suit. Are you getting the idea?

I didn't know who it was, but I had a sinking feeling.

"Kessie-poo!" came the voice, booming over my earpieces.

"Tiberius!" I said. "What the devil are *you* doing here, bursting in on my peace and quiet? I could have you fined for trespassing, you old villain, you!"

"Why, I just had a sort of philanthropic urge, you know. When one finds that one's old friends have retreated into the arms of some perfectly vile cult, what can one do? Although I must say you don't seem to be observing the rules very assiduously. Can I come for tea?"

"When have you ever failed to invite yourself where you're not asked?"

"Come now. Where does one park around here?"

"Put that hideous contraption on the other side of the azroid. The side with no windows. You seem to have lost what little taste you once had."

"Come, come, no harsh words." I heard the music swell up and the toyochev soared up and zoomed behind my azroid, out of sight. Meanwhile, the homing gizmo on my surfboard had worked its magic. I stood with the board tucked under my arm, subvoked a command to turn everything off; then I found a familiar cleft, artfully concealed between two beautifully crafted rock outcroppings of naugagneiss and naugagranite, and I dematted into my living room.

He was already sitting there, on the one comfortable chairfloat—the whole azroid was engineered for solitude, not for guests—snorting a sniffer of dream powder and calling for tea.

"You certainly haven't forgotten how to make yourself at home," I said archly. Pointedly I called the house comsim and told it to provide a chair for me; the only other one in the house was a cushion, not a float, and prickly on the arse besides. I looked at my guest. He hadn't changed. Oh, he was three or four times fatter. He was unbecomingly covered with clothing—feathers and leathers, belts, buckles, and buttons, and whirling holo-carbuncles as big as fists. He looked like the window of one of those kinky clothing stores. A red conical hat with a bell on it flopped from his head, and he wore a bushy beard of plasticottonwool.

"What sort of a costume is that?"

"Merry Christmas! Ho ho ho!" he said. "I'm Santa Claus."

"Collecting for some charity then? I should have known."

"My dear Kestrel. It is a little-known fact that Santa Claus, far from being a bell-ringing beggar as he is now always portrayed, was an ancient Roman emperor who used to shower the multitudes with gifts. Precisely what I have come to do to you."

I paused. I knew that Tiberius was in the habit of *paying* for everything, including friendship; that he never felt quite comfortable unless he was throwing money around. In his own funny way, then, this was a cry of desperation. I knew Tiberius far better than he ever dreamed.

"So how's life treating you?" I said.

"Very well indeed! Heh, heh, heh."

"Come on, I know you of old. You would hardly have looked me up if there weren't something wrong." This had always been true; for some reason Tiberius had trusted me in school, had even looked up to me. "Isn't the demat-booth factory deal going well?"

"So-so. Oh, all right. A huge shipment of my demat-booths, back on Earth, was being freighted across the Pacific Ocean when the flier burst a valve and plummeted into the sea. Do you realize how much—"

"You can afford it."

"Yes. But I have an uneasy feeling about it all, a sort of, I don't know—"

"I suppose the demat-booths were all sealed? Unbreakable? Can't be unsealed except by express sub-vocalized command of someone going through them?"

"Well, naturally. But suppose, just suppose—"

"You can't honestly tell me you're really worried about a thing like that."

"I have a terrible fear of the ocean."

"You've never even seen an ocean, Tiberius!"

"Yes, but all the same. Let's change the subject. Do you know about Copuland?"

"No. What's that? I've been closeted for years, remember?"

And then he told me. His eyes caught fire as the details of his magnificent creation came tumbling out. It was astounding— it *did* have a certain twisted creativity, I must say. For Copuland was a hybridization of two proven high-market entertainment concepts—the sex-mart and the amusement park. "I'm bringing sensuality into the purview of Everyman, Kessie! No longer shall they strive for a vapid dream. They shall all be as the ancient kings with their harems and pleasure gardens."

"And you, *you*—"

"Will rake in four megacredits every *minute* that my amusement park-theme brothel is in operation!" His beady eyes glinted. "Ho, ho, ho!"

"Then what's your problem? I want to go outside and ride some more eighteen-meter waves, and you're boring me now."

"Don't be like that, Kestrel, my only friend."

For a second he looked like a little kid. I did feel sorry for him, I really did; it was part of the training my copout guru had given me, that I was able to view his situation with compassion when before I would have been half full of envy, half of greed. "So there *is* a problem, Tiberius."

"Yes. It's the League of Sensual Standards."

"Oh, *those* old-fashioned guardians of the good old ways! What have they got to say?"

"I've been censured. By my very own cousin, Theresa barJulian! Cheapening sexuality, they said. Going for the lowest common denominator. Tackiness. Kitschification of kinkiness. Disneyfying of the meaning of life."

"Sounds true enough to me."

"It's a plot, I tell you! They've always had it in for me, ever since my own father, Clement barJulian the Fourteenth, traded in the equity on my parenthood and bounced me into a used kid lot!"

"Yes, but you *did* do something very naughty." The Clement barJulian branch had always had terrible luck with their children; I remembered the tale of Fred the vampire from many years back. Being rich isn't everything.

"So I speculated in dirty earthie governments. I was only ten years old, damn it, I didn't know better."

"That revolution you staged in Africa that violated the hands-off treaty between the earthies and the corporations that rule beyond, and nearly threw the barJulians out of power in the—"

"Fat lot you know about it," he said sulkily. "Bet *you've* never been to Earth."

"Whatever for?"

"It's a whole 'nother experience there, Kestrel! It's real! It's like...like surfing in real water."

I shuddered. "I think I'd puke." You didn't surf in *water.* For one thing, you'd get all wet.

"Look, will you come out of hiding and hang around with me for a few days? Till I'm out of this depression, huh? Come to Mallworld. Have some fun. I'll give you the run of Copuland. How long's it been since you had sex with anyone but the azroid androids, for god's sake?"

"...A while."

"Come on then. Cheer me up. Oh—" He leered horribly then. "Ever porked a porcupine?"

"What's a porcupine?"

I found out the next day.

A swift ride in his toyochev, popping through several transmat rings, and we were in the VIP parking lot of Mallworld—I was still naked from surfing and demurely clutching my surfboard, for I didn't expect to be there long.

We dematted into a grand concourse. I counted twenty-nine levels, swooping and swerving above me, before they became too tiny with distance to count. A thousand muzaks bawled forth from storefronts, newsstands, shrink shacks, autonumerologists, hamburger paradises, robot salesmen, barbershops...through the air flew flocks of winged shopping bags (the new style that year) with their masters hanging on to their leashes, Levitol zonkies, hands linked, spiraling like springs around the intertwisting slidewalks, and bevies of chattering comsims. It was sensory overload of the first order after the restfulness of the copout sect. I wanted to go back already.

"No, don't do that yet!" he exclaimed. "The barJulians are throwing a reception, we don't want to miss that, do we?" And I realized that he needed me for moral support. He was running with a crowd whose whims arbitrated the tastes of a solar system, and if they turned their thumbs down at his Copuland they could probably destroy him. I was there to watch him browning his nose, and to throw in a comforting line from time to time.

"Well, let's get on with it," I said, brushing off a talking ice-cream soda and idly watching an orchestra of Bible-thumpers as they banged their mallets on racks of resonant old books in a rousing commercial jingle for deodorant navel spray. Tiberius dragged me to a demat-booth, and we popped out in a wild landscape of giant flowers, big as trees. Meter-high ants scurried about. "Where the hell are we?"

"Oh, this is the Brobdingnag Suite of the Gaza Plaza Hotel. Don't worry about the ants—they're just comsims." Sure enough, we rounded a clump of roses and found a huge buffeteria piled with delicacies, cleverly disguised as a giant dead millipede. Hundreds of people were lounging about on flying carpets, quaffing from jeweled goblets; in and out of them flitted comsims and swarms of minimalists. I saw that the custom of having somatectomies and wandering around as severed heads on silver platters had come back into fashion again.

"The talking heads are back, I see."

"Yes, worse than ever. This time the Seven-veiled Sect reintroduced them; something to do with the cult of St. Salome the Baptist."

"How boring." As I came nearer I made out snatches of conversations: minimalists as a whole seemed to love to talk pretentiously about art. "But *is* it art?" one of them was saying to Tiberius at the very moment.

"Of course it is!"

"Surely Copuland represents a vulgarization of art, which by its very nature must elitify and superfluate within the microcosm of the societal individual," the head protested as it circled Tiberius's head like a hungry buzzard. I stalked off, looking for something more interesting, leaving Tiberius floundering in a maelstrom of pretension. As I was bending

over a platter of tentacle-waving chocolate sea anemones, a
seductive voice whispered in my ear.

"So who is Tiberius's latest friend? I've never seen *you* at
one of these things before."

I turned around. She was stunning. Her crimson hair had
been sculpted to resemble a nestful of writhing serpents and
was animated by some kind of remote control. I stared,
fascinated, at it, hardly noticing the bright scarlet eyes, the
jagged red lightning zagging down each cheek, the rosy lips,
the holographic gown that wasn't there that seethed with a
thousand serpents.

"Who are you?" I suddenly knew I'd committed a faux pas
of magnificent proportions. This obviously wasn't the kind
of person whose identity you'd ask; you'd just *know*. "Oh,
I've been out of sight for three years, and—"

But she just shrugged it off. "I am Juliana Julienne barJulian.
Your host, dummy!" She cackled prettily. "Oh, don't worry
about my manner, you handsome man. What a clever idea,
wearing a surfboard instead of a loincloth! Ever had one of
these?" She held out her palm; there was a pink crystal in it.
"They're simply the latest thing!"

"Mmmm?" I was confused. It must be some kind of drug;
frankly, I could have used anything at that moment, even
Levitol.

"Oh, they're simply the latest. They're called *oberons*. See,
they give you the most wonderful sense of wellbeing for about
an hour or so, and then, when you come to, you...fall in love
with the first person you set eyes on! Isn't that wonderful?
Aleatory eroticism, that's what it is! Here, take a couple." She
reached into her hair and pulled out a handful of the rubylike
pills, and thrust them at me. I had nowhere to put them, so I
cached them in the fusebox of my surfboard. "I don't need a
pill," I said suavely, "to fall for *you.*"

She laughed. "St. Martin Luther King's, Class of 666!"
When she saw me frown she added, "No, it's not what you
think. It's my idiot brother, he drops that line all the time."

Tiberius turned up. "Sis!" he said.

"You're not supposed to call me that anymore, Tiberoo! They've really got it in for you now, anyway." I turned to the sea anemones, chomping on one as it wriggled in its death throes.

"So why don't you lift the ban, huh?" So Copuland wasn't just being disapproved of: it had come under a Sensual Interdict! Tiberius went on, "How do you like old Kestrel here? He's a surfer, you know—"

Ha! I thought. *Crafty old bugger!* He had had it all planned, then. I, the sexy surfer, was to charm Juliana Julienne out of her mind. *She* would then use her influence on the League of Sensual Standards to declare Tiberius's kitsch kosher. He would then be free to up the entrance fees to Sensual (rubber stamp) approved standards, lining his insatiable pockets to the hilt. I was no fool.

But Juliana was already all over me. "You're a surfer, huh? Can you do the double-back-handspring from the top of a fifty-footer? Can you do a headstand while doing it? Can you—"

"Oh, sure," I said, although I was way out of practice. She was drinking me in, and I knew I'd made a conquest. I'd seen these types before, haunting the holo-beaches, waiting, panting, on the plastisand. And she was filthy rich, too.

But somehow it didn't feel right. It made me feel—well, *dirty.* To be used by Tiberius as bait for his sordid schemes—

I prevaricated. We discussed the finer points of surfing; she was knowledgeable, even did it a bit. She turned off her polyserpentine holo-diaphanon for a flicker so I could see her perfect body; then she accidentally "knocked the knob with my wrist, you know..."

Tiberius was stuffing himself with chocolate anemones; I became a trifle sick as I saw them fibrillating, struggling to get out of his mouth.

I popped an oberon.

And another.

"Look here!" I said, seizing Juliana by the wrists. "You're no better than those hustling groupies on level B46. You're all filth, you people, do you hear?" I felt wonderful. *"Feeeeeelth! Feeeeeeeeeeeelthhhhh!!"* I jumped up on the table that was elegantly holo-sculpted to resemble a rotting millipede. "Listen, you pretentious fools! How dare you have the temerity to condemn my good friend Tiberius barJulian-Sinistre, when you're just as gaudy, tasteless and kitsch-ridden as the rest of them?" I picked up a hamper of simufruit and began pelting the audience, now in an uproar. "I demand that you restore his good name immediately!" I did a little dance, slipping into a basin of Jell-O. "Behold! I baptise you all with whipped cream! O ye of little faith, you should all flee this den of commercialism and seek the copout sect!"

At the mention of *copoutism* the partygoers started to get angry. I should have known better than to preach the ultimate heresy here, but under the oberons' influence I was just past caring.

"Even you talking heads are just a ludicrous fad!" I screamed as a flock of them began to dive toward me. "Seek to contemplate the very navel of truth! Buy a condo-azroid in the Cluster of Austerity, and find the Meaning of Life—the true one, not some Schweitzerian heresy!" I was about to tell them to have their credit-thumbs amputated when Tiberius grabbed my ankles and I came toppling into the throng, whipped cream, Jell-O, chocolate anemones, and all.

"Let's split!" he whispered urgently. "Things are looking ugly. I don't know what I've done to deserve this, but—" He took my hand and began sprinting toward the nearest demat-booth, cleverly disguised as the snapping jaws of a Venus's-flytrap. The crowd was bearing down on us, cackling, hooting, and booing, as we jumped in and the thing closed around us and—

"Where the hell is this?" I said, dancing in circles around Tiberius.

What an amazing sight! A thundering muzak, built of layer upon layer of erotic sighs and sweet nothings, assailed my ears. We were at one end of a slidewalk stretching to infinity. A monster roller coaster twisted, flopped, looped, reeled, figure-eighted, spiraled and whirled with lights and seethed with frenetic holograms of copulating giants; the slidewalk, suspended in a nothing tube, whisked right through one of the loops like a thread through a needle's eye. As we popped out of the roller coaster (which soared above and plummeted as far as the eye could see) I looked around and saw floating brothels with singing maidens, flying king-size carpets, each bedecked with a siren beauty of either sex, sizzling with sensuality.

"Just showing you everything you've destroyed, you bastard!" Tiberius said, still shaking with rage. I was still under the influence, and I thought him incredibly funny.

"It's gorgeous! I want to try all the rides!"

"You might as well, mightn't you? Before I close down the whole shebang and sign up for credit clink."

"Yippeee!" I said, leaping from speedzone to speedzone of the slidewalk and waving my surfboard madly. From this vantage point I could see just how much he'd put into it. This theme brothel covered a whole sector of Mallworld, no doubt about it. The whole extravaganza was shaped like a gargantuan ice-cream cone, each level wider than the one below it; we were zooming through the as-it-were double-scoop of roller coaster and stardome overhead. The stars were projected on the holoZeiss, and a frieze of constellations that depicted the many amorous conquests of Zeus as Bull, Swan, Golden Shower, and what have you. It was pretty overwhelming, I thought, shaking the remaining oberons out of my surfboard.

"Hadn't you better stop?" said Tiberius. It occurred to me that he was showing surprising restraint—he was still acting as though I were his friend after what I'd done.

"Wheee!" I said, popping the remaining seven crystals.

"I guess I'd better give you the grand tour," he said morosely.

"Whoopee! Goshzooks!"

And we were off! First he took me to the Water-Sporty-
Flume-Ride, where I was drenched in golden liquid that proved
to be a mild aphrodisiac. He and I nabbed a couple foxy
androids and zipped through the Cave of Time and the Tunnel
of Sensuality and the Tower of Torment and the Chambers of
Chastisement, and we rode the Carnal Canoe through the Forest
of Fornication and the Dildo Dodgems through the Lake of
Lust. Customers seemed few. Tiberius kept cursing about it.
The Sensual Interdict was certainly having its effect; although
it had no genuine authority in our enlightened, utterly liberated
society, it had plenty of moral power as the arbiter of popular
taste.

"Those barJulians are just jealous," he said, "because they
didn't think of it first. They're spoilsports. They already own
half the known universe and they're mad they can't own it *all.*"

Then came the Copucoaster: soaring, whirling, junctions
snapping to and fro so you couldn't ever have the same ride
twice, fifty jumbled klicks of old-fashioned coastertrack. I
was breathless from gravi-wrenchings and oberon-synaesthesia
when we popped off it, but Tiberius seemed unaffected.

"See what you made me lose," he said grimly, catching up
with me on a lower level of the park.

"It's all fake anyway!" I said. "It's no fun!" I stuck my tongue
out at a passing couple as they made out on the back of a
chimerical half-Pegasus, half-beat-up-Chevrolet of the Ancients.
"Don't you have anything but androids and holograms here?
Besides"—I remembered something suddenly—"you told me
you were going to let me pork a porcupine, and you still haven't
shown me what one is! Come on, give this little old recluse
from the Cluster of Austerity some spectacle, you Pope's fallopian
tube, before I perish from boredom—"

"I guess there's nothing I can do until those blasted things
wear off." We found a demat-booth and matted down several
more levels, past the kinky vending machines to which effete
young things were hooked up in various places.

HIGH-CRED HALL, the sign sang to me. So this was where they kept their class ass. We matted into a chamber lined with cloudstuff. The raucous muzak of outside yielded to the quiet strains of ancient easy-listening, classically soothing yet not quite comprehensible to the ear. And on the floatbed, guarded by a bevy of comsim cupids, lay a person.

Nude, and quite extraordinary. For several dozen sex organs of every type (including many that were new to me) bristled and yawned all over the creature's body. It was genegeneering reduced to absurdity. The face—it was a woman's—was beautiful, though. Cold. Uninterested. A turquoise Afro with matched eyes and lips, the eyebrows arched and pointed like perfect wave-crests.

A number of clients were already on the bed, taking advantage of some of the cornucopious genitalia.

"Like her?"

"Her?"

"Yah. You can see why they're called porcupines though, can't you? This one cost me a gigacred or two, I'll tell you! I picked her up from the Center of Sin itself."

"No. She's an *Earthie?*" I got the picture. On Earth people are so deprived they can be bribed into depravement for a song. I shuddered.

"Her name's Ruth-Amyl Acetate. She's from Greater Calcutta. Well, shall we dive in?" He dissolved his clothes and leaped onto the bed.

At that moment she looked at me. For some reason I didn't feel so elated anymore. I'd left my nice azroid as a favor to an old friend, and all I'd seen was exploitation and nastiness. There was nothing here to make me want to stay in the big bad outside world.

"Ruth-Amyl," I said softly.

At that moment the drug wore off completely, and I fell head over heels in love with her.

"What the hell's with you?" Tiberius was shouting from the mound of bodies. "Can't get it up after all those years of copoutism?"

"She's...she's beautiful! You don't deserve her, any of you!" I said, angrily hurling my surfboard at the orgiasts. One of them toppled from the bed. Tiberius got up. "Kestrel, that was a customer, damn it! A *paying* one at that!" And Ruth-Amyl looked at me, long and hard. I wanted to protect her, I wanted her all to myself; I wanted—

"Come with me!" I pulled her off the bed.

"Party-pooper!" she murmured languidly. "Private session'll cost you triple, you know."

"Damn you, I love you." I kissed her hungrily, pushing several sets of genitalia out of the way.

"Wait a minute." She caught her breath. "This is for real, isn't it?"

"Yes! Come home with me to the Cluster of Austerity, be mine forever!" I said, just like on the soap-feelies.

"Please," she said. "So many people have lied to me. I was tricked into coming here with empty promises. I've prayed for you to come for so long. On Earth they surf the ocean waves, and their tanned bodies taste of salt, in my dreams they come to me...don't vanish into thin air, don't be another daydream—"

"Oh, Ruth-Amyl..." I never wanted to leave her. When she smiled, her turquoise eyebrows crinkled and she dimpled prettily.

But Tiberius was prying us apart. "You really do *everything* you can to mess up my life, don't you?" he said. "First you walk all over the faces of high society and now you go around disturbing my customers! And it's just a side effect from one of those untested drugs Juliana Julienne's always throwing at people to see them squirm!"

Ruth-Amyl slapped my face. "You liar! You're just a goddamn zonkie's what you are! And you had me fooled—"

"But I *do* love you!" Pope's boobs, it *had* to be true. At first, it might have been the drug, but now that she'd talked to me...I'd seen through to the suffering within her. She'd transmuted that pain into beauty, into loveliness that transcended the tawdry disfigurement that her profession had forced upon her. "I do, I do!"

"Get out of my life!" Tiberius and Ruth-Amyl both yelled at the same time.

"Who the hell asked you to come to my azroid dressed as Santa Claus?"

Just then, when love, fear, compassion and anger were all bursting inside me, an ear-splitting scream sounded and all the muzak fizzlepopped into silence.

The three of us froze, listening.

Some kind of crowd mad scene was going on outside.

"Quick," said Tiberius. We ran for the demat-booth.

We were on a balcony, about three quarters of the way down Copuland, looking down. An ominous sound—sploshing, burbling, like the water-muzak of a holosurf—was coming from below. And we could see little people on the lower levels, running around like ants, shrieking their heads off as they streamed into demat-booths.

"We'd better go down lower," I said. Back to the booth—

Then, near the lowest level, we saw:

The bottommost level of Copuland was flooded. And the level was slowly rising. Demat-booths bottlenecked and backfired as people jammed in, screeching the codes for higher levels. The pool of water was churning, seething. And then—

One of the ejected people was hurled smack into the pool of water, and as we watched, horrified, he floundered around, terrified of the unpredictable mass of genuine, natural water, and—

A huge gray triangle rose from the water. It made straight for him. He thrashed wildly, and then he was pulled under and then clouds of bright red were whirlpooling in the water, and the fin-thing was circling, circling...

A renewed exodus into the booths, but now the spectacle had awed them. They went in single file, their eyes never leaving the pool with the hungry shark.

"Amazing," I whispered. "So lifelike…in a way, you know Tiberius, you *are* a genius. Now if the League of Sensual Standards had seen *that*—love and death, Tiberius! The mystery of life itself!"

"I don't know what the hell you're talking about," he said. "I had nothing to do with that; and look, the water's still rising."

"You mean—"

"Yah. That thing in the water might not be an android." He was shaking. "Comsims! Come to attention, damn it, I want an explanation *now!*"

With a little *ping!* one of those little pink men materialized in front of our noses.

"Link up with Mallworld Centralcomp," said Tiberius. "I want to know what's going on."

"Hee! You're really in the swim now!" the comsim giggled. "Six-months—maybe a year, before we kiss this Mallworld good-bye!"

"What?" The comsim came and whispered in Tiberius's ear. I strained (still clutching Ruth-Amyl, who was standing around fretting) but couldn't hear. Then Tiberius gave the comsim some orders and it buzzed away.

"Well?"

"Well what?" Tiberius said. "Just think of it! Me, the shiftless, the one they bounced into a used kid lot! And look at me now. Apparently I'm about to be responsible for the end of the world."

"Come on, Tiberius!" I said.

"It really is that bad," he said as we made for the demat-booth. "You remember my shipment of demat-booths, the ones that fell into the ocean back on Earth?"

I nodded.

"Well…" He jerked his thumb at the incipient flood.

"No."

"Yes."

"The Pacific Ocean is slowly—"

"Emptying into Mallworld."

"But the booths were locked! They can only be activated by subvocalized commands! No one was near them, right?"

"That shark..."

"Preposterous!"

"Well, no. Whatever primitive thoughts were running through the creature's head—probably something like *food food food*—the booth, scanning the water for subvoke patterns, translated it as Mallworld level RR5 sublevel 0. And our end of it is under all that water, with that thing circling hungrily in between us. And that thing's still broadcasting *food food food* or whatever. It'll be months before Mallworld fills completely with water, but...I'm ruined! And so's every insurance company in the known universe!"

"What are you going to do?" Ruth-Amyl asked.

"Sign a contract with The Way Out Corp."

Suddenly I caught a familiar greed-glint in his eye. "That's it!" he said. "Ha, ha, ha! Sign a contract with them. They've never seen anything like...comsims ho! Business to transact! Contracts to thumb!"

"Hey! What's up? Don't you want to try and stop the flooding?"

"Of course not! At least, not yet! When the time comes, we'll figure out something. Meanwhile this accident has played right into my hands. It's the royal road to respectability. Thank god for primitive earthie animals! I'm in business again!" And he zipped into the booth and was gone.

"You're crazy!" I called after him.

And then I was alone with her. What had I ever done without Ruth-Amyl? No wonder I'd needed to cop out. As we stood on the overlook, with the water surging beneath and the shark fin slithering in the waves, witnesses to the beginning of the end of Mallworld, a burning urgency overcame me. I took her in my arms and crushed her hard to me.

"I love you," I said fervently.

"I think I believe you."

"I have a place," I said.

"What's your name?" she said.

Well, I'd come in Tiberius's toyochev, and she didn't have one, so we were stranded in Mallworld. So we just bummed around for a few hours, absorbed in each other, happy as clams. I'd never been to Mallworld, of course; and it seemed that *she'd* never seen anything but the inside of that room in Copuland since getting shipped from Earth.

We flitted through a level of body shops; she insisted on going into one and having all those working organs peeled off. "Don't you have a contract?" I said.

"Screw that! I'm happy now. I'm yours and I want to make sure of it. I'll talk my way out of it later, somehow. Besides, Tiberius barJulian-Sinistre is unlikely to come chasing after me from his cell in the credit clink." She was stunningly beautiful now. She had a classical somatype, perhaps a Storkways genegeneering blueprint the Earthies had pirated and added their own subtle spices to. She dissolved the static hair-controller that had held her Afro in place; now when she shook her head her hair, cerulean strands cool as spring water, shivered over her breasts. She was herself now; she wasn't some brothel-designer's creation. With a shock, I realized that the oberon-effect must have worn off, and that in my moment of madness I had discovered true love.

We made love in the comsim safari park. In the earthscape gardens. In a room in a sleazy mobile hotel which, in the shape of a huge winged serpent, tunneled through the crazi-gravi corridors of the department store level.

We slept.

When we woke up I said, "That rift in the transmat universe. It's still going, isn't it? Mallworld is still doomed, isn't it?"

"Honey, who cares?"

But something was tugging at me, willing me to return to Copuland. Perhaps my curiosity over what Tiberius had meant with his talk of the accident playing into his hands. Perhaps some deep fascination with depravity.

I wanted to return and see what was going on; there was nothing much else to do, so, my trusty surfboard in hand, I thumbed the motel's creditcomp and we matted out.

We popped in about midway down the cone of Copuland. The water had risen quite a bit overnight. But where Copuland had been all but deserted yesterday—

People were everywhere. Jamming the tiers, jostling, jabbering. We saw the center of the commotion, about three more levels down, and matted toward it.

DEATH! THE FINAL FRONTIER!
(a voice was announcing.)
YOU'LL NEVER FORGET THE SPECTACLE
OF THE LAST DAYS—
A COPRODUCTION OF COPULAND INC.
AND THE WAY OUT CORPORATION!
ASTOUNDING!
THRILLING!
MEANINGFUL!

Beaming, expansive, Tiberius barJulian-Sinistre pulled us out of the throng and showed us places in his private parapet.

"What the hell?" I shouted above the roar.

I looked below. The water was agitated now; it was caught in the cross-currents of Mallworld's many gravi-generators, so that waves veered up in white peaks and whorls of froth funneled up, vanished, reappeared. And through it all swam the silver-gray triangle, slicing the crests and streaking the water white. Now and then I could see more of him, lunging up from the foam like an ancient submarine. It was elemental. Powerful. Frightening. It had an art to it. No wonder the crowds had come…when I looked at them I recognized the banners of the Azroid Belt Eschatological Society, the Sun Myung Quetzalcoatl death-cultists, many other members of the Doom and Gloom Federation.

THE ULTIMATE DEATH EXPERIENCE
CAN BE YOURS
(the announcer blared forth)
FOR MINICREDS A DAY!
OR PAY A SMALL FEE JUST TO WATCH!
YES, HUMANS AND NONHUMANS,
HERE'S YOUR CHANCE
TO GO WITH THE END OF MALLWORLD…
TO HAVE A CLOSE ENCOUNTER
OF THE FINAL KIND…

"You're not going to try and turn it off?"

"What?" said Tiberius. "Oh, whatever for? In a few months this place'll become uninhabitable, we'll all collect the insurance and build a new Mallworld, and meanwhile I've cashed in on a one-of-a-kind experience…besides, there's nothing else to do."

"Isn't there some kind of central comp-controller for demat-booths?"

"Sure, but the shark's unreasoning brain patterns have overridden that. Computers must bow to people, and for all it knows, that *is* a person down there. Are *you* going to go down and tell our friend to think about something else?"

"No, but—"

"Shut up, then."

As he pointed, an enormous metal cage was being lowered from pulleys that had been rigged up on one of the loops of the Copucoaster. And there were humans inside. They must have paid good money to be devoured alive by a monster of the deep…

The crowd was cheering now, no longer individuals but windgusts of a mindless thunderstorm. I was chilled; fascinated, too.

Tiberius pulled out a diaphanous purple kerchief from his Santa Claus costume. With an imperious gesture he dropped it over the shark-pool, over which the cage hovered. The men and women in it, really hamming it up now, contorted themselves into artistic poses. The cage floor dropped.

The suiciders plummeted. One of them screamed, a sharp sound shattering the sudden hush. The shark zeroed in on her, a killing machine, jaws gaping. Arms and legs flew. And another animal roar burst unbidden from the audience.

"It's a success!" Tiberius said with a smirk.

"It's lovely, but what about the future of Mallworld?"

"Here today, gone tomorrow. Transience, karma, truth, the wheel of fortune. Surely you, a disciple of copoutism, see the beauty of this."

Although he had misquoted the theory of copoutism, I had to admit that this thing was a stunner. I was speechless. Ruth-Amyl moved closer to me. There were tears in her eyes.

"I thought," she whispered, "that no other world could be more barbarous than Earth. The dirtland. The mother planet that you spacies dump on. But now..."

I wanted to hide. I was ashamed of being human. No wonder the Selespridar had come. No wonder we had been denied the stars. We must truly be a fallen race.

Just then I heard another, half-familiar voice, soft and seductive, and clouds of incense billowed around us. "Kestrel, oh, Kestrel—"

It was Juliana Julienne! And when I gaped in astonishment she aimed a ruby crystal at my open mouth. I gulped. It stuck in my throat and I had to swallow it.

"I didn't get you last time," she said, sighing, "but I will now...my scientists have been working on the oberon, honing its effects. This is the new time-release formula—"

It hit me all at once. A few seconds of crazy synaesthesia, of kaleidoscoping emotions, and then I was passionately in love with Juliana.

"Oh, Juliana—" I cried, elbowing Ruth-Amyl out of the way in my haste to embrace my new beloved.

"God damn you!" Ruth-Amyl shrieked. "You filthy rich are all alike! You turn a poor girl's head, fill her with promises that you break in a few hours...I was right. You people *are* more barbaric than the dirty earthies! I'm going to—I'm going to—" She ran off, weeping, into the crowd.

"Never mind her," I said. "My place or yours?"

"Tiberius!" she said.

"Yah, Sis?"

She didn't get annoyed at him for calling her that. I could see that a complex round of barJulian family politics was about to be played.

"Tiberie-dearie," she said sweetly, "the League of Sensual Standards is prepared to reconsider its rating of your theme brothel, in view of the recent developments—"

"Ha! You should never have bought out Universal Insurance. And what's more, Clement should never have disowned me."

"That's all under the bridge, eh? I'm sure it can be brought up again at the next family board meeting."

"None of your stick-and-carrot promises!" Tiberius said. "I happen to have the upper hand, and—"

"No, you don't," she said, putting her arm around me. "You see, you've gotten us into this mess, but you haven't the slightest idea how to pull us out! I've known you since you were a baby, kid."

"Of course I can get us out!" Tiberius said, but he looked uncomfortable.

"Oh, baby brother," she said, *"I* have a plan. To save us all face, *and* to avert the End of Mallworld in a way that people will talk about all year."

"Crap! Something your bloody pet scientists have come up with, I suppose."

She pulled another pill out of her hair. "As a matter of fact..." She held it up. It was black, faceted, like a polished onyx. "No, it's not a drug, actually; it's a recalibrated vaculax."

"What!" Tiberius and I cried out at the same time.

"See, we have, in our labs, tissue samples of every known species, systemwide, and some alien ones besides. And *this* is a charcharadon-specific vaculax. It is, in short, sensitive only to the tissue of our friend down there. It will suck the shark right into the black hole at its heart and send it swimming into the next world. And may the Pope have mercy on its soul," she added piously.

"And if I arrange for a couple of clunkers to dive down there and pop the death-pill in its mouth," Tiberius said, "you'll revoke the Interdict and reinstate my family name?"

"W-e-e-e-ll...that's where your beautiful surfer friend comes in." I started to feel distinctly uncomfortable. The love effect was wearing off a little, and in any case I was learning to distinguish it from the real thing. I wondered where Ruth-Amyl had gotten to.

"You see, my two dears," she said, "we must put a little *art* into it. Imagine, if you will..." She closed her eyes, and I saw that she was reliving some private fantasy. "I have this vision. Imagine a surfer. No, not one of those namby-pamby ones of today, with their holo-imagistic sea, their gravi-waves, their space-tethers. I mean someone half-savage; nature in all its rawness and primitive splendor clings to him. He is beautiful, though, nothing like a caveman, but comely as the latest Storkways classic." And she looked at me. An almost evil look. As if she were clothing me with her eyes. I dropped my surfboard, restoring propriety by uncovering myself completely.

"Anyway," she said, "that's the price. I want *him* to do it."

Tiberius looked at me, pleading. "Kessie old friend—"

"No! That's *real water* down there! Not to mention a shark." But to be frank I was more afraid of the vast pool of genuine, *wet* water. "Ruth-Amyl was right!" I said. "You're all despicable! I'm going back to the Cluster of Austerity. I'll never come back. You've all used me—in the name of friendship, of love—when you don't know what any of those words mean!" So saying I started to push my way through toward the demat-booth.

I stopped for a moment because the announcer was booming on again.

FRIENDS AND MALLWORLDERS!
ANOTHER BAND OF
AESTHETICALLY INCLINED SUICIDERS
HAS JUST SIGNED UP FOR THE WAY OUT!
THE SPECTACLE WILL COMMENCE
IN TWO MINUTES,
BROUGHT TO YOU BY COPULAND
AND THE WAY OUT CORP.,
AND THIS TIME THE STARS ARE:
AMANDA CARRADINE!
DAMIEN KALAMAZOO!
MAYHUVIA C. BIRD! AND
RUTH...AMYL...ACETATE!

"Ruth! Ruth!" I cried as the whole crowd surged forward and I twisted around to see her standing stolidly in the cage—

I marched back onto Tiberius's parapet. I grabbed Juliana roughly and shook the crystal from her hand.

"You win, you vultures," I said, clasping my surfboard to my side, clutching the deathcrystal.

"Wait! You're not supposed to risk your life, I've planned a convoy of—" Juliana Julienne began.

But I was racing for the demat-booth, the cage of my beloved was descending slowly into the jaws of doom, and the announcer was already announcing my name and calling it the greatest stunt of the century.

When they saw me mat out onto the lowest undrowned balcony, already knee-deep, their chattering fell still. I looked up. There were layers and layers of onlookers, as far as I could see; at the very top they seemed no more than dots and splashes of color. And in the far height, suspended from the silvery sky that was a skin of Mallworld, I saw the serpent-Copucoaster, shifting, pulsing, twining, amazingly still functioning, and the tiny cage suspended, slowly coming down at me..."Ruth-Amyl!" I shouted, although I knew she couldn't hear me. The audience in the lowest tiers caught my cry and repeated it, until the walls resounded with her name.

Where was the shark? I knew I couldn't just throw the crystal at it and hope. I might miss. If it slipped off him I'd accomplish nothing. I had to bait it. And it would only be minutes before the trapdoor overhead opened and Ruth fell to her death, so I only had one chance.

Thrashing around attracts them, I thought.

The gravi-tides swept through the water, whipping up waves, huge ones. The water must already be a semiklick deep in the middle. Thirty-meter monsters, damn it! I reminded myself that the water was *real,* that this wasn't *really* surfing, it was some deadly game and I was a pawn in it, a hapless victim of the barJulians' family feudings.

But...

I felt the unaccustomed liquid lapping my legs. It was strange but not unpleasant. I threw down my board and swam out on it, relying on my instincts to adjust to the ubiquitous wetness. I'd go out maybe fifty meters, then I'd start paddling wildly and calling attention to myself, and then—

The water was warm, naturally warm; it had just left the sunlight. As I left the balcony behind, the crowd murmured.

Here came a wave! I sprang up, soared up, soared high, flinging up my arms. It was a singing, drunken feeling. It was different from actual surfing; it had a realness to it, a danger. I could actually drown. I began alternately riding the crests and beating about in the water, clenching the altered mini-vaculax tightly in my fist. And then I saw him.

Coming straight toward me.

I stood up. The shark came at me in an arrow-straight line, and its jaws were open and its teeth, hundreds of them, glittering, I was thinking, *This creature must be ten meters long,* and I steadied my aim and got ready to throw—

"No!" A shrill screech. I started, slipped for a moment, barely caught the edge of the surfboard. An enormous wave swept over me and I didn't realize I had to hold my breath. I spluttered horribly. The shark had been deflected for a moment, but when I looked up I saw the cage, getting nearer, nearer—

"Don't do it! Go back!" she was yelling hysterically.

"I love you!" I shouted.

"So do I! But it's too late!"

The shark circled, waiting—

And butted the surfboard! I tumbled, gave into the curve of a cresting wave. Suddenly I heard a *crack!* and I saw four people plunging into the water and I was kneeling on the surfboard and the hideous jaws were gaping wide, wide, and I was losing hold of the crystal and—

Pain exploded in my arm! I stared in disbelief at the stump of my arm and the blood coiling into the water and—

The shark, in midair, was deflating like a balloon as the vaculax sucked it into another universe. I could see that all the nonshark tissue wasn't being absorbed, that half my arm was floating in the water along with the half-eaten corpses of Way Out clients, that repairmen were already diving into the water to get at the demat-mechanism. The pain throbbed and throbbed, and I passed out as the standing ovation began to shatter my eardrums...

Well, whatever my motives, I *had* prevented the End of the World. Though I had begun the week an avowed copoutist, by the end of it I had become the savior of the very things I had stood staunchly against for so long. I supposed I would have to live with it.

Anyhow...when I recovered and got my arm back, the barJulians made such a big spectacle of it—triumphant parades in Mallworld, holovee specials, endorsements by the presidents of multiplanetary corporations—that I could hardly run away and hide again. Privacy was a lost ideal. I decided to marry Ruth-Amyl and make the best of it.

The barJulians made a spectacle even of *that*. The pauper-to-princess aspect of Ruth's life was played up in all the media. The operation to become a porcupine became preposterously fashionable, even though Ruth-Amyl wasn't one anymore.

And the wedding they gave us! The Pope herself blessed us and performed the ceremonial defloration of the bride and groom, and then we led half the in-crowd of the Solar System in a two-week-long holovised ritual orgy, while children dressed as cupids on puffy plasticlouds hosed us down with aphrodisiacs. It was a wedding to remember. Juliana barJulian, far from being jealous, fell in love with her brother; they went off to Earth to hatch some incredible fortune-making scheme that combined the concepts of Copuland, Suicide Parlors, Surfing, and Horticulture. Or something. And then there was the reception...

"I can't stand it!" I said, escaping with her into the Brobdingnag Suite at the Gaza Plaza. We stopped under the shade of a monster mushroom.

We had about a minute of privacy before the crowds found us again. Milton Huang, an obnoxious interviewer from the Holothrills-National Enquirer Syndicate, cornered us right into the rubbery brown stalk while his camera hovered in our noses.

"Let's have a few words, Savior of Mallworld! Handsome surfer-prince and Cinderella-princess! So where will you spend your honeymoon?"

"Earth," said Ruth-Amyl. "I'm going to buy my parents a nice estate or something; though they probably won't want to come out into space."

"And besides," I added, "I've acquired a taste for surfing. In the ocean."

Huang grimaced. "Now that you're rich and famous, are you going to live happily ever after?"

For a moment I longed for the old azroid. The week-long silences. The peace. I clasped Ruth-Amyl's hand. Would we live happily ever after?

I cleared my throat. All of a sudden everyone was silent. Ah yes, the conquering hero must have a few words, and they must be profound...

"Life," I began portentously, laughing inside as I saw them all strain forward to catch each pearl of wisdom as it fell from my lips, "life, and therefore Mallworld itself, which is after all a veritable microcosm of life, of the human condition...is like a soap opera. There'll always be another episode."

Just you wait.

Well, yes, indeed, O multi-tiered one. That was a salutary tale, was it not? Did you not feel the ug'unniethetic *stirrings deep within your perforated soles, when the fate of the entire Mallworld was at stake? Primitive, was it not? Primal, was it not?*

But you only want to know more about the ceremonial papal defloration? You want to know every detail? You want to know whether infibulation is practiced on the genital organs of—

Yes, Excellency, I'll shut up now.

Perhaps you'd like to get into the mind of Mallworld's spiritual leaders? At least then you will be divorced from all this carnal nonsense....

What, your multi-n'huatitude? Only if there's sex? Well, I think you can see from this holoprojection that the Pope of Mallworld is one of the most sexually attractive creatures of their species....

AUCTION NOTICE
EXTRAORDINARY ARTIFACT

To be offered at the St. Indiana Jones memorial annual antiquities auction, held on level ZZ-15.

A BOOK

What, you may ask, is a book? It is an ancient type of data storage and retrieval device in which the information seeker scans certain squiggles and marks optically, compares them to a brain-dumped data base to elicit individual words, and then pieces them together by means of an arcane left-brain signal manipulation to produce strings of words which then become coherent sub vocalized utterances.

The art of "reading" is a mystery now, known only to the very educated or the very obsessed. But experts tell us that this particular book is more than just a rather ineffective doorstop. It has magical predictive powers.

Dated 1984 A.D. (a date which our computers have variously identified as being one, two, three, or four millennia ago) this book appears to predict the existence of Mallworld itself, the barJulian family, and even the more well known space colonies such as Babylon-5 and Godzone. It appears to mention various people of our time by name. It even has a semi-nude picture of the Pope, done in a strange two-dimensional style of portraiture.

This is the perfect ritual object for your home, the perfect collectible for those who love the sublime mysteries of the past.

It's also the perfect combustible to bring to the next Fahrenheit 451 Theme Party!

No Reserve.

Bidding begins at one megacred.

A Mall and the Gneiss Visitors

Christmas comes but twice a year in Mallworld, but when you're the Pope, you can't really compartmentalize.

Everybody wants something. It's particularly true in Mallworld, of course—Mallworld the ultimate Mecca, Nirvana, and Holy Grail—the thirty-kilometer-long Cigar of Plenty that hangs out there, between the Belt and Jupiter, beckoning to the well-heeled of a hundred worlds, azroids, pseudo-planets and trailer parks, the one place where all dreams can still come true—at a price.

As my predecessor, Pope Moesha-Magdalene III, once said, "Religion is the opiate of the masses." That's according to one of the surviving texts; another says, "Derision is the onus of molasses." Take your pick. The variants are all written down in the papal archives, but then again, reading is a lost art.

Around Christmas, we get our share of pilgrims. Most just want a holy grail or fragment of the true cross; we send those down to the Sistine Chapel Souvenir Kiosk on Level X-99. Some want toys; we always have several Santas on duty, with a choice of Claus or Barbara. Some want to be priests—we offer several payment plans, including the celibacy option. But the papacy has been well-organized for a thousand years—even more so since our hostile takeover of Hinduism and our corporate merger with Shinto. Most pilgrims are processed by the bureaucracy...difficult cases sometimes get an audience with one of my computer simulacra. I don't usually deal with anyone personally...except, of course for the aliens.

The solar system has been walled off just beyond the orbit of Saturn by our extraterrestrial babysitters, the Selespridar, until such time as our primitive little old selves attain the requisite maturity to join the true community of worlds. As a result, aliens come here...but we can't go there. Any alien, therefore, is a VIP...even if he's just a rock.

"Schist, to be precise," said Cardinal Klang, my personal assistant, his voice set to maximum reverb. "The Petromorphs are the most hierarchical of the silicon-based life-forms. The sedimentary rocks are the drones and servant class; the igneous are the warriors—but the metamorphics are the ruling class, with gneiss and schist at the very top of the class structure. It makes sense to them; it takes millions of years to squeeze granite into schist, and—presumably in all that time a sentient rock may acquire the wisdom of the ages."

The cardinal fluttered over to my other side, proffering a cup of tea. He had recently received a ROM-refill from the Selespridon data banks, so he was very anxious to show off his knowledge.

Still, the creature that sat on the faux Louis XV chair in my audience chamber, under the watchful eye of the synthjade statue of St. Buddha, hardly seemed like a repository of million-year wisdom. He appeared, to all intents and purposes, like a large boulder. A dozen caterpillar-like creatures were attached to his hindquarters; they were symbiotically linked to him, and provided his means of locomotion. Two large lichens functioned as eyes, and he spoke by means of another symbiotically attached creature, a birdlike being rooted to his head. His name, at least, the name he was taking for the purpose of this interview, was Pious Boulder.

Two attendants—burly blocks of marble with golden caterpillar feet and sparrowhawks riveted to their heads—stood guard.

"Tea, Mr. Ambassador?" I said.

"Your holiness is too kind," the rock squawked. Cardinal Klang brought him a cup. The bird drank. "Perhaps—if I might be so bold—some hot chocolate for my feet. They can't get enough of this delicacy!"

"So...you're on a pilgrimage," I said.

"Yes, I am," said the schist, "but first, I'd like to say that things aren't quite what we expected."

"Oh?"

"Well...we were told that your system is extremely primitive...that you're still in the tribal stage, guzzling gas and shrinking heads...but our information seems to be a little out of date. And the thing is, you're a woman. And you're... naked."

I glanced down at my enhanced mammalia. The areolas had been circled in crimson, to represent the passion of our lord—the blood of suffering and sexuality. My pudenda were coyly covered with a communion wafer, symbolizing the noble truth that life issues from the womb, and that the bread of life is the gateway to eternity. It's all ancient, archetypal stuff, unchanged in a few hundred years. My job is really mostly a ceremonial one, and I suppose I might just as well be a robot, but everyone knows that the Pope's supposed to be a woman. "I am the Great Mother," I said. "You can't expect them to hire a man for the job." Why did that come out sounding so self-conscious? "Nudity," I added primly, "is purity. You can't expect the supreme vicar of the divine to go prancing around in a lewd, all-concealing potato sack."

"Well...the information that came to us has a patriarchal pontiff ruling over the spiritual needs of a people inhabiting a single planet, worshipping a single god," said the rock. "Yet I see several gods on display in this very room." Pious Boulder looked about my office...or rather, his eyes crept slowly around his face, taking in the data.

"Now that," I said, "is ancient history, very ancient history. Religion has gone through a few corporate mergers since then. Where have you people been in the last, oh, two or three thousand years?"

"Why," said the petromorph, "we've been on our way to see you, of course. We're looking for long-lost relative."

A slot opened in the boulder's side, and a two-dimensional hologram (if you can imagine so primitive an object) came sliding out. The cardinal plucked it out with a metallic hand and gave it to me. It had a greasy feel to it, and I realized that the photo had been imprinted on a paper-thin organism whose flat eye stared dolefully up at me...doubtless yet another symbiote.

"This is," said Pious Boulder, "my noble ancestor, Nickel-Iron Prime, lost to us many cycles of *n'huat* ago. I have been searching for him for virtually my entire existence. I have gone from world to world, from star system to star system...the recovery of my ancestor, and his return would trigger a renaissance among my people. We looked for aliens such as yourselves, with legends of a great stone that fell from the sky. So far, this is the most convincing."

The picture showed a massive crowd of people—hundreds of thousands, perhaps—thronging in a city square. At the center was a huge, rectangular black stone. It didn't ring a bell. But one thing was obvious. Teeming masses are not a fixture of human habitation, except in one place—Earth. The Old Country. The biggest slum in the solar system.

The other shocking thing was this—they were all fully clothed. From head to toe. Everything that ought, in chaste modesty, to be revealed, was lasciviously hidden behind robes—not even decent form-fitting ones, but billowing ones that would allow the most decorous somatype to appear libidinous to the filthy-minded.

Well—anything was possible. It was Earth. They are long on tradition in the slums—they have nothing else to cling to but the past.

I shrugged and handed the image to Klang. "Your analysis?" I asked him.

"Computing," he said, and a second later, went on, "this is an image of the ancient city of Mecca. The black stone is the ka'aba, said to have fallen from heaven...and the most sacred object in Islam."

"Islam," I said. "Islam, Islam, Islam...do we own that?"

"Apparently not, Your Holiness."

"Why not?"

"Oh, who knows? It's Earth...the Old Ways...quaint ancient stuff...you know how it is. We've managed to buy up most of the big religions, but this one held out. Their leader, Ayatollah Kurzweil, doesn't want the grand faith of the ancients held hostage to commercialism."

"You mean, they don't run their religion for profit?"

The robot shifted uncomfortably. "No, in fact, they consider us to be...what they euphemistically refer to as 'The Great Satan.'"

"Well, that's peculiar. Life on the reservation."

The robot chuckled—what a yes-man!—and the rock looked grim.

"I don't suppose they'll give up the stone, then. I mean, we can easily afford it...the church is almost as rich as the barJulians. Will they sell?"

"Not easily, Your Holiness," said the robot. "And as you know, we don't interfere with native affairs—those mud-eaters take cultural pollution very seriously."

This was a serious ecclesiastical crisis. These rocks had something we humans do not have—the Selespridar, guardians of the galaxy, considered them to be a real species, allowed to roam among the stars at will—while we, the subsentient, were still imprisoned within this pocket universe until such time as the human race matured enough to take its place among all those other beings. These rocks had come to Mallworld with the blessing of the Selespridar—giving them what they wanted, however peculiar, would surely lessen the human race's time in purgatory. And if the ka'aba was indeed, a living thing, it clearly was a violation of galactic law to hold it against its will, even if it was being worshipped.

In my twenty years as Pope, this was my first real challenge. A number of major moral issues were at stake. For the first time since things settled into the papal routine, I wasn't bored. I was even intrigued. This was better than hell night in Babylon-5.

Fat, gelatinous tears rolled down Pious Boulder's cheeks. I wondered what hidden symbiote was weeping. "Looking at that image is distressing to me," he said. "When I consider Nickel-Iron Prime, sitting in that square with those awful creatures—no offense—without a single symbiotic appendage, so that he can neither move, nor see, nor hear—three thousand years of the most appalling solitude—Your Holiness, you must help us. This is the last *n'huat* our ancestor can possibly survive without undergoing *uz'draftsi*."

"What's he talking about?" I asked the cardinal.

"Sex," he said. "The sacred stone has become somewhat...ah, frustrated over the last few millennia. So I gather. Without *uz'draftsi* every few thousand years, their life force drains away. They become...well, plain old rocks."

"And I have Nickel-Iron's bride with me," said Pious Boulder. "The most delicate-skinned marble you have ever seen—she is of the highest caste. What a fine coupling it will be! Mountains will crumble to dust in its wake. Trees will spontaneously combust. When our people mate, Your Holiness, they really mate."

"So let me get this straight," I said, mulling it over. "I'm going to Earth with a couple of rolling rocks in tow, and my mission is to abduct a sacred stone who would have walked away by itself long ago if it hadn't lost its caterpillars."

"Well, that's why we came to you," said the rock. "You are the source of all miracles."

"I am?" I said. It was so strange to see such piety. I mean, I am the Pope and all that, but we don't live in an age of miracles, and my job is less taxing even than that of a corporate CEO...it's almost all ceremonial. Okay, when my grandmother was a kid, every cheerleader wanted to as beautiful as the Pope when she grew up, but now with advanced genegeneering, everyone looks perfect anyway.

I won this job in the lottery. The DNA lottery that is—at the moment of conception.

Still, the very stones were weeping. I felt good about myself for once. I could be the comforter, the healer. I could be the redeemer of their race, the instigator of their golden age. And they weren't even Catholic.

It was with mixed emotions that I sought an audience with Klutharion, governor of the Solar System. He was attending a private clavichrome concert at the Gaza Plaza Hotel—the one inside the Great Pyramid in Mallworld's central level. Klutharion loved humans...was considered a bit off-the-wall by his fellow Selespridar. Of course, babysitting a backwater wasn't exactly a plum assignment in the Selespridon food chain.

It was duelling clavichromes, actually. One player was the famed Julian barJulian; the other was a comsim. They were flying around the interior of the pyramid on little Levitol-driven clouds, spewing their synaesthetic symphonies into the air.

Klutharion was ensconced in a chair float, surrounded by sycophants. I tried to follow him, but he was whirling around so rapidly I had to pop three Levitol to reach his level. The crazi-gravi field was set to alternate between areas of free fall and areas of high-gee...so my stomach got churned a few times before I reached him. Nevertheless, he seemed pretty pleased to see me, and gave me a quick peck on the pectoral area.

"Love your sexy nipples," said the ruler of the Solar System.

"Show some respect," I said, "I'm the Pope."

Indeed, many members of the audience were pausing to genuflect in mid-air. In fact, Julian broke off his playing and segued into a rousing rendition of Hail to the Chief, complete with stock holo-dioramas of crucifixions, nativities, and the cosmic dance of Shiva.

It's hard to keep one's cool with the Selespridar. It's the pheromones...for some reason, the chemicals they unleash upon our hapless nostrils happen to be the ones that cause homo *sapiens* sapiens to lurch into erotic frenzy. But I tried to control myself. With the crazi-gravi fields on, I didn't want to baptize some suppliant with a lubricious spray. "Listen, O Three-tired Selespridon," I said, "I need the benefit of your advice—seeing as you're a higher evolved being and all that."

"Gnarly," said Klutharion.

"Huh?"

"Oh…well like, I'm into ancient earth dialects this week. Totally awesome! Keeps me from dying of boredom among you simple souls."

"Get a grip on yourself, Klutharion. Your silicon-based friends have faced me with a profound moral dilemma." I explained the whole thing to him.

"Tough," said the Selespridon. "It's either destroy an ancient civilization—or piss off a pile of rubble. I don't envy you."

"Yeah, but what am I supposed to do?"

"One of the advantages," said Klutharion, "of being in a quasi-parental status to an entire species…is that occasionally one can say…'You're on your own.'"

"What a copout," I said.

"You can talk," he said. "You head up a religion, don't you?"

"I am a figurehead," I said, "in a vast, multiplanetary conglomerate that bears the same relationship to a religion as Mallworld has to a Neolithic lemonade stand. Religion's only one of our many departments, and in any case, I'm a symbol, not a leader—I'm a hereditary, superbly endowed Mother Goddess, grown from a sacred egg in a thrice-blessed holy incubator at Storkways Inc., and my job is to float around in the ceiling of the Vatican to induce a sense of catharsis and well being among my flock. And to cut the ribbon at the start of the Mallworld Christmas parade. Which happens to be next week."

"Well, then, my privileged daughter," said Klutharion, as the clavichromes began pouring waves of dense music and images into the cavernous darkness within the pyramid, "you're about to have a Big Epiphany…which is what all quests are ultimately about. You are going to know what it's like to be a Selespridon."

"Enlighten me—I was genegeneered for looks, not intelligence."

"You're about to know how Mallworld feels when it runs into your Neolithic lemonade stand, Your Holiness," said Klutharion.

"I think I get it," I said.

It isn't really possible for us humans to comprehend just how vast and unknowable the universe really is. The Selespridar have been there...well, further there than any human being...and yet they have the infinite patience to babysit our fledgling universe for us. Klutharion was telling me that, grand though the Selespridar were, they came from such as us; that a civilization like ours once gave birth to theirs. And I was about to experience the same thing in miniature. To breathe the air of earth—the primal, pure ancient air of antediluvian smog— was to return to my own roots—to come face to face with first principles—to find myself.

Well, I didn't see it all with such crystalline clarity at that actual moment, but hindsight is a great myth maker.

I sat back on my chairfloat and allowed the synaesthetic strains of the duelling clavichromes to invade my senses. I gave in to it all. After all, where was I going to find decent music on the home planet? How could the mud-eating earthies know the glories of Mallworld's cosmic culture?

And yet...we, with our toyochevs, our suicide parlors, our genegeneering, and our copucoasters had once sprung from such as those.

It was clear that this would be a journey into the dark heart of the human condition.

It only took a second to take the transmat to Luna—the last outpost of civilization before descending down to Darkest Terra—but the trip from Luna to Greater Calcutta seemed to last a lifetime. The vehicle was barely better than a canoe—it took almost a day, and there was actually a rotating star observatory—as though there were any stars to observe in these dark times—and in this observatory—I kid you not—a shelf of books. Actual books, with pages, and with lines and lines of wiggly little black things that once, in Neolithic times, people knew how to interpret.

Crescent Earth loomed ahead in the blackness of space, blue and shiny and well, big. My rocky friends, Pious Boulder and his henchmen, were extending their various sensory symbiotes to get a better look; my robot cardinal assistant was sitting around digesting more data capsules.

To my amazement, there was a wizened old man in a turban in the deck, hovering about in a chairfloat, and he was actually reading—or at the very least, doing a very convincing imitation of reading—I knew what it looked like, I'd seen it on old history tapes.

A number of other people in turbans were sitting around, whispering to each other in bizarre dialects. None met my gaze.

A bell rang. With Pavlovian suddenness, these people unrolled rugs, turned towards earth, and began prostrating themselves, mumbling what sounded like some kind of mantra, though it didn't match anything in the papal repertoire.

"What on Mallworld?" I asked.

"Bhakti," said Cardinal Klang. "Devotion. You are seeing an example of honest-to-goodness religious fervor. Kind of sends chills up one's spine, doesn't it?"

It did. I watched these natives for a long time. They moved their lips, bowed again and again to some unseen deity. And just as abruptly as it had started, it was all over; they rolled up their mats and returned to what they were doing before. For some reason, what I had just witnessed was a little, well, frightening. It was clear that the people of earth, for all their backwardness, were closer to the primal source than we were. They unnerved me.

But I am, after all the Pope—it's my job to be a people person. I decided to strike up a convo with the reading one.

"Excuse me," I said, "what are you reading?"

He didn't answer me.

I turned to the Cardinal. "How rude," I said. "What seems to be the problem?"

"I don't know, Your Holiness," he said, "but if you give me a moment to boot up some of my new data capsules...ah yes, I have it. He can't talk to you because...you're a woman. And you're naked. He's trying to spare you the embarrassment." He extruded a clothing nozzle and sprayed a pair of pajamas on me. "That oughta hold that...but as for your gender..."

"I don't have time for a sex change," I said. "We're due on earth in five minutes...and I still haven't a clue about what to do next."

"Don't worry about genital modification," said the cardinal. "In his culture, only the secondary sex characteristics matter." He pulled a false beard out of his armpit storage slot and slapped it in my face. "Now," he said, "you are truly the Pope."

The observation deck of the little shuttlecraft was instantly transformed. These earthies could see me now. The one who had been reading—as though he had only just heard me ask the question—said, "Oh, nothing, sir. I'm illiterate. But for some reason the tourists always like to believe we can read—mysterious lost arts of the ancients and all that. It adds to the mystique."

"I need a native guide of some kind," I said. "My friends and I are...journeying to..." I pulled out the two-dimensional hologram and waved it at the man.

"I see. You wish to make the Holy Pilgrimage," he said after some thought. "I didn't know there were any members of the faithful out there...it was my understanding that the universe beyond the orbit of Luna was a veritable Babylon of iniquity and perversion."

"Hardly," Cardinal Klang protested. "Do you know who you're talking to? This woman—ah, personage—is the spiritual leader of over fifty billion people, robots, and androids throughout the system. Your sacred places will be blessed a thousand fold by the manifestation of the Papal Presence. Where we come from, there are those who would thumb up a couple of megacreds even to be this close to the holy one."

The old man shrugged. "There is only one god," he said, "the merciful, the compassionate."

What a concept! I thought. How pristine! How primal! If only we could be this basic, this pure, back home!

"Nevertheless—" he continued.

The cardinal and I craned to listen as he dropped his voice. Our rocky friends lumbered closer on their symbiotic pseudopods.

"I can see what you want," he said. "You want to be smuggled into the holy city, at the height of the holy month...to profane the holiest of holiest with your infidel presence! You horrify me!" He seemed to be trying to make sure everyone in the chamber heard him.

"We just want to see our ancestor," said Pious Boulder.

"There are ways," the man said darkly. "It will cost you, of course, but I see that your thumbs are connected to the great credit network in the sky. There will be risks—you could be stoned to death, beheaded, or at the very least flogged to a pulp—but I daresay I can find a way to get you there, or my name isn't Rashid ibn Said ibn Edsell ibn Lollipop ibn Starbuck, the Younger."

I was glad this fellow had a price, after all. I was beginning to think that the earthies were too antiquated to understand such civilized concepts as self-interest, commerce, and bribery. Perhaps we weren't so different, after all. As a professional student of the human condition, I was glad to know that these living fossils of our gas-guzzling, tribal past could be just as venal as normal human beings.

The grandly termed Starport of Greater Calcutta was a rundown place. It was somewhat smaller than one of the thousand food courts of Mallworld, and it didn't have any demat-booths—you went from place to place in a sort of hydraulic chamber operated by a system of pulleys, and in order to know where to get off, you had to recognize the squiggly inscriptions on a bewildering array of buttons.

"The Mecca Express leaves from the third level," said our new guide, "but first we have to go to the souk for some disguises—that's on the twelfth floor." He pushed a button, and this little room began to descend.

"If you can't read," I said, "how do you know which button to press?"

"It's simple enough," he said. "The buttons are in sequential order; if you can count on your fingers, you can usually get where you're going."

More native mysteries! Pious Boulder and his cohorts had remained remarkably silent during the entire journey from Mallworld; I don't think they wanted to admit that they were scared—wouldn't do, what with them being higher beings and all, and under the Selespridar's protection—but the primitiveness of it all was even getting to me, and I'm a lot closer to Earth than a chattering gneiss from the stars.

The souk was a kind of Mallworld in miniature. In a room no bigger than a laseball stadium, hundreds of stalls touted everything from vaseline to vaculaxes. But instead of holograms and comsims, the salespersons were all actual human beings—as the stomach-turning odor of the place made clear. As we made our way through the throng, legless beggars on hover skateboards sailed past, importuning us for alms and promising to tell our fortunes. Tourists were everywhere—the off-earthers stood out by their freshly-sprayed garments and their perfect genegeneering, and they all stood at least a head taller than the natives. Cacophonous music poured from every tent.

There were several aliens slithering about, too, not to mention an honest-to-goodness whale with its retinue of human hangers-on, his mobile environment sailing majestically through the crowd on humongous levi-casters like some ancient juggernaut. With all this spectacle, few noticed a little old pope and a couple of talking rocks. Besides, the heat was too overwhelming for anyone to think much.

"Why can't they turn down that synthsun a couple of

degrees?" I asked the cardinal. At this, Rashid began cackling hideously.

"Oh," I said. "I take it the sun's not synth."

That really got to me. I mean, I was handling the rest of it pretty well, but now it hit me with a force beyond imagination...a lot of this stuff was real. I was actually basking in the unfiltered radiation of a star...the only star in our pocket universe...and I was absolutely at its mercy...and at the mercy of a thousand elemental, carcinogenic forces such as the wind, the humidity, and the pollen. I had heard of people actually living this way. Well, in ancient times, of course. But surely, even on Earth, people didn't actually go outside anymore! I wanted to turn back right then and there and reenter the cocoon of Mallworld.

"Your Holiness will endure far more than this," said Rashid, "before you arrive in the Holy City. There is even a chance— dare I say it—of permanent devivication."

"Death?" I said. "I don't think I've ever met anyone who died. Permanently, I mean." The idea had an almost sexual frisson...it was deliciously dirty. I shuddered.

Since we had unlimited funds—the church declines to place budgetary restraints on alien relations—it was simple to get outfitted for the expedition. I and the Cardinal would be robed from head to toe in white—I had never felt more obscene in my life, with every inch of my body covered, allowing people to think the most provocative thoughts about me—but Rashid informed me that this was simply the custom, and that it would actually render me more inconspicuous.

The rocks would not need to be disguised at all; they would pass for part of the scenery here. So after getting into our bleached potato sacks, and purchasing several camels from a car dealership—thank god the camels were at least automated, though they did guzzle gas!—our caravan was ready for the two-day journey through the desert toward the sacred city.

We also purchased several boxes of special food from a self-styled sacred food vendor. Have I mentioned the eating habits? Because this was some kind of holy month, our eating habits were totally dictated by the risings and settings of that huge, hot star. Many kinds of food were expressly forbidden, but since I had never heard of most of them, it didn't seem to matter that much. For the entire time that the sun-thing was shining, no food was allowed; at "night"—as these traditionalists insisted on calling it—eating became a veritable orgy. We sat out in the chilly desert—there were, of course, no stars—in front of a roaring holobonfire, knocking back platefuls of couscous and lamb substitute like there was no tomorrow. There were dancing girls and an entire orchestra of squawking and twanging instruments, courtesy of a holovision hookup in the main tent, and by midnight even the camels were trying their tonsils out at laser karaoke.

It was still dark when I felt something tickling my feet. It was one of Pious Boulder's symbiotes, a feather-like organism that extruded itself from his face like a sort of tongue. I hadn't had a good orgasm in some weeks, with all the pressures, even though it's my duty as the incarnation of the Great Mother to enjoy my sexuality at every possible moment. Still, I was intrigued that a large rock would have any kind of mammalian urges, and I wanted to know if there was any tenderness beneath his all-too hard exterior. I sat up quickly and subvoked the lamps on, but he doused them with another flick of a pseudopod.

"No need for luminescence," he hissed.

"How romantic!" I said, pleased by his unexpected coyness.

He laughed, a gurgling, gravelly laugh. "I see that Your Holiness thought that my intentions were somewhat…less than honorable. But I assure you that I've undertaken a vow of celibacy until my noble ancestor is recovered…besides, I'm not sure that it would be, ah, physically possible without some tissue damage."

"Pity," I said. As the religious symbol of eternal woman, it would not have been proper for me to refuse him, and the thought of a dollop of pain was not without its titillation.

"Come with me, Your Holiness."

He extended a stony appendage for me to hold on to. I grasped it, and he extruded a pair of rocket-thruster symbiotes. We lifted off as powerful jets of blue hydrogen flame spurted from his nether parts. A ledge slid out for me to sit on. His surface was surprisingly warm; as he burst through the tent-flaps, I huddled against him in the chill, pre-dawn air.

"Where are we going?" I shouted.

"Nowhere," he said. "Please, Your Holiness. You do not yet understand the passion that fuels my quest...I want you to see...your cosmos, your people, the profundity of the sentient condition."

I was about to protest when we rounded a sand dune...and I saw stars.

"Stars—" I whispered. For all around me, there was a sea of blackness, and in that sea were countless millions of pinprick light sources. I knew what the stars looked like—how many times had I dined in the view room at the Galaxy Palace in Mallworld, staring dewy-eyed at the unattainable?

"No," said Pious Boulder. "The lights of the Holy City...in the clear, black night of the desert."

I realized then that I had never seen a city...not really. The azroids are crammed with people, but always there's the vast vacuum of space. When I looked skyward, that same vacuum was still there...that same starless blackness enveloped these people as well as mine. The desert wind began to howl; my ungainly robes flapped against my skin; there was sand in my eyes. I thought of my ancestors, who had dwelled in a place as savage as this, whose nights were lit by atomic fission, who dressed in the skins of animals and hunted dinosaurs with ancient machine-guns...it was magnificent. I began to understand what the Selespridon had meant when he said I would know a little of what it was like to be a Selespridon among humans...to be humbled by the persistence of the past.

And the next day, our caravan made its way into the sacred city...our camels rubbing shoulders with thousands of others, their hood ornaments glinting in the dazzling sun, their hub caps polished and their humps freshly painted. There were even a few biological camels, harumphing and farting as their masters petted and brushed them; they were of course more for show than beasts of burden.

Rashid had gotten us to the Holy City, but he balked at the impiety of trying to help us kidnap the sacred rock; he bade us farewell at the gates, after I thumbed a liberal donation into his creditcomp.

The square was so densely packed that many of the faithful had taken Levitol in order to float above the crowd; they formed a secondary crowd above the first. In the center of the square was the sacred stone. Pilgrims were prostrating themselves. Weird, melismatic incantations filled the air. The spectacle of this many fully clothed human beings was almost too much to bear; I was fully aroused, and I hadn't even taken my pheromone booster tablets that morning.

The plan, such as it was, was simple enough. I, Cardinal Klang, and Pious Boulder would join the congregation of the faithful. There was no transmat nexus in the neighborhood, so we could not simply spirit the sacred rock away; we would have to plant a crazi-gravi modulator on it. Once Nickel-Iron Prime managed to levitate a little, we could get a fix on him from a tractor beam that was being broadcast from Vatican II, my orbiting palace—which hadn't been used much in the last few hundred years, but whose circuits still seemed active.

Then there was the small matter of ascertaining whether the ka'aba was, in fact, the venerable ancestor for whom Pious Boulder had been searching.

The Boulder was disguised as a sort of backpack, wrapped in a hand-hooked rug. Cardinal Klang was carrying him—as a clunker, he was the only one with the strength to bear that ton of stone and symbiotes—and we blended in pretty successfully with the throng. But how were we ever going to get close to the great rock? An inconspicuous heist was out of the question. We were going to have to make a spectacle of ourselves.

Now we were in the thick of things. The worshippers were so thick that they carried us along like a graviton tide. The babble was deafening. It came from around us and above us, and from holoscreens in the sky that projected images of hundred-meter-high Ayatollahs. Twanging music resonated; drums pounded. We were never going to reach the sacred rock!

I looked to my side. Pious Boulder was literally fuming—the rug he was wrapped in had started to smoke. I didn't have to be a xenopsychiatrist to know he was probably pretty stressed out.

"He's becoming igneous," grunted Cardinal Klang. "If he doesn't speak to the great one soon, he may explode. It's a hormonal thing; his species can't really take more than one or two emotional strains per century."

"This is a fine time to be learning about petromorph endocrinology," I said.

Plumes of steam were now spurting out of the rug, and I was trying to put out a little fire with the hem of my potato sack.

"I will perish before completing my quest!" said Pious Boulder. "I can feel my joints cracking open—"

The crowd was pushing and shoving every which way. The sun bore down on us. My robes were drenched with sweat. We needed a miracle. Suddenly, one occurred.

The hubbub was interrupted by a single voice that seemed to blare from every corner of the Holy City. It sang an eerie, meandering melody, and all at once, like clockwork, this crowd of a half million or so whipped out their prayer rugs and fell prostrate in prayer. Even the Levitol layer overhead were prostrate; their carpets, too, were spread out, each one fluttering a little in its own anti-grav field, carpet upon carpet, blotting out the very sunlight, so that a chill crept over the whole square.

"This is our chance," said Klang. "Let's make a dash for the ka'aba."

"But won't they try to stop us?"

"They can't—not till they've finished praying. We have a couple of minutes..."

Grabbing me by the arm, hoisting the flaming Pious Boulder above his head, the cardinal began making his way toward the center of the square, carefully stepping over the praying faithful, who were so ensconced in their religious ecstasy that they did nothing to prevent us from reaching the rock itself.

What a rock it was! An immense cube of blackness, it rested beneath an ornate marble canopy carved with a squiggly, ancient writing.

Reverently, the Cardinal set down the petromorph and unwrapped the carpet. He was no longer smoking. In fact, an immense calm seemed to emanate from him. He reached out a pseudopod toward the great rock. Rivulets of brine rolled down the ducts carved into his cheeks.

"Oh great-great-great-great-grandfather," he said, "I have come to take you home."

He extruded an extra pair of eyes and lips, and applied them to the face of the great stone; and so the ka'aba spoke for the first time since he had fallen from the sky...the language he spoke was like the wind whistling through the mountaintops (not that I had heard that before, but I knew of it from lonely childhood evenings at holofeelie palaces)...yet alien though it was, I seemed to understand it well...it must have had a telepathic component.

"Eyes," said Nickel-Iron Prime, "you have given me eyes...and lips with which to speak. I have been blind and dumb for millennia...you have awakened me." The eye-symbiotes revolved against his smooth black surface like little earths.

"Father of my fathers," said the petromorph, "we've come to take you home..."

"Home..." sighed the great rock.

I closed my eyes. All at once, I saw what the great rock saw. I saw stark valleys and millennial glaciers; cascades of colored lights; I saw a clear black sky thick with stars...more stars than you could ever have seen from Earth in the ancient times, for the petromorphs came from the heart of a rich star cluster. I was filled with wonder...and a terrible, aching envy.

"For a thousand *n'huat* I have wandered," said Pious Boulder, "and by this moment my existence is fulfilled. O great and glorious ancestor...you are free now. Come back to the homeworld, father of my fathers."

There was a long silence. I glanced behind me; the crowd was still prostrate in prayer. Time seemed to stand still...and indeed, I realized suddenly that while not completely stopped, time had slowed to a crawl around me. Time did not move the same way for these petromorphs, and I was caught up within their continuum. Around me, even amid the broiling sunlight, I also felt the icy star wind of Nickel-Iron Prime's homeworld. Two worlds superimposed upon each other...a past I had never known, a future I could never know.

"I will stay," said the sacred stone. "They need me."

I was inside the stone's mind now...reliving the terror of being lost in space...of slicing through the vacuum...of being sucked into the gravity well of a barbarian world...the atmosphere peeling away my outer layers, burning up my symbiotes, plummeting down to an alien surface...

Blind. Without sensation. Aeons passing, time stretching, snapping back, time a circle without ending, time slowing down, the river turning viscous...shutting myself down. Knowing there is no future. Outside time and space...outside sensation...an eternity...a recursive hell.

Then, after a time that is outside time, comes the pinprick of an outside consciousness. And another, and another, firefly minds that glow for an instant or two and then are silenced. But each momentary thought is an outpouring of devotion, of yearning, of love...

I understood now. For millennia, stripped of all sensory symbiotes, he had learned to feed on the adoration of millions of human beings...beings who believed in him, who worshipped him as a manifestation of divinity...

The people of the backwater planet, with their curious antiquated ways, were his symbiotes now. He could not leave them...and they could not be without him, for the fundamental tenets of their faith would be shattered, and they too would become like the debris of space, floating aimlessly in the cold and dark...

"My ancestor has gone mad," Pious Boulder whispered. "It is a terrible thing."

For another moment or so, I stood between two worlds...I felt the people's love, enveloping me with a warmth and profundity of passion that I, a creature of the most sophisticated culture of humankind, had never known possible.

Slowly, slowly the feeling faded, and, as the congregation roused itself from its prayers, the Cardinal, the Rock, and I blended back into the throng and slowly worked our way back to the gates of the city.

Christmas comes but twice a year, and here I am, ready for the big parade. In my nubile splendor, riding the foamy half-shell of my virgin birth, I will rise out of a holographic sea. A million Catholics around the solar system will watch me and adore me, and celebrate with me the rites of fertility. And yet...

Pious Boulder has not left Mallworld. He is ashamed because he cannot finish his quest. He has gone native, I'm afraid; gets zonked on Levitol at the barJulians' parties, has had a credit-thumb installed in one of his slots so that he can shop until he drops; he says he has no purpose anymore, and might as well live among the barbarians...

If he goes back, I told him, he can see the stars again. To which he replied, "I no longer deserve the stars."

But his malaise is deeper than that. I feel it myself, and the gulf between myself and the earthies isn't nearly as vast as the distance between his species and mine. We've touched a world where there is real power in people's beliefs, and where faith can really move mountains...or at least, prevent them from moving. How can I feel such pure, uncompromising faith? What must I give up to feel the same fire in my heart?

Perhaps we lost more than the stars when the Selespridar took over the solar system.

Perhaps we lost our souls.

...and so, O Many-Tiered Resplendence, we come to the final vision of this grand charade. I know you are impatient; I know you wish to leave this arena of puerile decadence and return to the vaulting nobility of your own homeworld. Yet surely, O great one, you will fulfill the terms of the great directive, and regard, at the very least, the ninth of the nine lives of Mallworld.

My, your resplendence, you seem impatient! You're shuffling through the chips as though crazed. Perhaps you think this race is actually capable of something? You're not on the verge of releasing them from bondage, are you?

What?

They're almost funny enough?

Since when was humor the criterion for this most difficult and awe-inspiring of decisions?

All right, Your Magnificence, I'll shut up.

Roll 'em!

(And now for a final word from one of our sponsors.)

(Again kids please do not read!)

Think You've Done It All?
Love-O-Matic presents
SEX SO REALISTIC,
IT ALMOST FEELS VIRTUAL

Have you had every sexual experience it is possible to have?
Hold on to your whips and chains, my friends, because there's
one more way to experience paid pleasure.

There is a comsim simulation for every possible sex act.

Male, female, alien, young, old, chubby, skinny, dead—
you've done it all. You've been raped by giant robots in the
back seat of a Stone Age Toyochev. You've had an onanistic
experience with a wet liver in the bathtub of a nineteenth-
century marmoset on Quaaludes. You've had a virtual sex
slave so real it made your hair stand on end and the Velcro on
your genitalia liquefy. And yet...you're still not satisfied.

Love-O-Matic has found a way to simulate virtual sex
with such verisimilitude...it's so fake, you'll never believe
it's real! It's a simple process. Young human beings—from
Earth itself, so that they are close to the primal essence of
the human condition—are captured from their native villages.
They undergo a rigid training process from childhood, with
porno-bedtime stories, cybersimu-orgies, and massive doses
of Levitol, placing them in a heightened, almost computer-
like state of sexual readiness by the time they are ready to
work. In other words, their brains are imprinted with vast
amounts of cybersex software, enabling them to simulate
virtual sex with uncanny precision—with the added frisson
of being unable to tell whether the sex worker is a comsim or
an actual human being.

It all adds just that extra bit of zing to your night on the
town.

Inherent in the human element is unpredictability. When
a human brain is rigged to simulate cybernetic activity, the
amount of RAM available within the gray matter is so vast—

and communication between neurons so relatively slow—that there is much random firing of neurons, resulting in a feeling of improvisation to the sexual activity that only the most complex virtual sex algorithms can encompass.

Yes, sex with a human being *can* be more exciting than sex with a computer—and we'll prove it to you—or twice your money back!

Bug-eyed in Mallworld

Of course I knew where I was. The toyochev I was riding in was slowly drifting down to Mallworld—the place where all dreams come true. I recognized it at once: thirty klicks of shopping center floating in space, gleaming against a night without stars. Already I was picking up a babble of jangling, pushy jingles on the car's communicator, and I could see the bumper-to-bumper traffic streaking across space all the way from the transmat nexus to the parking satellites that ringed the artificial world that lies between the Belt and Jupiter.

But I didn't know who I was. By the Pope's boobs, I couldn't remember my own name. Why was I here? My head was throbbing and I realized that it was stuck to the ceiling of the toyochev, even though the gravity was on full—all the furniture was firmly rooted to the floor, and there weren't any eating utensils, robots, or inflatable tongue ticklers swimming around as there would be if the gravity was off. I tried to shake myself free of the ceiling, but I seemed to be attached to it by a metal headband, and...worriedly I felt my scalp ...there were a couple of cables sticking into my skull!

"Who am I?" I shouted, kicking my legs and succeeding only in exacerbating my headache, as the spectacle of the traffic congestion around Mallworld swam in the view windows. "Tell me who I am!"

"I'm glad you finally asked," said a six-inch-high little man, popping into existence beside my ear. "I thought you were out for good! You've had...let's see...five levitols, three brevitols, two bottles of deep-fried chablis, a six-pack of squirtomatic filet-mignon-flavored chewing gum—"

I was starting to remember things vaguely. "A party?" I said. "At the barJulianses?" I tried to rub my head with my hands, but as I started to do so the ceiling sprouted an arm that brandished a washcloth, with which it proceeded to daub my face and scalp in ice cold water. I suffered this indignity for a while as the six-inch-high little man hummed a jerky ditty. "So answer the question—"

"I give up!" said the man, who was, of course, a computer simulacrum; that much had already impressed itself on my beleaguered skull. "You shmillionaires are all alike! Soap-box barons—bah! Seen one, seen 'em all. Just because you own virtually everything in the known universe, this side of the Selespridon barrier, doesn't give you the right to abuse us cyber-imagic constructs, you know! Under the Human, Alien, Cetacean and Mechanical Brain Rights Act of the Azroid Beltx Alliance—"

Suddenly I remembered who I was. I gave a whoop of pleasure. The comsim immediately gurgled to a stop. Of course it did. Machines never talked back to a barJulian! It must have had a grand old time complaining while I was fishing around for my identity.

"Just get on with your job," I said. "Go down to the locker and get me a fresh can of clothing."   .

"Yes, sir! Yes, master!" the comsim said, and winked out of existence. I yanked the din plugs out of my head and fell to the floor of the toyochev. An air stream jetted up to cushion my landing. The comsim matted right back and sprayed on the clothes; they didn't fit very well.

Then I accidentally saw myself in the room monitor in the control console of my car....

I was a giant insect in a trench coat!

"What is the meaning of this?" I yelled.

"Don't you remember?" came the comsim's voice. "It's the body you ordered."

Okay. That's my one passion in life, and one of the big advantages of wealth; you can get a new look whenever you want. But I'd never fancied the bug-eyed look before. This seemed to be a pretty elaborate somatic job. Suddenly I realized that—even with my identity more or less restored—I didn't quite remember everything about myself. The din plug cables had lowered themselves down from the ceiling and were crawling towards me. They were trying to tell me something. I seized them and stared wildly at them and they writhed in my fists like lunatic serpents. Well, at least I knew what they were now. Hastily I stuck them back in my head, jamming them hard so that the data stream would restart itself. Then I sat in lotus position and waited for the rest of my soul to infuse itself into my new body.

Losing your soul is not the brightest idea in the world. Especially when you've been dead for a couple of days. And dead was precisely where I'd been. I recognized the symptoms from all the other times one of my wild parties had ended up at The Way Out Suicide Parlor.

Most of the time I rarely went to my own parties. After all, a barJulian doesn't bother to frequent Mallworld: least of all Julian barJulian XV, direct heir of the Julian barJulian who, centuries ago and before the coming of the alien Selespridar, happened to win this ludicrous prize in one of those holofeelietape publisher's clearing house sweepstakes...one megacubiclick of empty space beyond the azroid belt...or a lifetime supply of deodorant soap! Well, as luck would have it, he opted for the former, and along came the transmaterialization technology from the Selespridar, and our little node of space just so happened to be the most densely packed nexus of transmat whiz lines in the entire solar system...and the only possible place to build a shopping mall the size of an azroid.

My family had been collecting the rent for a long, long time. It's a little known fact, but my grandfather, the famous clavichrome soloist, bought the earth from its bankrupt holding corporation. I guess being a slumlord as well as the owner of Mallworld's space made him feel a little closer to the masses. I've been trying to foist the earth off on someone ever since, but the only person ever interested in it was a schizophrenic whale. The Cetacean Council stripped him of his cetacean rights, and he's been forced to live like a human being ever since.

This whale (a humpback, I believe) had become so insane, by cetacean reckoning, that he had learned to think human thoughts and even talk more or less like one through a cumbersome voice-device. Of course, whale's brains being what they are, he was a lot smarter than humans, and he'd certainly acquired enough credit to purchase the earth from me. A sentient's a sentient, and I wanted to close the deal if at all possible, so I invited him to a party in his honor. The venue, of course, was to be the entertainment showcase of Mallworld—my most lavish suite at the Gaza Plaza Hotel, whose centerpiece was the Great Pyramid of Khufu, which my Great-uncle Clement had had hauled to Mallworld in bite-sized pieces and digitally reconstituted. Parties are a pain when you're constantly called upon to set the universal standard for lavishness, so I was already in a foul mood when I stepped from the demat-booth into the party room, which was an exact model of the White House, ancestral home of Genghis Khan, Johnny Appleseed, and other T'ang Dynasty Emperors of ancient earth history.

I did not, at that time, resemble a giant bug in the slightest. Indeed, I was the handsomest person in the room; I'd ordered the most streamlined soma money can buy, and all eyes turned to worship my magnificent, Storkways genegeneered physique.

The whale, who was known to all and sundry as Curly, occupied a vast tank in the middle of the hall. He was carrying on about fifty-seven conversations at once by means of a telepathic signal-splitter implanted in his baleen and outputting to various sofas, drinking booths and dialogue bathtubs all over the function space. He seemed to be an enormous hit. In one corner a whole bevy of minimalists—people who have had their bodies removed, and float around as talking heads on life support platters—had gathered around one of the outputs and was listening to the whale discourse eloquently about the nature of art. Simultaneously, Curly was expounding about earthie politics to a group of rapt maximalists, whose extra arms and legs writhed and flopped about their caterpilloid abdomens; in a corner, another of his extensions was emceeing a fashion show. I was delighted; like all my parties, this one was going to be a success. I popped a levitol and began to drift ecstatically ceilingward, pausing only to quaff a goblet of rattlesnake's tears that was winging its way through the air, offering itself to any guest that happened to float by.

"It's a success!" I screamed wildly. In the distance, the Pope waved at me. "A wild success!" I shouted.

It was at that moment that a Selespridon entered my party.

Now I hadn't invited any of the Selespridar. However, being our masters, however benign, they go where they choose. After all, the Selespridar had walled off the entire solar system at the orbit of Saturn and shunted us into a vacant universe "until such time as the human race is mature enough to confront the civilized races of the galaxy." You don't kick a Selespridon out of a party.

Anyhow, they have this odor, you see...they secrete this pheromone, or something, that excites the inmost erotic urges of human beings...as well as being two meters tall and entirely humanoid in shape but for the vivid blue color of their skins.

Everyone stopped talking right away.

Except for the whale, whose voice, in fifty-seven incarnations, continued to reverberate from all the different outputs of the telepathic signal splitter.

"I see," the Selespridon said very softly, "that there *is* another intelligent life form at your party, Julian barJulian XV." He pointed at the whale. "I'm glad you finally got around to inviting real people to these affairs of yours."

Everyone in the room waited for him to continue.

It's hard to tell the Selespridar apart—one is so overwhelmed by the scent that one can't think straight—but I recognized this one as Klutharion, who was and is the governor of the solar system. I wasn't surprised: Klutharion loved slumming. I wasn't thrilled, either; Klutharion's appearance invariably spelled trouble.

"Welcome, Klutharion," I said, catching the booze goblet on the fly and holding it out to him. "Have a drink."

"I think not. Actually, I have a little business to discuss with your friend over there." He waved languidly at the whale, who had begun to sing a doleful, keening song while never ceasing to pontificate from his fifty-seven outputs. "Nothing serious, really. Just the usual, carving Gaul into three parts, that sort of thing."

"I see."

"Carry on partying, by all means."

"Yeah. All right. Whatever you say."

I fluttered back down to the floor. The heady aroma was beginning to diffuse itself. Klutharion patted down the three tiers of his tunic (a signal of rank amongst the Selespridar) and approached Curly's tank. There were a couple of spare outputs, and he started talking into one of them. I crept closer but I didn't hear anything. Probably Klutharion was using whale talk—one of those supersonic languages—I mean, why not? One superior intelligence to another, I thought, rather bitterly. Being human often made you feel inferior these days. I guess it seems weird, I mean, what with being the richest person in the known universe and all and still feeling cut out of his own party, but that's the way it felt. I looked around for something to pop, and it soon came drifting my way: the self-opening, self-flambéing, self-photosynthesizing Flying Bong of Calcutta, a mind-altering device all the way from good old planet earth, vaculax of the solar system.

The party was soon in full swing again. There was a floor show of antelope strippers and a ceiling show of reverse-gravity dancing bears, so there was something for everybody. But I wasn't having fun anymore.

Despondently I decided to talk to the whale myself.

"Hi, Curly," I said.

The computer-enhanced thought waves started booming

in my ears. "Hi yourself, big boy," the whale said. "Having a good time. Wish you were here."

"I am here," I said irritably.

A robot climbed the tank and methodically began emptying a bale of plankton into the water.

"Yummy," the whale said.

"You know, I'm getting pretty fed up with you," I said. "You come to my party, you have all these people worshipping at your feet and treating you like the latest guru, and—"

"I don't have any feet, Jules," the whale chided.

"Shut up."

"OK."

I waited.

"Anyway," I said at last, "what's this hush-hush deal you're making with Klutharion? Don't tell me *he* wants to buy the earth too! What would one of them want with a rotten, stinking ball of dirt anyway?"

"What do *you* want with it, sonny?"

"That's different!" I said. "He can *get out* whenever he wants. I'll never be able to see the stars. Owning real estate is just second best." *Getting out* is the most important thing in the universe—*getting out* of this force-prison into which the Selespridar have cast us—seeing the stars again. I think it's the lack of *getting out* that makes the human race so frantic. We're stuck in this toy universe a few A.U.'s wide, and we *know* there's more and we can never break out of jail. "You ought to understand, damn it!" I went on. "You're just as system bound as any of us. You'll never see the stars either."

"That's what you think!" the whale said smugly. "But that's because you are unable to eavesdrop on this other conversation I happen to be having with Klutharion."

"What!"

"Our mutual friend, the governor of the solar system, is apologizing profusely to me and all the cetacean species for inadvertently locking us out. He has presented me with a key to the Selespridon barrier, which I can use whenever I want to.

Any space car that carries this thing on board will automatically be let through. He says that if they'd contacted us instead of you lot in the first place, you'd never be in this bind. But you guys were making so much noise in the belt and on Mars, the aliens never even noticed that you weren't the most highly evolved beings in the system."

"More cetacean propaganda!" I said angrily. "You vaculax! You...you fallopian tube!"

"There's no need for obscenity, Jules my friend. Actually, I don't give a shit about seeing the stars. For god's sake, I'm a whale! I don't think like you do. At least, I try not to. I mean, you naked apes are all stark staring bonkers. Go ahead, take the damn thing."

I felt something cold and metallic in my clenched fist. I unclenched it and looked at it. It looked like a cross between an ancient ninja throwing star and an impaled lizard. "You mean, with this I can—"

"Right!" said the whale. "Why don't you mat over to your toyochev and try it out right away?"

I could hardly believe it. I held in my hand the thing that every human longs for—the key to the stars—tossed into my hands like a silly bauble by a schizophrenic whale. I was shaking.

"By the way, it's a one way trip," the whale added. "And only one intelligent—I use that term loosely—being is covered by the key. If you're planning to take a friend, one of you will end up smeared across half the galaxy."

"So what?" I cried. I had heard all the songs, experienced all the romantic feelie tapes, been drenched in the propaganda since I was a little kid: "One day we will reclaim all that we lost." One day. It was the dream of all mankind. Though I clutched in my hand the key to the dream, it did not seem real to me. I pulled off my plastiflesh skull cap and stuck the device into my head. It rattled around for a moment before finding its niche. (Like most extremely rich people, I keep my brain in a safe-deposit box at the credit clinic, and I communicate with it by transmat modem.) Why would I even friend if I could realize mankind's ultimate dream? Getting out, I thought to myself, getting out, *holy getting out.*

"What's he saying now?" I asked the whale, noticing that Klutharion was still gesticulating wildly at the output.

"Oh, the usual," Curly said, "what a pain it is to babysit the human race, that sort of thing. It's all bullshit. He's a closet human-lover, that's why he's always at your parties. He'd love to be in your shoes, Jules—" he paused to take in a few tons of plankton....

Wild commotion! The tank was seething, vibrating...people were screaming...the whale was rising slowly from the tank! Water was splashing over the food. Comsims were fluttering about like insects, telling people not to panic. "What's going on?" I yelled, collaring one of the little pink men as he buzzed past.

"Some prankster has gone and laced the whale's plankton with levitol!" he squealed.

"This is fun!" the whale's voice boomed in my output. Panicking, I grabbed the cord and was hoisted up into the air. There were about a hundred of us hanging on wires for dear life, and each and every wire connected to the telepathic signal splitter implanted in the cetacean's cranium! "You humans sure know a good time!" said the whale. "This is just like being back in the Pacific, before you guys poisoned it ten centuries ago! Coolness!"

He then proceeded to crash through the wall, with about half of my lavish gathering literally hanging on his every word.

We were whizzing down the corridors of Mallworld. I felt sick. In a moment I was puking all over the swarms of customers with their shopping bags in tow. The signal splitter cable slipped through my vomit-smeared fists. I was falling, falling...past level upon level of shops that sold everything from cyborgs to cyclamates to detachable noses to bombast balloons...People were sure going to be talking about this bash for a long, long time.

Inevitably we were all going to end up at The Way Out for a few hours of agony and resurrection. How boring! I thought

as I landed. One of the robot monitors released an automatic air-cushion, so I didn't hurt myself. I got up and looked around.

The corridor was entirely empty. No, wait, there was someone…vanishing into a demat-booth. I squinted at the higher levels. People there too, but they were thinning fast.

"That's impossible!" I said softly. There isn't such a thing as an empty corridor in Mallworld. I looked again. There was someone, rounding a corner…no. Just a shopping bag, ownerless, striding purposefully onward. "Hey, you!" I shouted at it. "Where is everyone?"

"Big sale at Spacey's," it mumbled. "Level Y54."

"Spacey's?" I racked my brains. "Who are they?"

All at once, as though sung by a heavenly chorus, the sound of an advertising jingle permeated the air:

2-4-6-8

Spacey's plans to liquidate!

The shopping bag marched away. "Come back! I order you!" I yelled. It paused at the entrance to a demat-booth. I ran after it. I tried to trip it, but shopping bags can be pretty nimble when cornered, and it dematted before my very eyes, after squeakily calling for the level number Y54.

"Y54!" I said.

Nothing happened.

"Excuse me, mister! Are you going to stand there all day?" I was elbowed aside by one of the talking heads (quite a feat when you have no elbows) and I got out of the way. The minimalist said, "Y54, and make it snappy," and immediately vanished into the old hyperspatial wormhole network without a glitch.

I tried again and failed.

"Comsim!" I shrieked.

One of the little pink men popped into being, buzzing in my ear. "I am computer simulacrum MALLGUIDE 3425167—" it began.

"That's enough," I said impatiently. "Who the hell are Spacey's and why can't I get there?"

"Interesting questions, Julian barJulian sir!" said the comsim, who had doubtless scanned my retinas and knew just how important I was. "But as for answers..."

This was exasperating. "You know very well I can pay," I said, holding aloft my well-heeled credit thumb.

"I wasn't doubting your word," said the pink man. "Now, Spacey's is a new corporation that seems to be buying up this shopping mall at an alarming rate. They've already taken over the entire outer rim and they're moving in for the kill."

"How can they possibly afford to—"

"No one's figured it out."

"Well, don't just hover there! Take me to their leader, or whatever!"

"Well, yes, of course, but, you see, there's...ah...a problem, which is that someone seems to have reprogrammed the demat-booths so that they won't work for you...or any other member of your family."

"They've gained control of the—"

"Precisely."

I looked around. Curly the whale and the whole gang had long since vanished. They were probably at the suicide parlor already, experiencing the cheap and infinitely repeatable thrill of death. But even so bourgeois an entertainment seemed preferable to being stuck in this corridor. And someone was trying to take over Mallworld...to lock me out of my own kingdom! And Curly and Klutharion were probably in on it. Hadn't they been cosying up to each other all through my party? Never trust an alien. Pope's pantyhose! What would a Selespridon want with a shopping mall when he was already governor of the entire solar system? Stranger still, what would a whale want with one? Of course, Curly *was* crazy. For all I knew, so was Klutharion. Probably a requirement for being assigned to babysit the human race. Never had I felt more helpless. The more I thought about it, the weirder things looked.

Suddenly a sing-song voice, louder than the constant chorus of advertisements that chimed around me, whispered:

Come to Spaceys...
The most astonishing sale of all time—
For just twenty-four hours, you don't pay us...
We pay you!

I made a few more attempts to break through the demat-booth's recognition system. But I knew it was impossible. It was, of course, foolproof.

Available at Spacey's—
Hitherto unobtainable anywhere in Mallworld at any price—
Happiness!
And we pay you to buy it!

I looked around. Several department stores and a monopole skating rink bordered the corridor. Above me, slidewalks sailed in every direction, and there were levels and levels and levels, as far as the eye could see, and every shop was crying out a slogan or flashing an animated hologlyph to show off its wares, and the slogans rebounded from the chrome gilt of the walls, each one more sensuous and seductive than the next—

GET YOUR TALKING NECRONOMICON HERE
SPRAY-ON SKINS GIVE YOU A PEEL
YOU CAN SHED
LOVELORN? COME TO COPULAND!
YOUR HEAD EXAMINED AND
REPLACED FOR YOU IN SECONDS
BAD CREDIT?
GET A PHONY THUMBPRINT!

What could I do to trick them? A phony thumbprint was obviously the best solution...as long as the demat-booth didn't try anything more outrageous, like a retinal scan or a DNA probe. Now where was that jingle coming from?

I listened carefully. When you grow up with Mallworld in your blood your three-dimensional aural acuity becomes pretty intense. I pinpointed the commercial in a few seconds, then cursed in frustration. The thumb joint was four levels up, and

without the demat-booths there wasn't anyway of reaching it.
Except—

Maybe I had something on me...I tried my pockets, only to
realize that these monomolecular clothing films didn't have
pockets. The old spray-on Wear 'n' Wipe garments were great
for projecting the illusion of innocent nakedness while casting a
provocative, almost subliminal shimmer over one's perfect body.
Then I tapped my head, pulled open my skull compartment,
and there it was...right next to the Selespridon star traveling
device...my cache of drugs! I fingered the device, thinking of
the stars that have been denied men for so long...thinking how
wonderful it would be to leave it all behind and see all the things
that have been forbidden to us...I wanted to *get out* right then
and there. But I couldn't. The device had to be in my vehicle,
and right now I couldn't even reach the vehicle.

Obviously I'd have to deal with Spacey's first.

And then—the wide open spaces of the galaxy!

I popped a Levitol and started to float, using my
outstretched arms as steering rudders. There was the thumb
joint...I could see the rows and rows of thumbs hanging in the
window like strings of sausages. Higher and higher I went,
until...wait, I was sinking! I wasn't going to make it! I dumped
the remainder of my cache into my mouth and swallowed hard.
The euphoria hit me all at once. It took me a few moments to
realize I'd soared right past the right level and had no way of
stopping. Any other day there'd be a couple dozen other
zonkies gliding the hallways, and I could have braked and
reversed off one of them, but there was no one, and I was
going up and up and up—

There was something! A slidewalk ribboned between levels.
I somersaulted over it again and again, trying to wear off the
Levitol and mess up my own balance. At last I managed to
grab the handhold with my feet and we were off, careening
wildly through stomach-wrenching crazi-gravi corridors, stores
kaleidoscoping into other stores, levels whizzing past, exhibits
flashing by, all trying to sell me pet dinosaurs, kinky sex, aspirin,

religion, babies, tampons, robots, authentic rain dances performed in my home, designer hamburgers, condo-azroid options on easy credit, credit clinics, credit counseling, credit management, credit reestablishment, credit underwriting, credit necrophilia—

Getting my thumb redone was out of the question now. I didn't even know where I was. There are no maps of Mallworld; physical locations are just ideas in the mind of a computer; what you have to know is what level number to bark at the demat-booth.

At length the slidewalk stopped.

"End of the line," it said. "Wanna ride back? I can come and pick you up later if you want."

"Sure," I said, still dizzy. "I'll let you know." A vast building with Ionian columns, its gates guarded by statues of ancient earth gods like Anubis, Adonis and Elvis, stood before me. Torsos of men and animals hung in the windows. Still no people, though.

I was in front of *SomaTech—Exotic Body Shop—by special appointment to the Crowned Heads of the Greater Azroid Belt Area.*

"What a stroke of luck," I whispered. Why stop at the thumb? I told myself. Might as well get the whole body made over.

I'd been getting pretty sick of being the most beautiful person in any gathering all the time. My dad had paid gigacredits for my custom genegeneered Storkways soma, but there are limits to narcissism, especially when the future of all those gigacredits is at stake—and with the whales and the Selespridar in collusion, I could well end the day a pauper.

I entered the body shop. There weren't any humans inside at all. I mean, only the ritziest shops can afford human salespersons, but you'd expect at least a customer or two. There were none, but the place had the appearance of having been abruptly abandoned. Extravagant somas were sprawled all over the counter, as though someone had been in the middle of trying them on.

"I'm surprised you're not at the Spacey's sale," said a kindly clunker, materializing beside me. "Everyone else is. I mean, it's *almost* as though they were *sucked* away into some distant *vaculax*." The robot went on, "I suppose you'll be wanting a body."

I flashed my thumb at him. He immediately became more obsequious. "I'll fetch my superior," he said. "You're a *barJulian*." At least the thing knew its place.

Another robot, even grander than the first (he wore a pharaonic double crown topped by a silver-lamé propeller beanie) wafted into the room, its gold-plated tentacles waving sinuously. "Ah, so delighted to have such a distinguished customer...none of this crap for you!" Dramatically he began flinging the empty bodies to the floor. Then he clapped two tentacles and a curtain parted to reveal a spanking collection of exotics, each one spread-eagled on its own cadaver rack.

"I need something radically alien," I said. "Something my own mother wouldn't recognize...more importantly, my own mother's computer."

"Must be quite a party you're throwing," the robot said. I could have sworn he had an envious lump in his throat, even though he had no throat, resembling as he did a cross between an octopus, a lettuce, and an antique dishwasher. "But we can certainly accommodate you. This selection is our most exotic. Not one strand of mammalian DNA in any of 'em. This"— he gestured—"is a magnificent specimen. One of the silicon creatures of Arcturus VII, you know." It resembled a large rock, and I said so. "Now, that's not very gneiss," the robot opined. "How about that?" He pointed at something with six heads, dressed in a harlequin costume. I didn't like it. "My, you are hard to please. What...what sort of thing will you be doing in the new body?"

"Well...sort of a detective, I suppose."

The robot went into a frenzy of thrashing tentacles. "Oh, I have just the thing! The Mallworld Falcon!" he said, and clapped one more time. We stepped into an inner room, where, on display in a swath of glittering light, was the body of a giant insect wearing an ancient earthie costume. "This is the genuine thing," he said. "The actual, preserved-through-the-miracle-of-Selespridon-science corporeal remains of an ancient earth detective."

"But it looks like an insect," I said.

"Precisely! Humphrey Bug-Art, I believe it was called. The Bug-Arts were a sect of the Sherlockian religion, who practiced the unraveling of Zen enigmas by incarcerating themselves into meditation cells—hence the phrase 'locked room mystery.' This relic has been identified from a very faded fragment of an ancient filmstrip." The robot's voice took on a decidedly mantra-like tone. "This genuine soma was painfully reconstructed from a fragment of tissue only a few microns across—"

"But they didn't have sentient insects in the times of mead-drinkers and gas-guzzlers," I said, confused. Maybe this neolithic worthy had paused to swat a fly, and the mashed insect happened to be the only surviving fragment of the fellow. Such a mistake might seem contrary to common sense, but the annals of historiography are full of chimpanzee-headed diplodoci and other monuments to mistaken identity. Most people tend to think that, ever since Charles Darwin discovered that Piltdown Man was descended from a beagle and published his monograph *The Naked Ape,* we've found out all there is to know about the past. Being a barJulian and having had the best education that money can buy, I tend to know better. I was smug as I listened to the robot's exegesis on the subject of the Mallworld Falcon. (Besides, I know very well that a falcon isn't an insect. It's a dinosaur. I have one in my menagerie.)

The clunker chattered on: "And, of course, we guarantee our work, and if the new body doesn't work out we'll be happy to exchange it or give you full credit, good towards the reconstruction of your previous body or up to one half the cost of another selection, whichever is less, minus the cost of the brain dump."

"Yes, yes," I said. "Get on with it." I didn't care. As long as the demat-booth didn't recognize it. To make sure, I had my thumbs flayed and a fake I.D. superimposed on the insect's thumbs—or whatever they were. There was a convenient skull receptacle, so I stashed the thumbs there next to the interstellar device. The braindump took only a few seconds, and then I was watching my corpse as it lay unbreathing on the counter.

"Will you be wanting it embalmed, sir?"

"Nah. Trade-in." Since I wasn't *me* anymore, I had to get used to being cheap. Just before the dump I'd transferred two megacreds to the new thumbprints, but even so I felt uneasy. I wiggled my antennae. Looking through the compound eyes was weird at first, but the fractured appearance of everything was more than compensated for by the ultraviolet vision. The robot was radiating wildly in the ultraviolet. I wondered if it was their way of blushing.

"Come back soon," he said.

I paid no attention, but slipped back out into the corridor. Then I caught a glimpse of myself in the window of a store that sold old holofeelie tapes, and I was immediately entranced.

My skin was now gray and chitinous. I could see my mandibles...twitching...there was something quite dashing about the way they twitched. And those compound eyes really made the whole image. Of course a detective would have to see into the ultraviolet! For picking up extra clues. I was really getting into the part now.

But the mission was the important thing. I could imagine the chaos at the next family board meeting if they found out that Mallworld had been invaded from within. It had to be forestalled at all costs.

I found the first demat-booth, muttered the level number, and was whisked away.

What part of Mallworld could this be? The corridors looked the same yet not the same. People were everywhere. Children high on Levitol twittered as they soared and swooped. Level after level as far as the eye could see. A brass band tooting away in one corner, being conducted by an energetic six-legged tuba. Shopping bags marching about in pairs, holding hands or tugging at their leashes. A pornographer distributing tokens for kinky sex vending machines. Nothing unusual.

Up ahead, a row of demat-booths was spitting out shoppers faster than you could count them. They were in a festive mood, and they were all lining up in front of the portals of the most enormous department store I had ever seen.

WE'RE GROWING BY THE MINUTE
(sang an angelic chorus from somewhere within Spacey's.)
WON'T YOU COME AND BUY?
WON'T YOU JOIN US?

The line was long, but it seemed to be proceeding so rapidly that people were virtually being *sucked* into Spacey's. The vast portals, set in a facade of Babylonian friezes and dancing holographic images of Santa Claus, resembled the jaws of a gargantuan beast of prey, and the people had this crazed, glazed glint their eyes. I knew the look well. It's a kind of ultimate mass hysteria that seizes people at the onset of a giant sale. The crowd moves like a single being. The Spacey's jingle blared from every corner of the hallway like an anthem, and the people seemed possessed by an almost religious fervor. Brilliant rays emanated from the structure. Indeed, the light was so dazzling that you could hardly make out any of the other stores in this section of the mall.

Squinting, I tried to see what else there was...nothing unusual. A few restaurants...a topless sushi bar and a Buckerogeroo's SteakHouse...a little emporium specializing in nose jobs...a necrophilic brothel. But...were my eyes deluding me, or were the stores shifting, crumbling...were they, too, being inexorably sucked into Spacey's? How could it be? I rubbed my eyes. There. It was happening again. A corner of the Gimbel and Gamble's Department Store was actually melting, squishing up, being distorted along the axis of the light rays from Spacey's.

"This is weird," I thought. Was it just because I wasn't used to these insect eyes? But it seemed so real!

I was really getting into the role of the ancient earth detective. Investigate, investigate! I wondered whether I should join the throng. After all, no one would recognize me in this insect getup. And for some reason, the jingles, loaded though they doubtless were with subliminals, weren't pulling me in. Jingles rarely work on a barJulian. After all, we already own everything, and our method of collecting the rent is to go through Mallworld taking anything we want. If I slipped in, I could probably tune out the jingles and take in what was *really* happening. The Mallworld Falcon to the rescue! I'd save the family fortune before using my space travel key to set off for adventure in worlds beyond. A fitting end to a chapter in a life of excruciating boredom.

I barged into the line. No one seemed to mind. They were all smiling and gazing vacuously ahead.

Time to ask questions.

"What are you here for?"

"I can't believe I'm talking to a giant insect," said a man who'd had himself surgically altered to look like a slug. "You must be a member of the Society for Creative Anachronism." He oozed around me, peering curiously.

I said, "So what're you here to buy?"

"Oh, you don't know? But it's been broadcasting all through Mallworld all day."

"I was at a party."

"It's total awareness, man! It's the meaning behind the meaning of meaning! Life beyond life!"

"But they're advertising cheap underwear and biodegradable condo-azroids," I said, listening carefully to the music that wafted from the structure.

"Oh, that's nothing, that's just the old bait and switch," the slug said, slicking down the slidewalk with slime as he slithered about me. "Listen to the voices behind the voices."

I listened as the crowd pushed, farther and farther toward the jaws of the giant beast.

It was true. Behind the words that advertised toothpaste and vaculaxes, there was sort of a heavenly backup chorus, and they were singing, over and over, the words "the stars...the stars."

Now there's nothing more hypnotic than those words to people who have been denied the stars for all these generations. Even I started to feel the passion those words evoked, and the anger against our Selespridon masters, benign though they seemed to be. I listened more carefully, trying to separate out the subliminals—it's a knack. It was true! They were promising trips beyond the Selespridon barrier for "qualified creditholders"! But that was impossible, unless..."Klutharion's behind this," I thought. "That's why they're keeping me out. He and Curly are planning something big." It's easy to be paranoid when you know there are least two master races around and you don't belong to either of them.

I watched the slug-man. He was in the grip of tremendous ecstasy. It made me sick. The subliminals were starting to work on me now. Then I realized I had a cure for them. I already had the key to the barrier locked up in my skull. I rattled my head to make sure it was still there. Everything looked fuzzy through my compound eyes, what with the weirdly superimposed images and the ultraviolet light.

The crowd was moving, quicker and quicker. I struggled to tune out the influence of the jingles. Around me the storefronts became streaks as the beams from Spacey's disintegrated them.

The portals loomed up, and I saw words inscribed in flaming holographic letters in the doorway, and I knew I was the only one who could read them because reading is a lost art and only those like me who have been to snooty schools have taken the trouble to learn it—

ABANDON HOPE ALL YE WHO ENTER HERE

Flames danced everywhere. The heavenly chorus turned into the cackling of demons. We weren't inside a store at all...it really *was* the mouth of a giant creature. The people were being sucked into a gullet in the far back, and the slidewalk we stood on was a quivering, slime-drenched tongue...the crowd was running joyously toward the end of the dark tunnel, and I was caught up in the stream, I couldn't escape...

But did I want to escape? A tide of joy swept over me. The thing that was swallowing me whole was infinite and infinitely good. I was swept up in it. I could feel the collective ecstasy of thousands upon thousands of minds as they were all dragged deeper and deeper into the abyss that was giddier than levitol and more cosmic than brevitol. I didn't know that such a thing existed inside Mallworld...how could I not have known that there was such a powerful, pleasure-inducing vortex at the center of my own private kingdom? What was this thing that was trying to buy up Mallworld? Surely not a rival corporation with infinite credit...surely not even a plot cooked up by cetaceans and Selespridar. It was bigger even than that. It was conscious. It was all-encompassing. It was incommensurate and incomprehensible...it was perhaps a god...it was the ultimate alien.

So there I was, funneling down into a bottomless pit along with the souls of a million shoppers. And enjoying every minute of it. It was better than a roller coaster, better even than surfing the holoZeiss starfield simulator at the Cosmorama

Dome. Love was in the air—not exactly the air, as I'm not even sure we were inside any known manifestation of space time—but after a long long time (brevitol sort of time that is, time without meaning) I became aware that all was not quite as advertised. I suppose it must have been that barJulian ability to filter out the effects of subliminals, no matter how insidious…and these were *very* insidious. They weren't just your usual subvoke patterns stranded into the advertisements. They were working on some molecular level, I was sure of it, because even my blood felt different as it raced through my empty head—I have a nanochemistry monitor in a socket in my skull and it was definitely starting to give off "no-no" signals as it reacted to the bludgeoning of my endocrine system.

Closing my eyes, I pulled up the chart and dumped it to my left eyelid. The love arc was soaring off the end of graph, but underneath it was the throbbing, jagged black squiggle that clearly denoted the presence of Something Bad.

Beneath the protestations of love, beneath the breathtaking visions of the stars, I could hear an quiet ostinato drone of "I'm gonna eat you, I'm gonna eat you."

The people of Mallworld were being conned, and I was the only one who knew it, and the only one who could do anything about it—and I was spiralling down the vaculax of eternal love, not knowing who I had to fight and why…wearing a trenchcoat and the body of a giant insect.

I had to fight back. No wonder they had deprogrammed me from the demat-network! As my mind cleared, so did the illusion. Opening my eyes, I saw what was really happening around me. We were falling down a shaft into the heart of Mallword. Tentacles of metal were slithering out from the walls, reeling in people, plunging interface cords into their skulls as they writhed and thrashed in synthetic joy. The shaft itself was twisting and tying itself in knots…we were like a cloud of insects, flying though the oesophagus of some metal worm…suddenly, I realized that was precisely what was happening.

Mallworld was alive!

Somehow, the quadrillions of connections through the transmat nexus in this megacubiklick of space had all converged, mated, interwoven into a grotesque parody of sentience...Mallworld had acquired a soul, and that soul was as malevolent as they came, and it was trying to suck out the consciousness of every one of my happy shoppers!

As soon as the realization hit me, the spectacle became more and more horrific. You see plenty of gore at *The Way Out Corp.,* but never on this scale. People smashing into each other like a toyochev pileup in a condo-azroid parking lot, skulls cracking, brains spattering, limbs fluttering about looking for their lost bodies...and a lot of these humpties probably couldn't even afford to be put back together again. The crazi-gravi generators had gone berserk, and people were clumping together like grapes or flying apart like bowling pins.

I started screaming. I couldn't hear my own voice in the cacophony. And above this whole madness you could still faintly hear the siren song of the Spacey's shopping spree:

Down and down and down and down
Into the dragon's maw,
The stars are at the end of the tunnel...
Take the plunge.

Get out of my shopping mall! my mind screamed at the mega-consciousness that now possessed the cubiclicks of metal and transmat networking. *Get out!*

And then, abruptly, there was silence. I had landed somewhere. I had been pulled into a chamber somewhere at Mallworld's heart; the room was very much like a heart, in fact, a heart the size of a small azroid, metallic flesh that squeezed and wheezed and dripped a dark machine oil from its plated joints. I could still hear the spectacle I'd lately been a part of. The shoppers were still screaming. But it was all far away, and the sounds melded together so that they were like the sound your blood makes when you cup your ears—not *my* blood, of course, since my head is platinum and plastiflesh, but I remember, as a kid, listening to the blood rush and being told it was like the sea and saying "What's a sea?" and having my robo-tutor lecture me about the long-dead oceans of old earth.

Get out? said a voice, hollow and metallic. It came from the very air around me. It sounded uncomfortably like my own voice. Had I gone crazy, had I *caused* all this somehow? *Did I hear you say* get out?

"It's just as I thought. I suppose it was bound to happen sooner or later."

Welcome to my heart. Do you like it? I modeled it after yours; got the plans from the genegeneering blueprint in the Storkways memory banks. A pair of lips materialized in the air in front of me. They frowned, they smiled, they made kissy-kissy noises.

"How flattering," I said.

Aren't you the least bit concerned now that the thing you thought you owned, this mass of metal and cyber-connectivities, has finally acquired a soul—an intelligence that far exceeds that of any human? That I'm growing by the minute as I devour and absorb the memories of the millions of shoppers I've lured into my bowels with the promise of getting out? *That I may soon reach critical mass—be able to bud—perhaps even split into a pair of Mallworlds that could mate and eventually populate the known universe? Doesn't the image of two 30-click-long creatures of metal making love in the coldness of space stir you at all? It certainly stirred the Selespridar. And that whale fellow was pretty amused too; actually it was his plankton-eating habits that gave me the idea to suck the RNA out of human brains and learn everything about them from that…not that there's much to learn, as any Selespridon will tell you.*

"And you've applied to the Selespridon council for recognition as the third sentient species in our pocket universe—right?"

Please! Second. *You guys, as you know, don't count.*

The last thing the human race needed was *another* super-being lording it over us. How could we maintain a shred of our dignity if even our shopping malls could look down their noses at us? What would be next? Would robolushes sit around in cyberbars that had signs that said "We don't serve human beings?" Would Mallworld end up transmat-netting with every processor in the solar system, until the very known universe became a cosmic consciousness from which we humans were excluded? Was this what Klutharion had meant when he said that they were dividing Gaul into three parts—one for him, one for Curly, and one for a fast-talking shopping mall?

"I can't take this," I said.

You don't have to, said Mallworld. *According to my cetacean comrade, you've been given a ticket out of town.*

"That's true," I said. "As soon as I finish dealing with you, I can hop in my toyochev and make for the stars."

Perhaps you would care to stay for the traditional villain's expository lump?

"What's that?"

That's when I explain my dastardly plan to you while the buzz saw moves inexorably toward the virginal cleft of the gagged and writhing heroine. In this case, however, the heroine is the entire human race. This microcosm is just the beginning. I'm hungry and my synapses need more synapses. I've even hacked into central credit control; in just a few short seconds, if the virus I've engineered works correctly on its memory banks, you will no longer own the earth.

"If you're such a powerful, all-encompassing alien-type creature, why do *you* need to hack into the net to own my planet? Can't you just send an invasion of clunkers down to take over the place, evict me by force?"

Well, we all have our tragic flaws. You are a carbon-based life form. I am based on silicon. But even carbon life-forms have their differences. Some bacteria, as you know, are anaerobic; others are nitrogen-fixing, still others photosynthesize, and so on. In my case, there's a particular datastring that I need to absorb in large quantities in order to maintain self-awareness…it is a datastring found only in credit records. Human credit files, you see, are my equivalent of a smart drug.

"But you've also been eating people."

Oh, that, said the reverberating voice. *Mere sustenance...raw materials...they break down easily, I can put them together into new forms...this heart you're standing in, for instance...I extracted the hemoglobin from a couple of thousand people, reduced out the iron content, extruded sheetmetal out of it, warped it into a heart which, by the way, is a perfect copy of yours, Julian barJulian. As, indeed, I am...I am made in your image...though, of course, superior in every way. I too am a barJulian...the barJulian of the future...everything your family has ever aspired to be.*

"What do you mean—*you*—a barJulian? You're nothing like the way we are."

Indeed I am, said the spirit of the shopping mall, its lips tremulous in the ultraviolet. *I'm completely solipsistic. I'm sublimely attractive, yet I'm a parasite who sucks the life out of thousands of humans every time they come to this mall. There's no reason for my existence at all...except to devour...and to survive.*

I just couldn't accept this as a paradigm of myself. Did other people really see me in this way? Did even machines think of me as nothing more than a monster, I, the most beautiful of the beautiful people, the richest of the rich, most powerful of the powerful? Was I really feared and hated by the millions who thronged the corridors of my shiny-bright world...by the trillions upon trillions stacked up in their dungheaps on that other world I owned, the slummiest hellhole in the cosmos?

You got it, buster, said the shopping mall, and I realized that it had acquired telepathic abilities in the last few minutes. *You're the sleaziest, most ornery slumlord in this whole pocket universe. Toothless old crones curse your name as they live out their lives in their one-room dumpster-efficiencies. But what do you care? You've been given the means to* get out. *You may leave, and you may leave the rest of your naked ape friends to me; soon you'll be the only human being there is.*

"But you'll have no one left to eat—and soon all the credit accounts will be gone—you'll wither away and die!" I said.

Bullshit! Haven't you ever heard of evolution?

"You'll just eat your way through the earth, then Mercury, then Mars, you'll ooze down toward the sun and upward toward Saturn...but then you're going to hit a snag, because that's where the universe ends...that's where the Selespridon barrier is...and if you *are* anything like me, you'll feel trapped and you'll feel that even the vastness of the solar system is nothing compared to the things you can't have...and you'll start to die inside."

The shopping mall's voice was silent for a long time as he digested this. Alien though he was, in copying my genetic patterns from the Storkways memory banks he had also inherited the human capacity to dream, to desire, to burn with desperate longing for what he could never have. A prison will always be a prison to a human being; doesn't matter if its a single room in a continent-sized Calcutta on old earth...or a wall of force, 18 A.U.'s wide, big enough to contain the sun and seven of its attendant planets...a human being can only be satisfied if he knows that he is part of something infinite. That's why they used to have religion. That's why people worship the Selespridar.

And I knew what I was going to have to do to save the universe.

I didn't want to do it. I didn't want to give up attaining that longing that had been programmed—since Adam and Eve discovered America, in those neolithic times when Abraham Lincoln colonized the moon and set up the Statue of Liberty in the Sea of Tranquillity—into my DNA. But I had to do it. I had show that I was more human than a sentient shopping mall, no matter how much it tried to ape me.

I steeled myself. I thought of the first time I'd dined at the Galaxy Palace and watched the real-live stars, projected on the dome of the restaurant, as I dined on soft-shelled malaprops in a Bordelaise sauce. I thought of my childhood, hearing the stories of old earth from my nanny-clunker, her warm and loving synthvoice delighting me with fairy tales such as *The Stars My Destination, The Stars and the Styx,* and *A Life for the*

Stars. I felt terrible. I remembered my great-uncle Yitsakh, the misbegotten guru of Mallworld's lost children, who had taught that the only way to *really* see the stars is to purchase a non-reserval contract at the Way Out Corp.

Then I unlocked my skull and pulled out the key to the Selespridon Barrier. "I want you to have this," I said. I hefted the key in my hand: such a little thing, yet it was truly the Holy Grail, the ultimate object of the ultimate quest, tossed like a dog biscuit at me by a bored, schizophrenic superior being. I hesitated for a few seconds; then I threw the key at the quivering lips that hovered in the air in front of me; they opened wide; I saw teeth within teeth within teeth within teeth; and the key was gone.

Then things *really* got weird.

The lips started smacking. Then they winked out. Around me, the metal heart began to buckle. I felt the slight stomach-tingling that happens when your toyochev slingshots through the transmat nexus. The heart was pulsing; a liquid metal was spurting through its veins; a subliminal symphony hummed in the air; then there was major psychedelia. The heart exploded. I flew up in a cloud of metallic droplets. Suddenly I was racing down corridors again, slidewalks strewn with corpses, tunnels that were metal viscera. Then I was falling upward, and thousands were falling with me, gravity was upside-down, decapitated heads were rushing to rejoin their bodies, arms and legs were scrunching back into their bodies, brains squishing back into crania...time was flowing backwards...we were all pouring out of the mouth of the Spacey's department store...people filled the air like swarms of hornets...screams were sucked back into throats...my very thoughts were racing in the wrong direction....

And there I was, back in the Gaza Plaza, in one of the private rooms just off the White House suite...and there with me was Klutharion, leaning back on a chairfloat, calming, sipping a cappuccino volcano. There with us also was Curly, represented by a holographic image that hovered around one of his fifty-seven inputs; the rest of him, I was sure, was now back at the party, pontificating insanely to his fans.

"The good news," said Klutharion, "is that you, Julian barJulian the...XV was it?...you people are so shortlived, it's hard for me to keep you straight...you have passed a crucial test."

"A *test?*" I said. I was feeling testy all right. "Do you know what I just gave up?"

"Curly was sure you wouldn't do it," Klutharion said. "Whales, you know, they have a habit of underestimating humans...they have a lot of painful memories of the bad old days."

"What do you mean?" I shouted. I would have had a splitting headache if I hadn't left my brain at the bank. "I gave up the *stars,* Klutharion...I gave them up!"

"Yes," said Curly, "but you did it to save your fellow men. Maybe you guys didn't do to well at saving the whales, but there may be a little more compassion in your makeup than I had thought. You win, Klutharion...I'll transfer one credit to your account right away."

"Round? You bet the human race on *one credit?*"

I didn't feel very good. The human inferiority complex had been going on for centuries, and I felt all those downtrodden centuries weighing down on me, I mean me personally, on *my* shoulders. "Relax, Jules," said Klutharion, and I caught a whiff of that neurosis-inducing scent as he leaned over me. "The human race was never at risk. We tinkered with the timeline a bit and restored everything to normal. Well, almost. And Mallworld-turned-monster will never be back, thanks to your giving him the keys to the kingdom. This mad altruistic streak that you humans have...it's in your genes. Soon, Mallworld will be back to its good old soulless state; we've nanocrunched the self-awareness program into a sort of a human soma, and it's going to be leaving the pocket universe in...oh, five minutes or so."

"A human soma!" I said.

At that moment, I walked into the room. I mean, the body of Julian barJulian XV walked into the room. Julian barJulian himself, of course, was still trapped in the soma of the insectoid Humphrey Bug-Art.

"Yo, dude," said my body.

"Is this—" I began.

"Yup!" said my body. "I took the liberty of borrowing this soma, since you weren't using it at the moment. I've borrowed so much else from you after all, what with your psychological profile and all. Actually, I don't think I'll be able to get the body back to you, where I'm going."

"Keep it," I said listlessly.

"Thanks, dude," he said.

"Cheer up," said Curly. "You're about to see the spectacle of a lifetime—the temporary lifting of the Selespridon barrier. What a fitting climax to a party at the barJulians. But first, there's the little matter of the earth..."

"You can have it," I said. I was still seeing the image of myself as the slumlordosaurus, lumbering monstrously through the thousand-story tenements of Greater Calcutta. I'd given away the stars, why not the earth too? Perhaps I get something back out of this after all. My self-esteem.

Klutharion, I in my insect body, and the soul of the shopping mall in mine, emerged from the private room. Everyone was applauding wildly. Fireworks were going off. Champagne was raining from the ceiling. Oh, I felt empty, so terribly empty.

A small group of us took off in Klutharion's party-sized toyochev. We went right up to the rings of Saturn. We watched as a creature who looked exactly like me climbed into a private toyochev that belonged to me, and we watched that little vehicle pop from our docking bay, turn toward the great blackness beyond Saturn, and accelerate. And then the heavens opened.

I saw them at last. Millions upon millions of them, spangling the deep darkness in every direction, on and on toward infinity...I saw, with a special clarity because of these high-tech compound eyes of mine, reaching far into the ultraviolet range...great swirling galaxies beyond our own, incandescent quasars pouring their energy into the great emptiness, even the black hole at the heart of the Milky Way, sucking in the light of a million stars; I saw all these things for only a split second, and against them, the meteoric streak that could have been myself, fading into nothingness, and with it all I had ever yearned for.

"It's not so bad," Klutharion said as the prison wall closed around us once again. "I said it was a test; you passed with flying colors; I'm presenting this matter to the council and you'll probably have your waiting period cut by, oh, a couple of million years. It's great news!"

"Sure," I said softly. "Sure."

I committed suicide seventeen times that day.

Suicide always gives me a terrible hangover. Not to mention amnesia. Depression. Temporary insanity. But you know, it's not a bad way of clearing away the accumulated garbage of one's life. I had never committed suicide more than two or three times straight before, but this time was different.

Around the twelfth or thirteenth time was when I finally remembered who I was. Then, of course, after the initial exhilaration of knowing I was the richest, most beautiful, most powerful creature in the universe, I also remembered that I was a monster.

I killed myself again.

After a while, I remembered that I signed away the earth. I killed myself.

I remembered I had given up the stars.

I killed myself.

Then I remembered why.

I stopped killing myself.

They'd lopped a couple million years off our sentence. This was not hell the human race was living through; it was only a kind of purgatory. Maybe *I* wasn't going to be the one to break through that barrier...though I knew I was out there in the great starry yonder in the flesh, even if not in spirit...but because I'd been willing to give it up, the day when we would reach the stars had crept a couple of million years closer—*all* of us, together. Not just the beautiful and the rich and the powerful; but the lowliest creature that walked the earth that I no longer owned.

I had wrestled with aliens. I had shown them that we too, puny and backward though we were, could take the long view. Alien conquest—enslavement—the day-to-day ridicule of self-style superior beings—we were going to survive it all, if only our hearts stayed true. As my toyochev zeroed in on Mallworld, the place where all dreams come true, I knew that I had seen the stars once; that I had been granted a vision of the promised land; that to hold on to the power to dream is the only dream worth keeping.

I've never killed myself since.

Epilogue

Well, there it is. I think we've all had a thoroughly sickening time, haven't we? I shall be glad to take some time off, go back to the homeworld, contemplate the Navel of Z'Neugma for a while. I don't suppose there can be any doubt in your mind, my lord, that this race is hardly due for release yet.

Just put your seal here, my lord, and I'll process the official decision. Everything same as usual, I suppose. There, that's simple enough. And now I suppose you'll be wanting to get home; I'll have the shuttle bring you from the manse to the universe barrier, and we'll negotiate a temporary breach for you to make your exit, eh? Just a boring day in your endless round of judgments.

What? You think you'll stay for a while?

You're inviting all your friends?

You think that this is one of the finest repositories of the meaning of life you've ever seen?

My lord, my lord…your purity of vision is beyond poor miserable me! But that's only to be expected, isn't it? Perhaps in a couple of thousand n'huats I will attain something of your Ultimate Mellowness.

And now that the official part of your visit is concluded, lord, I've ordered a few classical entertainments from back home for your edification, purification, and ug'unniethic *enhancement.*

First we will have the Singing Stone Garden of Deneb IV, which will regale us with a three-hour symphony of silence composed specially for you by one of their most accomplished rock groups; their leader, a most engaging sentient gneiss, has been vying for your attention for some centuries now, and I thought it a golden opportunity to expose you to his work, combining as it were many different flavors of silence, from the starry silence of space to the awesome silence of the tomb itself…Next, something of the utmost intellectual stimulation, lord;

an exhibition of the tesseracted paintings of the existentialist artist Shmoefoot Coriandros; you will not be able to see these paintings, of course, folded as they are into the fifth dimension, but ah! you will be absolutely ravished by the exquisite program notes the artist has provided, illuminating as they do the profoundly paradoxical paradigms of the Selespridon condition. Then I've a distilled-water tasting setup, with waters distilled as long as fifty n'huat ago, so that you can really savor their temporal ambience undistracted by such trivialities as taste...what a feast of hometown delights I have for you, my lord!

You seem on the verge of losing your temper, my lord! Whatever is the reason?

You say you've no intention of being bored to tears by something you could be doing any afternoon back on the homeworld? You hate art? You call me pretentious, ignorant, stupid?

What do you mean, Your Lordship? What do you want to do?

Oh. You want the mind-magician back on. You want to peer into the minds of more of these primitive peoples. But we've done the nine minds, haven't we? You've made your decision, haven't you? We're shelving the human race for another thousand or so of their years? Come now; it's no longer necessary for you to sully your mind with these creatures.

You'll be the judge of that?

You know, sometimes I doubt the wisdom of all this. Maybe we're just voyeurs, really, fascinatedly watching those things which we have become too civilized to enact ourselves...have you ever thought of that? I mean, by what hubris do we set ourselves in judgment over these unfortunate creatures anyway? There you are, for instance; you've lived a million times longer than even me, and these funny little short-lived sub-Selespridar still amuse you.

Is there something in them that we haven't got?

If we were in their position, would we be banging our heads against the wall, knowing it's hopeless, yet still demanding release from the prison?

Of course not, you say. We're too civilized, you say.

Maybe that's our problem. Maybe that's why we roam the Galaxy, endlessly seeking this unattainable ug'unnieth.

I'll turn the machine back on now, lord, and you can spy into our little ant farm at your leisure. But those nine lives we've just examined will constitute the official record; everything else is between you and the machine. All right?

You want me to join you? No, thanks; I've had my fill.

I'm going back down to Mallworld for a few of their days.

The barJulians are having a party.

Author
S. P. Somtow's
Bio

Called by the Bangkok Post the "Thai person known by name to the most people in the world," S.P. Somtow is an author, composer, filmmaker and international media personality whose multitudinous talents and acerbic wit have entertained and enlightened fans the world over.

He was born Somtow Papinian Sucharitkul in Bangkok. His grandfather's sister was a Queen of Siam; his father is a well-known international lawyer and vice president of the International Academy of Human Rights. Somtow was educated at Eton and Cambridge, and his first career was in music. In the 1970s, while he was still in college, his works were being performed on four continents and he was named representative of Thailand to the Asian Composers' League and to the International Music Council of UNESCO. His avant-garde compositions caused controversy and scandal in his native country, though, and a severe case of musical burnout in the late 1970s precipitated his entry into a second career—that of author.

He began in science fiction, but soon started to invade other fields of writing, with some forty books out now, including the classic horror novel (voted one of 40 all-time greatest horror books by the members of the HWA) *Vampire Junction*, which defined the "rock and roll vampire" concept for the 1980s, *The Riverrun Trilogy*, ("the finest new series of the 90s—*Locus*) and the semiautobiographical memoir *Jasmine Nights*, which prompted George Axelrod to call him the "J.D. Salinger of Siam." He has won or been nominated for dozens of major awards, including the Bram Stoker Award, the John W. Campbell Award, the Hugo Award, and the World Fantasy Award. He now holds the post of president of the Horror Writers Association.

His most recent books are *Dragon's Fin Soup—Eight Modern Siamese Fables; Tagging the Moon—Fairy Tales from Los Angeles*; and *The Vampire's Beautiful Daughter*.

A media personality in his native Thailand, he has, in the U.S., been a frequent guest commentator on Sci Fi Channel talk shows, as well as the occasional "talking head" on documentaries for the Learning Channel and the History Channel. He has recently returned to music in a big way, composing Kaki, a ballet, for a Royal Command gala in Bangkok, as well as a number of film scores. He has just conducted the Bangkok Symphony Orchestra in a new symphony commissioned in honor of the King of Thailand's birthday.

He has also made a few incursions into filmmaking, directing the cult classic *The Laughing Dead* and the award-winning art film *Ill Met By Moonlight*. He will direct a new sci-fi film in 2000, *Little Savages*.

Interior Illustrator
Karl Kofoed's
Bio

Karl Kofoed is an illustrator, marketing designer, and art director with over 30 years of commercial art and marketing experience. Karl describes himself as working in two quite different professions. One is that of an art director with experience inside ad agencies such as NW Ayer Direct in NYC; in television as art director, director of news graphics, and scenic designer; as well as product design, development and marketing for a poster company. Currently Karl is principal art director for Orenstein Advertising in Philadelphia, PA. There he heads a creative team doing desktop publishing of advertising materials.

Karl's other profession is as a Science Fiction illustrator. He has used his skills as a water color artist in all mediums to produce scores of covers, interior book and magazine illustrations. Frequenting East Coast SF cons, he is well known to the SF community. This chapter of his life began with the Galactic Geographic© feature that premiered in Heavy Metal magazine in 1978. In 1998 Heavy Metal resumed publication of the feature. The latest incarnation of the feature utilizes all of Karl's skills in creating "photographic" magazine articles from the year 3000. With illustrated collage and digital art Karl has been able to achieve the look of credibility he has always envisioned for articles published "in the distant future". Karl and his wife Janet Kofoed, a popular jewelry designer whose work is at many eastern SF Conventions, live in Drexel Hill, Pennsylvania; a suburb of Philly. They each have a daughter named Lisa from a previous marriage.

Because of his professional career, Karl has to be selective about the Science Fiction assignments he undertakes. The first Mallworld stories were assigned to him when they appeared in Asimov's SF magazine in late 70s. The editor George Scithers, and Somtow, the writer, agreed that Karl's fanciful drawing style fit the flavor they wanted. For the recent incarnation of Mallworld, Meisha Merlin publishing was delighted to find Karl still available and eager to do four more original illustrations for Somtow's new tales. Says Karl of the assignment: "The challenge of illustrating Mallworld again was a double edged sword. It had been twenty years since the original drawings were done and, after going digital, it's been five years since I've actually drawn with ink and paper. The other problem was more eclectic, and as true now as it was when the original drawings were done; Somtow's writing is so fraught with delicious imagery and satire that it is almost impossible to choose what to illustrate."

You can visit Karl's entertaining Galactic Geographic© web site:

http://www.membershome.net/ggeographic